The
Water's
Edge

ALSO BY DANIEL JUDSON

The Darkest Place
The Bone Orchard
The Poisoned Rose

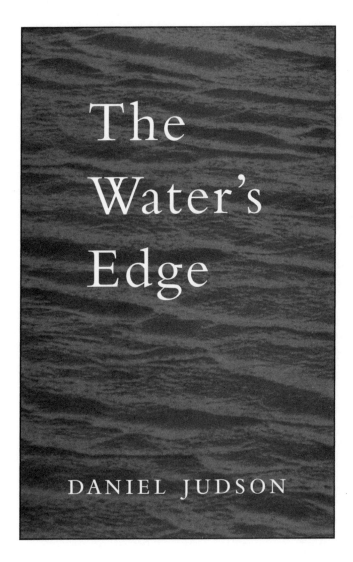

The Water's Edge

DANIEL JUDSON

St. Martin's Minotaur

New York

THE WATER'S EDGE. Copyright © 2008 by Daniel Judson. All rights reserved. Printed in the United States of America. For information, address St. Martin's Press, 175 Fifth Avenue, New York, N.Y. 10010.

www.minotaurbooks.com

Library of Congress Cataloging-in-Publication Data

Judson, D. Daniel.
      The water's edge / Daniel Judson.—1st ed.
         p. cm.
      ISBN-13: 978-0-312-35254-7
      ISBN-10: 0-312-35254-9
      1. Private investigators—New York (State)—Hamptons—Fiction. 2. Organized crime—Fiction. 3. Murder—Fiction. 4. Hamptons (N.Y.)—Fiction. I. Title.

   PS3610.U532W38   2008
   813'.6—dc22   2008012501

First Edition: July 2008

10 9 8 7 6 5 4 3 2 1

for William and Mary Peterson

Part One

Dark

One

HE COULDN'T SHAKE THE FEELING THAT HE HAD FORGOTTEN
something, and not long after walking through his door he narrowed it
down to whether or not he had turned off the quartz heater he used to
keep warm as he worked. It would have been easy, as beat as he was after
a long day of gutting the restaurant's bathrooms to get at a plumbing
problem, for such a thing to have slipped his mind. Grueling work, tearing out perfectly good drywall to get at pipe, more so because he had to
do it alone, couldn't afford to hire help. Plus he knew very little about
plumbing, was clearly in over his head, but a restaurant—a successful
restaurant—could be a gold mine, would set him up for life, if he was
lucky, and certainly that was worth doing whatever needed to be done.

Of course, he probably had turned the heater off, had done so without
thinking—so much of what he did these days was habit by now, and he
could see himself, if he thought about it, just walking right past the still-
running unit in his hurry to get out of there and get home, get himself
clean and warm and dry and then have nothing at all to do except rest
up for tomorrow's long day. But he couldn't chance that he hadn't
turned it off, knew *that* much at least; the last thing he needed was a fire
and the investigation that would follow. It would be likely, should his
place suddenly burn to the ground, that the authorities would suspect

arson—he was so far over his head financially, and Memorial Day was approaching fast, how could they not? But even if he had shut the damn heater off, even if he could to talk himself into believing that, into seeing himself doing that before he left, there would still be a doubt somewhere in his mind, and that would mean a night of troubled sleep. The last thing he *really* needed was that.

No, there wasn't any choice in the matter. He had to drive back and check.

He had parked his pickup truck in the lot behind his apartment building, hurried to it now through the rain—*rainiest March on record, the weatherman had said this morning*—and climbed in behind the wheel, cranking the ignition. The engine was running rough, but he expected that; there was a problem in the wiring he had been unable as of yet to fix. Everything he owned was a fixer-upper, but if the restaurant was a hit, if the summer was everything he hoped it would be, and if he made it through that first winter, when nine out of ten restaurants on the East End failed, then everything would change, everything he needed he could simply have, easily have, and he would no longer need to scramble around for money. And wasn't that what all this was about?

He shifted into gear, steered out of the back lot and made his way through the village to Hill Street. A little more than a mile later, where the two-lane road opened up and became Montauk Highway, the speed limit jumping from thirty up to fifty-five, he eased down on the accelerator and followed the shimmering road west, moving at an even sixty miles per hour toward violence.

The restaurant was on the other side of the Shinnecock Hills, on the eastern edge of the canal. He made the ride there in silence, didn't want to risk hearing anything more on the radio about the record-breaking rain; he'd live and die by the weather soon enough, when the restaurant opened. Just after he passed the hills and reached the bridge that spanned the canal—one of three, all within sight of his restaurant's deck—he veered right onto North Road. Tide Runner's, a single-story building on the water's edge, was the first left after that. He rolled into the lot, over the packed dirt and broken seashells and through the long puddles, parked and killed the lights. Grabbing his keys from the console between his front seats, he climbed out and headed for the set of plank stairs that led down to the restaurant's door.

Inside, the place was dark and cool, like a cave. He didn't bother to turn on any lights; the entire west side of the building was a series of large glass windows that let in the light from the canal, which was as brightly lit as a border crossing. Plenty of light, then, for him to see by. He made his way past the long bar and through the dining room to the kitchen. Pushing the swinging door open, he felt a current of dry, hot air against his face and knew that he had, in fact, left the heater running. The sound of the rain pounding on the roof had probably caused him not to hear the hum of the unit and therefore forget all about it in his rush to get home. He switched the heater off, then gave its power cord a tug, pulling its plug from the wall socket. Simply flipping a power switch seemed too little of a thing to have brought him all the way back here like this. He was on his way through the dining room, in a second rush to get out of there and get home, when he heard something that made him stop short.

He wasn't sure what it was, only that he had definitely heard something. Something strange. It came from outside, he knew that much, beyond the glass and wood that surrounded him. The restaurant, like most places by the water, was solidly built, but not so much as to keep outside noises from finding their way in. The more he thought about it, the more he thought what he had heard was a scream. A man's scream. Very little could be mistaken for that. Still, he immediately doubted himself— it could have been the cry of a gull or maybe even the squeal of a tire, from some car suddenly braking on the Montauk Highway bridge. Who, after all, would be out there on a night like this? The Montauk Highway bridge was visible from where he stood, and looking toward it he saw nothing, no cars stopped or about to crash, just the steel bridge standing solemnly in the rain. He looked then at the deck just beyond the large window. Empty now, in the summer it would be, he hoped, full of people eagerly and freely spending money. He looked for a gull but saw no sign of one, not sitting on a railing or riding the steady current of air moving through the canal. Finally, he looked toward the train bridge, which of the three bridges—Montauk Highway to the south, Sunrise

Highway to the north, the train bridge in the center—was nearest to the restaurant, no more than a hundred feet or so away. It was a narrow span of riveted steel that crossed the water, no more than thirty feet above it. Something there caught his eye, some kind of motion on the far side of it. Several long seconds of him staring at the bridge was what was needed for his brain to make sense of what his eyes were detecting.

Something was hanging from the bridge. Swaying, not rhythmically, as it would if its motion were caused by the wind, but frantically, violently even. Finally his mind was able to make sense of what he was seeing, put together what exactly it meant.

Someone was hanging from the bridge—not from its edge but well below it. A man, his head bent forward at a sharp angle and his feet kicking wildly.

There was no mistaking it then, as much as he wished this were a mistake, that this wasn't at all what was happening.

Someone was being hanged.

This wasn't the only motion, though. Directly above this dangling man was what appeared to be a scuffle among three men—two standing, one prostrate, each of the two standing figures bent at the waist. One of these figures dropped to his knees, raised his hand over his head and brought it down, then raised it again and brought it down a second time. A hacking motion more than a punch. Each time the man's hand came down, another quick scream broke and echoed, muffled by the rain, down the length of the canal.

The scuffle ended after that, and seconds later the figure of another man suddenly appeared below the bridge. This man didn't fall but was instead lowered slowly—first his legs came into view, kicking, and then his body till he came to a stop at the rope's end. The man hanging beside him, just a few feet away, was no longer moving now, simply hanging limp, his arms at his sides, his body twisting stiffly in the wind.

It was then, his breath beginning to fog the glass before him, that he witnessed two men running from the bridge, heading toward the other side of the canal, the Hampton Bays side. They were nothing more to him than two dark figures in motion, one right behind the other. Clearing the bridge quickly, they disappeared from his sight, following the train tracks west, leaving the two bodies hanging dead, or close enough to it, above the dark, rushing water.

Back in his truck—he had been overcome by the reflex to run, to just get out of there, and so he had bolted from his place as if it were on fire—he fumbled for the cell phone in the pocket of his jeans, dug it out and dialed 911 with trembling fingers.

Two

A HALF MILE EAST OF THE CANAL, IN A DARK COTTAGE, JAKE
Bechet awoke to the sound of rain. He lay still for a while, adrift, then finally sat up, careful not to disturb the woman still asleep beside him. The
darkness to which he had awakened was total, so he wouldn't have been
able to see the woman even if he looked for her, not that he needed to;
he knew by the sound of her breathing that she was still sound asleep.
Her name was Gabrielle Marie Olivo. Five foot ten, more beautiful, he
thought, than he deserved, easily more so than he was used to. Black hair
worn short because long hair was a bother, slender but not without
strength, naked now, the way she always slept, even in the dead of winter,
curled upon herself between satin sheets, the only carryover from her
former life as a daughter of privilege. The cottage was her place, a year-
round rental, the bed her bed. Bechet felt this way even though he had
slept beside her, without a single day's exception, for a little more than a
year. A long time for him—and for her, too, from what he gathered.
They didn't often talk about their pasts. What was there, really, to say? He
paused now, listening for Gabrielle's breathing, separating it from the
sound of the rain, heard no change in it at all. It took a lot to wake her;
she was, in this way, fortunate.

Finally Bechet moved to the foot of the bed, sat there on the edge of the sagging mattress and looked toward the window nearest to him. Normally, even with the curtain drawn, this window was a source of some semblance of light—starlight, moonlight, the lights of the town of Riverhead reflected off clouds, something by which he could see at least the shape of the room and the furniture around him. Familiar contours in a faint wash of blue. Tonight, though, there was nothing to see but utter blackness. He sat still within it, felt a little as if he had been swallowed up by it, as ready now to begin the arduous process of rising as he was going to get.

He, too, was naked, the air around him chilly, but the cold would do him good, help him more quickly shake off the effects of his too-long slumber. When it came to that, to waking and getting to his feet, he needed all the help he could get. He and Gabrielle had made love in the morning, during the quiet time between when she returned from work around four and they turned in at six, as the sun was only just threatening to rise. In the solemn predawn it always felt to them as if they were the only two souls left in the world, a sense that had the effect of somehow deepening their intimacy. No one to hear them, no one *but* them. Gabrielle was her most uninhibited at this time, almost raw. Fearless, intense. Bechet was powerful but restrained. Between them, the elements of a complex storm. There was nothing better than that hour they had together, the act of pleasure that both bonded them and finally, completely exhausted them, put an end at last to the workday. This morning, Gabrielle had fallen quickly into her usual deep sleep, had done so with her heart still fluttering, her dark hair matted with sweat. *Unable to move,* she had whispered, smiling, then *gone, asleep.* Bechet had remained awake for a time, took longer to relax afterward, but eventually found his way into blissful unconsciousness.

He usually awoke several times during the day but had no recollection now of having done that. Had he really slept from the darkness of early morning through to the darkness of night? That was a rarity, to say the least. The rain must have helped, covered up the daytime noises that usually lured him toward wakefulness. The overcast sky, too, no doubt had something to do with it, obscuring the sun to the point where noon must have seemed little more than dusk. Unbroken sleep, since he so seldom experienced it, was a treat for Bechet, but it was a treat that came with a cost. He was feeling that very cost now, sitting at the edge of his lover's bed like a boxer between rounds.

He had been a fighter, once, but that was a long time ago. Another lifetime. He and Gabrielle had that—lifetimes they had lived before meeting each other, lifetimes that had so little to do with who they were now—in common. Bechet had fought professionally, as a cruiser-weight, under the name Jake "Pay Day" Bechet. The nickname had been his trainer's idea—the rhyme of Pay Day and Bechet, the man had believed, would ensure that the press would get the pronunciation of Bechet's last name right. And, too, his trainer had thought, the nickname would sound good being cheered by an eager crowd. *"Pay Day Be-chet. Pay Day Be-chet."* Not that Bechet had ever fought to crowds, cheering or otherwise, and not that the press took much notice of him. Still, Bechet had come to embrace the nickname because he'd only really ever fought for the money, and so "Pay Day," therefore, had simply said it all. An identity that both did and didn't matter. There was real freedom in that, in having something, as it were, to hide behind, even as one was taking a beating. Bechet had hung up his gloves when his reflexes began finally to slow and his punch no longer carried the power he had once been able to call up at will but eventually only showed itself, seemingly, at random. Of all the things in a world, for a man like him, to be unable to count on. For the last year of his career he had become known, by the few who actually knew of him, for the punches he took and not the punches he threw, and that in itself was reason enough to get out. He was twenty-eight then. After six years of fighting for a living—brawling in clubs, working his way up to casinos, always, seemingly, just the right fight away from the big-time, a fight that never quite came about—after six years of this, *what was there for him to do now?* He didn't like thinking about those days. Nor, needless to say, did he like talking about them. Again, it was a lifetime ago. Actually, two lifetimes. And anyway, really, what was there to say?

Though he had stopped fighting well over a decade ago, Bechet was still in shape, more or less—arms and legs like heavy rope, a thick back and flat stomach, steady heart, strong lungs. Not bad for a man pushing forty. At least he still *looked* like a fighter, still carried himself like one, still had the walk. But of course he'd never lose that. *Once a fighter, always a fighter,* his trainer used to say. There were, at times, advantages to looking the way he did. Regardless of his physical condition, though, Bechet needed upon waking to work through long-abused elbow and knee and hand joints, all the parts of himself that had stiffened up during his rest, needed to do this before he could even think of rising to his feet. The unbroken sleep he had just enjoyed—long hours of stillness—only made matters worse. An object in motion tends to stay in motion, and all that. He straightened his back now, breathed in and out deeply, slowly, letting his ribs expand and contract with the movement of his lungs beneath. His ribs had been broken twice, the same two ribs savaged during different bouts toward the end of his career—savaged, in fact, by the same boxer, an up-and-coming kid made of nails with a left hook to the body like a hammer.

When the stiffness in his ribs eased as much as it was going to, Bechet then began to open and close his hands—heavy, broad, knuckles like rolls of quarters—till the faint creaking within even the smallest joints stopped. Hands, even ones as large as his, were fragile things, not at all meant for striking. After that he moved on to his elbows and shoulders and knees, rubbing and straightening and bending them till that particular stiffness, a bit like rusting metal moving against rusting metal, finally began to diminish. To be a fighter required a high tolerance to pain, and Bechet had that, to the degree any person could. Still, now, the less to remind him of his past, the better. And there was, of course, nothing like the battered parts of himself to remind him of who he once was, how he had turned into that.

Only after he finished his routine did Bechet feel ready to stand. He was six foot, weighed these days at just over two hundred pounds, and stood this evening like a building going up—slowly, and in stages. Once he was up straight he moved to the window nearest to the foot of Gabrielle's bed, pulled the long curtains apart. Her cottage—an art cottage, built a half century ago, maybe even more, back when this part of town was a sparsely populated community known as Art Village—was set at the top of a dead-end dirt road. No streetlights, no neighbors, nothing but the kind of darkness found so far from the heart of things. It didn't matter, then, that he was undressed because there would be no one around to see him. The view from her north-facing window was of the train tracks that cut behind the cottage, just fifty feet away. He ran those tracks in his effort to remain close to fighting shape, could follow them for miles in either direction and not see a soul. Or, too, be seen by one. He usually ran at night, did so in all kinds of weather, even as foul as this. Running was nothing less than a test of what was within a person. But tonight was Gabrielle's night off from the restaurant where she worked, some nights as a waitress, others behind the bar, whatever shifts she could get, working sometimes six nights a week. She had once been a medical student, had completed, with honors, a year at Harvard Medical School. Bechet knew that much about her. But the death of her parents, in a car accident years ago, had brought her schooling to an abrupt end, changed her life in that way only the death of a parent—in her case, both parents at once, in an *instant*—can. Since tonight was her night off, Bechet wouldn't go for his run. And anyway, in total blackness like this, why risk taking a potentially bad fall on the hard wooden ties and gravel of the tracks? The last thing he needed was even more injuries to slow his daily rising.

He stayed at the window for a moment, watched the frantic streams of rain pour down the panes. Gabrielle had said in the morning that she needed to get out and be waited on by someone instead of being the one to wait on others, to claim back just a little bit of her previous life of privilege. She had worked six days straight, really didn't mind working *just to support herself,* and though it would have been nice not to leave the cottage, particularly since she didn't have to, she had decided to opt for a little pampering. Whatever she needed, always, was fine with Bechet. He gave her what he could, was the least he could do.

With that in mind, he looked upward now. His eyes, in the time it took him to stand, had adjusted to the darkness to the point where he was able to detect, even if only barely, the weave of branches outside. A crowd of tall pine trees surrounded the cottage on all sides, shading it in the summer and winter. Beyond their branches tonight was a menacing sky, clouds as black as soot and riding low, much lower than they had been in the morning, when he and Gabrielle had turned in. Clouds that scraped the tops of the trees, Bechet knew, meant fog soon, possibly even within the hour, if the elements were right. Dangerous, particularly on the road below, which followed the sharp curve of the bay through the low-lying Shinnecock Hills. Bechet had heard—from a friend who owned a towing service and auto salvage yard—of the crashes that had taken place there over the years, the people who had been killed on that winding road. More than that, though, Gabrielle's parents had been killed on a night like this one, she had told him that much, killed not on the road below but on another road, in another part of the country, though really that hardly mattered. How could she even hear rain or glimpse a bank of fog through a car windshield and not recall what was better forgotten? He was protective of Gabrielle, as any man would be of the woman he loved—protective, that is, as much as she allowed him to be. Though her youth had been one of comfort and ease, she was by no means spoiled or, worse, incapable. She was, in fact, in all the ways that mattered, as capable as he. His matched opposite, as it were. Still, there was within him the need to protect her. Deep, primal, compelling. There was, too, the need to protect the life they had made, were making still— a pair of refugees, as they were, from the two extremes of brutal death.

This was a night, then, to stay in, keep dry and warm and play it safe. It was all about playing it safe, in every way possible. That, and keeping the past well behind them, keeping it from snapping at their heels like some hungry beast. He wanted, standing at her window now, staring out at the turbulent night, nothing less for them than that.

From behind him then, out of the darkness, muffled, came the sound of a ringing phone.

He turned, waited for the second ring, then followed its sound to where he had dropped his clothes on the floor in the morning as Gabrielle had watched from the bed. She often admitted, freely, that it was his body— the size of his frame, the strength his build promised—that had first attracted her. A simple voyeuristic thrill, then, his undressing as she waited stretched out on her sheets. He scrambled now to find his jeans, reach into the pocket and grab hold of the phone. As heavy a sleeper as Gabrielle was, she of course wouldn't sleep through the sound of a ringing phone in the room. He had his cell out of the pocket and in his hand by the end of the third, now unmuffled ring, flipped the lid open and looked at the number on the caller ID. The pale glow from the display was enough to light up the small room, and it took a second or two for his eyes to focus. Once they did, he recognized the number, thought first about not answering the call, letting it roll over to his voice mail. But by the time the fourth ring began, he had thought twice about ignoring it. The number was the cell phone of Bobby Falcetti, one of the men who worked for Bechet, drove one of the cabs that Bechet co-owned with his partner Eddie. For Falcetti to call Bechet meant that something was up. In weather as bad as this, knowing Falcetti the way he knew him, Bechet had a pretty good idea what that something might be.

He pressed the TALK button just as the fourth ring ended, then held the phone to his face, said in a half-whisper, "Yeah."

He heard a rush of what sounded like distortion, realized soon enough that it was the crash of the rain on the caller's end. Then, through it, a faint voice, "Hey, man, it's Bobby." Though faint, Falcetti was clearly shouting just to be heard.

"What's going on?"

"I need your help. I went off the road."

"You all right?"

"Yeah. A freaking dog or something ran out in front of me. I swerved, and then the next thing I knew I was nose-first in a ditch."

"How bad is the damage?"

"I don't think there's much, from what I can see. I think I just need someone to pull me out. I might be able to drive away from this."

"You drive too fast, Bobby. We talked about this. You're driving a cab, you're not in the smashup derby anymore."

"I know."

"It's Angel's night off, so Eddie's working the dispatch tonight. Have him call Scarcella, tell him to send a wrecker."

"Yeah, well, that's the thing. I'd rather not have to deal with seeing him tonight if I don't have to."

"You owe him money," Bechet said.

"Yeah."

Falcetti was a poker player, spent his nights off sniffing around the East End for private games. Bechet had known Falcetti for years, knew him to be the kind of guy who would try anything if it could make him money—or, better, if there was a chance that it might make him rich.

This is what had led Falcetti to give stock-car racing a try, at the track in Riverhead. When that didn't pan out, Falcetti had turned to the Sunday afternoon demolition derby and figure-eight races. That wouldn't make him rich but it was, for Falcetti, easy money, and therefore the next best thing.

Bechet had employed Falcetti back when Bechet owned a small housepainting business—Bechet, Falcetti, and a crew of six, mostly high school- and college-age kids, working fourteen-hour days all summer long, rushing from job to job, at the mercy of the weather, always seemingly just a day or two behind schedule thanks to one rainstorm or another. When he got tired of that business, decided he needed something that was more year-round, Bechet bought into Eddie's cab company, as a full partner, and hired on Falcetti—despite his stint crashing cars and school buses in Riverhead—as a driver. Falcetti was in his late twenties now, a good-looking guy with dark curly hair and eyes the color of summer skies. He was as close to family—a little brother, specifically—as it ever got for Bechet. Depending on which week you talked to him, Falcetti was either up or down, winnings-wise, though more often than not he was down. And when he was down, it was usually far enough to make him eager to the point of desperation to find the next game, his next chance to score and get himself, to one degree or another, out of the hole.

The holy game of poker.

Of course, of all the people in town to owe money to, Paul Scarcella was, Bechet knew, the last person anyone would choose. Scarcella was a friend of Bechet's, the very one who owned the local tow company and knew the details of every crash there had been in Southampton for the past thirty years. Scarcella also ran a repair shop out of his auto salvage yard out in the woods of Noyac, had in fact sold Bechet his decade-plus old Jeep. If Bechet was a capable man whose frame promised strength, then Scarcella was a generation beyond Bechet—capable to the point of menace, possessing a frame that more threatened violence than simply promised strength.

Bechet glanced toward Gabrielle's bed, could see by the light coming from the cell phone display the shape of her under the blankets—a long, curving ridge running alongside the emptiness he had left on his side of the mattress. No motion, from what he could see, so maybe she had slept through the ringing phone. He maintained his half-whisper.

"We have a service contract with Scarcella, Bobby," Bechet said. "Can't call anyone else."

"Yeah, I know. I'm actually not all that far from where you are, though."

Bechet let out a long breath. "Jesus, Bobby." He should have known that this was what Falcetti had been leading up to. He looked toward the window, saw the rain streaming down the glass. So much for staying warm and dry.

"You've got a winch on your Jeep, don't you?" Falcetti said. "It'll only take a couple of minutes."

"Yeah, all right. Where are you?"

"Just past Atterbury Road."

Bechet knew the place, could see it in his head. A broad curve in a relatively desolate part of Montauk Highway, less than a mile away.

"I'll be there as soon as I can."

"Thanks, man. I'll owe you one."

Bechet closed the phone, the room falling instantly back into total darkness. He held the phone between his teeth as he pulled on his jeans, then stuffed it into his hip pocket. He was pulling on his T-shirt when he heard the sound of Gabrielle stirring, her feet moving between the satin sheets.

"What's going on?" she said. Her voice was low, dreamy. Bechet instantly regretted having to leave, wished he was beside her right now.

"I've got to run out for a minute," he said.

"Something wrong?"

"One of our drivers went off the road."

"Which one?"

"Bobby."

"He okay?"

"Yeah."

Bechet looked toward her. The moment he had spent in the dull light of his cell phone meant his eyes would need to adjust once again to this dark. He more sensed Gabrielle there than saw her.

"What time is it?" she asked.

The clock was on the table by her bed. It was a cheap windup thing, noisy, though he hardly heard it anymore. He saw a faintly glowing dial and two hands, specks of green in the blackness.

"It's a quarter to seven," he said

"*Christ.*" She was still half-asleep, wandering, by the sound of her voice, in that no-man's-land between unconsciousness and awakened minds. "I guess I was tired."

Bechet had pulled on his socks, was stepping into his work boots now. He never ran in sneakers, always in work boots, an old boxer's trick that kept him—all two hundred pounds of him—light on his feet.

Gabrielle breathed in, then out, through her nose, a long, summoning breath.

"I love it when I fall asleep and it's dark out and I wake up and it's dark again," she said. "I don't know why."

Bechet crouched down, quickly laced his boots up, then stepped toward the bed, sat on the edge of the mattress. Gabrielle reached out for him, her hand coming out of the darkness. She touched his thick arm with the tips of her long fingers, then followed it to his shoulder, a cap of hardened flesh, moving finally toward his chest. She placed her hand flat upon it, loved the layer of the muscle there, loved more the feel of his heart beneath it, a beat per second when he was at rest, or close enough to it, close enough that she could easily keep time by it.

"Do we need anything while I'm out?" Bechet said.

"I don't think so. How long will you be?"

"He's just up the street. Fifteen minutes, maybe twenty."

"It's still raining, huh?"

"Yeah."

"It's so loud."

"I'll see you in a bit, Elle."

He leaned forward, toward the last sound of her voice. She must have sensed him coming toward her, lifted her head off the pillow to meet him. They kissed once, then again, her hand pressing lightly on his chest.

"Drive safe," she said.

"I will."

He leaned back then, stood, her hand falling away, disappearing again into the darkness from which it had reached out to him. He wished he could follow it, let it lead the way down to where she lay. *Fifteen minutes,* he thought. *Twenty, tops.* He'd beat the fog, no problem, and then, once back here, they'd have the whole night ahead, no reason at all for either of them to leave, nothing to do but stay close and talk and eat, pass the time it would take for their little corner of the world to make its way to another dawn.

Downstairs, lit by the glow of the dim light above the electric stove, Bechet grabbed his fur-lined corduroy jacket, pulled it on, then headed through the door and out into the confusing night.

He had expected to spot the cab easily through his rain-washed windshield by its headlights or taillights, depending on which direction Falcetti had been heading when he went off the road. But Bechet saw nothing at all till he was actually passing the cab, only then catching sight of it outside his passenger door window by the glint of its shimmering chrome.

He pulled over, then backed up till his Jeep was alongside the darkened cab. All of the cabs in their fleet were painted flat red, not yellow. The rain and the darkness somehow served to mute the already dull color. Grabbing a flashlight from under his seat and his work gloves from the center console, Bechet climbed out into the cold downpour. He didn't see Falcetti at first, assumed his friend was inside the cab, staying dry, but as he stepped closer to the vehicle he sensed someone moving somewhere in the surrounding darkness. He shined his light toward the motion, saw a figure leaving the shadow of the thick line of pine trees and scrub oak that bordered the far side of the shallow ditch. The figure, a man, was wearing black cargo pants, black boots, and a dark wool navy peacoat over a hooded sweatshirt, the hood pulled up against the rain. If not for his Maglite, Bechet would have not been able to distinguish the man from the darkness. The figure climbed down into the ditch, then up the opposing bank, stumbled once, regained his footing, and finally reached the roadside. He headed straight for Bechet, moving quickly.

"Hey, man, it's me," Falcetti called. "Thank God you're here. I'm freaking soaked to the bone."

Bechet kept the flashlight aimed at his friend. The hood of the sweatshirt was cinched tight, all but hiding Falcetti's face.

"What are you doing?" Bechet said.

"Waiting for you."

"Why over there?"

"In case a cop came by."

Falcetti reached Bechet. Though they were only a few feet apart now, they still had to speak in raised voices to be heard over the rain.

"Is that why the headlights are out?"

"Yeah. I didn't really want to call attention."

Scarcella had a service contract with the town of Southampton as well, so every accident within the town limits requiring a tow automatically went to his company. The cops were, Bechet knew, strict when it came to that detail. If Falcetti had remained with his cab and the cops got there before Bechet, he would have had to deal with Scarcella tonight. Not that abandoning his cab and lurking in the shadows would have really done much to prevent that since any automobile involved in an accident that required an investigation was impounded and towed to a police holding pen at Scarcella's salvage yard in Noyac. A crashed cab with its driver missing would certainly fall into that category. But that would at least have put off Falcetti's having to deal with Scarcella to a later time, and it was Falcetti's nature to put off everything he'd rather not face for as long as he could. Bechet wondered if the thrill that Falcetti got from gambling had been present in him as he waited in hiding to see whether Bechet or the police would arrive first.

"I thought the electrical system had gotten knocked out or something," Bechet said. That would have been bad news, meant possible days lost as Scarcella searched for the problem. Electrical shorts can be elusive bastards.

"No, the lights work fine. It was a pretty soft crash. I just went off the road and then kind of slowed to a stop. I have to tell you, though, I'm a little shaky, man."

He held out his hands, palms down, fingers together. They were trembling dramatically, as if from deep cold.

"You're okay, though, right?" Bechet said.

"Yeah. I never lost control of a vehicle before, though. And all for a freaking dog, man. Next time I'm just going to run the thing over."

Bechet stepped closer to his friend, aimed the flashlight so the edge of the broad circle of bright white crossed Falcetti's left eye. He turned the light away, then turned it back, crossing the left eye with it again. The pupils reacted normally, everything was as it should be. *You don't make a living taking shots to the face and not learn a thing or two about head injuries.*

"I'm fine, really," Falcetti said.

Bechet waited a moment, sizing up his friend. Falcetti seemed jittery, riled even. He was an emotional guy, always had been, compulsive, sometimes even a little manic. All part, Bechet supposed, of the gambler's nature, the gambler's disease.

He watched Falcetti closely for a moment more, then said, "All right, then, let's get this done."

Montauk Highway was one of only two main arterial roads connecting Hampton Bays and Southampton. Not a single car had passed yet, but it was only a matter of time before one did. It was only a matter of time, too, before a patrol car came by. The faster they got out of there, the better.

They moved quickly. The cab was sideways on the bank of the ditch, at the start of a curve in the road. Towing it out would be a simple matter of Bechet backing up straight along the shoulder. He maneuvered the Jeep till it was lined up directly behind the cab, then climbed out and released the cable from the motorized winch mounted to his front bumper, handed the heavy metal hook at the cable's end to Falcetti. Bechet fed the line as Falcetti reached under the back end of the cab and attached the hook to the frame. Locking the winch, Bechet then hurried to his Jeep. He looked back, saw that Falcetti was still standing by the cab's rear. He seemed to Bechet to be preoccupied. No, more than that. Bothered.

"Hey," Bechet said. "You sure you're okay?"

Falcetti snapped out of it, looked at Bechet, nodded. "Yeah." There was, though, still something of an absent look in his eyes. "I'm just a little shaky still, that's all."

"I need you alert for this."

"I'm okay. Really."

"Get in and start her up then."

Bechet climbed in behind the wheel. His clothes were soaked, he was cold. All he could think about was Gabrielle's warm bed. He waited till

Falcetti was in the cab and he heard its engine start and saw its bright lights come on, then flipped his lights off and on. Falcetti returned the signal, and Bechet eased out the clutch, backing slowly till he felt the tug of the cable going taut. The cab didn't move at first, then finally began to pull free. Bechet maintained a straight line along the shoulder till the cab was out of the ditch and on the pavement. When the red glow of the cab's brake lights lit his smeared windshield, Bechet kicked in the clutch and shifted into neutral. He got back out into the rain and met Falcetti by the cab's rear bumper.

Falcetti disconnected the cable from the frame and Bechet switched on the winch till the cable was fully retracted. After that Bechet hurried around to the front of the cab to have a look at the damage.

He checked all sides, saw nothing, not even a scratch. The engine was running smoothly, He crouched down by the front bumper. Nothing was leaking, no radiator fluid or oil. He shined the light underneath. The tire rods and shocks looked fine. The only question that remained was if the front end had been knocked out of alignment. But there would be no way of knowing that till the cab was in motion.

Bechet stood, switched off his flashlight. Falcetti hadn't followed him on the inspection, was in fact still standing by the rear of the cab, his hands in the pockets of his peacoat, his gaze fixed toward the curve in the road he had missed. But he wasn't distracted this time, he was listening to something, listening intently.

"What?" Bechet said.

"Do you hear that?"

"What?"

Falcetti didn't answer. He didn't have to. Bechet turned his head, looked in the direction Falcetti was already facing. He could hear then what it was that had stopped Falcetti in his tracks.

Sirens.

Faint, barely audible at first over the sound of the rain and the cab's running engine, but clearly approaching. It took a moment for Bechet to identify the actual direction from which the sirens were coming. From the west, he decided. Southampton.

"Cops," Falcetti said.

Bechet nodded, said softly, "Don't panic."

"What do we do?"

There wasn't time to do anything. The curve ahead was one of many in this part of the road, but by the rate the sirens increased in volume, it was obvious that the cops were moving at high speeds. So, then, *something bad*. The first cop car appeared suddenly, passed Bechet and Falcetti in the blur, churning the wet air into a frantic swirl. The second cop car was mere seconds behind the first, added a kick to the swirl as it sped through it, whipping cold, stinging drops at Bechet and Falcetti. The two watched as the cars disappeared around the curve to the west of them.

South Valley Road was of course only a half mile beyond that curve. Bechet in the next few seconds listened for any indication that the cops cars were slowing to make the turn. It was foolish of him to think that something could have happened to Gabrielle in the moments since he'd left her, he knew that, but all things were possible, and he *was* protective— of her, the life they had built out of their respective ruins.

He walked the length of the cab, passed Falcetti, stopped beside the driver's door of his Jeep, all the time listening. The sirens faded as the two cruisers moved farther west but remained audible for the time it would have taken them to reach South Valley Road. To Bechet's relief the sounds continued on till they were finally lost altogether to distance and the hard rain.

"Jesus, that was close," Falcetti said.

"It's time to get going, Bobby."

"I wonder what's going on."

Bechet said nothing. Falcetti was looking toward the western curve now. He seemed suddenly focused, as if the scare had startled him from his confusion and into a real clarity.

"You know, I bet you Eddie can tell us," he said.

Falcetti hurried toward the cab then. Everything about him had changed. Bechet knew right away what was on his friend's mind. Video-tape of celebrity hijinks was potentially worth a lot of money these days, so Falcetti had begun to carry a videocamera with him, in case ever he found himself in the position to catch some famous person misbehaving. It wasn't altogether unreasonable, Bechet supposed, to expect that video-tape of a crime scene might be worth something to someone. Still, it was dangerous stuff, he thought, tailing the cops, recording them at work.

Southampton police were known to be a secretive bunch. But there was no point in telling his friend that. This was a chance at free money, and Falcetti never passed up a chance at that.

"You coming?" Falcetti said.

Bechet shook his head.

"You sure?"

"Yeah. You know, your front end might be out of alignment."

"If there's a problem with it, I'll pull over before your road. If not, I'll keep going. I've got a feeling about this, man. Something's up."

Again, Bechet said nothing.

"Thanks for the tow, man. I owe you."

Falcetti tugged the heavy door closed. The cab made a wide U-turn, headed west. Bechet knew that Falcetti was probably already on the dispatch radio, finding out from Eddie where the cops were going. Eddie monitored the police scanner, day and night, always had.

Back in his Jeep, Bechet wiped his face, then shook his large hands dry, or as dry as they were going to get. He gripped the steering wheel with one hand and the gearshift with the other, made a U-turn of his own, rounding the curve and heading back toward South Valley Road. There was no sign of Falcetti, on the road ahead or parked alongside it. The front end must be fine. Either that, or Falcetti simply didn't care.

As he slowed for the turn onto Gabrielle's road, Bechet heard even more sirens in the distance, out on Old North Highway, by the sound of them, though it was difficult to tell in which direction they were headed. Still, Montauk Highway and Old North Highway converged at a particular place that was of interest to Bechet. He stopped short of the side road, pulled onto the shoulder and waited a moment. He took a breath, then another. He didn't care one way or another what was going on, it was none of his business. But if something was up, and in that part of town, then he'd probably be better off knowing about it. He'd be better off, too, keeping Falcetti—in a cab with the name of a company he co-owned in large letters on the driver's door—out of there.

He dug his cell phone out of his pocket, dialed Eddie's number. A dispatch radio was mounted under his dashboard, but he didn't want to use that; it was an open channel, and anyone, including Falcetti, could easily listen in on their conversation.

Eddie answered on the second ring.

"It's me," Bechet said. "What's going on?"

"In Southampton?" Though he had lived on the East End for close to forty years, Eddie's Jamaican accent was still present, as heavy, Bechet had been told, as it had been the day he arrived.

"Yeah."

"Someone found two bodies."

"Where?"

"The canal."

Bechet nodded, though of course Eddie couldn't see that. He waited, then said, "An accident?" The canal was a dangerous waterway, and this was, with the heavy rain and growing fog, a dangerous night. Bechet kept all hint of hope from his voice, though. Not that he wished an accident on anyone, he simply wanted the news of two bodies being found at the canal to mean something other than the only thing it could mean.

"Doesn't sound like it," Eddie said.

Bechet nodded again. "Bobby knows about this?"

"Yeah. He just radioed in. Where are you?"

"At the bottom of her road."

"Good night to stay in."

"Yeah."

"No one's going to be able to see a thing in an hour or so, according to the weather."

Bechet checked his watch. It wasn't yet eight o'clock. He looked through the blurred windshield. The road ahead was a straightaway that ran along the edge of the bay for about a half mile. Bechet could see stray strands of fog coming in off the shallow water. He said nothing for a moment, just listened to the background static coming from his phone and the crashing of the rain on his Jeep's fiberglass top.

"You there?" Eddie said.

"Yeah. Listen, I need Bobby to get out of there right now."

"What's wrong?"

"I don't know, and I don't want to know."

"Do you want me to call him?"

A cell phone call wouldn't be any better than radio chatter. For right now, even more caution that usual.

"No, I'm right here," Bechet said. "I'll take care of it."

"You sure?"

"Yeah. I'll see you, Eddie."

"Get home safe, my friend."

Bechet returned the cell phone to his pocket. The sirens on Old North Highway were louder now, definitely heading in the direction of the canal. Bechet waited a moment more, then steered back out onto the rain-swept road, headed toward the one part of town he did his best to avoid.

The canal was brightly lit, as always, glowing gray-white under the low ceiling of gathering fog, sparkling in the falling rain like something brand-new. He'd seen this sight often, but there was an added element now: the frantic flashing of police lights, throbbing like a quickened pulse.

There wouldn't be a lot of people out and about tonight to witness who came and who went. No fishermen along the length of the canal, no pleasure boats drifting through, no diners on the deck of that restaurant on the eastern bank. Bechet could then roll in and out again without anyone knowing he had even been there. He approached the bridge, and for a second time tonight Falcetti wasn't where Bechet had expected him to be. Bechet was certain the cab would have been parked there. The Montauk Highway bridge spanned the southern end of the canal. From it Falcetti would easily have been able to record the newly arrived police, wherever they may have gathered along the canal below.

Bechet stopped just shy of the halfway point, switched on his emergency flashers. He looked to his right, saw through the dotted glass of his passenger door window the cop cars gathered below, on the western side of the canal. Four of them, parked at haphazard angles directly beneath the train bridge, the center of the three bridges, on the access road that ran alongside the waterway. It all looked to Bechet, at first glance, like chaos, nothing less. He checked the rearview mirror once more, then got out for a better look. He moved around the back of his Jeep, so as to not cross the headlights, and stood at the metal railing. He saw now the cops, in bright orange slickers, standing along the canal's western edge. They stood together, all in a row, looking upward and aiming their flashlights, the beams visible in the sodden air, at the underbelly of the bridge.

Bechet followed the lights to their destination, saw what it was these cops were staring at.

"Christ," he muttered.

He'd seen horrible things in his life, terrible things, some up close, too close, but he still wasn't prepared for this, not by a long shot. He stared at the two bodies hanging side by side at the end of ten or so feet of rope, twisting slowly in the wind, their arms stiff at their sides. Dead. The whole thing looked surreal, like some bad dream being acted out. He could see no details, the bridge wasn't close enough for that, and the lights from the cops' flashlights came up from below and behind, making silhouettes out of the two bodies. Still, this was enough. More than enough. Bechet checked his surroundings, quickly but carefully, saw everything there was but nothing he didn't want to see, then hurried back inside his Jeep. He was reaching for the gearshift when his cell phone rang.

The number on the display was Falcetti's number. Bechet pressed the TALK button, spoke as he drove. A concrete divider separated the east and westbound lanes of the bridge. He couldn't make a U-turn till he had crossed over to the Hampton Bay side.

"Where are you?" Bechet said.

"I saw you on the bridge."

"Where are you, Bobby?"

"I'll tell you, someone's going to pay big money for this footage."

"You've got to listen to me, Bobby. Wherever you are, you need to get out of there, right now."

"It's cool, man. There's no business tonight anyway—"

"Where are you?"

"The cops can't see me, if that's what you're worried about—"

"Where are you?"

"I'm at Tide Runner's."

The restaurant on the eastern edge of the canal, Bechet thought, the one with the outer deck. He made a U-turn, headed back across the bridge. He didn't want to go there if he didn't have to. He had risked enough already.

"Get out of there, Bobby. Now."

"It's okay. I'm here with the owner. He's a buddy of mine. He saw the whole freaking thing. Can you believe that—"

Bechet snapped the phone shut, tossed it onto the passenger seat. There was no point in arguing. Falcetti was a pain in the ass, but he was also a friend. Bechet didn't have too many of those. Friends were a luxury he couldn't quite afford these past few years. But that was the way it had to be.

Once he was clear of the bridge, Bechet made the left-hand turn onto North Road, spotted the cab right away next to a pickup in the restaurant's dark lot, steered through the mud toward it.

His Jeep was leaving tire tracks alongside the cab's tire tracks, but there was nothing he could do about that.

The front door was ajar. Bechet stepped through it and into a dimly lit restaurant, saw Falcetti across a large, empty dining room, standing by a row of ceiling-to-floor windows that overlooked the narrow outside deck. Beyond the deck was the canal. The only light source, Bechet noted, aside from the canal lights outside, was a row of long fluorescent bulbs mounted above the sinks beneath the long bar to his right. These bulbs gave this part of the room, farthest from the windows, the dull, almost pale glow of the last moments of dusk.

Not far from Falcetti stood another man. Falcetti's buddy, the owner, Bechet assumed. This other man didn't hear Bechet at first, was on his cell phone, talking, his back toward the door. He turned, though, when Bechet had moved close enough for his footsteps to be heard. The man looked at Bechet for a moment, uncertainly, but Bechet was used to that. Then the man glanced at Falcetti before turning away to continue talking. By the content of the side of the conversation Bechet could hear, it was clear the owner—thirty, tops, longish dark hair and a slight frame, dirty jeans—was talking to a girlfriend or wife. He kept repeating that he was okay, that he had to wait for a detective to come talk to him before he could leave.

Bechet reached the center of the empty dining room, remained there for a moment to take a look around. The place was obviously being renovated—stacks of tables and chairs lined the wall to his left, cans of paint on top of a spread-out paint-spattered canvas, a stepladder and carpenter's box not far from that.

Falcetti was standing at the window nearest to the right-hand corner of the room. It was the window that would offer him the best view of the foot of the train bridge. He was holding the camera up, level with his face, watching the small video screen. It had his full attention. Bechet doubted Falcetti had even heard him enter. After a moment, Bechet walked to Falcetti, the floor planks creaking beneath his weight. Falcetti didn't even hear this—or, if he did heard the noise, he didn't pay any attention to it. Bechet stepped to Falcetti's side, kept a few feet between them. The last thing he wanted was to be seen on that videotape.

"Turn off the camera, Bobby," he said. He spoke softly, calmly, tried to keep his voice as neutral-sounding as possible. The voice of *any* man. He didn't want to be heard on that tape, either. Still, calm and neutral, he made his seriousness clear. "Turn off the camera," he said again.

Falcetti was too caught up in what he was seeing to respond. Bechet waited a moment, giving Falcetti a chance, but when that moment was up, Bechet moved, crossing the distance between them with two quick, determined strides. There was no point in courtesy now. He yanked the camera from Falcetti's hands, searched for the power button as he took a step back, found it and switched the camera off. Falcetti, startled, turned and faced Bechet. For a moment it looked as if he was going to reach out and grab the camera back. But he caught himself, stayed where he was with his empty hands hanging at his sides.

"What the hell, man," he said.

Bechet moved away from the large window, gestured toward the owner. Still on the phone, the owner had stopped talking when things had suddenly grown heated.

"What's your name?" Bechet said.

The owner said into the phone, "I have to call you back. No, I'm fine, I just have to call you back. I will, I promise." He closed the phone, glanced at Falcetti, then back at Bechet. "I'm Dennis," he said.

"Dennis what?"

He waited a moment, uncertain whether or not to answer, then said, "Adamson. This is my place. I own it."

"You saw what happened, right?"

"Yeah."

"What did you see exactly?"

"Two men on the bridge. The first body was already hanging below it. Two men were standing up, struggling with another guy."

"What do you mean, struggling?"

"One of the two guys got down and hit that other guy. Or something. I saw him raise his hand up, then bring it down a couple of times. The next thing I knew they were lowering the second guy down by a rope. Then the two guys took off."

"In which direction?"

"That way." Adamson pointed across the canal. "To the west."

"And that's all you saw."

"Yeah."

"Would you be able to identify either of the two men?"

"The ones who did this?"

"Yeah."

"No, they were too far away."

Bechet nodded, waited a moment, then looked back at Falcetti.

"A TV show is going to want this footage, Jake," Falcetti said. "Cable or even network news, they pay money for stuff like this. Good money."

"It's safe to say that whoever did this doesn't want to get caught, right?"

"Yeah."

"When they hear someone has a tape of this and is looking to sell it to the highest bidder, what do you think is going to happen?"

Falcetti shrugged. "I don't know."

"They're going to come looking for the person who made the tape. They're going to want it for themselves."

"You don't know that."

"Yes, I do."

"How?"

"Just listen to me, Bobby."

"But I got here after they left. All I saw was the crime scene, not the crime."

"They don't know that, though, do they?"

"Jake, you're acting like an old man. We're talking ten thousand dollars, maybe more. Maybe a hundred thousand."

"It's not worth your life."

"I need the scratch, man. I'll take the chance."

"Not while you're driving one of my cabs."

"Jake, c'mon. You're being paranoid."

Bechet ejected the microcassette from the recorder, handed the device back to Falcetti, and slipped the tape into his jacket pocket.

"You're going to have to trust me, Bobby. I'm doing you a big favor."

"Man, c'mon. You're killing me here."

Bechet said nothing more, just stood there, staring.

Falcetti turned to Adamson to plead his case to him, as though there was something Adamson could do. Falcetti was, of course, desperate now. Every second he wasn't taping was a second something was happening that might just make the videotape as valuable as he dreamed it could be. He said nothing to Adamson, who was a little dumbstruck himself. Finally Falcetti looked back at Bechet. It was clear, though, by the way Bechet was standing there—nothing short of a wall—that Falcetti would get no sympathy from him.

Finally, genuine pain on his face, Falcetti shook his head in frustrated resignation, then looked once more out the large window.

Bechet looked, too, not at the bodies hanging from the bridge, he didn't care about that, but at the scene along the access road below it. A fifth car, an unmarked sedan, had arrived. Among the uniformed cops now was a man in a dark overcoat. The head detective, Bechet assumed. Two cops were talking to him as he stared up at the bridge. He pointed down at the rushing water, said something to one of the uniformed cops. The cop listened, then ran to his cruiser. The detective gave orders to the other cop, and that one rushed off as well, took the remaining two cops with him. Probably to set up roadblocks, close off the perimeter, secure the scene.

A second unmarked sedan pulled in then and parked behind the first one. The man that stepped out of that car, from its backseat, was wearing jeans and a tan jacket that hung to his thighs. He opened an umbrella, held it up against the rain. The driver of the second sedan was a uniformed cop, dressed, like the others, in rain gear. Together, he and the man in the tan jacket hurried toward the detective at the canal's edge. When they reached him, the detective nodded at the man in street

clothes in a way that told Bechet he was the detective's superior. Roffman, then, the chief of police. Who else could it be? *So this was big
enough to bring him out,* Bechet thought.

He didn't like what this was starting to add up to. The sooner they got
out of there, the better.

The detective pointed toward the bridge's underside, and the uniformed cop, a female, not a male, Bechet realized by the way she walked,
shined her flashlight there, waving it a little till she found her target. She
and Roffman and the detective just stood there for a moment, staring up
at the two dangling men.

"Get going, Bobby," Bechet said. "Go home and change, then get
back out on the road. The cops will be stopping the trains in Hampton
Bays for a while, so they can get the bodies down and check the bridge
for evidence. Late commuters from the city are going to be stuck there,
need rides to Southampton and points east. It looks like you're going to
have a busy night after all."

Falcetti watched the scene for a moment more, then turned to Bechet.
"That's not exactly the kind of windfall I was hoping for," he said.

"Go on, Bobby, get going," Bechet said.

Falcetti looked at Adamson once more but said nothing. What was
there left to say? Finally he started toward the door. Bechet listened to
him cross the empty dining room. His footsteps were heavy and fast. *Angry,* but Bechet didn't care. When Falcetti was outside, Bechet turned to
Adamson.

"A detective is coming to take your statement, right?" he said.

Adamson nodded. "That's what I was told, yeah. I'm supposed to wait
for him here."

Adamson was nervous, seemed even more uncertain about Bechet
now that they were alone. Bechet made no effort to make him feel at
ease. He wanted Adamson scared. There was, in his experience, a particular kind of clarity that came with fear. It would be better for all involved, Bechet thought, if Adamson knew that clarity.

"If you could leave Bobby out of this, I'd appreciate it."

Adamson nodded. "Yeah, sure."

"I doubt he will, but if Bobby comes back after I leave, do yourself a
favor and don't let him in."

"What do you mean, do myself a favor?"

"In fact, you might want to lock the door behind me. And when the detective shows up, make sure you see his badge."

"What's going on?" Adamson said.

Bechet shrugged. "You'll just want to be careful, that's all," he said. He turned and started toward the door. The hard soles of his work boots echoed in the empty room. He made a point to step on the tracks he had left as he entered. Reversing treads in this manner was a way of making it difficult for someone to get a clear print, should it come to that. Falcetti's two separate sets of tracks remained, but there was nothing Bechet could do about that.

Adamson called, "Wait a minute," but Bechet didn't answer. He'd said all there was to say. Adamson called a second time, but Bechet was already at the door. He stepped out into the night, paused for a moment under the overhang, surveying the dark parking lot. Falcetti was long gone. The poor guy must have all but felt the money in his hands. Torture, no doubt, for a man like him. Bechet thought of the tape in his jacket pocket. How many minutes had Falcetti been there before he had arrived? Too long, however long it had been. Bechet knew he needed to get rid of the tape as soon as possible, but tossing it out of his Jeep window as he drove back to Gabrielle's wasn't good enough. The thing needed to be destroyed. Gone forever. And now.

The noise of the rain was like static to Bechet's ears. But it wasn't just the rain, he realized. There was another noise, a hiss, lower pitched than the rain but just as steady, a rumble, almost. It mixed with the rain like the two notes of a dial tone. This second noise was the sound of the water rushing through the canal on the other side of the restaurant. The locks were open, the rumble told him that. This water, moving fast from Peconic Bay to the north to Shinnecock Bay to the south, was his best bet at getting rid of the tape in a way that would guarantee it wouldn't, somehow, come back to haunt anyone. He had learned a long time ago, from the cruel men who had taught him everything he knew, to leave nothing to chance.

Bechet stepped to the building's southern side. Most of the lights along the canal were to the north, so the shadow cast by the restaurant would conceal him. He made his way to the canal's edge, pulling several feet of tape from the cassette as he went, then tossed the entire thing into the water. He watched it land on the rough surface, get caught instantly by one of the countless whirlpools that swirled just below the chop. It spun for a few seconds, then was pulled under.

Gone.

Once, years ago, a fisherman had fallen into the canal while the locks were open. His body, bruised and broken from having been yanked to the channel's bottom and dragged along it, hadn't been found till several hours later, and then not far from the inlet that connected Shinnecock Bay with the Atlantic. There was no reason, as he stood on the edge of that water, to doubt its danger and power tonight.

Bechet watched the churning surface where the cassette had disappeared, then looked across the canal, not toward the police gathered near the support column of the train bridge, but directly across from where he now stood.

To take a look, see it for himself. Face it, the past, *his* past, if only for this quick moment, then leave it far behind again.

It stood there on the western edge of the canal just as it always has, or at least had for these past six years: a dark and dormant mammoth, three stories tall and sprawling out, all its windows boarded over, its white paint and red shingle roof long since faded. Close now to a century ago, it had been a hotel, a fashionable one, and then, decades later, in the wild eighties, it had become a popular dance club. But when the heyday of the dance clubs came to its end, the club closed down and was quietly sold to a South American family, reopening a few years later as a gin mill that quickly became a popular hangout for locals, a place called the Water's Edge.

There was, of course, more to that gin mill than selling drinks. There was more to pretty much every business the Castello family had their collective hands in. Even now, black smoke was rising from one of the three crumbling chimneys. Not wood smoke, Bechet would have smelled that, and anyway it was too heavy black for that, too thick. A running furnace, then—and a badly running one, at that. So much, Bechet thought, for this building being dormant.

He didn't stay for long; there wasn't any point. He turned and headed back to his Jeep. It was time he got himself out of there, before anyone had the chance to see him. Prior to getting in behind the wheel he scraped the sediment out of the soles of his boots with a folding knife he kept in the console between the front seats. Dark dirt and shell fragments came out in clumps. He hurriedly got as much as he could, then climbed into the driver's seat and, before swinging his feet in, grabbed a bottle of spring water and poured it over the soles, till they were as clean as when they were new. Steering across the parking lot, he thought about the second set of tire tracks he was leaving behind. Falcetti's cab had no doubt done the same. He thought, too, about the boot prints he had left on his way to and from the canal's edge. A good detective was likely to ask Adamson to account for them. Others, clearly, had been there tonight, had come and gone. What time were they here, what did they see, who were they? But these prints couldn't last long in this rain. Maybe the detective would arrive too late to see them, or he would arrive in time to see them but not make the connection. Or not care. Maybe, knowing what Bechet knew about the cops in Southampton, the detective would have been told not to care about such things at all.

A lot of maybes. Too many.

Bechet felt now as if he was leaving something to chance. Doing so was like disobeying his deepest nature. Soon enough, all that would remain to prove he had been at Adamson's restaurant were his prints on the floor. He had done his best to blur them, though that might not be enough. His work boots were common, he had bought them with that in mind. *Old habits.* They were sold in a thousand stores across the country. If it came to it, he would simply dispose of them, just as he had been taught to do, just as he had done before.

He hated thinking like this, having been put once again in this situation. *Fucking Falcetti.* Bechet had to remind himself that this crime wasn't his crime, that it had nothing at all to do with him, that it had only crossed his path because of Falcetti's desperation. Still, here he was, covering his tracks, doing what was necessary to outthink the cops, looking to make a clean getaway from the scene of a crime.

As he headed back toward Gabrielle's he watched his rearview mirror carefully, making certain he was not being followed. He even pulled over and came to a stop just before South Valley Road, waiting for headlights—anything—to appear in his mirror. But he saw nothing. He waited a moment longer, again, just to be certain. Finally he made the left onto her road, started up the long incline toward its darkened end.

He found the foot of her bed in the darkness and began to undress. His T-shirt was dry, except for around the collar, so it came off easy enough. His jeans, though, were soaked through, the heavy fabric clinging to his legs like cold hands. Removing them was like peeling off a second skin. He got down to his boxer briefs, then got out of them, tossing them onto the floor next to his jeans and shirt. He was now back exactly where he had started his night, standing naked in the cold, Gabrielle asleep just feet away, in the darkness. Hardly an interruption at all, really, this folly with Falcetti. Still, Bechet felt as if he had strayed too far from his life, had come too close to what he'd left behind, what had to remain behind at all costs.

He looked out her window, saw again nothing but the darkness, heard only the sound of the rain. Perfect cover, this moonless, noisy night, for a lot of things. Perfect cover, too, should someone want to come for him. But why would they, and how would they find him?

If Falcetti only knew the havoc he had come close to unleashing. Bechet could barely stand to think about that. *The South American way,* Castello, Sr., used to call it. Brutal but effective, yet that was Castello, his son, the men he employed.

That was, too, once, Bechet. *But not anymore.*

This wasn't over, that much he knew. If this was what it appeared to be—and what else could it be?—there would be more violence tonight. Terrible violence. Adamson, no doubt, wouldn't live to see morning, but there would be more than just that, much more, much worse. There was, though, nothing Bechet could do about that. Nothing he *should* do about that. He knew that.

Closing his eyes, he willed these thoughts away. He could do that, when he needed to, *disconnect.* When he reopened them again he took one more look through the window, out of habit more than anything else. *What would he see now but just more blackness?* Then he sat on the foot of the bed, found his T-shirt on the floor, picked it up and began to wipe his head and face and the back of his neck with it. His hair was short, buzzed close to his scalp, little more than stubble. White beginning to take over the brown, mostly around the temples, more of it with each year. And in the three days' growth on his face, too. He was lucky; Gabrielle loved it, thought it was distinguished. He'd looked a lot of things to a lot of people before, but never distinguished.

When his head and face were dry enough he wiped off his hands, felt as he did Gabrielle's feet moving beneath the blankets, searching for him at the foot of her bed.

"You there?" she said.

"Yeah."

"How'd it go?"

"Fine."

"I must have fallen back to sleep."

"You were tired."

"I feel like I've been asleep for days."

"You can sleep more if you want."

"No. I should get up." She took in a long breath, let it out. "I dreamed about sirens."

Bechet said nothing.

"How is it out there?"

"The roads are washed over in some places. Fog is coming in."

"Bad."

"Bad enough, I think."

"We should probably stay here then, huh?"

He'd forgotten about her plans for the night. "Yeah," he said. "That's probably a good idea."

She said nothing for a moment. Bechet listened to her breathe in and out again, shorter breaths this time. She was waking. Another set, even shorter than the one before, then: "Are you okay?"

"Yeah."

"You sure?"

"Just cold."

"C'mere, then."

He heard motion, knew that she was reaching for the reading lamp on the table beside her bed. It came on, barely lighting more than their corner of her room. The window near Bechet became a smoky mirror. He saw himself—as much shadow as man—reflected in it.

Gabrielle pulled aside the blankets on his side of the bed. He tossed the wet T-shirt onto the floor, then made his way to his indentation, lay in it, on his back. She pulled the blankets over him, and he felt the touch of satin sheets on almost every inch of him. Cool now, but the warmth would come soon enough. Gabrielle turned onto her side, moved close to him, draped her left leg over his and her right arm across his chest. Like embracing the trunk of a tree, she'd once told him. He felt her breasts press against his shoulder, the soft strip of her pubic hair brush against his thigh. *The warmth of her.*

"We should stay like this all night," she said. "I can't believe how tired I am."

"You work a lot."

She nodded. He looked at her, hadn't seen her since the predawn light. A long time. Her face was oval-shaped, her features soft, almost delicate. Her short dark hair was a mess, as it always was after a long sleep, and her gray eyes—more sunrise silver than colorless and somber gray—shined like wet stones in the dim glow of her small lamp. Bechet sensed her body alongside his. She had that length of bone that came with generations of good nutrition. Strong, athletic, yet leisurely so—existence hadn't depended on physical strength, not for her; hadn't, for a long time now, for those who had come before her. A body built for tennis, long swims, weekend hikes. Sleek, well-tended, smooth to the point of polished. Unlike Bechet, then, and those who had come before him—rough, and built for survival, for a world that was far different from the one into which Gabrielle had been born.

She lay her palm on his chest, felt his heart beat. She was always drawn to that, the steadiness of it. *Like a clock,* she liked to say. Then she moved her hand to his left arm, followed it to his forearm, where the tattoo of a star, dark black and the size of a nickel, lay. She'd asked once what it meant—all tattoos, she had always assumed, meant something—but he wouldn't tell her. By his reaction, though, it was obvious that it meant something. She had even mentioned some time later that she was thinking of getting one herself, a dark star just like his, in the same place on her body as his. A matching set, as it were. He had simply shook his head from side to side, left it at that. She had never mentioned it again—they weren't ones, as a rule, for talking about their pasts, and she, if for different reasons, wanted to leave hers behind as much as he wanted to leave his. But she went for his tattoo, he noticed, whenever she could, straying to it and touching it in a way that told him she couldn't really help herself, that she was drawn to the thing as if it were a wound she secretly, maybe even desperately, wanted to tend to, always would.

Finally, as if realizing she had strayed there yet again, she returned her hand to his chest, did so quickly, held it there for a moment before moving it down his hard stomach and reaching between his legs.

"You *are* cold," she whispered.

Afterward, she slept beside him, needed to, she'd said, for just a bit more. Maybe she was that tired, after six days of work, or maybe it was something more, a need, perhaps, to get away from the rain. Her life had been changed by rain—more than changed, it had been shattered, and she lived now among all the broken pieces of *what used to be,* did so without complaint or self-pity. Bechet loved her for that, admired her for her strength and her ability to accept a reduced life, to find, as he did, the comfort in existing. Still, though, this much rain was probably just too much to ask of her—this rain and the sirens, not to mention the fog waiting to descend: reasons enough, all of these, for her to want to indulge herself in the comfort of unconsciousness.

Bechet lay still in the darkness, listened to the downpour. Doing so helped him to not think about the things *he* didn't want to think about. So, they had this in common as well. His matched opposite, Gabrielle Marie Olivo. And anyway, what else was there for him to do? They were together, in the same room, and that was all that mattered. If he did fall asleep—willed himself into it, since he wasn't at all tired—he would probably dream of violence, he had that sense now, and he didn't want that, not tonight. It was always there, though, that deepest part of his nature, inherited at first, passed down to him from his father, and then ingrained over the years—as a boxer, and then as what he had become after that—into his very being. But that wasn't his life now, and everything he did was, he believed, a testament to that. A conscious choice to be something other than what he had been made to be. What he was maybe even meant to be. Everything he did—every thought, every gesture—was designed with that very denial, that very resistance of fate's hand, in mind.

At some point, though, the heavy rain began to ease, eventually coming to a stop altogether, leaving a silence that was nothing short of remarkable. The world was suddenly as quiet as a graveyard, the kind of noiselessness that has its own echo. But it was a false stillness, Bechet knew that; somewhere on the East End, in this dark that surrounded them, roamed two men with blood on their hands. Whenever Bechet closed his eyes he could see them as if they were right there with him, standing quietly in that room. He could see, too, the men who employed them, the father and son who had likely ordered two more killings—at least two, possibly even more, whatever it took to protect what was theirs—orders that were to be carried out certainly before morning, were maybe even being carried out right now, at this very instant, as Bechet lay still.

The South American way.

But, again, there was nothing he could do about that, so there was no point in thinking about it, in doing that particular disservice to himself. *This had nothing to do with him, with the life he had built for himself and the woman asleep beside him, the first and only woman he had ever truly loved.*

Safe for now in his lover's bed, Bechet imagined this brush with his past as a near collision at sea, in the darkest of nights. He had seen his past, had been close enough to reach out and touch it, but maybe it hadn't seen him, maybe it had been blind to him and was drifting now farther and farther away, blessedly ignorant of him as it receded into the blackness, all possible distances growing between them. There was comfort in all that, seeing tonight's events in his mind as such—if only he could be certain it was true. He'd gotten used to certainties, the probable outcome of his *every day.* Predictable, as much as anything can be, as long as he remained cautious, did what needed to be done.

But he had no such assurances now. The rain resumed eventually, falling as heavy as before. *More than enough racket to conceal all manner of approaches,* he thought. But also more than enough to conceal all manner of escapes.

Unable to sleep, still silently adrift, in his mind, on that empty sea, Bechet listened for the first sound he didn't like, the first hint that he had been wrong all along, that his past had seen him, was not moving away at all but in fact coming nearer, swift and unseen, on the hunt for him like some single-minded predator, like the very thing he had once been made to be.

Three

IN SOUTHAMPTON, TOMMY MILLER WAITED TO TAKE ANOTHER painkiller. He had heard the sirens earlier, about an hour ago by now—cop cars, by the sound of them, moving away from town, to the west, moving fast—but hadn't really paid all that much attention to them. If the sirens had been coming toward him, then he probably would have taken notice, gotten up and walked to his window for a look. Not that seeing the cops coming would have meant much as far as advantage went, and not that he had any reason to expect that they would be coming for him now, certainly not with sirens wailing. Better, if that were the case, to do something other than just lie there on his unmade bed and wait blind for a hard knock on his apartment door. But sirens moving away was something Miller could quickly forget all about, and so he resumed what it was he'd been doing before the sirens had sounded at all: riding out the hours till he could take another Oxycodone, feeling with every minute that passed the precious effects of the dose he had taken five hours before diminish like the memory of a dream.

Of course, the last thing he needed these days was an addiction. He was playing on the edge of one as it was, he knew that, but his knee was killing him, had been every day for weeks now. *This fucking rain.* It used to be that his knee bothered him in the cold—whenever the temperature neared freezing, a limp he could pretty much conceal otherwise grew suddenly, decidedly worse. He had undergone surgery a year ago, to replace his torn-up joint with a state-of-the-art mechanical device, but as a result the pain he had always felt in the cold was replaced by one that afflicted him whenever there was even a hint of dampness in the air. Winter rain, summer humidity, it didn't matter—any rise in moisture meant a pain that reached deep. The past month, then, had been difficult, to say the least—just to get from morning to night and back to morning again required an extra dose, bringing him up to three a day. A dangerous thing, but what else could he do? He had played football in high school, had been a blue-chip athlete with a bright future in front of him, so he was used to pain, to giving it and receiving it. But high school was a long time ago, and anyway, somehow, this was different. Maybe it wasn't even the pain so much as the monotony of *being in pain*. There was, he'd come to realize, a subtle but important difference between the two—one a state of body, the other a state of mind, the latter easier to ignore than the former. He was, these days, though, out of work—in fact, at the age of twenty-nine, he was retired, had now, if not a bright future, then at least a comfortable one ahead of him—and this was, he'd be willing to admit if anyone asked, the problem. There was little else for him to do on any given day but pass the time between morning and night, and nothing at all to do on these days in particular—these days of steady rain—but to deal with a pain that reached into the deepest parts of him like clawing fingers.

He had thought repairing his knee would have meant that he was done having his well-being subject to the changes in weather, but no such luck, it seemed, not yet, anyway. Since he was sixteen, when his knee had been ripped to shreds—not in a game or during practice but in a late-night fight, one he in his own arrogance had started—the cold had always been a lonely time for him, a period of days, for the most part, even in the worst of winters, in which he was forced to slow down, if not come to a halt entirely, and, for a change, think. Now it was rain that caused him to stop and face his ache and remember the foolishnesses of his past. So far this month he had endured not just days and nights of this but weeks of it, and having nowhere to go, no job to occupy him and no one in his life to expect a thing from him, there was really no reason at all for him to resist the temptation to take a pill sooner than the eight hours between doses he was otherwise strict about observing, no reason not to let himself be *just a little numb*. There was, in fact, no reason at all for him to wait the remaining three hours, when he could take his third pill of the day without risking addiction. In the long run, really, what would it matter—to him, to anyone—if he were to lie around his own apartment more than just a little stoned? What would one night's infraction mean to a man who was otherwise so diligent? And who would blame him at all, what with *this fucking rain*?

The amber-colored bottle and glass of water were on the windowsill near his bed, within easy reach. He lay still on his back, looked at the bottle for a long enough moment, then finally reached for it. Unscrewing the cap, he tossed a pill into his mouth, downed it with what was left of his stale water. *There, then, done.* Nothing left now to debate. Lying back down, his two-hundred-plus pounds compressing the springs of his mattress, he told himself as he waited for the effects of this pill to begin that rain like this wouldn't last forever. It couldn't, right? Spring was coming, wasn't it? When this patch of late-winter weather was finally done, he wouldn't need this *shit* anymore, these pills, not like this, maybe not till summer even, when that first stretch of humidity came, as it always does. And who knows, maybe by then he wouldn't need these pills at all; maybe by then he would have finally healed. Once this long patch of rain passed, then he'd deal with whatever problems may have arisen from his current overreliance. Till then, though, not much else that he could do except *lie back, feel the pain drift away, and enjoy the ride.*

It wasn't long after he took the pill that he felt a blue flame in his chest. The advantage of waiting eight hours between doses—two hours longer than the label suggested—was that his body didn't develop a tolerance and so the effects didn't diminish all that much. Maybe that was all in his mind, but maybe that was all it took. Whatever the case, the sensation of a flame flickering in his chest was where it always started for him—a soft, glowing warmth that was not unlike, though he'd only known it once, falling in love. After that he felt a numbness in his lips and a tingling in his fingertips, a kind of lazy busyness, a buzz of activity inside him and no outward signs of motion to show for it. Soon after that came the first hints of lightness of being, the feeling that he was about to float up and out of his body. A little like death, maybe, like that very moment when the brain floods itself with doping chemicals, but enjoyable nonetheless.

Here it was now, painlessness, and that rush moving through him that was both giddy and melancholy.

Turning onto his side, waiting now for unconsciousness, he looked toward the window next to his bed, saw through it the very end of the long train platform that stood across the street from his place. A picture-postcard, this train station, a quaint place, sometimes bustling but mostly dead still, like now. It was the place he had last seen *her,* or rather the place where he had watched her stand and wait for a cab the night she had finally left him. The night she finally had enough of *being alone.* Of course his mind, unwinding the way it was, went there now, to that very memory, the one pain that no amount of prescribed medication could dull. *"What are you trying to prove, Tommy? It's like you care more about strangers than you do me. I need you, too."* There wasn't a day, clear minded or otherwise, when Miller didn't think of her, didn't look at that station and remember. There wasn't a night when he didn't stand in any one of his empty rooms and be reminded of *something.* She had left four years ago, back when his work had meant much too much to him. Not just a job but *salvation.* He cringed now just at the thought of that, the choice he made, night after night, to leave her at the mercy of her own fears while he went out to help others—strangers, most of them, just like she'd said—deal with theirs. *A private investigator, but more than just that, if only in his mind.* They had been together for a little more than two years, a one-night stand that just took. For him, there had been no one else in the two years since, not a soul, not even close. It was a long time to be alone, maybe, but there were, of course, worse things for a man to endure, Tommy Miller knew, than self-imposed exile.

He lived above a restaurant called L'Orange Bleu, a French-Moroccan place run by a Frenchman named Oberti. Miller owned the two-story building, the last one on the north end of Elm Street, had bought it as an investment after selling the house his parents had left him. The apartment above was all he and Abby would have needed, now it was all he had, the limits, more or less, of his world. Being Monday, L'Orange Bleu was closed, so there would be nothing for Miller to listen to—no murmured voices coming up from below to occupy him, no happy chatter and occasional bursts of laughter, no cars now and then on the street beneath his front windows, people coming and going. Soothing sounds, for the most part. *Humanity, not all that far away.* Tonight, though, it was just him—the parts of him that he could still feel—and the rain and the view of the train station outside his window and the hours between now and morning.

He let himself drift in and out of consciousness as the effects of the painkillers deepened, moving, he imagined, like roots steadily reaching downward into dark, cool soil. Finally he slipped into sleep. Motionless, dead to all of the world, he had begun to dream of the touch of a woman whose face he could not see, only to be torn away by the sound of someone pounding three times on his downstairs door.

He lifted his head, listened, but did little more till he heard the pounding a second time. Three bangs in a row, fast, just like the ones that had awakened him. *Boom, boom, boom.* He sat up, waited a moment more, then stood. His knee felt fine now, which meant he was feeling nothing, or close enough to it, so he moved less with a limp and more with a stagger across his bedroom. The entire world, as far as he was concerned, was the rolling deck of a ship caught in a storm.

He paused in the doorway to regain his balance—standing up was always the worst part, took at first pretty much everything he had—and then entered his living room, heading toward the row of tall windows on the other end of the room. His apartment spanned the entire top floor of the building, the living room a wide-open space that was easily several times the size of his small bedroom. From any of his front windows he would be able to see if a car was parked at the curb below and, more than likely, determine who it was that had come knocking. He went to the window that was directly above his street door, saw no car below, looked across the wide street and saw one was parked at that curb. It was an old Ford Bronco, well maintained and rigged for beach riding. He didn't recognize it, heard as he studied it a third round of banging on his street door. Fast, like before, heavy. *Authoritative?* He'd grown up among cops, was the son of the former chief of police, had a long time ago learned to distinguish the difference between the knock of a friend and the knock of a man carrying a badge. He knew all the cops in town, officers as well as detectives, some since he was a kid, knew, too, what each one of them drove when off-duty—or at least he used to know this, back when it was his business to know such things. So, then, maybe it wasn't a cop at his door now, maybe not the commanding knock of an authority figure but something else, the urgent knock of someone in trouble. Whatever the emotion of whoever it was down there, Miller simply wasn't in the frame of mind to deal with anything, least of all someone in trouble enough to keep pounding on a door like that.

He moved away from the window, in case whoever was below decided to take a step back from the door and look up, search his row of windows for some sign that he was home, some reason to keep at it. Waiting for another round—or, better, the sound of the person below crossing the wet street, returning to the waiting Bronco—Miller heard neither of these things. What he heard instead was the downstairs door opening and then closing. An old door, rotting, hanging loose on its hinges, it had no working lock. The building was a fixer-upper when Miller had found it, still was, for the most part. After the sound of the door closing came the sound of footsteps on the wobbly stairs. Moving slowly, evenly. After a half-minute or so the footsteps reached the top landing, stopped. Nothing for a moment more, and then, finally, knocking.

Not pounding this time, though, nowhere near it, in fact. Knocking. *Civilized.*

Miller stayed where he was, had no clue now what was going on, who this could be. This door, of course, had a lock, and all his lights were off, so sooner or later, if he didn't make a sound, the person in his hallway would assume no one was home and go away. That he could do, stand there and say nothing and wait—well, barely. The Oxycodone was in him now, numbing some parts of him, causing others to tingle as if caressed by fingertips. It was then, of course, at that very thought, that Miller wondered if this might be *her.* A wild, irrational thought, but that didn't matter. She knew, though, that the downstairs lock didn't work, wouldn't have bothered knocking on it, even after all these years. Still, *what if*? He took a step toward the door, then stopped himself, pushed away any hope that it was her, that it was Abby needing him, suddenly, for whatever reason. He stood paralyzed now, as much by the thought of her as the drug surging through his system, shutting him down from the center out. He was standing there, dumb and wavering just a little, no thought of doing anything other than that for as long as it took, when from behind the door a voice said, "Miller, you there?"

It was a male voice, muffled slightly but clear enough. Though it was immediately familiar, Miller couldn't quite place it, not yet. Remaining silent, he did the only thing he could do—he continued to stay put.

"Miller, it's Spadaro," the voice said. "Open up."

So, the pounding of a man with a badge after all, Miller thought. Still, he didn't answer. No way now.

"Look," Spadaro said, "your truck is parked around back, and I doubt you went out for a walk, on a night like this, with that knee of yours, so I'm fairly certain you're in there." A pause, then: "It's important, Tommy. Okay? I think you know I wouldn't be here otherwise."

Miller closed his eyes, reopened them. Somebody was dead, or dying—why else would Spadaro be here? The question, then, was who? Miller and Spadaro had only one person in common, a dear friend Miller hadn't seen in a while. A long while. So maybe this had something to do with her. At this moment Miller couldn't think of any other reason for Spadaro to be here.

Finally, Miller said, "Yeah, all right." His voice, rough-sounding, was full of concession. It took a real effort for him not to slur his words. "Hang on."

He took the time required to cross the large front room to focus, pull himself out of the muck—warm, comforting, but muck nonetheless—that the painkillers made of him. He reached the door, flipped the dead bolt, then gripped the antique glass knob, cold against his palm, and turned it, pulling the door open. He wanted to give a clear sign to Spadaro that this needed to be quick, so he remained in the doorway. Leaning against the door frame, Miller tried to look as much as possible like a man who had been roused from sleep, and nothing else. Spadaro didn't need to know about the current game with painkillers that was being played. No one did.

"What's up?" Miller said.

Spadaro looked at him, studying his face. "You all right?"

"Yeah. I was sleeping. What do you want?"

Spadaro wasn't in uniform tonight, was instead wearing jeans and a red-and-black checkered jacket, a hunter's jacket, and dark sneakers. He was in his mid-thirties, had black hair, curly but thinning, and a square face. He was as tall as Miller but not as powerfully built, stood now with his hands deep in the pockets of his jacket and his legs apart slightly. *A cop's authority, even in street clothes.* But Miller was used to that, had seen it in his father, and all of his father's friends, had grown up surrounded by it, among it.

Spadaro glanced past Miller, into his apartment. "Anyone in there with you?"

"You said this was important."

"I just need to know if we're alone or not, Tommy."

"Yeah, we're alone."

He nodded but was still looking, not that he could see much since Miller all but filled the doorway. Finally he focused on Miller again. "You up for a ride?"

"Not really."

"Too bad. I was sent to get you, bring you somewhere."

"Where?"

"You'll see."

"Has anything happened to Kay?"

"Not that I know of," Spadaro said. "Why don't you grab your shoes and coat."

"What do you mean, not that you know of?"

"Don't give me a hard time, Tommy. I don't like this any better than you do, trust me."

"Am I under arrest?"

Spadaro looked closely at Miller's eyes. After a moment he glanced down at Miller's knee, then looked up again. Miller knew by this that his eyes were glassy, his pupils dilated. How could they not be? How could Spadaro, even in this dim light, not see that?

"Just get your things, Tommy," he said. "There isn't a lot of time."

Miller didn't know Spadaro all that well, but he assumed that if something had happened to Kay, if she was hurt or needed help, Spadaro wouldn't be behaving in this manner, would have just come out and said that she was in trouble. Concern for her well-being was the one thing they had in common. Something else, then, was going on, had to be. Miller remembered the sirens he had heard hours ago, moving away from town, toward the west, realized that if not Kay, then there would be only one other person on whose behalf Spadaro would be acting.

"Tell him you couldn't find me," Miller said.

"Can't do that. Please just get your things. As a favor to me."

Miller waited a moment, then said finally, "Yeah, all right. Hang on." He stepped away from the door, grabbed his shoes off the floor. Black Skecher's, half sneaker, half boot. Slip-proof sole, steel-toed, years old but still new-looking. Bending down just now to pick them up told Miller not to try to put them on standing up, so he sat down on the coffee table just a few feet from the open door. Spadaro stepped into the doorway but made a point of not crossing through it. A sign of respect, maybe. Or the caution of a cop concerned about contaminating a crime scene? Miller wasn't sure which. Spadaro stood there and watched as Miller began to tie the laces of his sneakers.

"You all right there, Tommy?"

Miller knew his wobbliness was showing. But the cat was already out of the bag. He nodded, said nothing. Spadaro stayed where he was, watching Miller. When he was done lacing up his shoes, Miller stood, carefully, focused everything he had on the way he moved, trying his best to do so with some degree of fluidity. Spadaro knew, certainly, but he didn't need to know how bad, how far away from the world Miller really was.

A military field jacket lay across the arm of his nearby couch. It was old, worn, a hand-me-down. Above the left pocket was a patch with the name *Hartsell* stenciled on it in faded black letters. Miller picked it up, put it on.

"I'll follow you in my truck," he said.

"I don't think so," Spadaro stated flatly. "From the look of you, the last place you should be right now is behind the wheel. Besides, it's getting pretty bad out."

"I'm fine, Ricky."

"Sure you are. Anyway, it doesn't matter. Your truck stays here."

"Why?"

"Because it does. C'mon, Tommy. Like I said, there isn't a lot of time."

Miller followed him down the dark stairwell, holding on to the railing tight, then through the rotting door and out into the night. Nothing to hold him up out there. It was cold, and the rain was gone for now, but, again, the mist was enough. They crossed the wide street, climbed into Spadaro's Bronco. It was warm inside, more so than back in Miller's apartment. A place so open was difficult to keep comfortable in the winter, so he had given up a long time ago, got used to the chill, the *edge*. He sank into the passenger seat, sank deep, his jacket wrapped around him. He was feeling much heavier now than his two hundred pounds. He knew he would feel that way for the next few hours. If only he had waited to take his last pill, he'd be fine right now. In pain, but fine. In his current condition, though, pain probably would have been an advantage. Kept him clearheaded, keenly alert. Nothing cut through like pain. But he had taken that pill, and he was at a disadvantage now, this much at least was clear. It would take all he had to hide his weakness. *Weaknesses.* Wherever it was they were going, whatever it was Spadaro and whoever had sent him wanted, Miller would need to do at least that.

He checked his watch. It was just past ten.

Spadaro drove them through the village. At one point Miller thought they were heading for the new police station, but Spadaro made a left instead of a right onto Windmill Lane, then a right onto Hill Street. They were heading west now, in the same direction as the sirens Miller had heard hours before.

Once they were clear of the village Miller looked over at Spadaro. He couldn't remember ever having seen Spadaro in anything other than his cop's uniform. In street clothes he looked like a different man, but that had always been the case for Miller; his father had almost always been in uniform, but those times when he wasn't, he seemed just a bit out of place in the world, somehow reduced. Spadaro looked a little like that now.

"You make detective?" Miller said.

Spadaro shook his head. "No. It's my night off. I got called in. By the chief."

Miller nodded, thinking about that. He looked ahead, through the windshield. The edges of the glass were still dappled with raindrops. "Last I knew you were on the top of his shit list."

"Still am. No offense, but chauffeuring you around is a shit job."

Roffman was like that. When you were on his shit list, you knew it, were never allowed to forget it, in fact. Miller had been on that list for years.

"So where are we going?" he said

"The canal."

"What's at the canal?"

"A double homicide."

So someone was dead after all, Miller thought. He considered all this. He considered, too, the fact that he had been taken out of his apartment in the middle of the night by an off-duty cop, the only cop in the entire department with whom he was on anything close to friendly terms. There was only one question that arose from these thoughts.

"Any idea what this has to do with me?"

Spadaro shook his head. "Thought you'd tell me."

"Who's in charge at the scene?"

"Mancini is head detective, but from what I can tell, it's the chief who's calling the shots tonight."

"Roffman's there?"

"Yeah."

"That's . . . unusual."

Spadaro nodded. "A little bit, yeah."

Miller looked out the passenger door window then, saw that the top halves of the ancient trees lining this side of Hill Street were completely lost in the descending cloud. The large houses beyond them were barely visible, too, looked to Miller like ships receding into a bank of fog. It was then that the Bronco came to Moses Lane, the street on which Miller had grown up. He glanced down it as they passed, couldn't make out his former home only three driveways down. He had lived there with his mother and father till they were killed—his father by hired killers, his mother, two years later, by cancer—then had lived there alone for many years, till Abby showed up and moved in with him. She had stayed with him till he sold the house and had moved with him to the apartment by the train station.

She was everywhere in this town, everywhere he went, in everything he saw, or, in tonight's case, couldn't see. Even now, years after she had left him, and riding with Spadaro to meet Chief Roffman at the scene of a double murder, Miller was thinking of her, wondering where she was, what she was doing right now, if she was, at this moment, happy and safe.

Always there, on any given day, just a sight or sound or thought away.

They were passing the college, about to enter the Shinnecock Hills, when Miller said, "Any idea who's dead?" His voice was quiet, almost solemn. He sounded to his own ears like exactly what he was: a man who had to ask the question but wasn't at all certain he wanted to hear the answer.

Spadaro shook his head. "No." His frustration was clear. After a moment he said, "All I know is that the two victims are male. White, in their early twenties. Apparently the whole thing is a fucking sight to see."

Miller nodded at that, thought of asking what that meant exactly, *a fucking sight to see,* but didn't. He'd know soon enough. He said nothing more as the Bronco followed the curving road west though the low hills. Every turn tugged at him, pulling him deeper into the passenger seat. The blue flame in his chest burned steady and warm, and his lips tingled as though he had been kissed roughly for hours.

Always there, Abby was, just a thought or two away.

Even before they reached the bridge Miller saw the lights. Unnatural, garish even, glowing white beneath a thickening ceiling of fog. A brighter than usual canal up ahead, which meant police floodlights, a lot of them, by the look of it. A full-fledged investigation, not that a double homicide didn't call for that, but this was Southampton and the police were, at times, *peculiar.* As the Bronco approached the bridge, the bright white loomed, filling the windshield. Like a flash of lightning that, instead of ending, endured. It was, Miller knew, more than enough light for him to be seen by, and seen clearly, for anyone at the scene to determine by a mere look at him his current condition and its likely cause.

No place to hide.

He was used to that, hiding in his apartment, having little reason to leave it, and when he did, rarely going farther than the restaurant below. And now this. If it had been any cop but Spadaro. But, of course, that was why the chief had sent Spadaro.

Crossing over the bridge, Miller glimpsed from the passenger door window the access road below, saw the floodlights set up in a wide circle around the crime scene. He remembered the last murder scene he had been to, felt a chill move suddenly through him at just the memory of it. A dull chill, though, thanks to the medication. Once off the bridge, Spadaro turned onto Newtown Road, steered past the building that had once been a bar called the Water's Edge. Miller looked at it—windows boarded over, parking lot empty, just a solemn hulk standing a lonely guard along the canal. Passing this close to that building made him just a little nervous, and this surprised him. He tended to want to keep his promises, even the promises he hadn't ever fully understood, promises that couldn't by now matter, not anymore, not after so many years. Still, straying this close now to a place he had promised to steer clear of felt a bit like betrayal, a bit like brushing close to something that was fiercely dangerous.

The first right past the Water's Edge was Holzman Street, which connected Newtown Road with the access road that ran parallel to the canal. A police barricade was blocking Holzman, two patrol cars parked at angles behind it, their blue and red lights flashing. Two uniformed cops were standing by the open driver's door of one of the cruisers. They turned to face the approaching Bronco, one of them holding up his hand to indicate to the driver that he should halt. But Spadaro was already pulling over to the shoulder. He parked, kicked in the emergency brake, and killed the motor and lights.

"We'll have to walk from here," he said.

Outside, the cold, damp air felt good on Miller's face. Bracing. He needed that. He sunk his hands into the pocket of his field jacket and walked beside Spadaro toward the barricade. The cops looked at Spadaro, then at Miller. The looks on their faces were the same no matter who they were looking at. It was clear—made clear by hard stares—that these cops held Spadaro and Miller in more or less the same low regard. Contempt, even.

Not the warmest of welcomes, but Miller hadn't expected one.

Directly ahead, at the end of the block, was the canal. The fog hanging a dozen or so feet above the water reflected the harsh white of the floodlights, creating a sharp glare that almost hurt Miller's eyes. He squinted against it as they approached. The painkillers, no doubt, his pupils dilated. When they reached the end of Holzman they stopped, stood shoulder to shoulder. To their right, not far down the access road, was the support pillar of the train bridge. Made of stone, wet from the rain, it shimmered like a monument in the bright lights. Around it was yellow police tape. Within the perimeter made by the tape, near the footing of the pillar, lay two bodies. Miller's eyes went straight to them, he couldn't help it. He looked for a moment, almost sheepishly, then turned his attention away.

A half dozen cops were standing along the outer edge of the tape, their backs to Miller and Spadaro. Spadaro told Miller to wait where he was, then approached them. Four of them were uniformed, wearing bright orange slickers and hats covered with clear plastic bonnets. The other two wore street clothes—one a long black overcoat, the other a tan horseman's jacket. Even with their backs to him, Miller was able to recognize Detective Mancini and Chief Roffman.

They turned as Spadaro approached. He spoke to Roffman, but Mancini listened closely. Miller was too far away to hear what was being said, so he stood there, watched and waited. Every one of the uniformed cops turned and looked back at him. The looks weren't unlike the ones he had gotten from the two cops back at the roadblock. Miller noticed then that one of the uniformed cops was a woman. Tall, slender, a thick strand of wet hair hanging from beneath her cap, dangling in front of her face. As she looked at him she reached up with her left hand and brushed the stray strand away, tucking it behind her ear. The resemblance was striking, but of course this wasn't Kay. She had quit the force a year or so ago, all but been forced to. Roffman had obviously replaced her. He obviously, too, had a very specific type.

Miller looked back at the three men in street clothes. Roffman was in his mid-fifties, Mancini about the same, maybe a little older. The chief was tall but slimly built, had been considered, back when he came on after Miller's father was murdered, as more of an administrator than an actual cop. He had promised to end the deep corruption that had plagued his predecessor's department, but it didn't take long at all for rumors of all new levels of corruption to emerge.

Mancini was one of the first cops Roffman had brought in. Built a little like a bull—solid, from his shoulders straight down—he was an experienced street cop, everything Roffman wasn't. He had quickly become Roffman's right-hand man. Right now Roffman was talking to his detective, who was listening and nodding, his eyes, though, fixed on Miller. Roffman talked for a while, then finally said something to Spadaro that Spadaro clearly didn't like. He shook his head, as if in disbelief, looked down at his feet. Roffman took a step toward him, was inches from him now, spoke again, this time sternly. Spadaro looked up from his feet and toward the two bodies, then back at Roffman. When Roffman was done talking, Spadaro turned away and started back to Miller.

When he was within Miller's earshot, he said, "You're on your own, Tommy."

"What do you mean?"

Spadaro kept walking, was obviously not planning on stopping. "Roffman and Mancini are going to talk to you in a minute."

"Wait. Where are you going?"

Spadaro stopped short. "Home. I've done my part, apparently." He glanced back, then said to Miller, "Something's not right. The chief is up to something."

"What do you mean?"

"Like I'd fucking know. Listen, if you don't mind, I'd like to know what Roffman wants from you. I'd like to know *something*. Who knows, maybe we can help each other out."

Miller thought about that, then nodded and said, "Yeah, okay."

"Watch your back," Spadaro said. He took one last look at the cops gathered behind him. An outsider, looking in. Then he left without another word, headed back up Holzman, walking fast.

Miller watched him go, then looked at Roffman and Mancini. Roffman was talking again, Mancini nodding. The detective wasn't paying attention to Miller at all now. After a moment, Mancini turned away from Roffman, pulled his cell phone from his coat pocket, made a call. Roffman looked directly at Miller then, gestured toward an unmarked sedan parked along the canal's edge, just a few yards behind Miller. Miller nodded and started toward it.

The canal locks were closed, the water slow-moving, its rippled surface steely under the lights. Miller faced the water and listened to the small waves lapping on the concrete wall of the channel as he waited for the chief of police to meet him.

He stood as still as he could, his mind reeling just a little. He felt as if the edge he was standing upon now wasn't mere feet above tranquil waters but instead hundreds of feet, thousands of feet, in the night sky, up in those relentless currents of buffeting winds, as cold as space, racing like frantic ghosts high above Long Island.

"This won't take long," Roffman said.

He had reached Miller, was standing beside him, facing him. Miller continued to look out over the canal, his hands deep in the pockets of his field jacket. He didn't turn to face Roffman, kept his left shoulder pointed toward him. He didn't know which was more of a concern to him—hiding his condition from the man or not having to look at him. Probably both.

"What do you want, Chief?" Miller said.

Roffman nodded toward the sedan. "C'mon, let's get in."

"I'm fine here."

"I'm not," Roffman said flatly.

He was looking around, checking his surroundings. Miller caught this from the corner of his eye. It was clear by the way Roffman was searching the area that he was checking to see if there was anyone around—anyone other than his people—to see him talking with Miller.

"C'mon, it doesn't have to be this way," Roffman said. "Get in and we'll talk. Like I said, this won't take long."

He walked to the sedan, opened the back door, waited for Miller. Scanning, still, but not as blatantly as a moment before. Head held still, his eyes moved as casually as possible—toward the bridge to the south, the darkened restaurant on the eastern side of the canal, and the bridge to the north, the Sunrise Highway bridge. All the areas that offered clear views but were not secured by his cops. Miller waited a moment, then stepped away from the canal's edge and climbed into the sedan. Roffman swung the door closed behind him. It sealed more than shut. He walked around the back to the other side, opened the door, got in, pulled the door closed. Again, it sealed tight, cutting off the sound of the waves and the hiss of the occasional car crossing over the nearby bridges, all the subtle noises of the canal on a wet night.

Just the two of them now, sitting side by side in silence.

"I appreciate you coming," Roffman said. He had dark hair and a mustache, the face of an intelligent—if not forever doubting—man. But maybe that was the administrator in him, this expression a means of ensuring that those beneath him worked always for his approval. *You wear a mask long enough, it becomes you,* Miller thought. It was hard to tell how much of this was a well-practiced act and how much of it was the actual man, but really it didn't matter either way to Miller. Roffman was little more than an abstract idea in his life now. Miller had every intention to keep it that way. He owned his building outright, paid his taxes, rarely strayed far from his end of Elm Street, what was for him *a sovereign state.* Roffman had no reason to want anything from him, or to give a damn about him. He lived his days now, or so it seemed at certain times, with this ambition, and this ambition only, in mind.

And yet, here he was, confined in this small space, smelling the man's cologne, close enough to hear the man breathe, no choice but to look at his skeptical face. Almost . . . *fatherly.*

"Why the hell am I here?" Miller said.

"First things first, Tommy. I need to know if you happen to have a recording device on you right now."

"Jesus."

"Do you?"

"No."

"Spadaro said he didn't see you grab anything as you got ready. Of course, you're a resourceful type and might keep something in your coat, a just-in-case kind of thing. You mind if I check?"

Miller raised his arms. They felt heavy, as if he had just lifted weights. "Knock yourself out."

Roffman patted the four pockets of the field jacket, felt nothing. Miller lowered his arms as Roffman leaned back into his seat.

"We don't have a lot of time," Roffman said, "so I'll get to the point. I could use your help with something."

"I'm not interested."

"You will be."

Roffman reached into the pocket of his coat, pulled something out. Miller glanced down, saw from the corner of his eyes a thin stack of Polaroid photographs.

"Living the good life these days, huh?" Roffman said.

Miller didn't answer.

"It certainly looks like the good life to me. Retired before thirty. The rent you collect from that restaurant pays your property taxes, keeps you fed and warm. What more could a man want, right?"

What man didn't want more than that? Miller thought.

Roffman sorted through the photos in his hand. Four of them, from what Miller could see. He shuffled them like playing cards.

"How long ago did you give up your license?"

Miller said nothing.

"Like I said, Tommy, there isn't a lot of time. You have your reasons for disliking me, just as I have my reasons for not trusting you. I think we're both clear on that part. But the sooner you cooperate, the sooner we'll be done here. The sooner we're done here, the sooner you'll be free to go."

Miller took a breath, let it out. Finally, he said, "I gave up my license two years ago."

"And you haven't been doing any unlicensed work, right? Off-the-books kind of things, favors for friends?"

"No."

"Why would you, though, right? It's not like you need the money. And it's not like you have a lot of friends or leave your apartment all that much."

Miller looked at him. There was no need, by the look on his face, to say what was now on his mind.

Roffman nodded, almost apologetically. "You're a pretty easy man to keep track of," he said. "So, you're out of the business, right? No back-road work, nothing like that."

"No."

"Good." Roffman sorted through the photos, picked out one, held it up for Miller to see. "I'd like to know if this guy looks familiar to you."

Miller glanced at the photo. It was a close-up of the face of a dead male. White, in his twenties. He had been beaten, but not so much to have made the face unrecognizable.

After a moment, Miller said, "Never seen him."

"You sure?"

"Yes."

Roffman showed a second photo. Just like the first one. White male, in his twenties, face badly beaten.

"How about him?"

Miller glanced at the face, the eyes swollen shut, the cuts in the skin. He shook his head. "No."

"You're sure about that?"

"Yeah."

Roffman looked at the photos, put them back on the thin stack with the others. "There are some things you don't ever expect to see," he said. "You know. Even as a cop, you don't expect to see them, they're just not part of . . . I don't know . . . modern life."

Miller waited, saying nothing.

"About three hours ago these two men were hanged from that bridge over there." He pointed through the window, toward the train bridge. "Hanged by their necks. Like a lynching. I've seen pictures of hanged men, but I never expected to see the actual thing. It's . . . disturbing, somehow."

Miller looked toward the bridge. Nothing there now, of course. He tried to imagine that. *Supposed to be a fucking sight to see,* Spadaro had said.

"Suicides?" Miller asked. His doubt was audible.

"No."

"What tells you that?"

"A witness saw one of the victims being lowered down by two men. Not pushed, so his neck would break at the end of his fall. Lowered down, nice and easy, so he'd strangle."

Again, Miller waited.

"Of course, we don't really need the witness to tell us this wasn't some suicide pact," Roffman said.

"Why not?"

Roffman removed the two remaining photographs, held them up side by side. Miller looked at them but couldn't believe what he was seeing.

These weren't close-ups of the faces like the two previous photos but rather full body shots of the victims stretched out on the wet access road. Their hands were missing, had been cut off at the wrists.

"They weren't bound in any way," Roffman said. "I can't help but imagining these poor guys, you know, out of reflex, reaching up to grab the rope tightening around their necks, nothing there but two bloody stumps. Jesus, just the thought of it."

Miller turned away from the photos. He thought then of the beaten faces.

"Were their teeth knocked out?" he said.

"No."

"So this wasn't done to conceal their identities."

Roffman nodded. "It seems that way. The rain, of course, washed away any footprints up on the tracks. Some blood remains, but not a lot."

"You think the hands were severed up there."

"The statement from the witness indicates that. He saw one of the two men making what sounds to me like hacking motions right before they lowered the victim down. And we found fresh cut marks from some kind of hatchet in the wooden ties. I imagine the hands are somewhere in the Shinnecock Bay by now."

Miller looked toward the slow-moving water. "Were the locks open when this happened?"

"Yeah."

"Then they're probably out in the Atlantic by now."

"We're getting some divers from the coast guard to search the bay, just in case. It's going to be like looking for a needle in a haystack, though."

"Any identification on the victims?"

"Oh, yeah. No problem there. No cell phones, but wallets, with everything we'd need to know who they are."

"Money, too?"

"Yeah. In fact, one of the victims had over two hundred dollars."

So not robbery, Miller thought. It was doubtful that anyone would go to such lengths just to steal a cell phone or two.

"Whoever did this clearly wanted the identities of their victims to be known," Roffman said.

Miller almost didn't want to ask. "So who are they? The victims, I mean?"

"One is named James Michaels. He has a record, one bust for stealing a car two years ago. The other is named Richard Romano. He has no record at all. Both of their driver's licenses have upstate addresses, so we have nothing local to check out. At first we assumed, because of their ages, that the upstate addresses would belong to their families."

"How old are they?"

"Twenty-three. We got the numbers currently listed to those addresses and called but no one had ever heard of them."

"They're from the same town?"

"Yeah. Colonie, outside of Albany."

"So they were friends," Miller said.

"Probably, yeah."

"What about Michaels's arrest form from two years ago?"

"The address listed is one of those rental houses across from the college. According to the landlord it's unrented right now. Apparently a lot of those houses are empty now that the college is closed. According to him he never had a lease with either name on it."

"Maybe Michaels had been a student at the college. Liked it out here, stayed around after. That happens."

"We're checking on that."

"And the name on the lease for the time Michaels was supposed to be living there?"

"Yeah, we're on that, too."

Roffman returned the photos to his jacket pocket, was quiet for a moment. Then he reached into his jacket, removed from an inside pocket a clear plastic Baggie. At first Miller couldn't see what it contained. Finally he made out what looked like a business card.

"So the names and faces of these victims don't ring any bells with you," Roffman said.

"No."

"Neither of them were ever clients of yours?"

"Obviously, no. If I've never seen them or heard their names, how could they have been?"

Roffman nodded. "Then we have a bit of a problem."

"What?"

Roffman held up the Baggie for Miller to see.

"We found this in the wallet belonging to the onetime car thief. James Michaels."

Miller looked at the card, recognized it at once.

Tommy Miller. Private Investigator.

Printed below that was a phone number and an e-mail address. The card was a heavy stock, gray, the lettering raised.

"Any idea how this got into his wallet?" Roffman said.

Miller shrugged. "No. It's an old card, though. From four years ago."

"How do you know that?"

"The number is the business line of my house on Moses Lane. When I moved four years ago I printed up new cards, replaced that number with the number to a cell phone."

Roffman turned the card, looked at the number, then held the card up again for Miller to see. He pointed to the e-mail address in the bottom-right corner.

"But this account is still good?"

Miller nodded. "Yeah."

"So if we figure out where Michaels lived and get access to his computer, we aren't going to find e-mails from you to him?"

"No."

"Any idea how he happened to get hold of one of your business cards?"

"One of my old business cards," Miller corrected.

"Any idea how he happened to get hold of one of your old business cards?"

"No."

"Who did you give these out to back then?"

"The usual. Clients."

"How many cards, roughly?"

"I don't know."

"Four years is a long time for someone to hold onto a business card, don't you think? And it's not like his wallet was filled with business cards. Just the one, in fact."

"You said this would interest me, Chief. So far it hasn't."

Roffman returned the Baggie to his inside pocket, then lay his hands across his lap and looked out his window, toward the bridge foundation, the cops around it, the yellow tape and floodlights.

"Aren't you curious how this kid ended up with a four-year-old business card of yours in his wallet?"

"Not really."

"Yeah, well, I am."

"So find out."

Roffman smiled. "Ah, see, that's the trick."

"Funny, I thought that was your job."

"For the longest time, Tommy, my job was cleaning up the mess your father had left behind. There were a lot of people in this town who were used to a certain kind of treatment. Who had paid well for that over the years, assumed they'd get the same consideration from me, didn't necessarily like the idea that they wouldn't. Some were determined to get what they wanted at all costs."

Miller said nothing, just sat there and waited for the point.

Roffman looked again toward the bridge foundation.

"If you kill somebody," he said, "if you know what you're doing, you don't kill them in a public place, right? And you certainly don't string them up for everyone to see. God knows there are plenty of places out here to stash a couple of dead bodies, right? The Pine Barrens out in Westhampton. The Northwest woods. Hell, take them out in a boat, miles offshore, feed them to the sharks. You don't do this, go to all this trouble, unless you want what you did to be seen, unless it being seen benefits you somehow. Walking somebody onto a bridge, in view of two other bridges, not to mention that restaurant over there, that's a big risk, and you don't take risks like that unless you absolutely have to."

Again, Miller waited, saying nothing.

"To me," Roffman said finally, "it's obvious that this is some kind of warning. From someone, to someone. It has to be. And it's not just that those two poor bastards were hanged there for everyone to see, but that their hands were cut off first. Hacked off. In certain places in the world that's still the punishment for stealing."

Miller nodded absently. So maybe it wasn't a coincidence after all, the bodies being here, within sight of the Water's Edge. The thought crossed his mind—how could it not?—but he didn't grab on to it, just let it pass through and then be gone. *A promise was a promise.*

Miller thought back then to what Roffman had said just a moment ago about certain people expecting a certain kind of treatment from the police, doing what it took to ensure that they got it. What exactly had Roffman meant by that? What had he been trying to tell Miller?

"We haven't had a murder here in six years," Roffman said. "And now this fucking mess. Barbaric, like something out of the Dark Ages. The kind of thing the press will eat up and still want more of. And I'm not talking just the local press, either, the weekly papers, the radio. I'm talking national coverage. We got the bodies down as fast as we could, before anyone had the chance to take any pictures, but it seems to me that word of this alone will be more than enough to bring us some un-wanted attention."

Miller knew then why he was here, the reason Roffman had sent for him.

"I don't believe for one minute that you don't have an interest in knowing what your connection is to all this," Roffman said. "There's something very . . . cautious in the way you live these days. Like a man with something to lose, as opposed to what you used to be, a man with something to gain. I'll tell you, I don't miss that guy, he was a pain in my ass. But I simply can't imagine you sitting there in your apartment, pop-ping those pills of yours, content to hope that this, whatever this is, doesn't rush up from behind and bite you on the ass. I just don't see you doing that."

Miller took a breath, let it out. He wondered what exactly had given his current condition away. Had he been slurring his words? Reacting slowly? Had Roffman seen his eyes, the wild look the drug brought to them? Of course it was foolish to wonder about this at all. Really, what was there about him now that *wouldn't* have given him away? Administrator or not, Roffman was intelligent enough to identify a person half-lost in the warm haze of painkillers. One didn't need to be an experienced street cop to do that.

"I have a brutal double murder and no leads to speak of," Roffman said. "No leads, right now, that is, except for you. It seems for now our interests might be somewhat aligned. Since we both know you're going to end up looking into this, I'd be interested in knowing what you find out about our two victims here. In exchange, I'd be willing to look the other way should you need to . . . cross the line in the course of your investigation."

Miller looked at him. "Cross the line?"

Roffman shrugged. "You don't have a license to protect these days. There are advantages to that, you can go places you couldn't go before. Do things you couldn't do before."

"Things you can't do. Places you can't go. That's what you're really saying, isn't it, Chief?"

"Like I said, people are going to be watching this closely. A lot of people. I'm asking for your help, Tommy. Help yourself and help me at the same time. I'll give you a window of twenty-four hours. If at the end of that twenty-four hours you need more, we'll talk."

"Why twenty-four?" Miller said.

"Because you know full well that if we don't find who did this by then, we probably won't ever find them. Those are the unfortunate statistics. Besides, you're a Miller. Like father, like son, right? You can't give a Miller too much free rein, he'll only end up wanting more. Or making a mess of things. After the twenty-four hours is up, if I don't hear from you, we're all back to business as usual."

"And what does 'business as usual' mean?"

Now Roffman said nothing. He looked at his watch, adjusted the cuff of his jacket. "Don't contact me directly," he said. "Anything you need to tell me should go through Mancini. He speaks for me from this point on. Do you understand?"

Miller nodded. It was more of an indication of his desire to *get the fuck out of there* than an indication of his complicity in what Roffman was proposing. Miller had heard more than enough, more than he needed to hear, more than he could right now handle. His mind was reeling.

"Amnesty doesn't mean you don't need to be careful, Tommy. Eyes will be upon us, remember that. Crossing the line is one thing, but going too far, that's something else."

Miller said nothing for a moment. Then, finally: "I need to call a cab. You sent my ride home."

Roffman took one last look at Miller, sizing him up.

"Officer Clarke will take you back." Roffman knocked on his window with the knuckle of his middle finger. Miller's door opened then. He got out, was face-to-face now with the female cop he had seen earlier. How long had she been standing there? He felt suddenly that everyone around him was steps ahead of him, and he didn't like that at all.

He rode in the back of the cruiser, like a criminal. He and Clarke didn't speak. What was there for them to say? There was cross-chatter on her dispatch radio, but nothing that told Miller anything he didn't already know. Every now and then he'd look through the steel grid separating the front and backseats and notice that Clarke was looking at him in the rearview mirror. She was young, pretty. A few years out of the academy, at the most. Roffman's driver, no doubt. *The privileges of being chief.* The man had a type, though, that much was clear; Clarke looked enough like Kay to be her kid sister. Miller realized something then. His whole life he had been younger than the cops on the force, but now here was a new recruit, and one that was obviously younger than he. Significantly younger. A fact, he thought, worthy of noting.

He was twenty-nine now. His father hadn't lived to see sixty. Granted, the man hadn't died of natural causes, but still, for the sake of argument, it was safe enough for Miller to claim that he was halfway through his own life now, give or take. Another fact worth noting, he thought. But it felt to him as if a lifetime was already behind him. It felt, too, that another one, a life he could not quite imagine, was ahead still. Somewhere, waiting, beyond sight and grasp. *A comfortable, if not promising, future.* But what future, exactly? Who to be now that he wasn't who he used to be?

At one point on the ride to Southampton, Miller met Clarke's eyes in the mirror and held them for a moment. He couldn't help but wonder then what she knew about him. About his past. The good *and* the bad, though, more than likely, of course, she would have heard only the bad. Who really talked about the good? What was that line from Shakespeare, about the evil that men do?

It didn't really matter, though, what she may or may not have been told. Miller knew that. He had made his peace, paid his debt, in doing so sacrificed what should never be sacrificed. He owed nothing to no one, least of all an explanation.

He turned away from her stare then—the stare, for a change, of some- one younger than he. The rest of the way home he watched the gather- ing fog drifting past the windows of the cruiser like long puffs of lingering smoke. The world he knew so well, the landmarks that had been there his entire life, were almost completely obscured now, hidden behind these gathering banks of reflecting white. *Unearthly, like the land- scape of some bad dream.* If he didn't already know where he was—on Montauk Highway, winding through the Shinnecock Hills, one turn shy, by his count, of the long straightaway that ran past the college—he would have felt utterly, terribly lost, little more than a stranger adrift in some foreign and dangerous land.

Back in his apartment, Miller stood in the empty front room, by one of the tall windows that let in the street light, looked down at the train sta- tion, or what he could see of it. Finally he got tired of all the open space, wanted the comfort of four walls close around him, that and a little more darkness, so he retreated to his back bedroom and sat on the edge of his mattress. Too much to think about, too much to take in, still. He consid- ered calling Spadaro, as he had been asked to, and fill him in on what the chief had said. Several times he even reached for his phone and then stopped himself. Spadaro's feud with Roffman was real, Miller knew this much. Still, this whole thing felt somehow wrong. He couldn't put his finger on it, couldn't find words to explain his feeling, but *this just seemed wrong.*

Miller glanced at the amber-colored bottle of pills on the sill near his bed. Eventually he reached out for it, held it for a moment with both hands, then opened the drawer of his nightstand and tossed the bottle in. It was then that he saw the photograph, lying in the bottom of the drawer. He picked it up and looked at it in the weak light of his room.

Abby. Taken in this very room, as she lay beneath the covers of his bed. *Their bed, back then.* The very same covers, in fact. Her bare shoulders, her long brown hair, her arms folded across her stomach, something she did whenever she was nervous. But she was laughing, almost wildly, happy. She was twenty-one when they had met, twenty-three when the picture had been taken, months still before she would leave him. She was, what, now? Twenty-seven? He thought about that for a while. *Life passing him by.* He had lost her because of his job, because of his commitment to it. His obsession, really, he knew that. He often wondered if things might have been different had he quit sooner, back when she was still with him. She was afraid of being alone, hated it, and he had thought a restaurant full of people below would have made the nights he worked and she waited for him easier on her. It hadn't. There was no point in wondering about what he should have done; he had done the only thing he could do at that time, and she was gone now, long gone. Still, if he knew where to find her, he'd do so, tell her about the changes he had made in his life, tell her that she had been right and he should have listened to her, that he wished he had listened to her, wished he could simply go back and find a way to pay his debt and not, as she saw it, abandon her, not leave her alone night after night till she finally left him. . . .

He looked at the photo for a moment more, then returned it to the drawer. He needed to think this through, see where it came out. *Whom to trust?* Roffman or Spadaro? Both were cops, so there was, really, no reason at all for him to trust either.

He needed answers. And there was only one person to whom he could turn.

Miller checked his watch. It was a few minutes before eleven. Late, but he didn't care. He stood, crossed the small room, opened the top drawer of his bureau and dug through its contents till he found what he was looking for. A calling card, years old by now, but maybe it was still valid. He left his apartment, hurried across Railroad Plaza to the train station, hardly limping now, hardly feeling a thing at all. *Dangerous, to be out in the world like this, impaired as he was.* But he had no choice.

If something *was* heading his way, then he wanted to see it coming. Needed to. Roffman had been right about that much.

From the solitary pay phone on the long, empty platform, Miller made the call.

Four

THE CAB HAD YET TO ARRIVE.

She thought it would have been there by now, had, in fact, expected it to pull up in front of her place just minutes after she'd hung up the phone. That was how it had always gone in the past. Concerned now that the cab wasn't going to show at all, she wondered if she should call for another. Finally, though, she told herself to give it one more minute, and when that minute had passed, she told herself to give it one more. She wasn't supposed to drive her own vehicle, that much she knew, and anyway, she didn't know where it was they were supposed to meet. He hadn't told her that, had only said that he needed to talk to her and that he was sending a cab to get her. He was never one for saying much over the phone; eavesdropping on calls was just too easy these days. But this wasn't a recent thing, he'd always been that way, for as long as she'd known him. She was asleep when he had called, dead to the world, half-naked in her warm bed, there for the duration. Now, minutes later, she was in jeans and a thermal shirt and boat shoes, her oversized green parka wrapped tight around her narrow torso, the fur-lined hood pulled up over her head against the damp and cold. If she had known the cab was going to take this long to arrive, she would have waited upstairs, in her apartment, watching from her front window. But how could she have known that? How could she have known that this would be any differ-ent from all the other times she'd been called to meet him like this? Still, she felt a little silly, standing there on her dark front porch, watching her quiet residential street and listening for the sound of tires on wet pave-ment, drawing her parka tight around herself to hold on to what re-mained of the deep warmth she had carried down with her from her bed.

She'd heard the sirens earlier tonight, was home from work by then, but hadn't thought twice about them. She began to wonder now, though, exactly what they had meant. Four patrol cars, racing westward, by the sound of them. That was every cop on duty. Add to that the call from Miller a few hours later—after all this time. And add to that the overdue cab. Even in the summertime, when the streets were congested with tourists, cabs came faster than this. Any one of these things sepa-rately was enough to tell her that something was going on in town. *Something big—or big enough.* All three of them together, though, well, there was just no way that could be anything but bad news for someone.

She was about to head back inside, call for another cab from her third-floor apartment and wait for it there, where it was warm and dry, but just as she was turning toward her door she caught sight of the familiar sweep of headlights crossing her street, knew by this that a car had made the turn from Meeting House Lane onto Lewis Street a block away. She heard then the sound of tires on the pavement, started down the path that led from her front door to the curb even before she actually had seen the cab. But who else could it be at this time of night? She reached the end of the path as the cab pulled to a stop, climbed into the back and pulled the heavy door closed. Though it was warm in the cab, she kept her hood up, settling back in her seat as the cabbie made an illegal U-turn, then returned to the end of Lewis. Once there, he made a left on Meeting House Lane, heading west, toward the village. He was driv-ing just a little bit above the speed limit, but she ignored this, as she had done with the illegal U-turn.

Such things were no longer any of her concern.

The cabbie had been told where to take her by Miller, so there was no need for her to say anything. She sat with her parka wrapped around her and looked out her window. She didn't glance at the driver once, even though she sensed that every now and then he was looking back at her in the rearview mirror.

Halfway down Meeting House a call came in on the radio.

"Dispatch to Bobby." Even with the voice distorted by static, muffled as it came through the single small speaker, she could hear a Jamaican accent.

The driver picked up the handset, responded, "Go ahead, Eddie."

"Got a pick-up in Wainscott. That bar called Helenbach. How soon can you get there?"

"I'm about to drop off the Southampton fare. Better tell them a half hour. The weather's getting pretty bad."

"If they can't wait, I'll radio back."

"Okay."

"Eddie out."

The driver replaced the handset to the radio mounted under the dashboard. They came to the stoplight at the end of Meeting House. As they waited, she looked to her right, down Main Street. Visibility was less than a block in all directions. About halfway down Main, all she could see was the shimmering black pavement feeding into a blur of soft white.

A severely limited world tonight, but that was fine with her.

"Busy night," the cabbie said then.

She was still looking down Main, at the end of the world. Hypnotic, almost. "Oh, yeah," she said flatly.

"They had to stop the eastbound trains in Hampton Bays, and the westbound trains in Bridgehampton. I've been running people stuck in Hampton Bays to their cars at the stations in Southampton and Bridge-hampton. Had to take one guy to East Hampton. Boy, was he pissed. Crazy night, man. Crazy night."

She nodded politely, wasn't going to ask but finally couldn't help herself, a part of her had to know. "Why'd they stop the trains?"

"The cops found two people murdered at the canal. On the bridge there."

She nodded at that, thoughtfully. It was clear why Miller wanted to see her. Something to do with this, no doubt, what else could it be? But what she didn't know was why Miller would now, suddenly, care about something like this. Last she knew he was out, retired, done with all this.

Last she knew he had gotten what he needed to finally be able to live with himself.

Another question came to her mind. She waited a moment, wondered if she could live without knowing the answer, told herself she'd find out sooner or later, that much was certain. But, of course, in the end, she asked. Like she could have stopped herself.

"Any idea who the victims are?" she said.

"No."

She glanced forward then, met the driver's eyes in the rearview mirror. He was young, maybe Miller's age, maybe a little older. Younger, then, than she was, by a few years at least. Caucasian, a mop of curly black hair framing, from what she could see of it, a long but handsome face. Steady eyes, remarkably so, piercing even. Pale blue, though maybe that was a trick of the dashboard lights. *A practiced stare,* though. It had to be. Though he was sitting she estimated his height and weight, just as she had been taught to a long time ago. Five-eleven, one-eighty. Only an inch taller than she, but outweighing her by a good sixty pounds. She had lost too much weight over the winter, had become too slight, significantly weaker. When she was a cop, she had worked out, run, stayed strong. Now she didn't do much but work at the liquor store and sleep, started her days not with a blend of vitamins designed specifically for runners but with the pill her doctor had prescribed to ease her depression.

She broke from his stare, glanced down at his license mounted under clear plastic on the back of his seat. *Falcetti, Robert.* It wasn't a name she'd seen or heard before. Nothing worse than coming face-to-face with someone she had once arrested or helped to process at the station house. Seeing them walk into the store, then ringing them up at the register, wondering if they were staring at her because she was a woman and they were men or because they recognized her, or almost recognized her, had seen her somewhere before but just couldn't figure out where. Nothing, really, worse than that.

Falcetti was still looking at her in the mirror. Still staring with that stare of his. Her face was framed by the fur-lined hood—faux coyote fur, army surplus. A perfect oval of eyes and nose and mouth, nothing more. She knew how she looked in that hood—coy, almost—was wearing it not for that reason, never wore it for that reason, but just to keep warm and dry. And, too, to feel concealed. *Private.* She knew, also, that stray strands of her hair—brown, straight, long—had slipped out of the pony-tail she had pulled it into before coming downstairs to wait for the cab, were now peeking out from the fur-lining, hanging here and there in front of her face. It used to interest her what men had found attractive about her. The more unkempt she looked, it seemed, the more they stared. *A woman on the verge of wildness?* Was that what they saw? Was that what she was?

"You look different out of your uniform," Falcetti observed.

Barton nodded, said nothing to that.

"I guess everyone does, though, huh?" Falcetti added.

"Yeah."

"You're . . . Katherine, right?"

"Kay."

He thought for a moment more, still watching her, then: "Barton, right?"

"Yeah."

"I'm Bobby."

She glanced at him once more, nodded briefly. No reason to be rude. But she said nothing. No reason, either, to say anything. Something about the way he looked, though, the way he looked at her, unnerved her. His *stare.* So . . . practiced. But there was always the chance that she was being oversensitive. She was like that these days, wary of men, all men. Contemptuous, even. But how could she not be? Her current in-teractions with men, fortunately, were limited to her customers at the liquor store. Regulars, for the most part, many of whom came in not for the prices or the convenience of the Job's Lane location but, obviously, for her. The store's owner had hired her because he liked the idea of an ex-cop behind the counter, hadn't anticipated a bump in sales, though, looking back, he realized he probably should have. Men are, after all, men. But Barton didn't care about that, wanted nothing to do with any of it. Love, lust, the whole damned mess—these were simply things she had no interest in anymore. *No room for that.* Besides, she was tired. So tired. Her pills, mercifully, kept her numb to the parts of herself that had once demanded there be a man beside her, that had driven her to need all that and to risk—and, finally, lose—everything for which she had worked so hard.

"So what the hell's at the beach at this time of night?" Falcetti said. "And on a night like this?"

Barton continued to look out the window to her right, down what she could see of Main Street. "I'm meeting a friend," she said. Her love affair with Roffman, when it was finally revealed, had been headline news in the local papers, remained so for months. She had stayed on the force for as long as she could, quit finally when it became clear to her— when it was *made* clear to her, once and for all—that she would not advance. Ever. She doubted that there was anyone in town, this cabbie included, who didn't know of her years-long affair with her married boss. Hadn't heard at least *something* about that. Her saying what she had just said, she hoped, would stop Falcetti from asking any more questions. A late-night meeting in an out-of-the-way place—how could that be anything other than this Barton woman—this *home wrecker*—up to her old tricks?

Let him think what he wants to think, as long as he leaves me in peace.

The light turned green then. Falcetti made another left, onto South Main Street. The ocean was less than a mile away. As they headed south and approached the water, the fog deepened, became quickly a shifting curtain that surrounded them closely on all sides. Barton looked forward, through the windshield, careful to avoid the rearview mirror. There was nothing to see, though, except the glare of the cab's bright headlights reflecting back, unable to penetrate the harsh, solid white that was now all there was ahead of them.

A right onto Gin Lane, then onto Dune Road. Barton could hear the ocean now, even over the hiss of the tires cutting across the wet pavement below, even with the cab's windows closed tight. Rough seas crashing into the beach, heavy waves sounding like the long rumble of approaching thunder. The cab turned into the large parking lot at Cooper's Beach, a public beach area where Cooper's Neck Lane met Dune Road. The lot was empty and unlit, which was, of course, why Miller had chosen it as their meeting place. Anyone that may have followed either of them here would easily be seen if they entered the long lot or, if they tried to hide their intention by continuing past it, be clearly visible on Dune Road for the time it would take them to cover the length of the lot. Also, with the noisy ocean to their backs, Barton knew that she and Miller could talk without fear of being eavesdropped upon by some high-tech device. Anyone who desired to get close enough to filter out any covering background noise would be unable to do so without making themselves seen.

This was the world in which Miller lived—or *used* to live. The world, Barton thought, he had given up in favor of the life of a landlord, a life of leisure.

So what, then, were they doing here?

The cab crossed the lot, pulled to a stop at the foot of a steep dune. Falcetti shifted into park, looked back at Barton once again in the rearview mirror.

"Is this good?" he said.

She nodded. "How much do I owe you?"

"It's covered."

"I should give you something."

"No, it's all taken care of. Orders. Don't take a dime from her."

Barton nodded again. "Tell Eddie thanks."

"I will. I should wait, though, till your friend gets here."

"That's okay."

"I can't let you just stand out here all alone."

"It's okay, really. My friend might be a while. Besides, you have a fare waiting."

She opened the door, slid across the backseat and got out, then swung the door closed and took a step back. Falcetti was looking at her through the driver's door window. He nodded once, then drove off. The cab crossed the parking lot, disappearing into the fog less than halfway across. All she could see now were its lights, growing duller as it got farther away. She saw it turn right onto Dune Road, after that fading from sight completely. Barton was alone now. She put her hands in the pockets of her oversized parka, drew it tight around her. When she exhaled, she could see her breath, watched it as it quickly rose upward and dissipated into nothingness. The ocean was louder now that she was out of the cab, now that there was nothing at all to hear but the sound of it. A hundred feet behind her, and angry, brutal even, made so by the recent late-winter rain.

A few minutes after the cab drove away, another vehicle appeared. This one was heading straight down Cooper's Neck Lane, its headlights visible as two blurs in the distance. The lights stopped at the end of Cooper's Neck, then crossed Dune Road and entered the parking lot. Out of the fog, halfway across the lot, emerged Miller's pickup. Mid-sized, beat-to-shit. It didn't approach Barton but instead headed for a spot a good hundred feet from where she was standing at the foot of the dune. Of course, there was no doubt in Barton's mind that he had seen her. Miller quickly killed the motor and the lights but didn't get out right away. Barton knew he was watching for any indication that a car had followed him. She looked toward Cooper's Neck Lane, couldn't see it at all through the ground fog, couldn't even see the entrance to the lot. She knew, though, that she would have seen headlights, just as she had seen Miller's, which was why he had chosen that approach, she was certain, in the first place. She stared but saw nothing except a wall of white, no sense of any world at all beyond it.

Eventually she heard Miller's truck door close, turned and spotted him crossing the distance between them. Tall like his father had been, as solidly built as ever, wearing that same old hand-me-down military field jacket he always wore. But there was something different about him now. Dramatically different. He was bearded, hadn't been when she last saw him. A thick beard, full. His dark hair, too, was longer than she had ever seen it. The change was nothing less than jarring. He reached her finally, stood with his hands in the pockets of his jacket, only a few feet between them now. They faced each other but didn't make a move to embrace, never really did that in all the time they'd known each other, as close as they were.

"Thanks for meeting me, Kay," he said. His tone was serious, solemn. He had to speak up to be heard over the sound of the waves but didn't dare speak too loudly. *A razor's edge.* To her, Miller didn't only sound grim, he looked it, but maybe that was an effect of the beard and the unruly hair.

"Long time, no see, Tommy."

"How've you been?"

"Good. You look different with a beard."

"Yeah?"

"It makes you look older. Less of a boy."

"That's good, right?"

Barton shrugged, smiled. It was, despite the changes in his appearance, the circumstances of their meeting, good to see him. "How's the new place?"

"Falling apart."

"You get used to the trains yet?"

"Can barely hear them. How's the liquor store?"

"Busy. All this rain, everyone drinks."

"You look good." He was lying, she could hear it.

"You look stoned," she said flatly.

Miller smiled. He looked away, checking for signs of a car in the fog. He was concerned about them being seen, this much was clear to Barton. She wasn't ready, though, to know why.

She glanced down at his leg. "How's your knee?"

"Hurts in the rain. All that money and time so it would stop hurting in the cold, and now it hurts in the rain." He looked back at her.

"How are you right now?"

"I feel good."

"Yeah, I bet. You shouldn't be driving like this, Tommy. Especially in weather like this."

"I'm okay."

Barton waited a moment, watching his face closely, looking for the man she had always known, always trusted. He was sixteen when they had met, she twenty-three. He was the son of the then-chief of police, had once been the worst kind of juvenile delinquent, was trying to straighten himself out. He was already shattered by then. Barton was a recent hire, brought in as the first of the "new blood." Chief Miller was just starting to clean house, trying to quiet rumors of corruption—corruption that had caught the attention of the FBI, among others. Three months later Chief Miller was dead. In the months that followed, the actual depths of his department's corruption—"vast," the newspapers kept calling it—began to be known.

Still, Chief Miller had invited Barton to his house for dinner when she had first arrived, had, along with his wife, opened his home to her, treated her, so far from her own family, like a daughter. She and Miller had stood together at his funeral, then stood together again, two years later, at Miller's mother's graveside. Till recently, she and Tommy had been a significant part of each other's lives, always there, always checking in on each other. Whenever possible, Barton had done what she could to help Miller out with his investigations, even had gone as far several times as to get him copies of police files—statements, police reports, coroner's reports—when he had needed them.

She looked at him now, was at last ready for the one question that mattered to be answered.

"Why are we back here, Tommy?" she said. "What's going on?"

He took one more look around, quick but thorough, then looked at her and said, "I had a little meeting with Roffman."

"When?"

"Just a little while ago. He sent Spadaro to pick me up."

"What did he want?"

"Two bodies were found at the canal tonight."

"Yeah, I heard."

"How?"

"The cabbie mentioned it."

Miller thought about that, then continued. "The victims were two males in their early twenties. They were hanged from the bridge. Their hands had been hacked off."

"Jesus."

"Yeah."

"What do you mean by hanged exactly?"

"Just that. Hanged, by their necks. Like an execution."

"Did you see them?"

"No. I mean, not hanging. The cops had them down by the time I got there."

"You went to the canal?"

"Spadaro took me there. Walked me right in. That's where the chief was."

Confused, Barton shook her head. "Wait. Roffman had you meet him at the scene?"

Miller nodded. "Yeah."

"Jesus," she muttered.

"I know."

She waited a moment. "Who were they? The victims?"

"One is named Michaels. He has one arrest for auto theft. The other is Romano. No record. Both are from up around Albany."

"I don't understand what any of this has to do with you."

"Roffman found one of my business cards in the wallet belonging to the car thief."

"Michaels."

"Yeah."

"Did you know him?"

"No."

"So how'd your card get there?"

"That's what the chief wanted to know. It's an old card. Four years old, actually. I didn't give out a lot of them back then. Basically only to clients—people I had worked for already—and a few friends. Any one of them could have given it to Michaels, I suppose."

"And you saw the card?"

"Yeah. Roffman had it in a Baggie."

"He showed it to you?"

"Yeah. According to him, it was the only business card Michaels had in his wallet. He found it significant that the only business card some kid would have in his wallet is one of mine."

"But that's the thing, though, you know."

"What?"

" 'According to Roffman.' I mean, I don't have to tell you how un-usual it is for him to come out to a crime scene. And to have you brought there. This is just so strange."

"Tell me about it."

"Who was the detective in charge?"

"Mancini was there, but it looked to me like Roffman had taken charge."

"I'm not sure I like this, Tommy."

"You think Roffman could have planted my business card in Michaels's wallet?"

"It's possible."

"Why, though?"

Barton shrugged. "Pick a reason."

"But how would he get one of my old cards?"

"From one of your clients. Or one of your friends, even. The same way, supposedly, this Michaels guy was supposed to have gotten it."

"But I don't do this anymore, Roffman knows that. What would he gain by trying to trick me into getting involved in this?"

"Maybe it's more than trying to get you involved. Maybe he's trying to set you up."

"Why *now,* though? Why *this?*"

"I don't know, Tommy. One thing is for sure, though. Roffman wouldn't be doing whatever the hell it is he's doing if he didn't stand to gain *something* from it. It's not like you were going to read in the paper that some dead guy had your business card in his wallet and then put yourself in the middle of this. He wanted you to know, went out of his way to tell you."

Miller thought about that, said nothing.

"What else did he say, Tommy?"

"He offered me amnesty. In case I needed to, as he put it, cross the line. For the next day I more or less have free rein."

Barton had suddenly heard enough, felt a rush of powerful emotions: fear and deep concern for Miller, but also anger and resentment toward Roffman, for what he was doing now, for what he had done in the past, had done to her. She hadn't experienced feelings like this in a long, long time, not since the day her doctor had taken one look at her and handed her a prescription for her blessed Lexapro.

She took in a breath, calmed herself, then let the breath out.

"Roffman's desperate," she warned. "Something has him scared."

"It's a little hard to imagine someone like Roffman scared."

"I don't know, Tommy, if you ask me, I think men in power are the ones out of all of us who are the most afraid. It's an awful big thing to lose, you know. Power. Everybody wants it, and when you have it, everyone around you is looking for ways to take it away from you, to grab it for themselves."

Miller looked at her for a moment, saying nothing. She wondered if he was thinking of his father. Roffman had been brought in all those years ago to turn things around, put an end to all the corruption, make things right again. How long, Barton wondered, till he had made his first back-room deal? How long had he held out? What was it that had finally turned him around? She gave Miller credit, always had, for not becoming like his father, but more than that, for standing up against the man who had been appointed to replace his father, only to become exactly what Miller's father had been. Most men didn't have the sense to avoid the traps fate put in front of them, didn't have what it took to *beat the odds.* Miller had done that, at a terrible cost to him, yes, but really what in this life came cheap?

Miller glanced once more in the direction of the road. He couldn't see it, could barely see halfway across the lot. Barton sensed that the nervousness he had come with had increased. More than before, more than ever, the last thing he wanted, for her sake, was for someone to see them together.

Always concerned about the right thing. Noble to a fault. But she could hardly blame him. It wasn't like she didn't run to extremes as well, so she could live with herself and the things she had done. Once she had been a cop, sworn to keep order. Now she sold booze, the cause—the *legal* cause, at least—of most disorderly conduct. Once she had been a woman in love with a man. Now she couldn't remember the last time she had touched or been touched, couldn't for the life of her imagine the next time she would.

"Listen, I know I haven't been . . . available that much lately," Miller said. "And then suddenly I show up out of nowhere, asking for help."

"My phone works both ways, Tommy. I haven't called you either."

"I think of it, all the time. You know? I just don't ever seem to get around to it. Something holds me back, the next thing I know it's too late to call, that kind of thing."

"I think it's easier to . . . suffer in private, you know. No one watching, no one listening." She shrugged. "At least it is for me. Anyway, I'm part of your old life, Tommy, and you're part of mine. We haven't found a way yet to include each other in our lives the way they are now, that's all. I'm not too worried, though. I figured we'd figure it out sooner or later, when the time was right for the both of us."

Miller nodded. "I'd like that, Kay." He looked toward the road again, turning his head fast this time, as if he had heard something he didn't like. He stood perfectly still. Barton did as well, couldn't help it. She felt, though, only calmness. *The freedom that comes from not caring, having nothing left to lose.* After a moment of them standing still it became clear that there was nothing there for them to worry about.

"We shouldn't push our luck," Miller said. "We should get you back." He was still looking in the direction of the road, though. She knew then that there was a part of him still, a part deep down inside him, that was unable to let go of his fear of doing wrong. Maybe he would never be able to let go of that.

"Listen, Tommy, the thing you need to know about Roffman is that he's made his share of deals with the devil over the years."

Miller looked at her. He waited, saying nothing.

"You're not the only one with a promise that shouldn't be kept."

Miller studied her for a moment. He was trying to work this out, she could see that. He had it, she could see that, too, knew just what it was she was saying to him. Still, he needed her to say it aloud, needed to hear it. *The painkiller, no doubt.*

"Think about it, Tommy. About where the bodies were found, on display like that, the *fact* that they had been put on display to begin with. The hands cut off, hanged from a bridge at the canal, for everyone to see. Who else could that be but that friend of yours?"

"He's not my friend, Kay."

"I know. I was being ironic. When you first went into business for yourself, you took people on. A lot of people. And head-on, too. You were fearless. A little too fearless, if you ask me, but that's a zealot, right? That's what a zealot does. Of all the people you went after, though, there's one person you left alone. One person you never went anywhere near. It's the one person I would have expected you to go after. When you finally told me why, I understood. You were being you, you couldn't help it, even if it was a stupid promise to make. But don't think for a moment that certain people in town didn't notice that this one man went ignored by you. And don't think they didn't form their own conclusions as to the reason why."

Miller shrugged. "People will think what they want to think. There's not much I can do about that."

"As long as *you* know you're right," Barton offered. "Right?"

"Yeah."

"I love you, Tommy, I really do, you know that, but all this honor stuff, it doesn't get you anywhere. You don't get points for doing the right thing. If anything, it's just the opposite."

"I know, Kay."

"So what are you going to do?"

"I'm not really sure what it is Roffman expects me to do. A four-year-old business card in the wallet of someone I've never met isn't really much to go on. To be honest, I'm more concerned about what Roffman is up to than anything else. I don't really care one way or another about who committed these murders and why."

"Who are you, and what have you done with Tommy Miller?" Barton joked.

Miller smiled, but it didn't last very long. Too much was on his mind. Barton could see on his face the strain of all this information, all the questions, see in his eyes—wild eyes, thanks to the painkillers—that he was trying with everything he had to make *some* sense of all this.

"I meant it when I said I wanted nothing to do with this anymore, Kay. Life isn't so bad right now. I could live with things the way they are, for a long time. Minus the rain, but you can't have everything, can you?"

"So go away for a couple of days. Let this blow over."

"I don't think I can do that."

"Then let me come with you. Whatever you're going to do, you shouldn't be behind the wheel the way you are right now."

"Your buddy Spadaro asked me to let him know what Roffman wanted. He thinks maybe we can help each other out somehow. If I need any help, I can get it from him."

Barton nodded. "Okay."

"I need you to tell me something, though."

"What?"

"I need you to tell me if I can trust him."

"Ricky dislikes the chief as much as you do. Maybe even more. He's stuck working for the guy, even though it was made clear to him that he'd never advance either."

"But he *does* work for him. The whole thing between them tonight, that could have just been . . . theater."

"I doubt it. Ricky's not the type to hide his feelings very well."

"Even if it means keeping his job?"

"When it ended between Roffman and me and everyone turned against me, Ricky was pretty vocal about the way I was being treated. It got him in a lot of trouble, but he couldn't help himself. They say hell hath no fury like a woman scorned. Let me tell you, that's nothing compared to a chief of police scorned."

"So you think I can trust Spadaro."

"I think Ricky doesn't need to make things worse for himself by doing favors for you. But, yeah, you can trust him. You're two of a kind, if you ask me."

Miller nodded. Barton watched him for a moment.

"Don't underestimate Roffman," she said finally. "He's a man with a lot to lose."

"I won't."

"Talk to Ricky, tell him everything you told me."

"I'll need his number."

"Okay."

Miller reached into the pocket of his field jacket, removed his cell phone. "I'll call Eddie first, have him send the cab back for you."

"It's on its way to Wainscott right now."

"How do you know?"

"The call came in over the radio while he was taking me here."

"Eddie probably has more than one driver on tonight. Especially with the trains shut down."

"Tommy, enough," Barton said. "Just take me home yourself, okay?"

"It's for your own protection, Kay."

"I don't really care."

"I do."

"Then take me as far as the hospital. I can walk from there."

"We have to be careful, Kay."

"We're not doing anything wrong, Tommy. I'm done living like a guilty person. I've been done with that for a while now."

A wave came in, crashing into pieces just beyond the dune behind them. It was louder than any wave they had heard so far.

"C'mon, Tommy," she said, "let's just get the hell out of here, okay?"

The warmth flowing from the heater vents and collecting around them in the cab of his pickup caused Miller to sink even deeper into his numbness. Barton had refused to let him drive, so he was sitting in the passenger seat. In all the years he owned his truck, he'd never sat there before, not once. It was just a little strange, no steering wheel in front of him, no pedals at his feet, but not driving allowed him the freedom to look out the window as they headed back toward the village. Not that there was much to see, of course. When he wasn't looking at the fog around them, or at the twelve-foot hedges lining Gin Lane just beyond the passenger door window, Miller was glancing at the mirror mounted outside his door, looking in it for any sign of headlights peeking through the white curtain behind them.

He was suddenly very tired. Maybe Barton had been right about his not really being in any condition to drive. He was a big guy, though, and his body had been getting gradually used to the effects of the pills, so this stupor wouldn't last for too much longer. He would have felt better during these days of rain had he added a fourth pill to his daily routine, but he knew that that was how people got into trouble with this shit—their bodies became tolerant, the pain wasn't so easily taken away anymore, so, they told themselves, *just one more pill, just for today, just to get through.* Life was just too good, Miller thought, to wake up one morning suddenly addicted, to find that his mind and body weren't his own anymore.

At the hospital parking lot—empty this time of night, the emergency room entrance on the other side of the building—Barton parked. No big goodbyes, nothing really at all anyway left for either to say. She climbed out, looked at Miller for a moment, then closed the door. He watched her as she crossed the parking lot, then he moved across the seat and got in behind the wheel. She exited the lot and turned left, starting down Lewis Street. Her place was less than a block away, the street was a well-lit residential street, she'd be fine. Still, Miller waited for the time he figured it would take her to get to her door, then steered across the parking lot and turned left onto Lewis, heading toward her place. He'd come this far, so there wasn't really any point in bothering to pretend anymore. And anyway, no one had followed them. Despite the fog, he would have seen their headlights.

Miller slowed as he passed her place, saw a light go on in the third-floor apartment, glimpsed Barton, still in that parka of hers, as she crossed in front of her living-room window. She was fine, locked in, safe. He hadn't been inside her place in a long time. Even before they had fallen out of touch he hadn't been there more than a few times. So much of their friendship then had to be in secret. Back in those days she was a cop and he was a private investigator, so it wouldn't be good for her if they were to be seen together all that much. But it hadn't been just that, it had also been because of Roffman and the secret, so-called, that she had shared with him. Miller back then wasn't supposed to know but did, of course he did, and Roffman couldn't know that Miller actually knew— a ridiculously complicated time, to say the least. Miller was glad that it was over. It was a dangerous, foolish thing for Barton to have done to be-gin with—enter into an affair with Roffman—but who was Miller to criticize. He'd done worse than love the wrong person. Much worse.

Miller remembered the last time he had been inside Barton's apart-ment, remembered the wall in her living room dedicated to her achieve-ments as a cop: her diploma from the academy, where she had graduated first in her class; the certificate she had received upon passing the sergeant's exam; a similar certificate she had received for acing the detec-tive's exam. Not any of these achievements had come to anything in the end. Miller wondered if that wall was as it had been when he was last in her place, or if it had been stripped bare, everything that had been hung upon it packed away in a cardboard box in some closet.

He returned to his place, didn't turn on any lights as he went into the bathroom. There he filled the sink with warm water, splashed his face with it. When he was done he leaned over the sink, water dripping from his beard, and looked at his reflection in the mirror. He wished then that it wasn't Monday night, that the restaurant below was open. If it were he could sit at the bar, relax, numb himself even further by adding a little booze to the painkillers in his blood. A night of forgetting—everything he knew, everything he'd just been told, every question that each detail brought to his mind. He supposed he was lucky that downstairs was in fact closed. He had no choice now but to face what was before him, whatever it was, and try to see where it would take him, if he could, what it all really meant. He had right now no idea at all what he should do next, aside from informing Spadaro, as he had promised. He always kept his promises, no matter what. But beyond that, nothing, no path to follow, no lead to pursue. As far as he knew, he was home for the night. In his current condition, and the weather being what it was, that notion at first appealed to him, greatly. But then he realized that staying home would mean he'd be left with nothing to do but to wait and wonder, and these were the last things he wanted to be doing.

Barton had given Miller Spadaro's home phone number, which he had stored in his cell phone. He would, of course, need to place the call from the pay phone at the train station, using his calling card. If all this went to shit—there were many ways it could, always were—the cops didn't need to find a record of a call from Miller to Spadaro. Miller dried his face and hands, looked at himself once more in the mirror, then grabbed his field jacket and was putting it on, about to step back outside, when his landline rang.

He checked his watch. It was fifteen minutes to midnight. Stepping to his phone, he glanced down at the caller ID. The number displayed wasn't one he recognized. Above it were the words *NY Wireless*. A cell phone, then. And a Long Island area code. After a moment, Miller finally picked up the phone. There wasn't any point now in his refusing to answer. The caller would only keep on trying, or, worse, come pounding on his door. One such visit in a night was enough.

On the other end of the line, a male voice, unfamiliar. "Miller?"

A pause, then: "Yeah."

"It's Mancini."

Miller's first instinct was to hang up, but he didn't. *Mancini speaks for me,* Roffman had said. And anyway, Miller needed something, a lead, anything, somewhere to go, something to do other than wait. He was hungry for it, a feeling he hadn't known in a long time, a feeling he had thought he'd never have to know again.

"What's going on?" Miller said.

"I need to talk to you. In person."

"When?"

"Right now."

Miller took in a breath, let it out. What choice did he have? "Where?"

"I'm coming over."

"No." He was shaking his head. "I'd rather we met somewhere else."

"I don't care. I'm around the corner, and this can't wait. I'll be right there."

Miller looked around his dark apartment, thought of Mancini standing in it. Just the thought of it felt like an invasion. Being out in that world again was one thing, letting it into his place was another.

"Meet me at the restaurant below," Miller said.

"I prefer privacy."

"The restaurant's closed tonight, no one's there. I have a key. The back door will be open."

"Be there when I arrive," Mancini said. There was an edge to his voice. A strain. Miller didn't know Mancini all that well, but he knew a man under pressure when he heard one.

"What's going on?" Miller said.

The call threatened to drop, Miller heard only a stutter of half-words.

"I didn't get that," Miller said. "You're breaking up."

The signal strength returned, and Miller heard Mancini clearly now.

"It seems we've got ourselves another dead body," he said.

Miller wanted to ask who, the word was on the tip of his tongue, but he could tell the line was already dead. Either the signal was lost or Mancini had hung up.

Miller kept the phone to his ear for a moment, just in case, then finally returned it to its cradle. It took another moment for him to start toward the door.

In the restaurant below he waited by the large storefront window, could see from where he stood both Elm Street and Railroad Plaza. He kept the lights off, but just like his place above, the lights of the train station were more than enough to get around in. Only a minute after he had let himself into the empty restaurant, Mancini's unmarked sedan appeared on Railroad Plaza, turning onto it from North Main. Miller watched the sedan pass the long railroad platform, at the end of which Railroad Plaza, crossing Elm, became Powell Avenue. The sedan continued along Powell, passing the restaurant and disappearing from Miller's sight. He stepped away from the window but not by much. He had left the door to the kitchen ajar, waited till he heard its hinges squeak, then heard footsteps in the kitchen. Soon enough Mancini stepped through the swinging doors, spotted Miller standing at the far end of the long dining room, headed toward him.

He was wearing his dark wool overcoat, dark pants, and dress shoes. The shoes were, Miller noticed, remarkably clean, but that was Mancini. Always well groomed, always well dressed. Still, clean shoes on a night like this, no small accomplishment. Mancini was looking around as he walked toward Miller, making certain, Miller assumed, that they were alone. Built like a fire hydrant, his footsteps landed heavy on the plank floor. He wasn't as tall as Miller but easily the same weight. About halfway down the room Mancini came to a stop. He glanced now at the tables placed close together throughout the room— a European sensibility, this proximity—and at the long bar that ran along one wall. After that he looked up at the ceiling of old, stamped tin, the building's original ceiling. He wasn't making certain that they were alone now, was instead checking the place out, like a prospective buyer. Maybe he was simply hoping to determine the value of the place and thereby get an idea of Miller's value. It was safe to assume, by the way Mancini dressed, by what Miller knew of him, that such a thing mattered to the man. Southampton was, after all, a town of haves and have-nots. The treatment one got often depended on just how much or how little one had.

"You own this?" Mancini said. He was still studying the ceiling.

"The building, yeah," Miller answered.

"But not the business."

"No."

Mancini nodded. Miller waited, saying nothing.

"It's always been amazing to me how nine out of ten restaurants out here don't make it past their first winter," Mancini said. "This place seems to do okay, though, huh? Oberti certainly seems to be doing okay, driving his fancy car, running around with that young girlfriend of his."

"It's busy most nights, and Oberti pays his rent on time," Miller said. "That's about all I know."

"I've always wanted a restaurant of my own. I've always thought of starting one up after I retire. It's such a risk, though. A guy could lose his shirt."

Miller had had enough of this small talk. "Who's dead?" he demanded.

Mancini was looking at Miller now, was still only halfway down the long room. It was as if he didn't want to go anywhere near the front window.

"A guy named Adamson," he said. "Did you know him?"

"Never heard of him."

"A few months ago he bought Tide Runner's, that place on the canal."

"He was your witness, wasn't he?"

"What makes you say that?"

Miller shrugged. "Roffman said there was a witness. It adds up."

"But you didn't know him, right?"

"Right."

Mancini nodded, thought about that, took another quick look around, then said, "Where'd you go tonight? After you left the canal."

"I went home."

"I tried to call you a few times but there was no answer."

"I wasn't picking up."

"So you've been home since talking to Roffman at the canal."

"Yeah."

"I drove by a few times, too. Figured you might not be picking up. Didn't see your pickup out back, but it's there now."

"I loaned it to a friend of mine. He just brought it back."

Mancini nodded again, thoughtfully. "Well, that explains that, then, doesn't it?"

"Look, if I was a suspect, Detective, you wouldn't be here alone, would you? You would have showed up with another detective or a uniformed cop, that's procedure. Then you would have invited me down to the station and asked me these questions with a video recorder aimed at my face. So why don't you save us both some time and tell me what you're really here for? It's been a long night, it's late. I'd like to get some sleep."

"You do look a little beat." Mancini studied Miller, then said, "I'm here because I thought maybe you could help me figure something out."

"What?"

"There are some things that don't make sense. Lots of things."

"Like?"

"Like Adamson was found beside his truck, in the parking lot of his restaurant, not all that long, actually, after he was questioned by Roffman."

"Roffman interviewed him himself?"

"That's right. It seems that after he talked to Roffman, Adamson called his girlfriend, told her that he was on his way home. When he didn't show up after a half hour, she got worried and went to look for him, found him dead in the mud. That's got to suck, huh?"

"How was Adamson killed?"

"Strangled."

"With what?"

"Bare hands, it seems. I know that Adamson's parking lot isn't paved, and that at least a few vehicles were in and out of it at some point tonight. The rain, though, has washed away most of the tracks."

"What about inside the restaurant? Footprints, debris?"

"Roffman is going to have crime scene techs check it out. Not sure if they're going to find anything, though. Not sure even if they do find anything that anyone is going to know about it."

"What do you mean?"

"Roffman interviewed Adamson alone."

"Where were you?"

"I was sent back to the station. By Roffman. To double-check the information we got from the DMV. Not exactly the best use of the head detective, wouldn't you say?"

"You think Roffman is up to something."

"Just like you do."

"What makes you think I think that?"

"You ran to Barton tonight because you missed her all of the sudden?

It's pretty obvious that's where you went. It's a pretty safe bet. I'll tell you, she's the one I'd run to first if I thought Roffman was up to something. Who would know him better, right? Who might have a dirty secret or two, maybe even be dying to share those secrets with someone, be the cause of Roffman falling flat on his face."

Miller said nothing. Mancini took one step toward him.

"You're a smart guy, Tommy, we all know this. Roffman has always been scared by how smart you are. More than scared, though, it threatens him. Me, I don't give a shit who's smarter than who, all I care about is the fact that three hours after two men are brutally murdered, the only witness we have was himself murdered. That's fast work, if you ask me. Too fast."

"What do you mean, too fast?"

"It could be that the killers were someplace where they were able to keep an eye on the whole scene, saw Roffman going in to talk to Adamson, waited for him leave and then made their move. Or it could be something else. Something worse."

"Like they were tipped off by someone."

"Like they were tipped off by someone in the department, yeah."

"Why someone in the department?"

"It's doubtful the killers could have seen Adamson from the bridge, but even if they had, the distance was too great for him to have been able to identify them as anything other than two figures running away from him. So why would they risk hanging around and watching? And why risk killing him? Killing him right there, across the canal from a crime scene?"

Miller could think of only one thing, the obvious thing. "To cover their tracks," he said.

"And push their luck by leaving all new tracks? The bridge was brilliant—solid wooden ties and gravel means on a rainy night they'd leave no footprints. But the parking lot outside the restaurant is dirt and crushed seashells. That means nothing but footprints. It just seems to me like an unnecessary risk. The only thing that would have made it necessary was if Adamson had somehow actually seen something and told Roffman. But how would the killers know that? And so soon after Roffman questioned him."

"Unless it was Roffman who told them."

"Exactly."

"But why?"

"That's what I'd like to find out."

Miller waited a moment, thought about all this, then said, "The first part of your theory, that the killers were waiting somewhere nearby, watching the whole scene—" He didn't complete his thought. He didn't have to. Mancini was watching him closely.

"We all know who owns the Water's Edge," Mancini said finally.

Miller muttered the name: "Castello." Even saying it aloud felt a little like betrayal. Foolish, he knew, but the need to keep his word was steeped in him.

"This time of year you can easily see the canal from its upper windows," Mancini said.

Miller thought then of what Barton had said, about Roffman keeping a promise he, too, really shouldn't be keeping.

"You think Roffman is involved with Castello?"

"I think he's busy covering up for somebody, yeah," Mancini said. "And Castello's from where? South America somewhere? They play by their own kind of rules down there, don't they? They have their own particular forms of punishment." After a pause, he added, "They aren't like us."

Us? Who exactly was Mancini talking about? Miller wondered.

"The dead guys at the canal had worked for Castello," Miller said. "That's what you're thinking, right?"

"That they worked for Castello and betrayed him somehow, yeah."

"But to display their bodies so close to a place he owns, that a lot of people know he owns, that's kind of bold, don't you think?"

"South American types are hotheads, aren't they? Besides, if you had the chief of police in your pocket, wouldn't you feel a little bold? Hell, from what I hear, having a chief for a father had made you plenty bold yourself once upon a time."

Not bold, just stupid, arrogant, violent. A troubled kid out of control. *But I've long since made up for that.* More than made up for it, more than repaid that debt.

"So what are you going to do about all this?" Miller said.

"I'd like to find out what's going on inside the Water's Edge."

"Get a warrant."

"Can't, you know that. Besides, it's best that Roffman doesn't know what I'm thinking."

"Wish I could help you, Detective," Miller said flatly. He knew where this was going, why Mancini was really here.

"You can, though. You're not a cop. You don't have a PI license to protect anymore. You could . . . let yourself in, have a look around."

"Can't."

"Can't or won't?"

"It doesn't matter which. I'm not going to do it."

"I thought you'd want to help. After what Roffman did to your friend. After the stuff he uncovered about your father, the posthumous beating that poor man took."

"What was said wasn't untrue. Anyway, I don't fix other people's problems anymore."

"Not even Barton's?"

Miller said nothing.

"What about your own problems, then, Tommy?"

"My only problem right now is you. Let me make this clear: I'm not breaking into the Water's Edge. Not for you, not for anyone. There's nothing you can say that will change my mind."

"Even if it means exposing Roffman."

"You're the cop, not me. You catch the criminals."

"And if in the meantime Roffman somehow connects you to all this?"

"Is he trying to?"

"I don't have a fucking clue. All I know is *he* searched the wallets, *he* was the one who found your business card. What did he say when he talked to you?"

Miller thought about Roffman's proposal. *Amnesty, free rein, the sharing of information.*

"Not much," he said.

"Yeah, I'm sure." Mancini studied Miller, then reached into the pocket of his overcoat, pulled out a business card, placed it on the nearby bar. The bar was made of oak, had a dark marble top and brass trim. Older than Miller, older than Mancini, even—older than all of them.

"If you change your mind, give me a call." Mancini took one more look around. "Smart investment," he said. "You set yourself up nice here. Most people your age would have opted for flash, you know. Sold their parents' home for two million bucks and blown it all on cars and a lifestyle." He nodded, then looked at Miller once more. "Smart guy."

He turned and walked back toward the kitchen, stepping finally through the swinging doors. Miller waited till he heard the back door close before he left his spot by the front window and went back into the kitchen. Something told him not to go out that way, something in his gut, so he locked the door and returned to the front of the restaurant, let himself out through the main entrance, locking it behind him. He stepped to the corner of Elm Street and Powell Avenue, looked down Powell. The fog wasn't as thick here as it had been at the ocean's edge. He could see the taillights of Mancini's unmarked sedan just as it reached the end of the street a long block away. The sedan turned right, then disappeared from sight. Miller was then, as far as he could tell, alone in his little corner of town.

He waited a moment, thinking. It took everything he had. Finally he crossed the street to the train station, used his calling card and dialed Spadaro's number from the pay phone on the platform. Spadaro's phone didn't ring, went instead straight into his voice mail. Miller didn't understand why Spadaro's phone would be shut off—no ring and being sent straight to voice mail, that's what that meant, right? Miller hung up without leaving a message. Something, again, something deep in his gut, told him to do that.

He returned to his apartment, and once inside he found that he didn't know exactly what to do with himself. His dilemma, though, didn't last too long. Less than a minute after stepping through the door his landline rang.

The number on the caller ID was a local number, one that Miller recognized. The pay phone on the corner of Cameron and Main Streets, in the heart of the village. He had called from pretty much every phone in town, at one point or another, remembered their numbers, or enough of their numbers to be recognize them and recall their location when he saw them. He answered his phone right away.

"It's me," Barton said. "I'm calling from a pay phone."

"Yeah, I know. What's going on?"

"I called Ricky, to let him know you'd be calling. He wanted me to give you a message."

"What?"

"Michaels had a girlfriend."

"How'd he find out?"

"He didn't want to say. He was leaving, wanted me to give you an address."

"Where was he going?"

"He didn't want to say that, either. He thinks you should go to this address and have a look around. It'll be a few hours at least before the cops get this information, he said, so you have a window. He's afraid that evidence might disappear once the cops go through the place, thinks you should get there before that happens."

"I don't know, Kay—"

"You have to promise me something, Tommy."

"What?"

"I'm not going to give you the address unless you promise to let me come with you."

"I'm not even sure I'm going anywhere—"

"Just promise."

"Listen, I'm a little uncomfortable with a cop telling me to break into the home of the girlfriend of a murder victim. First Roffman wants me on the case, offers me amnesty, then Mancini tries to get me to do something only an idiot would do, and now Spadaro."

"What do you mean, Mancini wants you to do something only an idiot would do?"

"He just gave a big pitch. Thinks Roffman is up to something, wants to find out what. Maybe he's on the level, or maybe he just wants to be the next chief. I don't know and I don't care."

"When did this happen?"

"Just now, after I saw you. He met me downstairs."

"Jesus."

"Yeah."

"I almost don't want to tell you now."

"What do you mean?"

"You won't be able to sit still once you find out who the girlfriend is, Tommy. And until we know what's going on, you probably should sit still. It looks to me like all the big boys want the playground tonight."

"Back up, Kay. What do you mean, once I find out who the girlfriend is?"

"If Roffman knew about this, I'm sure he would have told you. Same with Mancini. If they were trying to get you to act, this would certainly do it. You're going to find out sooner or later, though, so I guess I should tell you now. Better me than any of those clowns. But you have to promise to let me come with you."

"Kay, what's going on?"

"Just promise me, Tommy."

"Yeah, all right, I promise, whatever. What the hell is going on?"

The line went quiet for a moment. Miller looked toward his front windows. His unlit apartment was chilly. He waited for what felt to him like a long time.

"Jesus, Kay, what?"

"Michaels's girlfriend was Abby."

Miller's next word was little more than a desperate whisper. "What?"

"Your Abby, Tommy. According to Spadaro she was going out with the Michaels guy. She was his girlfriend. And Spadaro thinks she might be missing."

Miller closed his eyes, then opened them again. Nothing in his living room had changed, and yet suddenly everything looked so different, so foreign.

"What's the address, Kay?"

"It's not as easy as all that, Tommy."

"What does that mean?"

"I'll explain when I see you. I'll be at your place in two minutes. Okay?"

Miller nodded, though of course she couldn't see him.

"Tommy?"

"Yeah. I'll be here," he said.

"I'm leaving now."

She hung up. Miller returned the receiver to the cradle. After a moment he looked at his watch. It was midnight, and the blue flame in his chest was gone now.

Part Two

Midnight

Five

IN DARKNESS, BECHET SCRAMBLED FOR HIS RINGING CELL phone. He found it and quickly looked at the number on the display, saw that it was Falcetti calling. Of course it was. *Who else could it have been?* Bechet answered right away, for the sake of his still-sleeping lover stretched out between her soft satin sheets. He had been unable to sleep at all, had gotten up to use the bathroom and was on his way back to bed when his phone had started to ring. He stood now in the middle of the small bedroom, naked, speaking as softly as he could.

"Yeah, Bobby," he said.

"I need your help." A cell phone to cell phone connection was usually bad, but this was terrible. It sounded to Bechet as if Falcetti wasn't speaking directly into the phone at all.

"What'd going on?" Bechet said. "Where are you?"

"I got a flat."

"How?"

"The tire stem must have broken or something when I crashed, started a slow leak. Everything was fine, and then the steering started to feel funny. Next thing I knew, I was flat." He was speaking quickly, sounded out of breath even.

Bechet thought to ask why but wanted to keep Falcetti focused. "What about the spare tire?"

"It's fine, but I can't find the lug key."

Most of the cabs Bechet and Eddie owned were used, purchased, back when Bechet had bought into the business, from a cab company in the city. Each wheel on each of these cabs had a locking lug that prevented the wheels from being stolen. A lug key, which fit like an extender into the lug wrench and matched the pattern of slots on the lug, was needed to remove each tire. Each cab had its own particular key, of which there were only two copies. One was kept in the respective cab, the other in a lockbox in Bechet's Jeep.

"It should be in the glove compartment," Bechet said.

"I know, man. I looked. It's not there."

Bechet didn't bother to suggest that he call Scarcella, have the cab towed to Scarcella's salvage yard and then deal with it in the morning. No point in going over all that again.

"Where are you?" Bechet said again.

"Wainscott. Helenbach."

He was farther away than Bechet had hoped he'd be. A good half hour, each way. Not a quick trip like the first had been, or at least had promised to be.

"I'll get there as soon as I can."

"Thanks, man."

Bechet started to say, "You're a real pain in my ass, Bobby," but even before he got halfway through, the line went dead.

He closed the cell phone, held it in his fist as he stood there in the darkness. He listened to the silence that he still wasn't used to, then sat on the edge of Gabrielle's bed, the phone still in his hand, the cold and the pure dark of her room all around him. Something about the call bothered him. He couldn't put his finger on why exactly, though. Maybe it was just the bad connection. Or maybe it wasn't that at all. Maybe it was Falcetti, the fact that he was speaking very quickly, quickly even for Falcetti. Manic, almost. Or maybe it wasn't even any of that. Maybe Bechet was just bothered by the fact that he was being bothered again and was looking for something other than that. Falcetti had always been an excitable boy.

There were times when Bechet wondered how the hell the guy, being the way he was, won even a single hand of poker.

From behind him, Gabrielle said, "Who was that?" She sounded more alert than she had the first time the phone had awakened her.

"Bobby. He needs my help."

"Again?"

"Yeah." Bechet stood, gathered together his clothes, pulled them on. His skin was cold to his own touch.

"How long will you be this time?"

"He's out in Wainscott. An hour, at least. I just have to hand him something. Why don't you sleep some more?"

"Maybe I will. I'm so tired. I don't know what my problem is."

"It's stopped raining," Bechet said. He figured he'd let her know that, in case she hadn't noticed, so she wouldn't worry about him out on the roads. He didn't know about the fog waiting for him on the bayside road below.

"Has it stopped for good?" Gabrielle said.

"I don't know. Probably not. I'll listen to the weather on my way."

Bechet was dressed now—jeans and a T-shirt, socks. He seldom wore more than that, even on the coldest night. All that was left now were his jacket and boots. His jacket was on the back of a chair in the kitchen below, put there to dry. His boots were on a piece of newspaper inside the downstairs door. He hadn't wanted to track in any of the mud that had collected in the treads as he ran from his Jeep to the cottage. And there was always the chance, as thorough as he had been prior to leaving the canal, that something from the parking lot had remained, something that might indicate that he had been there. This way, if it came to it, all he would need to do was get rid of his boots and the single page of newspaper and he'd be as good as gold.

An old way of thinking, old skills that would always be there, just below the surface.

He sat on the bed once more, facing her. "I'll be back as soon as I can."

"Be careful."

"Always."

He leaned down, found her lips in the darkness. They kissed.

"You taste good," she said.

He kissed her again, could feel her smiling. He waited till her smile eased, then kissed her once more. Finally, he stood. She held on to his hand, her fingers wrapped around his. They lingered like that for a moment, in the dark, a man fully dressed, a woman naked between expensive sheets.

"I love you," she said.

"I love you, too, Elle."

Downstairs he pulled on his boots and jacket, buttoned it up, then hurried to his Jeep. Under the backseat was the lockbox containing the lug keys. He opened it, found the one that belonged to the cab Falcetti drove, slipped it into his jacket pocket, then closed the lockbox and laid it on the passenger seat.

It wasn't till he was halfway down the dirt road, gutted severely by these months of winter rain, that Bechet saw the fog below. It clung to the narrow two-lane road, looking as he approached it like the very edge of some mythical world.

He descended into it.

Forty-five minutes later Bechet reached Wainscott. The fog, close to nothing in places, was like a winter whiteout in others; it all depended on how near the water Montauk Highway happened to curve at the moment. Driving through the whiteouts was nothing short of treacherous, Bechet unable to do more than creep along at ten miles an hour. He was glad he hadn't known about that fog, that he'd left Gabrielle with the impression that the bad weather had passed. The last thing he needed right now was to think of her alone *and* worrying about him, waiting nervously for his return—or lack of return. Doing so would only have made the trip feel even longer than it was already turning out to be.

Helenbach's parking lot—paved, thankfully—was surrounded on all sides by a line of trees and bushes. Its single entrance, off Montauk Highway, was just wide enough for two cars to pass through side by side. The lot, unlit, looked empty to Bechet when he first turned into it. Like most places this time of year, Helenbach was closed on Mondays, so Bechet didn't think twice about the total lack of cars. But he had expected to see Falcetti's cab right off. There was no sign of it at all.

Bechet coasted into the lot, crossed twenty feet or so, then came to a stop and looked around. The building was designed like a fort—two separate structures, one a two-story restaurant, the other a single-story dance club, both surrounded by one six-foot wall. The entrance to the complex was a gate that, when closed, was all but indistinguishable from the wooden wall. Bechet saw that the gate was open—no, more ajar than open. He wasn't sure what to make of any of this. After a moment he shifted into first gear and continued deeper into the lot, passing the entrance to the complex, then running the length of it till he was past the compound all together. Now, to his right, was an extension of the lot that ran behind the restaurant. He spotted Falcetti's cab there, parked at the far end of the extension, well out of sight of the road. Bechet wasn't sure what to make of this, either. Nor was he sure what to make of the fact that, just like before, there was no sign of Falcetti anywhere.

He could see as he approached the cab that the back tires were fine. The damaged tire more than likely would have been one of the front tires, so he steered around and came toward the cab head-on. One of the front tires—on the passenger side—didn't appear so much flat as simply underinflated. Still, Falcetti had been right not to drive on it, particularly tonight. Bechet killed the lights and the motor, stared at the cab through the windshield. Could Falcetti have fallen asleep as he waited for Bechet? Bechet took his heavy Maglite flashlight from under the seat and got out, walking toward the cab. He switched the light on, and the bulb flickered, then glowed dully. The batteries were dying. He reached the cab and shined the light inside. It gave enough illumination for him to see that there was no one in the front or backseats. There was nothing unusual at all that Bechet could see—excepting, of course, the absence of the cab's driver. The keys hung in the ignition, and Falcetti's jacket, which he often removed when driving, was on the passenger seat. No sign of a struggle, though of course that didn't mean anything one way or another.

Bechet looked around the lot once more, then looked toward the back of the restaurant. Nothing to see there. He went to the bad tire, knelt down and spit on his index finger, then rubbed the spit on the tire stem. No bubbles, so the stem wasn't leaking. Or wasn't leaking anymore. This could have been a case of higher pressure inside the tire causing it to leak, then stopping when the pressure ran low. There was only one way to be sure.

Bechet returned to his Jeep, opened the back hatch and searched through the tool bag he kept behind the rear seat for a can of Fix-A-Flat, a large aerosol canister that contained compressed air that inflated flat tires but also contained a thick foam that sealed any small punctures or leaks. He found a can, removed the lug key from his jacket pocket, tossed it onto the console between his front seats, then closed the hatch. He didn't want the lug key to fall out of his pocket as he worked. Back at the flattened tire, Bechet attached the clear plastic tube to the stem, then pressed down on the nozzle and watched the white, foamy liquid rush into the tire. He studied the stem as it did. No bubbles, no leaking foam, nothing. *Could someone have let the air out of Falcetti's tire?* For what reason, though? And how, exactly, without Falcetti knowing? It took more than a minute for the tire to inflate, and during that time Bechet could think of no answers to his questions. He only, in fact, thought of more questions.

When the canister was empty, Bechet detached it from the tire stem and tossed it into the back of his Jeep, closing the hatch door. The tire was inflated enough that the cab could be driven. Bechet had half-expected to see Falcetti wander now from the dark edge of the lot, as he had earlier. But there was still no sign of him. Bechet stood at the rear of his Jeep for a moment, watching the restaurant now. Where else could Falcetti have gone but in there? The gate *was* ajar. But from what Bechet could see there were no lights on anywhere inside the small complex. What did that mean? What reason could Falcetti possibly have had to go inside?

Bechet switched off the flashlight but carried it with him as he approached the entrance. He wanted to spare the batteries, but he also knew that the last thing he needed was for someone passing on Montauk Highway to see him—a man with a flashlight—lurking around a darkened restaurant. Bechet reached the entrance, which was open just wide enough for him to pass through if he turned sideways. He looked through it, saw the brick courtyard between the restaurant and the dance club. It was empty. He slipped through, stopped just inside the gate and listened. There was enough light from the streetlamps that lined the road for Bechet to see by. Halfway down the courtyard, to his left, was the door to the restaurant. The door to the dance club was on his right, almost directly across from the restaurant door. He walked down the center of the courtyard. The restaurant was glass—double glass doors, an atrium dining room that looked out onto the courtyard—so Bechet could easily see that there were no lights on inside. He doubted there was anyone there but thought he'd better check. He stepped to the door, used the cuff of his jacket as a glove as he pulled on the handle. The door was locked. He turned and looked at the dance club.

This building had no windows at all, was built solid like a bunker, no doubt to keep down the sounds of the music that boomed within when the club was in full swing. There was no way, then, to have a look inside except by opening the door. Bechet crossed the courtyard, used the cuff of his jacket sleeve again and pulled on the handle. This door was unlocked. Bechet opened the door just enough to look in. All he saw, though, was a darkness as total as the one into which he had awakened tonight back in Gabrielle's cottage.

He switched on the failing flashlight, aimed the weak beam inside, following it with his eyes as he moved it around the room. To the left of the door was an elevated DJ's booth, to the right a small bar, between them a sunken dance floor. The walls were mirrored, the glass smoked, the room only big enough for maybe eighty people if they stood shoulder to shoulder, which, of course, they did on busy summer nights. Bechet stepped inside, guided the door slowly closed, didn't want it to slam shut behind him. He made another sweep with his flashlight, held it on the DJ's booth for a moment, then on the bar. Nothing, no one. He listened for a moment more, just to be certain, was about to turn and get out of there when he finally heard something.

His name, said in an urgent whisper.

"Jake."

Bechet stopped.

"Jake, that you?"

He shined his light in the direction of the voice. A door just past the bar, in the corner at the far end of the room. He had to take two steps forward to see it fully. This door, like the gate, was only partially open.

"Bobby?" Bechet said.

"I'm in here." The same urgent whisper.

Bechet crossed the room, stepping down into the sunken dance floor, then back up again. The air inside the club, particularly down in the dance floor, was cool and damp, like a cave. Bechet stepped to the door, pushed it the rest of the way open, shined his light into what looked to be a storage room. It wasn't much bigger than a closet. Falcetti was seated in a chair, toward the back of the narrow room, blinking against the bright light shining in his eyes. Bechet could see right away that Falcetti's face was bruised and swollen. His hands were tied behind his back, his feet to the legs of the chair. He was naked, his chest and stomach streaked with dried blood that had dripped from his battered lips and nose.

"Jesus," Bechet said. He hurried into the room, removing his jacket and placing it over Falcetti's lap. He knelt down beside Falcetti, laying the flashlight, flickering again, on the floor. Falcetti was shivering, from the cold, yes, but from fear, too. Bechet could sense it, had learned a long time ago, as a boxer, to recognize when another man was feeling terror.

Falcetti muttered, "I'm sorry, Jake." His voice cracked; he was on the verge of tears.

"It's all right," Bechet said. He reached behind Falcetti, began to untie the ropes around his wrists. It was nylon-coated rope, military-spec. "Who the hell did this?"

"Just get me out of here, man."

"I will."

"I'm sorry, man."

"It's all right, don't worry." They were still whispering. Bechet did his best to keep urgency from his voice. "How many?" he said.

"What?"

"The people who did this to you, how many are there?"

"Two."

"You sure?"

"That's all I saw."

"Do you know where they are now?"

"No. They just put me in here and left."

"How long ago?"

"I don't know."

Bechet got Falcetti's hands free, started on the rope binding his feet.

"They took my clothes," Falcetti said.

"It's okay. You're going to be okay."

"Hurry, man. I just want to get the fuck out of here."

"Is this about money you owe?" Bechet said.

"Just get me out here."

Bechet got one foot free, began work on the remaining one.

"I need to know what's going on, Bobby. I need to know how serious these people are. Are they punks or are the professionals?"

"I don't know. I never saw their faces. I have no idea who they are."

"What do you mean?"

"All they wanted was for me to call you."

"What?"

"They kept hitting me, telling me to call you, get you to meet me."

Bechet stopped.

"Who kept telling you to call me?"

"*They did.* I don't know who."

"What did they look like?"

"I don't *know.*"

"Did they speak with accents?"

"I'm sorry, Jake."

"*Did they speak with accents?*"

The flashlight blinked out then, leaving them in total darkness. Falcetti said, "Shit." His voice was urgent like before, but it wasn't a whisper this time. Bechet had thought Falcetti was panicking because the flashlight had gone out, but when Falcetti said again, "Shit, Jake, shit," Bechet knew that it was more than the darkness that was causing his friend to panic. Bechet looked up at Falcetti, couldn't see him but could sense somehow that Falcetti was looking toward the door behind him. He could sense, again, the deep fear. Bechet's attention quickly shifted, and he knew that someone was there now, in the doorway. His heart began to pound, adrenaline hitting his blood, but before he could move, before he could think to move, he felt something press against the back of his head. It was cold and hard, and he knew instantly that this was the muzzle of a gun.

"Don't move," a voice said. It spoke calmly, but there was an edge to it, too, a contempt. Bechet ignored that, had nothing but his hearing now, listened for the accent and recognized it—Algerian—at once. He had expected to hear exactly that, but he didn't recognize the voice at all, and that stumped him. Still, he didn't dare let himself think that this could be anything other than what it seemed to be. There was no reason to do that. He'd been half-expecting to hear or see something from his former life since he'd learned of the bodies at the canal—some sign of the man for whom he had once worked, or worse even, the man's son, some *stirring in the air to indicate that Castello was near, or getting near.* Expectations or not, Bechet was nonetheless surprised by the swiftness with which his past had apparently found him, had come up behind him like this. What did they know? How long have they known it? If not the Algerian he had once known, then who was the man behind him? But more than all this, more than surprise and a flood of questions, Bechet was angered by how suddenly years and years of meticulous precautions could be rendered so pointless, so utterly and sadly pointless . . .

Bechet calmed his heart, kept his adrenaline from pushing him into panic. He could do that, the boxer in him, the man he used to be, knew how.

"I will put a bullet through your head if you do not do what I say," the Algerian said. A young voice, Bechet thought, not sure why, exactly. "Do you understand me?"

Before Bechet could react, the muzzle of the gun was gone, removed from his skull. Only an amateur would have left it there any longer. Bechet heard footsteps, and then lights came on, not in the storage room but outside it, overhead spots mounted above the dance floor. Dim, shining through colored filters, these lights made a gloomy mix of reds and blues and greens that didn't really reach into the small storage room, couldn't make it past the Algerian in the doorway. The Algerian's shadow fell across Bechet and Falcetti, was large enough to cover the both of them. A second shadow appeared in the room as the man who had turned on the lights joined the Algerian in the doorway. Bechet looked over his shoulder at them—his first act of defiance—but lit as these two men were from behind, it was impossible for him to see anything more than their respective shapes. Two shadows standing side by side, one stout but solid, maybe an inch or two shorter than Bechet, but easily as wide, the other as tall but slighter. Bechet scrambled for every detail his senses could collect.

Even though he hadn't been told to—*because* he hadn't been told

to—Bechet rose to his feet. His second act of defiance, to let the Algerian know that even though he was the one holding the gun, he wasn't
necessarily the one in charge. It was the only hand Bechet had to play. It
was, of course, one he would have to play with care, even when it looked
otherwise.

He turned and faced the two men, defying them again in the only
way he could. On the outside he wanted—needed—to appear bold, fearless. On the inside, though, feelings he hadn't known in a long time were
beginning to stir, the feelings of an animal trapped in a corner. Scared,
desperate, ready to fight, if necessary, and do so with brutality.

It was not a good place at all for a man like Bechet to be.

"What do you want?" Bechet demanded. He still wasn't certain whom
he was facing. The only thing he knew was that he was, in some way or
another, facing a thread that threatened to reconnect him with his past.
This was more of a concern to him than the gun in the Algerian's hand.

"Did I tell you to stand up?" the Algerian said.

"Go fuck yourself."

"You're going to do what I tell you to do, do you understand this?"

"Where are my friend's clothes?"

"I don't think you should be worrying about your friend right now."

"I don't give a fuck what you think. Get my friend's clothes."

Bechet turned, intending to untie the last remaining rope around Falcetti's ankle. He stopped short when the slighter man finally spoke.

"You're going to want to take what my friend here says seriously," the
man warned. "He's a vicious little bastard. Almost as vicious, in fact, as
you used to be, Pay Day."

The slighter man's South American accent and clear, educated English
were immediately recognizable to Bechet. There was no possible way to
mistake what was going on now.

Bechet turned to face the shadow of the slighter man again. Just as he
had done back in Gabrielle's dark bedroom, he saw this man's face clearly
in his mind. It took a moment for Bechet to speak.

"Long time, no see, Jorge," he said.

Castello nodded. "Long time, no see, my brother." He reached out,
found the light switch on the wall, flipped it up. The only light in the
storage room was a bare bulb mounted on the ceiling at the far end. Its

light was both dull and glaring. Bechet turned away from the sudden light, giving his eyes, so used to the darkness, a chance to adjust. As he was turned away, he looked down at Falcetti, saw that he was struggling against the light as well, his eyes blinking rapidly, as if he were afraid to let them close for longer than a second. There was fear in everything about him—in his expression, in the way he sat on the chair, holding Bechet's jacket over his lap with two trembling hands.

Finally, Bechet turned and looked once more toward the doorway and the faces—clearly visible now, not just imagined—of the two men standing squarely in it.

Castello was dressed in an overcoat, wool slacks, and a dark fisherman's sweater. Expensive, as always. His thick, dark hair was combed back, his face recently shaved, his skin taut, healthy, pampered. He was only a year younger than Bechet, but he was aging in that way the wealthy often age. No gray hair, no softness under the eyes. Tooth and nail all the way. The Algerian at Castello's side, out of Bechet's reach at the moment, was in his late twenties at the most. He was dressed in a black field jacket, black cargo pants, black boots, and his hair, light brown, was a military buzz cut. Everything about him said military. Not a wanna-be, though, Bechet could tell that. The real thing. It was obvious by the way the Algerian was holding his Desert Eagle .50 caliber semiautomatic. With two hands, muzzle aimed at the floor between his legs, elbows cocked so that the butt of the handle was level with his belt buckle. Bechet thought of Castello's warning: *vicious as you used to be. Almost.* Castello had the money to hire the best—and the worst—there was, and the Algerian seemed made to fill that order. Built like a wrestler, low and compact, thick. Designed for knocking things over. Bechet studied the man's—the *kid's*—face: square, with a low hairline, eyes that were narrow, giving him the appearance more that he was taking aim at Bechet than looking at him. The contempt Bechet had heard in the kid's voice was just as visible in his face. He was thick, from top to bottom, but his neck was particularly thick, held up a head, in keeping with the proportions of his body, that was the size of a crash helmet. Bechet had never seen this kid before, yet he was nonetheless, somehow, familiar. It wasn't simply the type of man he was that Bechet recognized now—a type Bechet had encountered many times in his past. It was something more than that.

The look of half-recognition was visible on Bechet's face.

"The resemblance is amazing, isn't it?" Castello said.

Bechet immediately looked back at Castello, said nothing.

"Don't tell me you don't see it, Pay Day. His father is a little taller, yes, but other than that, he's a mirror image, don't you think?"

Bechet glanced at the Algerian again. He was staring at Bechet with hard eyes, standing rigidly, as if his spine and shoulders were iron bars that formed a cross. Even though the man was wearing a field jacket and loose-fitting pants, Bechet sensed powerful limbs. He sensed, too, an eagerness to use them. This was obvious, maybe too obvious. It was an indication of confidence and a desire to get to work, or else a need to prove himself, to dominate. Either way, this kid clearly relied on the power his frame promised, counted on it to get him through everything life put in front of him. Bechet could tell that much just by looking at him. The kid was more than likely, then, someone who, when he fought, fought to win, expected to do so quickly, decisively, was therefore the kind of man who went all out, balls to the walls, from the start. The question, though, was did he have the heart and lungs required to last in a fight that went on for longer than seconds? Bechet had fought men like that before, in the ring but also out of it. The fights outside the ring were, of course, the ones that mattered. As for the Algerian, as for this moment, *right now*, there were, Bechet knew, certain weaknesses that came with the kind of strength this kid so proudly possessed. Bechet focused his mind on the ways to disassemble—when it came to it, which it likely would, was just a matter now of when—the machine that was this particular opponent.

All machines can be taken apart.

"He's LeCur's kid," Bechet said flatly. He didn't need to look at the Algerian a second time.

Castello nodded. "Good to know all those punches you took to the head haven't taken their toll yet."

One LeCur—a younger, more powerful LeCur—was bad enough, but two LeCurs would have been very bad news indeed for Bechet. He needed to know if the father, too, was here, or even just nearby. What Bechet would do next depended on that.

"Where's his old man these days?" he said.

"Oh, he's still around. He was looking forward to seeing you again, actually. But he had something else he had to do tonight."

"Whatever it is you're up to, Jorge, it doesn't have anything to do with my friend. Let him go. Okay?"

"Well, we don't really want him running to the police, do we? Something like that wouldn't be good news for any of us. He stays here for now."

"Then at least give him his clothes."

Castello waited a moment, then looked at LeCur. "Go get his things while Pay Day and I have a talk."

LeCur hesitated, glanced at Bechet, sizing him up.

"We'll be fine alone," Castello assured him. "Pay Day wants to know what's going on, so he'll behave himself just fine till he finds out."

"I should check him for weapons."

"It's obvious he isn't carrying a firearm. And if he had a knife, he wouldn't have wasted time untying the ropes. Anyway, like I said, he wants to know what's going on, so he won't do anything foolish. Will you, Pay Day?"

Bechet didn't answer. LeCur studied Bechet once more, then holstered the Desert Eagle under his field jacket and disappeared from view. Bechet listened as he crossed the dance floor, waiting till he heard the door open and close before kneeling down and starting to untie the last rope around Falcetti's ankle.

Despite Castello's lingering shadow, Bechet could see that Falcetti was looking in the direction of the doorway. It was as if he was unwilling to take his eyes off Castello. Bechet could see, too, that there was shame in Falcetti's eyes. And fear. As dangerous as he might have thought his life was, there simply was no way that he was prepared for this kind of violence.

Once Falcetti was free, Bechet stood, dropping the rope to the floor. Falcetti remained seated, though; standing would only have exposed him even more. Not long after that LeCur returned with Falcetti's clothes, all bundled together in a clump. He entered the narrow storage room, but Bechet kept himself between him and Falcetti. It was partly because of the design of the room, but mostly on purpose, an act of protecting the weak and defying the strong. This was, after all, the true man, the real

Bechet. He wasn't what Castello and his father and the older LeCur had once tried to make of him, *had* for a time made of him.

"C'mon out of there, Pay Day," Castello said. "LeCur will get him dressed."

Bechet looked down at Falcetti. "You all right, Bobby?"

Falcetti nodded. His eyes, though, were wild with uncertainty. He looked almost bewildered.

Bechet said to Castello, "He can dress himself."

Castello nodded. "LeCur, give him his clothes."

The Algerian threw the bundle at Falcetti. There was contempt in the way he did that, of course. There would be contempt, Bechet knew, in everything he did. Falcetti caught the clothes, clutching them to his chest and almost losing Bechet's jacket in the process. LeCur backed out of the doorway, making way for Bechet. He kept his eyes fixed on the onetime boxer, sizing him up. Bechet placed his hand on Falcetti's shoulder, felt skin that was cold and slick with sweat.

"Everything's going to be okay," Bechet told him. "I'll be right outside the door. We'll be out of here in a few minutes."

Falcetti, still clutching his clothes and Bechet's jacket, was unable to look Bechet in the eyes. He nodded once, quickly. Clearly all he wanted at this moment was privacy in which to get himself dressed.

Bechet stepped out of the storage room. Castello was standing by the bar along the left side of the room. Bechet looked at LeCur, then walked to meet Castello. LeCur didn't follow him, remaining by the storage-room door to keep an eye on both the washed-up boxer and the pathetic cabbie. He thought of them only in that way: a man past his prime and a scrawny and easily scared punk. They weren't men to him, weren't *people,* couldn't be even if he wanted to think of them as that. They were simply a collection of weaknesses, things to be exploited for the gain of the man for whom he worked.

Castello gestured toward the bar, like a host. "A drink?" He'd been educated at Oxford before coming to America to learn his family's business. He was articulate, never anything less than polite, though this had always seemed only to add to the sense of menace he carried with him like a well-worn affectation. Bechet shook his head, refusing the drink. He knew Castello well, knew his way of doing things, his tricks, his need to make a person feel at ease while at the same time keeping him or her just a little uncertain as to what may happen next.

But Bechet wasn't going to play that game.

"How did you know Bobby worked for me?" he said. His partnership with Eddie was a secret—well, as secret as a legitimate business could be. There was a paper trail: tax forms, insurance forms, registrations. Still, only a handful of people at the most knew about it. As Bechet waited for Castello to answer, he made a point of finding LeCur in his peripheral vision and keeping him there.

"There isn't much in this town we don't know about," Castello said. He nearly always referred to himself and his family as one. He'd once told Bechet he did that for the same reason a president was referred to as Mr. President and not by name. It took the individual out of the equation, made things that needed to be done easier to do. *On behalf of the office, part of the job.* Not that, as far as Bechet had ever seen, Castello had any difficulties, family or no family to hide himself behind, when it came to doing what needed to be done.

Bechet waited for Castello to offer more, knew when Castello didn't that this was as much of an answer as he was going to get. And really, for now, it didn't matter how Castello had found him. What mattered was exactly how much more Castello knew, how badly Bechet—and Gabrielle— were exposed.

"It looks like you're getting some gray hairs there," Castello said. "We're not kids anymore, are we?"

Bechet ignored that. "Your father and I had a deal," he said.

Castello nodded. "We know. It hurt him that you could turn on him the way you did. You know that, right?"

"I did what I had to do to get out."

"What you're saying is we gave you no choice in the matter."

"Something like that."

Castello nodded again, glanced at the tattoo of a dark star on the inside of Bechet's left forearm. He looked at it for a moment, then said, "He loved you like a son, Pay Day. And to me you were a brother. You were a part of the family. I always thought we made that clear."

"Nothing has changed, Jorge. Not as far as I'm concerned. The deal still stands. If anything happens to me, the evidence I have gets turned over to the FBI. It's all in place, nothing can stop that from happening."

"Actually, Pay Day, everything has changed, you just don't know it yet."

"What do you mean?"

"My father is dead."

Bechet thought about that for a moment, about what it meant, could possibly mean. His brain scrambled to imagine and understand all the variations. But there were just too many, they kept coming, radiating out like endless ripples on the surface of a quiet lake. Finally, Bechet said, "How did he die?"

"Natural causes. He became ill, knew he was going to die, wanted to do so at his home, wanted his family around him."

"He died in Argentina?"

"Yeah."

"I didn't know."

"It was kept quiet."

"When?"

"About a year ago."

Bechet thought to ask why Castello had waited so long to come after him but didn't. There was something *he* needed to make clear.

"The evidence is just as damaging to you as it would have been to him," he said.

"Do you really think we didn't come after you because we were afraid of the FBI?"

"Then why didn't you?"

"Like I said, my father loved you like a son. He let you walk away. It was an act of compassion—one, I warned him, that would probably come back to haunt him. Plus we had invested money in you—in training you, feeding you. But he didn't care about that."

"I don't believe that you're not afraid of the FBI, Jorge, not for a second."

"Any evidence you have against us also implicates you. The problem with a détente based on the threat of mutual destruction is that the destruction is mutual. Anyway, if we wanted to, we could have gotten our hands on the evidence."

"How?" It was as much of a dare as it was a question.

"Everyone has his weakness, my brother. Your particular weakness would have made things especially easy."

"And what's my weakness?"

Castello smiled. "It has always amazed me how vital a target the heart is. In every way possible."

Bechet waited, saying nothing.

"A pretty woman, everything you've ever wanted, would have made her way into your life," Castello explained. "Taken you places a woman has never taken you before. All your dreams come true. It may have taken a while, but sooner or later she would have asked the right questions, found out all your secrets, shared them with us. We taught you everything you know, Pay Day, but not everything *we* know. Not by a long shot."

All around Bechet now precautions—*the very things that defined his life*—were being rendered pointless. He felt foolish, wildly vulnerable. More than that, though, he sensed the pressure he felt whenever he was in a corner, felt it starting to build within him.

Like a fuse being lit.

This was the time to stay calm and swing smart, not wild.

"You would have had to find me first," Bechet said.

"You spent the year after you left us in hiding. Maybe you started running low on money, or maybe you were feeling a little confident in your ability to make yourself invisible, but whatever the reason, you began working as housepainter, did that for two years, then started your own business. There were women here and there, nothing too serious, nothing a beautiful woman couldn't have lured you away from. You sold your business a year and a half ago, disappeared for a little while again, then showed up again when you bought into your friend's cab company. No woman after that, not that we knew of anyway, though, of course, there was always the chance that actually meant there was someone special, someone you were taking care to keep hidden. We weren't able to ascertain where you lived, or what you drove. I suspect you changed vehicles a lot. Every, what, six months? Smart, in a place like this, where everyone is known by the car they drive. It's amazing the wealth of personal information you can get with just a license plate number and the right connection, but of course you know all about that, don't you? For the past year it was like you had disappeared again. We knew you were out here still, somewhere, but of course we weren't really trying all that hard to find out exactly where. We didn't need to know that because we knew we could draw you out through that buddy of yours if the need ever arose, which it did tonight."

"The two bodies at the canal," Bechet said.

Castello nodded. "I think you know us well enough to know that we wouldn't dispose of a problem in such a way. We certainly wouldn't string up two bodies in our own backyard, as it were, for everyone to see."

"You had nothing to do with that."

"No. The victims, however, did work for us. Did some . . . courier work. Not long ago we discovered that they were, in fact, stealing from us, something we allowed to continue in hopes that we would find out who they were working for."

"What makes you think they were working for someone?"

"These two young men weren't particularly bright or ambitious, which is why they did what they did for us. A lack of imagination is a good thing when someone is transporting certain items of value from one place to another. It is our belief that someone coerced them into stealing from us."

"Why coerced?"

"They knew what would happen if they betrayed us."

Bechet nodded. *Not just the betrayers, but their women, their families. The South American way.*

The heart was a vital target indeed.

"It's hard to imagine they'd do something as foolish as to steal from my family," Castello said, "knowing, as they did, the consequences."

"But who could do that? Who would have the power to coerce them into doing that?"

"That's what we would like you to find out."

Bechet glanced at LeCur, still standing outside the storage room, then looked back at Castello. "You've got plenty of resources to draw from, Jorge. You don't need me."

"I will, of course, pay you for your time."

"I'm not interested."

"I went to considerable trouble to get you here tonight, Pay Day. Too much trouble to simply take no for an answer."

"That's not my problem."

"It is, actually. Someone is making a move against my family. Do you really think I wouldn't pull out all the stops, do what I had to do to protect the people I care about, protect the business my father spent his life building?"

Bechet felt his heart race just a little then. "What are you saying, Jorge?"

Castello looked at LeCur, nodded once. LeCur removed a cell phone from the top pocket of his field jacket, opened it, held down a single button, then brought the phone to his face. After a moment, he said something in French. He listened to the answer, then looked at Castello and announced, "He's in place. We're all set."

"What's she like, Pay Day?" Castello said. "Is she pretty? Does she know what you used to be? Does it turn her on a little? Some women are like that, no?"

Bechet's heart froze. He said nothing.

"Since you've gone to considerable trouble to keep her secret, I take it she means something to you, not like those other women." Castello spoke to LeCur but kept his eyes on Bechet. "What's the name of the street again?"

"South Valley Road," LeCur answered. "The last cottage at the top of the hill. Door around back."

"It didn't really take much for your friend to tell us everything we needed to know," Castello said. "Ironic, that the great Pay Day Bechet would be friends with someone who couldn't take a punch. Maybe not ironic, maybe just funny."

Bechet looked toward the storage room then. Falcetti was standing now in its doorway. He was dressed, holding Bechet's coat in one hand. He could barely keep his head up.

"So should we send the old man in?" Castello said.

Bechet looked back at him.

"He touches her and I will kill you."

"I'm sure LeCur over here would have something to say about that.

And anyway, no one's going to go near her—unless, of course, you give us no other choice. But you know all about having no choice, don't you?"

"Don't do this, Jorge."

"You should have expected it the moment you saw my face, brother. You know me, you know the way I think, how ahead of everyone I have to be. You should have known this was coming."

"But why me?"

"Do you really need to ask that?"

"Because I'm not connected to your family. If this goes to shit, it won't come back to you."

"Look at it as karma, Pay Day. If you hadn't left us, hadn't . . . disconnected yourself from us like you did, you wouldn't be in this situation. You'd be valuable to us, not dispensable."

"I wouldn't even know where to start looking for whoever is behind this," Bechet said.

"You're rusty, I understand that. It's been a while. Our couriers had girlfriends. Find them, find out what they know, everything they know. I'm sure you remember how to do that. It's likely that whoever killed our couriers knows about the girlfriends as well, so there probably isn't a lot of time to waste. If they know the price we charge for betrayal and are intent on making certain people think this was our handiwork, then it just might be too late already."

"And if it is?"

"Let's hope for your sake it isn't."

Bechet looked at Castello for a moment. "You don't want to start this, Jorge."

"It seems neither of us has much of a choice here. Just find the girls, find out who is behind this, and you and your lady can just slip away. I give you my word on that."

The word of Castello's father was one thing, but the word of his son was something else altogether. The difference between gold and fool's gold. Bechet knew this, felt the fuse that had been lit getting shorter and shorter the more he thought of it, with each second that passed that he wasn't in motion, doing something.

But not now, not yet.

"Where do I find them?" he said finally.

"LeCur will give you an address. It's where our two couriers lived. I doubt the police will find it any time soon, so you should be able to come and go as you please. Still, you'll want to be careful."

Bechet thought about that. "What were their names?"

"Why?"

"Because you've been very careful this whole time to avoid saying their names. It sounds a little like you don't want me to know."

"Why would I want to keep that from you?"

"You tell me."

Castello nodded, then said, "James Michaels and Richard Romano. Those were their names. Not friends of yours, by any chance."

"No."

"I'm sorry, I don't know the names of their girlfriends. But I'm sure once you have a look around the apartment you'll be able to pick up their trail." Castello looked at Bechet for a moment, then said, "I'm sorry about this, Pay Day. I really am."

Bechet said nothing.

Castello nodded toward LeCur. "Start the clock." LeCur said into the phone, "All clear," then flipped the lid closed. He held on to the phone, his hard eyes fixed on Bechet.

"Just so you know, his old man remains outside your place till we hear from you. You've got a little over six hours till first light. We expect to hear something from you by then. LeCur will call his old man every half hour, on the dot, and if he fails to make a call, even by a second, his old man goes inside. Do you understand?"

Bechet nodded.

"If your lady tries to leave, the old man will stop her. And if LeCur here calls and his old man doesn't pick up, then your buddy here dies, and we make certain the cops have plenty of reasons to blame you for it."

"You've thought of everything, haven't you?"

"Like I said, we've taught you everything you know, not everything we know."

"How do I contact you?" Bechet said.

"You don't. LeCur will give you a number to call. I doubt you'd be fool enough to go to the police or the FBI, but if you do, your friend here and your lady friend are dead. In very unpleasant ways. And don't forget, protective custody is still custody. You've gone to too much trouble to live free just to throw it all away in a moment of panic. We clear on all this, Pay Day?"

Again, Bechet nodded.

"A few minutes after I leave you'll be free to go. Don't want you thinking you can somehow get out of this by following me and running me off the road." Castello looked toward LeCur, who was on his cell phone again.

"The car's here," LeCur said. He flipped the cell phone closed, then returned it to the top pocket of his field jacket.

Castello nodded, looked at Bechet one last time, said, "I'm not my father, Pay Day. I won't let you off the hook as easily as he did. Do us both a favor and remember that, okay?"

He waited a moment more, then walked to the exit and stepped outside. Bechet glimpsed the dark night beyond through the open door. He had almost forgotten about the bad weather, the slick roads and the patches of blinding fog. But there was nothing he could do about that. Once the door swung closed Bechet made a quick check of his watch. It was 12:57. LeCur had ended the call to his father less than a minute ago. The clock, then, was ticking. Bechet needed to make his move against the Algerian, needed to make it now, there was just no other way out of this.

Once again, Castello had left Bechet with no choice but to find a way of escape.

The fuse was close to its end now, Bechet just seconds from exploding.

Falcetti was just outside the storage-room doorway, LeCur only ten feet away, both men looking at Bechet expectantly, waiting for his reaction. *An animal in a corner, dangerous, unpredictable.* Bechet glanced at Falcetti, then at LeCur, his hard face blank, his body, except for the movements of his head, motionless. Suddenly, though, Bechet flung himself into motion and headed straight toward Falcetti, rushing at him fast, like a man who had given in to an irresistible and violent rage. The instant Bechet began to move, LeCur reached under his jacket for his Desert Eagle, stepping back as he pulled it out, putting a safe distance between himself and Bechet. He aimed the muzzle at the floor ahead of him and tracked Bechet with his eyes, turning his torso so his shoulders were always square with his target. Bechet didn't stop at the sight of the drawn firearm, though, didn't even slow, just continued straight for Falcetti like a man who could simply take no more.

"Hold it," LeCur ordered.

"Fucking shoot me," Bechet snapped.

Bechet reached Falcetti, it took only seven or eight determined strides to close the distance, grabbed him by his shirt with both hands, almost lifting the guy off the floor. Falcetti flinched, his eyes even more wild with fear than before, as Bechet angrily shoved him back into the narrow room. Once they were through the doorway the jacket Falcetti had been holding, Bechet's jacket, fell to the floor, his hands rising up instinctively to cover his head and face. Bechet made a quick quarter turn, driving Falcetti into the wall, hard, pressing him against it. The doorway was to Bechet's left now, and in his peripheral vision he could see LeCur on the dance floor. He was moving toward them, his gun, held muzzle down still, firmly in two hands. Bechet began to shake Falcetti, cursing at him, yelling, a man gone wild. *"You're fucking dead, Bobby. You're fucking dead."* From the corner of his eye Bechet glimpsed LeCur, saw him raise his handgun to the firing position, then let it down, only to raise it again and keep it there. *So much uncertainty.*

LeCur stepped into the doorway, commanded, *"Let him go. Now."* But Bechet ignored him, kept Falcetti against the wall, continued to shake him violently, to vent his rage.

"You're fucking dead! You're fucking dead!" LeCur gave the order again, to which Bechet snapped, *"Fucking shoot me. Fucking shoot him. I don't fucking care."* LeCur maintained his firing posture, his elbows bent, tucked tight to his body, one leg forward, the other back slightly, knees loose. Bechet pulled Falcetti from the wall then, made another quarter turn, was facing the doorway now, facing LeCur with Falcetti, stunned, frightened, between them. LeCur removed his supporting hand from the butt of the gun, held it out to keep Falcetti at a distance. Bechet was shaking Falcetti back and forth now, like a schoolyard bully, and LeCur reached out for the collar of Falcetti's shirt, intending to pull Falcetti from Bechet's hands and separate them, get control of a situation that

had so suddenly spun out of his control. The instant he began to pull, though, pull with all his power, everything changed, and changed fast.

Falcetti went from being shaken back and forth to moving backward only, moving faster than LeCur was able to pull. Falcetti, off his feet now, little more than a human projectile, closed the distance LeCur had left as a buffer and slammed into LeCur with the force of a tackle. LeCur stumbled backward, his gun now pressed flat between his body and Falcetti's. He quickly regained his footing, though, stabilized himself as Falcetti, his balance lost from Bechet's sudden, violent shove, began to fall. LeCur tried to retreat several steps, reclaim distance and a good firing position, get his gun clear and put Bechet square in the sights, but it was already too late for that.

Bechet was all over him.

And LeCur was candy.

Bechet had moved around Falcetti as he collided with LeCur, got in next to the young Algerian before he even knew Bechet was there. Bechet landed a right hook into LeCur's ribs that made LeCur almost fold. Crouched low for the body shot, Bechet recocked his torso as he rose with all the power he had in his legs, then landed a second right hook, this one landing just a bit too high, striking LeCur's cheek and not his jaw. LeCur stumbled back, Falcetti still against him, still falling, but Bechet was tight on the Algerian, right there beside him. A full second had yet to pass since the blow to the ribs had struck, and now an overhand left was coming down, Bechet's full weight behind it. The overhand landed right on the button, flush on LeCur's chin, and it was like hitting a switch. LeCur's legs turned instantly to rubber, his knees buckling. He went down as if a trapdoor had been opened beneath him, was unconscious even before he and his Desert Eagle hit the floor.

Bechet didn't waste any time. He followed LeCur down to the floor, mounting him and striking him three times in the head with his right elbow. *One, two, three.* Each blow bounced LeCur's head off the boards of the dance floor like a ball. Bechet then rose, striding LeCur. He kicked the handgun out of reach, and grabbing the collar of the field jacket, he dragged LeCur into the storage room, turned him so he was facedown on the floor.

Bechet looked toward Falcetti, who was scrambling to get to his feet. He was beyond startled now.

"You okay?" Bechet said.

Falcetti didn't answer, couldn't.

"*You okay, Bobby?*"

Falcetti shook his head. He was standing now, staring at Bechet, what Bechet had done, made of the Algerian with a gun.

"I need your help," Bechet said.

He placed LeCur's hands behind his back, then peeled off the field jacket, tossing it aside. He grabbed a chuck of rope off the floor and began to tie LeCur's hands together at the wrists.

Falcetti didn't move.

Bechet glanced at him. "Bobby, c'mon. I need your help."

Falcetti entered the room, stopping just inside the doorway.

"Get a piece of rope," Bechet ordered. "Tie his feet together."

Falcetti hesitated.

"C'mon, Bobby. There isn't a lot of time."

Falcetti nodded. He knelt down, picked up a length of rope, began to wind it around LeCur's ankles. He looked and moved like a man in shock.

"You okay?" Bechet said again.

Again, Falcetti nodded. He was looking at something out of the corner of his eye. Bechet, working fast to secure LeCur's hands, followed Falcetti's line of vision to LeCur's left arm. His inner forearm, specifically. He saw three tattoos. Dark stars, identical in every way to the single tattoo on Bechet's inner left forearm.

"You guys have the same . . ." Falcetti didn't finish his sentence.

Bechet glanced at LeCur's forearm but ignored the comment. When he was done securing LeCur's hands, he helped Falcetti finish up with LeCur's feet. Every now and then Falcetti glanced at the tattoo on Bechet's forearm. When LeCur's feet were bound, Bechet stood, stepped deeper into the room and searched the shelves until he found a stack of bar rags. He grabbed several, found on another shelf a small toolbox. Inside was a roll of duct tape. He returned to LeCur, shoved one of the rags into his mouth, then, using the remaining rags as gloves, stuck the end of the tape to the side of LeCur's face and wound a long strand around his head like a gag, did this several times, just to be certain. He did the same around LeCur's eyes. The only flesh exposed was LeCur's nose and chin.

Bechet quickly searched LeCur's pockets, found a folding knife and a Zippo lighter, a ring of keys and a wallet. He shoved them all into the various pockets of his jeans, along with the roll of duct tape, then picked up the last remaining piece of rope and his Maglite off the floor, tucked the butt end of the flashlight and the rope into his back pocket before grabbing his own corduroy jacket and putting it on as he stood.

Falcetti had retreated to the doorway, was looking now at his friend. Bechet moved around him, hurried to the field jacket, picked it up.

"Any spots in your vision, Bobby? Ringing in your ears? Loss of balance? Nausea?"

"No."

"If you start feeling sick to your stomach, go to the emergency room. Other than that, I don't care where you go, Bobby, just go somewhere and stay put, okay? Stay out of sight." Bechet checked the jacket, making sure the cell phone hadn't fallen out of the top pocket, then opened the coat and used it to pick up the Desert Eagle, careful not to touch the gun with his bare hands. He folded the jacket around the gun and looked at Falcetti. "Do you understand?"

Falcetti nodded. Bechet turned and headed toward the door, could hear Falcetti moving behind him. After a pause to take in a deep breath, Bechet pushed the door open a crack with his foot. He waited, heard nothing, then opened the door enough to slip through. Falcetti followed close behind. They crossed the courtyard to the gate. It was closed now. Bechet nudged it open, studied what he could see of the parking lot. It was empty. He slipped through the gate and walked the length of the fence to the parking lot behind the restaurant. His Jeep was still there, nose to nose with the cab. He bolted for it. When he reached it, Falcetti was right behind him.

"Where are you going, man?"

"Get somewhere safe, Bobby."

"What are you going to do?"

Bechet ignored the question, pulled the Maglite from his back pocket, tossed it onto the Jeep's floor. "Check into a motel, leave town, do something," he said. "I'll let you know when it's all over."

"What do you mean all over? What are you going to do?"

Bechet climbed in behind the wheel and laid the jacket containing the handgun onto the passenger seat, then cranked the ignition till the motor caught. He pulled the door shut without another word and tore like a shot across the empty parking lot.

On Montauk Highway, heading west, he checked his watch. It was 1:01. Even on a clear night the ride from Wainscott to the Shinnecock Hills took longer than a half hour. But, again, Bechet had no choice now. He worked through the gears, taxing the old engine, shifted finally into fifth, then gripped the wheel with both hands. He was doing eighty, the old Jeep shuttering around him as wildly as his heart was shuttering within.

There wasn't much fog till Bridgehampton, but when it finally did appear, shocking white in the beams of the Jeep's headlight, it was like a barricade. There was nothing Bechet could do but slow down and inch his way through. He was doing twenty now—even that was too fast, but he didn't care, and it took him several long minutes to reach the other side of town. There the fog broke, and Bechet once again worked up to fifth gear, pushing the Jeep to its limits on the still-slick roads. He tried to make up for the time he had lost, but just before the village of Water Mill, just as he felt he was regaining precious moments, he came to another barricade of shifting fog and was forced to slow to a crawl again. Halfway through that village he checked his watch. It was now 1:14. *Shit.* By the time he was out of that village and on the long, straight stretch of road that would take him to Southampton, it was 1:17. Less than ten minutes now till the phone call from LeCur to his father was due, and South Valley Road was, at best, still fifteen minutes away.

Just outside of Southampton, Bechet turned from Montauk Highway onto Sunrise Highway, a route west that would take him around the heart of the village, but also away from the water, so there would be, he hoped, less fog to slow him. He pushed the Jeep well past the speed limit, aware of the places cops were likely to be waiting for speeders, though he hardly slowed for them, how could he? At the crossroads along Sunrise he got lucky, caught some green lights, and the few red lights he came to, after stopping and looking all around for the sign of a cop, he jumped, racing through the empty intersection. At the college he turned onto Tuckahoe Road, followed that south to Montauk Highway, turned right onto it and continued west. He was close to the water again, and though the patches of fog that crossed the road here were significantly less than the barricades he had encountered farther east, they were still enough to require him to drive much more slowly than he wanted, than his heart required. He was only five minutes away now, just the winding, two-lane road through the Shinnecock Hills, a road with which he was very familiar, but it was already 1:26. Time was up.

He thought then of calling in a fire, giving the address not of Gabrielle's cottage but of one of the other cottages on her road. The presence of fire trucks and cop cars might scare LeCur off, or at the very least delay him from making his move against Gabrielle as scheduled. But that, along with the absence of the phone call that was at this moment due, would certainly appear to LeCur as a clear indication that something had gone wrong with their A plan and that it was time for him to carry out their B plan. There was no knowing exactly what LeCur would do then. Play it smart and slip away? Or, at the first sign of the fire trucks, storm the cottage and wait inside—with Gabrielle—for Bechet to arrive? Anyway, it was too late now; it would still take several minutes at least for the fire trucks to reach South Valley Road, and by then LeCur would be well into plan B.

Still, Bechet had to do something. *Something.* He grabbed the field jacket, found the cell phone in the top pocket, dug it out and scrolled through the outgoing calls, stopping on the second-to-last call made. The last call had been to Castello's driver, but the one before that had been to LeCur's father. It was a gamble, a bluff, and a poor bluff at that, but it was the only hand that was his to play.

Bechet hit REDIAL, placed the phone to his ear. Two rings, and then a voice from his past, instantly familiar.

"*Oui.*"

Bechet saw LeCur in his mind now, the father, not the son, saw his face. He was in his late forties when Bechet had left, so he would be in his mid-fifties now. An early model of the man Bechet had just taken apart. Bigger, too, and more experienced. In many regards, age only made a soldier better. Youth, the power that comes with it, these were all well and good, served their purposes, but a veteran was always worth more than a new recruit, no matter what the situation. LeCur, when Bechet had last seen him, had nine nickel-sized stars tattooed on his inner forearm. One dark mark shy of a double ace, if he were a fighter pilot. How many more, Bechet wondered, would LeCur have now? How much more experience had he gained?

Never an easy thing, killing a man in cold blood.

Bechet kept the phone to his ear but said nothing. The sound of LeCur's voice had triggered a dozen different memories, none of which he had time for now. Still, these memories—fragmentary non sequiturs—ran around in his head like echoes. *That life long ago.* Bechet had barely known his own father, hadn't had much need or time for father figures, but the closest anyone had come, really, to filling that role, to being a surrogate father, were the two men who had trained him—his manager, who had taught him to box, and the older LeCur, who had taught him, among other things, to fight.

Bechet held the phone an arm's length away from his mouth, said in French—he knew a little—"Can you hear me?" He tried to muddy his accent, sound like—or enough like—LeCur's son. He repeated himself, then hit the button marked END. His heart was in spasms now, his blood pure adrenaline. He waited a few seconds, then hit REDIAL again. This time LeCur answered on the first ring. Bechet held the phone an arm's length away again but said nothing. He hoped that the noise of the Jeep—wind racing around a square, fiberglass top—would sound enough like the static of a bad connection. After a few seconds he hung up again. He was just minutes from South Valley Road now, approaching the curvy section where just hours before Falcetti had gone off the road. He opened the center console, dug out his winter gloves, pulled them on as he steered, then unfolded the field jacket and removed the Desert Eagle, laid the heavy gun on the floor between his seat and the pedals. The last thing he needed now was to hit the brakes for some reason and have the loaded gun go flying off the seat. He picked up the cell phone once more, pressed REDIAL again but hung up halfway through the first ring, then laid the phone on the console between his seats. His only hope was that these seemingly dropped calls had caused enough confusion to buy him the minutes he so desperately needed.

In the sharp curves he twice lost control of the Jeep, almost fishtailing off the road. But he couldn't let up now. Gabrielle was a half mile away. Each time he nearly spun out, he'd fight to regain control of the Jeep, then press on, his heart pounding, each hard throb just another dose of adrenaline for his blood.

The minute it took him to cross the remaining half mile, down the stretch of road that ran along the edge of Shinnecock Bay, was the longest minute he'd ever known.

He killed the headlights as he pulled to a stop on the shoulder at the foot of South Valley Road. If he had made the turn onto the road, his headlights would have been visible from anywhere above. If this was going to work, LeCur couldn't see him coming. Bechet got out, hurried to the road, careful to remain out of sight, and looked up the long incline. All he could see, of course, was darkness, the very darkness to which he had awoken tonight. He had to assume that LeCur was in his vehicle, and that his vehicle was parked close to the cottage. That was what Bechet would have done, where he would have parked, so no one could see his vehicle from the main road below. If Bechet thought this way, then the man who had taught him to think that way—who had taught him how to hunt others—would have thought this way as well.

Back at the Jeep, Bechet removed his corduroy jacket, tossed it onto the rear seat, then grabbed the black field jacket from the passenger seat and put it on fast. It fit him well enough. He then took the Desert Eagle from the driver's side floor, ejected the clip, checked to see that he had a full load, then slapped the clip back into the grip and pulled on the slide, chambering a round. Just as he did that, the cell phone on the console began to ring. He grabbed it, checked the display. It was the older LeCur, calling back. Bechet found the volume button, pressed till he silenced the ringer, then pocketed the phone. It vibrated against his wild heart as he grabbed the Maglite off the floor and started up the incline, heading for the darkness at its end.

He stuck close to the edge of the dirt road, making use of the cover provided by the thick scrub and crowding trees that lined it. The phone in his pocket vibrated two more times, sounding like the buzzing of some giant insect, then stopped. Bechet hurried up the gutted road, eventually leaving the influence of the lights that lined Montauk below and entering the near total blackness that was by now so familiar to him.

His eyes adjusted as best as they were going to, but it was enough for him to see the dull shine of a car bumper up ahead. An older Ford sedan, nondescript, probably stolen or bought at an auction and registered to a false name and address. Castello had access to a fleet of those. It was parked on the other side of the road, only twenty feet down from Gabrielle's cottage. He couldn't tell if there was anyone in the car, but as he got nearer he made out the shape of someone sitting in the passenger seat. He understood, if this was in fact LeCur, why he would be in the passenger seat and not behind the wheel. A man sitting in the passenger seat of a dark car was likely to appear to anyone who might see him as someone who was waiting for the car's driver. Every little diversion helped. But Bechet couldn't be certain yet if the man in the passenger seat was LeCur. For all he knew, LeCur was inside, this man had stayed behind to keep watch. Bechet continued forward, as quickly as he could while still being careful, till he was in a position to see the cottage through the trees. Its windows were as dark as they had been when he'd left it. Certainly, if someone was inside, moving through the unfamiliar darkness, there'd be some hint of light visible from the outside, the flicker of a searching flashlight in one of the windows, something.

But nothing, just the stillness and darkness of a place so far from the heart of things.

With someone seated on the right side of the car, Bechet knew he would have to enter the scrub that ran along the road or risk being seen. If the waiting man had been in the driver's seat, Bechet could have continued up the edge of the road, confident that he was safely within the car's blind spot. Moving through the scrub was slow and noisy, but there was no other approach that he could make. It took him two minutes to get close enough to where he could cross the open road quickly enough to surprise the passenger. Once there—once alongside the car, the man a dark profile in the passenger window—Bechet waited for an opportunity to show itself.

As he waited, though, the phone in his pocket started to vibrate again. The noise was, in the silence that surrounded him, nearly as loud as a ring would have been. If the car's windows had been open, the man inside would certainly have heard it. Bechet clutched at the phone in his pocket to quiet it, though that did little good. The phone went still after the third vibration, but Bechet didn't need to look at the display to know who had called. He could see the passenger taking his cell phone away from his ear, see his face by the glow of the display. It was LeCur. His features, visible for a few seconds only, disappeared when he flipped the lid of the phone closed. He sat still for a moment, thinking. Bechet knew what it was the man was considering. *Stick to plan A or switch to plan B.* It wasn't long, though, before the decision was made and the passenger door clicked open.

No interior light came on. LeCur would have disconnected it. The door hung ajar for a few seconds, open by only an inch or so, then finally swung out on well-oiled hinges. LeCur emerged, stood by the open door, his eyes fixed on the cottage. After a moment he swung the car door till it was almost closed, then stopped and gently nudged it with his knee till it clicked shut. He reached inside his jacket, removing his gun, looked down the length of the dark road for a moment, then back at the cottage. Bechet held his breath as he waited for LeCur to start moving, needed LeCur's motion to cover the sound of his own. Finally, LeCur took one step, but before he could take another, Bechet was rushing out from the cover of the brush. He crossed the dirt road with two long strides, came up beside LeCur, put his left hand on LeCur's right shoulder and pressed the muzzle of the gun against LeCur's right temple, did both things with enough firmness not only to make his intent clear but to edge LeCur off balance.

LeCur stiffened.

"Face the car," Bechet hissed.

Nothing for a moment, no movement or words, and then, softly, LeCur's voice: "Pay Day, that you?"

"Face the car."

LeCur turned slowly. Bechet was now behind him, the muzzle of the Desert Eagle pressed hard against the base of LeCur's skull. Bechet knew he couldn't leave it there for long.

"Grab your gun by the barrel with your left hand, then hand it back to me butt first." Bechet spoke in a whisper. So far not enough noise had been made to awaken Gabrielle. Bechet wanted to keep it that way.

"That was you who called all those times," LeCur said. He made no effort to match Bechet's whisper.

"Shut up."

"That was brilliant. You really had me guessing."

"Just give me the gun."

LeCur handed the gun back to Bechet as instructed. Bechet ejected the clip, then tossed the gun into the woods. He stepped back, putting himself just beyond LeCur's reach.

"Take off the coat, toss it over there."

LeCur was wearing a midlength leather coat. He slipped it off, tossed it toward the edge of the road. It landed heavy. There was probably a flashlight and some spare clips in the pockets.

"Hands on your head, palms down, fingers locked."

"You must have flown back here," LeCur said.

"Now spread your legs."

LeCur widened his stance, was leaning now with his full weight against the passenger door.

"Cross your thumbs."

LeCur did. Bechet stepped to him, wedged the inside of his left foot against the inside of LeCur's right foot, then grabbed hold of LeCur's thumbs with his left hand. He tucked the Desert Eagle into the waistband of his jeans and quickly searched the man. In his pockets was a folding knife, identical to the one Bechet had taken from the younger LeCur, and a wallet. He tossed them in the direction of the leather jacket.

"Is my son alive?"

"For now, yeah," Bechet said. "Do what I say and you'll see each other again. You understand?"

LeCur nodded. Bechet looked toward Gabrielle's cottage. It was still dark. Right now all he wanted was to get LeCur away from her. He stepped back two paces, drew the Desert Eagle.

"Open the door and get the keys out of the ignition," Bechet ordered.

"What for?"

"We're going for a ride."

"Then why do you need the keys?"

Bechet didn't answer. LeCur glanced toward the trunk, then looked back at Bechet.

"Get the keys," Bechet said.

LeCur opened the passenger door, reached across the seat, climbed back out with the keys in his hands.

"Open the trunk," Bechet said.

LeCur walked to the trunk, opened the lid. Bechet removed the Maglite from his back pocket. Its dull bulb was still flickering, but it was enough to do a quick search of the trunk. A spare tire, jack, and tire iron. To the left of the tire was a stack of large, heavy-duty garbage bags. On top of them was a hacksaw.

The sight of it made Bechet's gut tighten.

He looked at LeCur. *Carry only what you need for the job*—this LeCur had told him years ago. *Travel light, don't overprepare.* He had stressed that. The garbage bags and hacksaw, then, were there for a reason, for *this* job, for what would have been done with Gabrielle when she was dead.

Bechet looked at LeCur for a long time. He wanted to kill the man right now, right there, drag his dead body to the woods beyond the train tracks at the end of the road, leave it there to rot. The urge to do just that was powerful. But Bechet forced himself to keep still, keep his adrenaline in check. Now wasn't the time for emotion. Now wasn't the time for mistakes. He needed to stay cool, think, do what needed to be done to get Gabrielle away.

It was his only concern. Nothing else in the world—nothing at all—mattered.

Finally he reached inside the trunk, never taking his eyes off LeCur, and grabbed the hacksaw with his gloved hand. He flung the saw into the woods, heard it land with a *thump,* then grabbed the tire iron, just to be safe, did the same with that.

"Get in," he said.

"Pay Day, c'mon."

"Get in."

LeCur climbed into the trunk. His weight significantly compressed the rear shocks.

"On your side, hands behind your back."

LeCur complied, curling into the fetal position, his knees to his chest. Bechet pulled the roll of duct tape from the pocket of the field coat, secured LeCur's wrists together, then closed the trunk. He removed the

keys from the lock and hurried in behind the wheel of the sedan, starting the engine and turning on the headlights.

There were no dashboard lights—the fuse had probably been pulled—
so the interior of the Ford was dark. The only light was the glow flowing
back from the headlights.

LeCur never left anything to chance.

Neither, now, would Bechet.

At the bottom of South Valley Road Bechet eased down on the brakes,
bringing the sedan to a stop. He looked both ways several times, just to
be careful. The last thing he needed was to get into a fender bender
while driving a car with dubious registration, if any at all, and a hired
killer bound up in the trunk. Visibility was limited still, but better than it
had been earlier. Bechet would have preferred the fog to be heavy now, a
thick blanket to conceal him as he made his way to his destination, but
what remained would have to do. Besides, there was no one out tonight,
not at this time of year, at this hour, no waking souls except for himself
and this one connection to his past.

Bechet made a left onto Montauk Highway, heading east. Past the first
bend was Peconic Road, a narrow side street that wound northward
through the Shinnecock Hills. It wasn't much more than a mile long,
and the few houses to be found along its edges, lower-middle-class cottages, were mostly unoccupied this time of year. At its peak Peconic
crossed the train tracks, and just beyond that was a secluded area. No cottages to be found there, only a bridge that crossed over Sunrise Highway.
On the other side of the bridge, Peconic wound its way back downhill
till it ended at North Road.

Bechet made the turn onto Peconic. After a moment he reached the
top of the hill, crossed over the train tracks, then turned into a narrow
pull-off, followed it as far as the terrain would allow. Beneath the tires
gravel, spillover from the train tracks, crunched. The sedan was parallel to
the tracks now, just a few feet from it, twenty feet in from the road. This
was as private as it was going to get. Bechet killed the motor and lights,
leaned across the seat and opened the glove compartment, shining his
flashlight inside, searching for anything that might pass for intelligence.

An address, a phone number, anything. The glove compartment was empty, though, didn't even contain a fake registration. Bechet shined his light into the backseat. It, too, was empty, spot-clean. Finally Bechet searched the front seat, saw a folded-up wool blanket, several inches thick, there no doubt to keep LeCur warm on long stakeouts. Beside it was LeCur's cell phone. Bechet grabbed the phone, slid it into the pocket of the field jacket, and was about to get out when he spotted something sticking out from under the blanket.

It looked like the corner of a book. Bechet moved the blanket aside, saw a pocket-sized Moleskine notebook on the seat. It was open, lying facedown. Bechet picked it up and turned it over, read what was there on the page.

It stopped him dead in his tracks.

He was looking at Gabrielle's license plate number. Below it was the make and model of her car.

Shit.

Up to this point Bechet had been planning on running, leaving LeCur alive in the trunk with a message for Castello, a warning to leave him and his friends alone. All Bechet cared about was getting Gabrielle safe first, then figuring out what to do from there. He had a year ago set up a way of escape for them, complete with several routes laid out and a place for them to hide, everything they would need ready to go, ready to be grabbed at a moment's notice. But this was all contingent on Gabrielle's identity remaining unknown to Castello and his men. No name, no trail for them to pick up, nothing. With Gabrielle's license plate number in Castello's possession, all that was blown. Bechet had run before, could easily do so again. But lying low and starting over, that was one thing. Outrunning the price of betrayal, outdistancing a man of means like Castello, that was something else altogether. You can't look where you're going—*really* look where you're going—when you're too busy looking over your shoulder.

Bechet closed the notebook, pocketed it, then looked down at his lap. He closed his eyes, breathed in and out a few times, then opened his eyes again, lifted his head and looked through the windshield, down the tracks that led straight past Gabrielle's cottage, the tracks he had run night after night as part of his preparation for this.

He opened the door, grabbed the folded-up wool blanket from the seat, and stepped onto the gravel. He would leave no tracks on such a surface. He took a look around, quick but careful, then stepped to the rear of the sedan, slid the key into the lock and popped the trunk open.

LeCur had turned onto his back. He looked up at Bechet, but saw only a dark figure with an equally dark sky behind him. Barely distinguishable, one from the other. He could, though, make out the gun in Bechet's hand, see it moving toward him. He felt the cold metal of its muzzle pressing hard against his head.

"Who else knows her license plate number?" Bechet said.

"What?"

"Did you call it in to anyone? Does anyone other than you know her license plate number?"

LeCur was quick, sensed the change in Bechet, sensed his intent. Bechet was aware of this, as aware of LeCur as LeCur was of him. They had been, once, *family*.

"Yes," LeCur said.

"Who?"

"I made a call while I was waiting."

"To who?"

LeCur shook his head. "Kill me and you never find out."

Bechet stepped back, removed LeCur's cell phone from his pocket, scrolled through the recent calls. Incoming and outgoing were listed in one file. There were the calls from his son's cell phone a little before one, then nothing till the calls Bechet had made from his Jeep and the calls LeCur had made to his son's cell phone as Bechet made his way up the driveway. Nothing else in the span of time between those calls.

There wasn't a lot of time to argue this point. Either LeCur had told his son when they had last spoken, when LeCur had told him that he had arrived at Gabrielle's, or else he had told no one at all. Whichever was the case, it was clear to Bechet what needed to be done so he could make his escape.

Nothing left to chance.

"I'm sorry, Jean," Bechet said.

He stepped to the trunk again, placed the folded-up blanket over

LeCur's head, then pressed the muzzle of the Desert Eagle deep into the fabric.

"Jesus, Pay Day, wait," LeCur said.

Bechet ignored the plea, pulled the trigger without hesitation. The gun kicked hard against his palm, and the flat crack of the shot, muffled even as it was by the blanket, rang out in the still night.

Bechet didn't bother firing a second round, even though he'd been taught to do just that. A double tap, as it was called, to be certain of fatality. But there would be no need for that with a .50 caliber round; LeCur's skull was easily in a dozen pieces now beneath the thick blanket. And anyway, one rupture in the quiet night, however muted it may have been, however isolated Bechet believed himself to be, was more than enough.

Bechet dropped the heavy gun into the trunk. It landed with a thud. He grabbed one of the garbage bags beside LeCur's body, then swung the trunk closed and made his way over the gravel and up onto the train tracks.

As he had done hundreds of times before, he ran those tracks, though tonight he ran them with everything he had, a lone man cutting fast through the darkness toward the only thing that mattered.

A hand gently touching her shoulder awakened Gabrielle.

She opened her eyes, looked up and saw Bechet by the light of her small reading lamp, sitting on the edge of their bed, leaning over her.

"You need to get up," he said.

She was groggy from oversleeping but still heard something in his voice, heard it right away.

"What's wrong?" she said.

"We need to leave."

"What happened?"

"We're okay right now, but we don't have a lot of time. Do you have your grab bag?"

She nodded. "Yeah."

"Where is it?"

"In the closet, on the top shelf."

Bechet stood, crossed the small room, opened the closet door and stepped inside. He reached up to the top shelf, pulled down a nylon ditty bag, carried it by its draw cord and placed it on the foot of the bed.

"Get dressed, okay?" he said. "Wear layers, just in case."

Gabrielle swung the blankets away and rose from the bed. She was naked, instantly felt the cold of the room on every part of her. Yesterday's clothes were on the floor; she stooped down to gather them together. When she stood she saw that Bechet was kneeling in front of her bureau, reaching under it. He pulled something free and then stood up, stepping aside so Gabrielle could access the drawers. As she opened one she looked at him, saw that he was holding a metal container the size of a paperback book. He pulled off the tape that had held it to the bottom of the bureau, discarded it and then opened the box, making a quick check of its contents. All Gabrielle had time to see was a stack of twenty-dollar bills and several brass keys. Shiny and new. Bechet closed the metal container and dropped it into the pocket of the black jacket he was wearing. Gabrielle realized then that she had never seen that jacket before.

"Meet me downstairs," Bechet said. "And don't forget all your documents."

Gabrielle nodded. She was still naked, her clothes in a clump in her arms. Bechet hurried down the stairs, his footsteps hard on the planks. Gabrielle dressed, a combination of the clothes she had gathered up from the floor and items from her bureau. Jeans and T-shirt, over that a thermal shirt and a white fisherman's sweater. Layers, like Bechet had said. She dressed fast, didn't bother with a bra, had never really needed one, only ever wore one when it was required, for propriety's sake. There were advantages in having small breasts, she thought now, moving fast, just as there were advantages in having short hair. No need to fuss, so much less to carry. Everything she would need to live for a few days, in fact, was in the ditty bag—essential toiletries, changes of underwear, a half dozen Clif Bars and a large bottle of water, a decent first-aid kit and a battery-powered charger for her cell phone. Under her bed was a pair of insulated boat shoes. She grabbed them, pulled them on, then felt under the mattress for the watertight pouch that contained her passport and

Social Security card, checkbook, and recent tax returns. She grabbed that, too, then yanked her cell phone from the charger on the table by her bed and headed down to the stairs.

Her bills—utilities, credit cards—were kept in a tray on her kitchen counter. Bechet was collecting them when she entered. He handed them to her as he dialed his cell phone and waited for his call to be answered. She put the bills and her document pouch into the ditty bag. All her mail was sent to a post office box in town, not to the cottage. Bechet had advised it; this way no one could stake out her place and steal her mail if they ever had to leave in a hurry, collect information on her that way. Bechet, too, had suggested that she shred all her paid bills and junk mail. He had even brought a shredder over not long after he had started sleeping there.

Finally, whoever Bechet was calling answered.

"I need you to pick me up," he said. "At the Hampton Bays station. The trains are running from Southampton now, right? Both directions? Okay, good. In your own car, though." He looked at his watch. "As soon as you can. I think we can just make the last train. All right, thanks, man." Bechet closed his cell phone.

"Jake, what's going on?" Gabrielle said.

"I need you to go somewhere."

"Where?"

"I'll tell you on the way."

"Just tell me now. Please."

"We're okay, Elle. I promise. We just need to hurry."

He didn't give her a chance to respond. He took her coat—a snug denim thing with a fur-lined collar—off the hook by the door and handed it to her. As she put it on he took her by the arm and led her from the cottage and up the incline to her Rabbit. He moved more steadily than fast. She noticed as they walked that Bechet was holding an empty garbage bag but didn't bother to ask him what that was for. He told her to get in behind the wheel, that she was going to drive. She hurried to that side of the car. Instead of heading for the passenger door, though, Bechet walked past her car and out into the dark road. He picked something up off the ground—two things, in fact—and stuffed them into the pocket of the black jacket. Then he picked up something else. It was a leather coat. He stuffed it into the garbage bag as he walked to the passenger door.

He opened the door, laid the bag on the seat, then walked behind her car, scooped some mud with his gloved hands and packed the handful onto the rear license plate, obscuring some of the numbers. He went around to the front of her car, did the same there. Back at the open passenger door, he removed his gloves and threw them into the garbage bag, then tossed the bag into the backseat and climbed in.

He told her they were going to the Southampton station.

"But you said the Hampton Bays station on the phone."

Bechet nodded. "I know. Drive nice and slow, okay. We should have twenty minutes." The Southampton train station was a fifteen-minute drive at this time of night. If the fog continued to lift, returning to tree-top level, they shouldn't have a problem.

At the bottom of the gutted road, Gabrielle turned left. Bechet looked behind them as she carefully handled the winding road. Shreds of fog, the menace that killed her parents, here and there. Though she wasn't the type to panic, her heart was pounding.

"Jake, baby, what's going on?" Her voice was even and calm. This, she noted, pleased her.

"I need you to lay low for a couple of days."

"Are you in trouble?"

He nodded, turned forward, dug the book-sized metal container from his pocket and opened it. "Yeah."

"What kind of trouble?"

"I used to work for somebody, a long time ago. He wasn't a good guy. He found me, wants me to something for him, something I don't want to do."

"What does he want you to do?"

Bechet was going through the container, didn't answer. He was, Gabrielle could tell, focused on this moment, on what he was doing, what was *at hand*.

Beneath the stack of twenties was a narrow manila envelope and a pen. Bechet took them out, closed the container again and used its surface to write on the outside of the envelope.

"Here's an address," he said as he wrote. "You're going to take the train to Penn Station, from there take a cab to this address. It's a safe part of town, you'll be okay. There's a security system, too, so I'm writing down the code. I want you to wait there till you hear from me."

"You're not coming?"

"I'll be a few hours behind."

"Jake."

"There's something I have to do first. One last thing."

"What?"

"Just listen, Elle, please." He finished writing, then opened the container again, grabbed the stack of twenties—all of them—and stuffed it into the envelope. He did the same with two of the brass keys, held together by a small, curling wire.

"This is five thousand dollars," he said, "and the keys to the door. You have thirty seconds to punch in the code. After you've done that, lock the door behind you and reactivate the alarm system. It's not the coziest place in the world but it's safe. There's food and bottled water, so you shouldn't have to leave for a while."

He laid the envelope on the console between their seats. Gabrielle glanced down at it, caught one word.

"Brooklyn?" she said.

"Yeah. Williamsburg. You'll be fine."

"Who's place is this?"

Bechet looked behind them again.

"It's my place. My father left it to me. Like I said, it's not much, but it'll do for now. I wrote a phone number on the envelope. Call me on that number when you get there."

He looked forward again, returned the pen to the container and closed it, put the container back into the pocket of the jacket.

"I don't have that phone on me yet," Bechet said. "I should have it in about a half hour, though. I will only call you from that number, okay? If your phone rings and it's any other number but that one, I don't care if it's someone from work or a friend, don't answer, okay? Do you understand?"

Gabrielle nodded. "Yeah."

"If for some reason I need to call you from a number other than that, I'll call, let it ring twice, then call back and let it ring once. If I call a third time after that, it's safe to answer."

Bechet looked behind them once more.

"Who is this man?" Gabrielle said. "The guy you used to work for?" Again, her voice was even and calm.

"I'll tell you everything when I catch up with you."

"Tell me now."

"It's the past, Elle," Bechet said. "I thought we didn't want to talk about our pasts."

"It doesn't seem to be in the past anymore now, Jake. I love you, you know that, but you're asking me to take off in the middle of the night and hide out in some strange place. I need a little more here."

Bechet looked forward then. After a moment he nodded once and said, "His name is Castello. I used to work for his family."

"What do you mean, family?"

"They ran a number of businesses."

"What kind of businesses?"

"Drugs, prostitution, money laundering, extortion. You name it. There were some legitimate businesses, too, but they mainly served as fronts. It wasn't small-time, either. The family was involved in some major international deals. Big-time money. I'm talking tens of millions sometimes for one deal, for one day's work."

Gabrielle didn't want to ask her next question, but she had to know.

"What did you do for them?"

Bechet shook his head, a gesture, he hoped, of respectful refusal. Finally, he shrugged and said, "I was a boxer, Elle. What kind of work do you think I did?"

Gabrielle said nothing, just looked through the windshield and drove. They had reached the village, and she steered her Rabbit through its empty streets toward the train station. Once there she parked in its empty lot, shut the motor off.

She sat still now. With no sound from the motor or the heater or the occasional swish of the wiper blades, there was only silence between them. She stared at the long train platform ahead. Finally, though, she spoke.

"So you were, what, hired muscle?"

Bechet nodded. "Yeah. It was a long time ago. I didn't know how else to make money back then. I didn't do it for long, if that makes a difference."

Gabrielle took a breath, let it out, then took another, let that out.

"Did you ever kill someone?" she said finally.

"Would it matter?" Bechet said. "If I had, would it matter?"

"I don't know."

"Have you ever felt anything other than safe with me?"

"No."

"Nothing has changed, Elle. I'm still the man you know. I'm the same person who's slept beside you for the past year. Nothing has changed, and nothing is going to happen to you, that much I promise."

"How can you be so sure?"

"Because I'm going to make sure."

"How?"

"I just need you to trust me, okay?"

Gabrielle looked at him. He had a long, thick face, heavily boned. A hard face, even when he smiled. But she didn't care. There were small, thin scars beneath his eyes and on his cheeks, as if someone had sliced at him here and there with a razor. She knew, though, that these were the scars of the punches he had taken during his years as a fighter. She knew, too, that she had never once sensed anything but caring and tenderness from him, except for those moments when she wanted something other than a light touch. When she wanted the feeling of being taken. But even then, as he obliged her, he had never become a man out of control, never for a second confused passion with violence or degradation.

Still, it was difficult not to feel shaken by what was happening now, by what, as little as it was, had been said. It was difficult, too, not to see that, despite his assurances otherwise, things were going to change—*had* changed. How could they not? How could she and he go back to the way things had been, to the life they had as much set up for themselves as fallen into—two people pretending, for reasons unspoken, that their lives had only started more or less on the day they'd met.

Gabrielle, try as she might, couldn't see them going back to that. A life of pretend can only last for so long. It was as much her desire to live that way as it was his. But now, suddenly, that desire was gone.

"No more secrets, Jake," she said, "okay?" No incrimination in her voice, no judgment, just decisive, certain, calm, as though she were sharing with her lover a New Year's resolution she was determined to keep.

"Not if we're going to keep sleeping beside each other. From now on, I tell you all about my life, and you tell me all about yours. I think that's the way it needs to be, don't you?"

Bechet nodded. "Whatever you need, Elle."

"You'll be a few hours behind me?"

"If everything goes well."

"And if it doesn't?"

By the way Bechet looked at her Gabrielle knew he understood what she meant. *How long would she have to wait before she was to conclude he wasn't coming?* Like the night her folks were killed.

"It will," Bechet said. "Everything will be fine."

As they waited on the platform for the train they stood close to the station house to keep themselves out of sight. Gabrielle had her ditty bag, Bechet his garbage bag with the leather jacket in it. *Two refugees,* she thought. Bechet studied the handful of buildings that were visible from the station, watching their windows, their doorways, did this for several minutes. Then he watched the various directions from which a car could approach. There were three, Gabrielle counted—Powell Avenue to the east, Elm Street to the south, and Railroad Plaza via North Main. Bechet studied these directions carefully, splitting his attention evenly among them all. Gabrielle watched him do this, standing close to him for warmth, his arm around her shoulder, both her arms around his waist. The train arrived after five minutes, and Bechet got on with her, sat with her, she by the window, he on the aisle. From the conductor he purchased a single ticket to Penn for Gabrielle, but he wasn't charged when he told the conductor he was just on till the next stop.

There were three other passengers in the car—a young couple and, a few seats behind them, a man in his sixties. The young couple was nestled together, the boy sleeping, the girl staring absently out the window. The older man, in a wool suit, was reading a newspaper. Bechet watched them all as the train headed west, looked at them, Gabrielle thought, as though he were reading them, as though he were looking *into* them. When he was done, satisfied that they were in fact what they seemed, he relaxed a little, slouched in his seat and leaned into Gabrielle as she leaned into him. Eventually she rested her head on his shoulder, felt the vibrations and rocking of the train moving through them both.

Within a minute they were crossing over the canal. It took only a few seconds to reach the other side. Just minutes after that the train was pulling into the Hampton Bays station. Bechet sat up in his seat, and Gabrielle felt a sudden twinge, a kind of anticipatory fear, at the thought of his pending absence. She'd traveled like this before, late at night, at times alone, was accustomed to that. She had done her undergraduate work at Columbia, so she knew New York—well, she knew Manhattan, or parts of it. So she could cram in as much studying as possible she used to take the late train back to Boston on holidays to visit her parents. And one summer, with her sophomore year roommate, had backpacked through Europe—hostels, trains, meals with strangers, an encounter here and there. Her year in Hampton Bays, working as much as possible, staying in that cottage with Bechet, staying put—*that* was what was uncommon, not *this,* a late-night journey with only what comforts she could carry. Still, there was no avoiding the fact that this was different. This wasn't *going to,* it was *running from.* Running for her life. Bechet hadn't said that this was what she was doing, but he didn't have to. From what little she apparently knew about him, she did know him, could read him, could tell that this was serious, a matter of life and death.

"I'll see you in a little while, right?" she said.

Bechet nodded. "Yeah. Call when you get in. And remember everything I told you."

"I will."

He looked at her, placed his hand on the side of her face, then kissed her.

"I love you, Elle."

"I love you, too. Be careful."

"Always."

He got up as the train came to a stop, walked with his garbage bag down the aisle to the exit, hurried onto the platform. He did this, Gabrielle could tell, so he could observe who got on. No one did; very few people were headed for the city at two in the morning. As the doors closed and the train pulled away, Bechet looked for Gabrielle through the green-tinted windows. He saw her and half-smiled. It was meant to be an assuring smile, Gabrielle knew this, but she would need more than just that. She watched him slip past as the platform slid away, and then he was gone from her sight completely.

She settled into her seat and pulled the fur-lined denim coat around herself. A poor substitute for her lover, but it was all she had, would have to do. She thought about the fact that she was on her own now, for the first time in more than a year. Bechet was always there when she left for work, always there when she came home. Somehow he knew she needed that, knew without her having to say it. It was more than a comfort, his being there, always, it was an anchor, something solid upon which to rebuild—no, not rebuild, the life she had known was gone for good, there was no changing that—so, then, something solid upon which to start over, create something new, something else. Out of the darkness, out of the nothing. But of all nights to find herself suddenly alone—a night not unlike that night her life last changed, a *foggy night*. What would she do if Bechet didn't come back? When would she know he wouldn't *be* coming back? Where after that? What after that? A life in Brooklyn? In some other place, as of yet unknown to her?

But she didn't want to think about that, think *that way*, so she went over in her mind everything Bechet had told her, every instruction, every detail, every little thing that gave her reason to believe that she wouldn't have to wait long before she once again sensed him in the empty space beside her.

Falcetti's jaw was badly swollen, and there was blood in one eye. He took Bechet as far as South Valley Road, then, as instructed, disappeared, heading west on Montauk Highway. Bechet didn't know where Falcetti was staying, didn't want to know. As far as he was concerned, his friend's part in this was done. All the guy needed to do now was lie low and wait for his face to heal and to forget what had been done to him. As swollen as Falcetti's face was, Bechet could still see the look in his eyes, had seen that look in a hundred defeated boxers, had seen it in his own eyes as his career was grinding down, as he lost his speed. He saw that look in his own eyes again on the night the dark star was carved into his forearm by a tattooist. It was that look that had made him plan his way of escape.

Bechet pushed all that out of his mind as he drove toward Southampton. He put in a call to Paul Scarcella as he went, asking Scarcella to tow Gabrielle's Rabbit from the Southampton train station to his salvage yard in Noyac, then lose the plates. "No problem," Scarcella told him. The only question Scarcella asked was if Bechet needed a new vehicle. Bechet told him he might, then ended the call. Taking the long way to the village, Bechet crisscrossed down side streets, watching his rearview mirror as always, checking to see if he was being followed. When he was certain he wasn't, he drove to Hampton Road, a few blocks south of the train station, and from there to a small garage he rented from an old lady who took cash and didn't ask for names. It was behind a house and next door to Red Bar, where Gabrielle waited tables. Inside the dark garage, at an old workbench, Bechet sorted through the things he had accumulated, putting what he didn't need into the garbage bag and what he did need into a small shoulder pack. He kept the knives, the cell phones, the contents of the wallets, and the notebook. He removed the black field jacket and his gloves, put them into the garbage bag, then grabbed a pair of leather gloves from a drawer below the workbench counter, put them on. From active chargers waiting on the workbench he removed a cell phone and a handheld radio scanner, turned them both on and tossed them into the pack. Next to the workbench was a locker. From it Bechet grabbed a hooded sweatshirt, a black mechanic's jacket, and a new pair of boots. He put them all on, tossing his old boots into the garbage bag with the jackets and gloves and empty wallets.

On the other side of the room, in the bottom drawer of a standing tool chest, hidden within a box of sockets, was a second stash of cash. Five grand, this time a mix of twenties and fifties. He put some bills in the pocket of his jeans, some into the pack, and the rest in a jacket pocket. Back outside he tossed the garbage bag into the Dumpster behind Red Bar. It was Tuesday morning, garbage pick up was just hours away, not long after dawn. Soon enough everything connecting Bechet to LeCur—everything but the contents of his wallet and notebook— would be gone. A piece of luck, this, Bechet thought. He welcomed it, hoped that it wouldn't be his only piece today.

In his Jeep he headed eastward, back toward Wainscott. It started to rain again, not a downpour like before but close enough. The fog was still breaking, so he made the trip quickly. A half mile from Helenbach he parked his Jeep in the lot of a garden center, shouldered his pack, and made his way as quickly as he could along the scrub that lined the two-lane road.

He reached the edge of the unlit parking lot in just under five minutes. The gate was still open, exactly as it had been when he left. He crouched down as he opened the pack and removed one of the matching folding knives he had taken from the LeCurs and slipped it into the back pocket of his jeans. The hunk of rope was still there. It connected him to the younger LeCur, so he flung it into the woods. He was about to make his move and sprint across the parking lot toward the gate when something made him wait.

A sound emerged from the noise of the rain.

Hissing tires coming from Montauk. A car approaching, moving fast along the wet pavement. Bechet stayed low, expecting the vehicle to pass. It did, a pickup, followed a few seconds later by another vehicle. Instead of passing, this second vehicle slowed and made the turn into the parking lot. Its headlights swept past where Bechet was hidden, and he crouched down even lower out of reflex. The vehicle was a dark town car, and it came to an abrupt stop by the open gate to the compound. Its driver got out, took a quick look around, then opened the back door. Castello emerged, talking on a cell phone. He and his driver—the driver's handgun drawn—hurried through the open gate.

Maybe they had a system in place, Bechet thought, a timetable in which the younger LeCur was to check in with Castello. That seemed likely; they had covered every other possibility. But what had brought them back here didn't matter now, they were here, at this moment freeing LeCur. Bechet stayed low, watching, not making a move. He had a wild hope that maybe LeCur had suffocated, but less than a minute after Castello and his driver had entered, LeCur appeared in the open gate, moving like an animal sprung from a trap. He had a cell phone in his hand, was dialing. When he was finished dialing, he brought the phone to his ear.

Suddenly, from Bechet's pack, the muffled ringing of a cell phone. It wasn't loud enough for LeCur to hear over the sound of the rain, and across the parking lot, but Bechet nonetheless scrambled to locate and silence it. The phone ringing was one of the LeCurs' phones. The father's, more than likely. No name on the display, just a number and the initial C.

Bechet now had Castello's cell phone number.

He didn't answer the phone. What would be the point? The only real advantage he had now was that neither LeCur nor Castello knew for certain what was going on. The longer Bechet kept them guessing, the better. When the time was right, he'd make certain they knew exactly what he needed them to know. But only then.

Castello and his driver emerged from the club. Castello tried to calm LeCur down but couldn't. The man was in a rage. The driver scanned the parking lot, his handgun still drawn. Even though he was scanning their surroundings, the driver was also keeping an eye on the thug ranting nearby. Bechet was able to determine, without hearing what was being said, that Castello was demanding LeCur hand over the cell phone. It was, after all, Castello's cell phone, and he had to know that Bechet would have taken the phone belonging to LeCur's father as a matter of procedure. Castello and the Algerian argued for a bit, and then finally LeCur obeyed, but unhappily.

The Algerian obviously wanted blood. For what Bechet had done to him, but also for what Bechet had most likely done to his father.

LeCur and Castello talked some more, Castello standing next to LeCur, his hand on LeCur's shoulder, like a coach consoling a player riled by a foul. Finally, Castello talked LeCur into getting in the town car with him. Only then did the driver holster his handgun. Exiting the parking lot, the car turned left, heading east.

Bechet noticed that one of the taillights was out. He also got a long enough look at the license plate to get its numbers, memorized them, though little good it would probably do him; he didn't have the connections Castello had. Still, collect what you can, everything you can, you never know. Bechet hurried back across the half mile to his Jeep, remaining as always in whatever darkness was available, even if it meant veering from a straight line. He knew now that killing LeCur would no longer guarantee Gabrielle's anonymity, no longer serve to sever his wanted future from his unwanted past. More than just a simple killing would be required now.

He waited at the edge of the garden shop parking lot before approaching his Jeep, checking to see if anyone was lying in wait for him. But there was no way to be certain, so Bechet took a breath and bolted across the parking lot. He half-expected at any moment to hear a shot or feel the knockdown punch of a bullet, but he didn't. The night, with the exception of the sopping rain, remained quiet. He climbed in behind the wheel and cranked the ignition, getting out of there fast, his Jeep the only vehicle to be seen anywhere on the drenched blacktop.

Returning to Southampton, Bechet checked into a motel on the edge of the village, not that far from his garage, leaving his Jeep behind the single-story building, out of sight from the road. His only hope now was that there was something in the items he had taken from the two LeCurs that would give him an edge. Something, anything. He needed to take the offensive, couldn't afford to sit and wait for them to come to him. This was, for now, the only hand he had to play.

Bechet got out of his wet clothes, laid them to dry on the heating unit, then, naked, tipped his shoulder pack upside down and spread its contents out onto the motel bed. By the weak light coming in from the street he began to sort through what was there.

Six

IN HIS APARTMENT, MILLER WAITED FOR BARTON TO ARRIVE. Though the blue flame was gone there was still a lightness in his head, as if he had just awakened and was no longer in the world of dreams but not yet in the waking world either, drifting instead along some narrow, twilight edge between the two. He knew he wouldn't feel this way for long, that the effects of the painkillers would dissipate and that sense of lingering in a kind of no-man's-land would, like the blue flame, be gone. But there was nothing he could do till then, so he closed his eyes and listened anxiously for the sound of Barton's car on the street below his front windows. Of course, when he closed his eyes, all he saw was Abby.

He had been able, for a while, to keep track of her after she had left. Doing so had nothing to do with his being a private investigator, or his being the son of the former chief of police, with the certain set of skills that were no doubt in his blood. It had, instead, everything to do with Southampton being a small town, especially during the long, desolate winters. After leaving Miller, Abby had waited tables for a few months at LeChef, the French restaurant on Job's Lane, met an older man while working there, a regular customer, a man with money and a boat, or so the rumors said, with a house in Sag Harbor and all the time in the world to spend with Abby, keep her company day and night. Even now, all these years later, Miller found himself cringing at the idea of the nights she and this older man must have spent together. Abby was, when Miller had been around to receive it, when he wasn't too busy with furthering his personal redemption through PI work, a dedicated lover, willing to do anything, to become just what the man she loved wanted. It was all Abby wanted not to be left alone at night, and so she made love as if doing so kept back the darkness and all the monsters that roamed within it, kept it all at bay. It was difficult for Miller, then and now, to imagine another man receiving Abby's devoted attention and sometimes bold curiosity and eagerness—an almost wild need—to please. It was even more difficult for Miller to imagine this occurring night after night, imagine this other man—this *older* man—free to explore and enjoy what Miller, because of his business, his *quest*, had been unable to.

Miller learned where in Sag Harbor Abby and her lover lived but refrained from ever going there to get a look at the man, to glimpse a happy Abby, happy in a way Miller had been unable to provide, happy in the way she had always wanted. Now, of course, in Miller's mind, the man was everything Miller wasn't. Whether that was the case or not didn't really matter. Miller wasn't sure how exactly Abby had come to learn the truth about her lover, but after six months or so the older man with money and all the time in the world to give turned out to be a not-yet-divorced man with nothing but dwindling credit and crushing debt. A man on the run from a life he had grown tired of. The security Abby thought she had found—the security, Miller knew, she sought from all the men she loved—turned out to be anything but secure, so she fled in the middle of the night, just as she had fled Miller. Miller half-hoped that she would show up at his door, but she never did. This was in the summertime, and she simply disappeared into the crowd, into the anonymity of summer shares and off-the-books work. Eventually Miller learned that she had found a job as, of all things, a housepainter. Rumor had it that she was involved, to some degree or another, with her boss, and as much for her as for himself, Miller checked up on that man, found some things he didn't like. It had taken him a while to piece the man's past together, follow it to the one place he didn't want it to go, the one place Miller couldn't go, but by the time he had all the information he needed, and before he could even decide what exactly to do with it,

Abby had moved on again. Miller didn't know what had happened to make her flee, worried for several long nights that some harm had come to her through her boss, but then she turned up on his radar again, working as a bartender out in Montauk, living with yet another man. When that relationship eventually failed, Abby disappeared once again, this time, it seemed, for good. No rumors about her, no reported glimpses of her, no trail. Miller kept his ears and eyes open, read all the local papers looking for a mention of her, or a mention of some unidentified Jane Doe recently found by the police. Nothing, not even a whisper. A part of Miller saw this period as his chance to forget about her, put his foolish choice, the choice that had made her leave, behind him. But try as he might, there wasn't a day, then and now, that he didn't wonder what had happened to her, where she had gone, who she was with now. There wasn't a day when he didn't say her name aloud at least once, half the time without even realizing he had until he heard himself speak.

Now, though, suddenly, after all this time, he not only had a lead to her but the knowledge that she might be in danger. Miller could feel his heart in his throat and a surge in his legs that made sitting there and waiting an almost unbearable thing to do.

Finally he heard a car come to a stop outside on the street below, then a car door close. At last Barton was here. The downstairs door opened and closed, and then Miller heard her climbing the steep stairs to his apartment door. A light knock, and then she entered. They were family, she didn't usually even bother to knock, but it had been a while since she visited, a while since either was anything more than an absence in their respective lives.

Miller was standing, ready to go, his heart like a clenched fist. Barton walked through the kitchen to the wide entranceway of his large living room. Miller got the sense almost immediately that they wouldn't be rushing out the door, that Barton needed to tell him something first.

"What?" he said.

"I've been thinking that maybe you shouldn't get involved in this, Tommy. That you're *too* involved, you know? Maybe you should leave this up to Ricky and me."

"We're wasting time, Kay."

"I'm not sure I like any of this."

"It's Abby, Kay. You can't possibly expect me to just sit here and do nothing."

"You're not responsible, Tommy. You have to know that. You're not responsible for all the bad luck she ran into after she left you. She's a grown woman, she makes her own choices. Bad choices, in her case. But you can't save people, not from themselves."

"I'm not trying to save her from herself. If she's in trouble—real trouble—I want to help her."

"I just don't want you to get hurt, Tommy. She's maybe not the person she used to be. You might even find out she wasn't ever the person you thought she was."

"Do you know something you're not telling me, Kay?"

Barton didn't answer. She waited a moment, then said, "The address Spadaro gave me is where the second victim's girlfriend, Romano's girlfriend, lived. It seems that your Abby has gotten very adept at covering her tracks."

"What do you mean?"

Barton shrugged. "She's a ghost. Off the grid."

"Then how does Spadaro know that she was going out with Michaels?"

"He wouldn't say over the phone. But I have the feeling that Ricky has been doing some moonlighting."

"What kind of moonlighting?"

"I have a feeling he's been keeping an eye on this, whatever this is exactly, for a while."

"But why would he be doing that? He's just a uniformed cop."

"He's a uniformed cop with ambitions to be more, and a strong dislike for the chief. Whatever is going on, Tommy, it didn't start tonight."

"It seems we have some catching up to do. All the more reason for us to hurry, don't you think?"

"Hurry and do what exactly?"

"Maybe Romano's girlfriend and Abby were friends. If so, then it's possible there's something in her place that would lead us to Abby. We find Abby, maybe we can begin to piece everything together."

"Like I said, are you sure you want to do that?"

"Do I have a choice? If Roffman is up to something, I need to know what it is."

"I don't think you're seeing where this might be going, Tommy."

"What do you mean?"

"I think your eagerness to find Abby has you blinded to something."

"To what?"

"Roffman has a weakness for adoring young women. You know that."

"Yeah. So?"

"Someone taught Abby how to hide her tracks. Maybe it was someone who had something to gain from her knowing how to hide her tracks."

Miller looked at her for a moment. "You think Abby and Roffman are involved?"

"It would explain Spadaro knowing what he knows about her. About someone who's obviously so determined to be make herself hard to find. If he's been following Roffman in his spare time, keeping tabs on him, and if Roffman and Abby were having a secret affair, then that would explain Spadaro knowing what he knows."

"But I thought Abby was with Michaels, according to Spadaro?"

"A small-time criminal. A dumb kid, by all accounts. Not exactly the father figure type she's been hooking up with since you guys split."

Miller could think of nothing to say, nothing to do. He just stood there, stunned into dumbness. His heart, so active a moment ago, felt like a dead weight in his chest.

"What were the odds, you know?" Barton said after a moment. "My ex and your ex ending up together. Who could have done that math?"

"I just don't see it, Kay," Miller murmured. It took all the air in his lungs just to get those six words out.

Barton took a step toward him, entering the large living room. "Let me ask you a question," she said. "Those four-year-old business cards of yours, did you ever give one to Abby? Did she maybe take one with her when she left?"

Again, Miller could say nothing.

"Maybe I'm all wrong," Barton offered. "Maybe your Abby has nothing to do with Roffman. I just thought you needed to know what I was thinking. I just needed you to know going in that you might not be happy with what we find out."

"It's not about being happy, Kay."

Barton nodded. "Love rarely is, it seems. That's why I get my love in pill form these days."

Miller looked at her then. He'd known her longer than anyone—anyone who was still around, still alive. So many people gone, so many people dead. The last two souls on a dwindling frontier, the two of them, in an abandoned place. It was, this he had to admit, both a good and a bad thing. She'd seen him at his worst, as a troubled young man, then had seen him at his best, a man taking on the troubles of others, try-ing to help, trying to do good, to *make up*. He was neither person now, and here was Barton, witnessing that, too. Was this the reason for his part in letting their friendship ebb? Was it as simple as him seeing her see him and somehow being defined by that?

It was easier to be no one in the presence of no one.

In her oversized military surplus parka, Barton seemed to Miller, de-spite the fact that she was older than he, like some kid lost in hand-me-downs. She'd shed so much weight since quitting the force, not that she'd had any to spare. With it, certainly, had gone much of her strength, her *power*. Once, surprisingly strong, wiry. Now, thin, on the verge of frail. Was this what she had been trying to hide from? Trying not to face it by not facing him, seeing him see her, a woman faded into uselessness?

"I need this," Miller said. "If I hadn't . . . abandoned Abby, she wouldn't be where she is now."

"You don't know that."

"No, I do. Please, Kay. We have to assume we don't have long before the cops find out that the victims had girlfriends. If we're going to do this, we need to do this now."

"It means breaking the law, you know that, right?"

"Yeah."

"I thought you didn't do that."

"It wasn't ever about Abby before."

Barton looked at him, thought about that. She never would have thought that either of their lives could come to this—she a clerk at a liquor store, he a landlord, both of them popping pills, one to feel nothing, the other, something. Who were they in the scheme of things? What would it matter to anyone if either or both of them just ceased to be?

"You maybe have amnesty, but I don't," Barton said. "If we get caught, I'm going to jail. Considering my relationship with everyone in the department, I'd rather that didn't happen. I'd rather not have to stand there at their mercy with my hands cuffed behind me."

"Then let's make sure we don't get caught."

She looked at him once more, this time through squinted eyes. Doubtful but, too, a little curious.

"And how exactly are we going to do that?"

"Let me show you," Miller said.

He told Barton to leave her parka because she was known by it, had been seen wearing it by a lot of people in town for a long time. From his bedroom closet he removed a black leather jacket, a gift from him to Abby that she had left behind the night she took off. His reason for hanging on to it was, of course, obvious. Barton put the jacket on; it fit as though it had been cut especially for her. For himself Miller grabbed a dark raincoat that he had found in the thrift shop in town and hadn't worn in years, and an insulated vest to wear beneath it. From a footlocker at the bottom of the closet he dug out two pairs of rubber galoshes and two dark baseball hats. Barton could see that there were several more pairs of galoshes inside the footlocker. Miller grabbed two pairs of cotton work gloves, then one final item before closing and locking the locker. As they left his bedroom, Barton glimpsed the unknown item just before Miller slipped it into the pocket of his raincoat. It was a Brockhage pick gun, a device locksmiths used to pick tumbler locks quickly.

In his kitchen, from a cabinet beneath a counter, he removed a box containing a large salad bowl. He took the bowl from the box, then carried the empty box into his living room, got a roll of bright red Christmas wrapping paper from the closet there and proceeded to wrap the box with it. Barton watched him, saying nothing. When he was done, they left his apartment together, Miller carrying the wrapped-up empty box with him.

The address provided by Spadaro was a cottage near Conscience Point, out in North Sea. Barton insisted that she do the driving, but Miller would agree to that only if they took his pickup. That made sense, considering Roffman's promise to Miller that his men would be looking the other way for the next day. He wasn't likely to be pressed to explain the presence of his vehicle anywhere, and even if he were, he was Tommy Miller, known for showing up in places he shouldn't.

On the way to North Sea, passing through patches of dense fog, neither Barton nor Miller spoke. Quiet, each lost in their thoughts for minutes at a time, just as Miller's pickup was now and then lost to the curtain of grainy white that crossed in front of them, surrounded them. Barton had never been on this side of an investigation before—Miller's side—and so she had no idea at all what the next hour might bring. As a cop she had been bound by laws and rules, remained bound by them even when she began to realize that many of the men around her weren't. Not that she was an angel, of course—her affair with Roffman was wrong, there was just no way around that, and every now and then, when he needed them for a case he was working on, she provided Miller with copies of police reports, coroner reports, crime scene reports. Still, those infractions aside—in the name of love, she told herself, always in the name of love—she had never strayed far from the pledge she had taken the day she was given her badge. Tonight was, then, new for her. Heading to a private residence to break in before the authorities arrived. *A step into a foreign world.* It was, of course, new for Miller, too. Back when he had a license to protect, he had been bound by a strict code of conduct, a code he had set for himself and clung to like a zealot to holy doctrine. Unwaveringly righteous, that was his way, though she had always forgiven him for that, had always understood that this was who he was, who he had to be. But now that he was no longer a private investigator with a license to protect, and she was no longer a cop bound by a pledge, just how far over the line would they be willing to go? Was this breaking and entering an exception out of necessity, or was it merely the start of something more?

But as concerned about all that as Barton was, what occupied her thoughts most as they neared Conscience Point was the question of how much to heart Miller would take the notion of amnesty. Knowing him as she did, if she had ever wanted to set him up for some kind of fall, freeing him from the consequences of his actions and dangling the woman who haunts his dreams in front of him would certainly be one way to go. How much, Barton wondered, did Roffman know about Miller? How much had she herself told Roffman during the course of their affair?

Romano's girlfriend's place was a small single-story cottage set on a narrow lot in a neighborhood crowded with small single-story cottages set on narrow lots. As was the case with many of the areas on the out-skirts of town, there were no streetlights lining this road. As they approached the cottage Barton slowed, but Miller told her to continue past and park several houses down. Once she did, they slipped their galoshes on over their shoes, put on their baseball hats, bills low, and the cotton work gloves. Miller then handed the empty box to Barton. She now understood what it was for—to any one of the neighbors who may have been looking, she and Miller would appear as nothing more than a couple bearing a gift, arriving for some late-night party. Barton felt an odd exhilaration, a rush she could only describe as a mix of appreciation and pride. As minor a detail as the present might be, the guy knew his stuff, that much was certain. She stepped out of Miller's truck and, shoulder to shoulder, they made their way casually toward the cottage. Halfway there, to complete the illusion, Miller reached down and took Barton's hand, held it as they walked the rest of the way. This was the first touch Barton had felt in a long, long time. She barely even felt her own touch these days, thanks to the Lexapro. The urge to come came infrequently, and when it did, the result was hard-sought and less than earthshaking. Miller's hand, though, was warm, his grip strong. A male's touch. It seemed both familiar and alien. Still, this intimacy, however much for show it was, was enough to send a chill through her, to cause goose bumps to rise along her thin arms. Her reaction—a sudden break in a dull but real tranquility, the kind of tranquility only a state-of-the-art drug can provide—caught her a little off guard.

There was a light on inside the cottage, somewhere toward the back of it, Barton could see that. They followed the brief sidewalk and climbed the three steps up to the porch, approaching the door. Barton wasn't sure what exactly would happen next. Would Miller knock while they stood like a couple on the porch? What would they do if the door was answered? And if it wasn't answered, how long would he wait before he picked the lock?

In the end, none of these questions mattered. The front door was closed, but not all the way, not to the point where the catch had slipped into the notch. Lightly, Miller pushed on the door with the knuckle of his middle finger. That was enough to send the door back an inch or so. He waited a second, listening, then pushed the door again, this time with all five tips of his gloved fingers. The door swung open a few feet, enough for them to glimpse inside.

It was as if a violent storm had moved through the interior of the cottage. Everything that Barton and Miller could see had been turned upside down, maybe even more than once. It was nothing short of chaos.

Miller slipped inside, Barton following closely. Her heart was racing. Miller remained just a few feet from the door for a moment, was once again listening. Barton listened, too. The only light on was in the kitchen, at the back of the cottage. It spilled down the narrow hallway and into this front room.

"Stay here," Miller said quietly. He walked across the living room, stepping over a coffee table that had been turned onto its side, making his way around a couch that looked as if it had been dropped from a height. He paused at this end of the hallway, listened again, then started down, stopping halfway to look in the bathroom to his left. After a moment he continued past it, looked into the lighted kitchen, then came back down the hallway, returning to the living room. He walked to the entrances to the two bedrooms, looked inside each. Finally, he looked back at Barton, nodded an all clear. She stepped away from the door, looking down at the wreckage at her feet.

"Looks like someone got here ahead of us, huh?"

"Looks that way," Miller said. He was preoccupied, studying the scene.

Barton took a few more steps. Everywhere she went, there was something under her feet.

"Well, it obviously wasn't a robbery," she said. "The stereo and TV are all still here."

It was then that Barton looked up from her feet and saw what was occupying Miller's attention. There were holes in the walls. Too large to have been made by fists. Below each one of them, mixed in with the debris of someone's possessions scattered on the floor, were chunks of Sheetrock.

Miller said nothing, continued looking around. Barton sensed that he was puzzled by something, moving almost hesitantly, the way someone would when trying to reconcile in his head what could not be so easily reconciled.

"What?" she said.

Miller shrugged, looked around some more, then said, "The walls in the bedrooms had the same holes punched in them. The bathroom and kitchen, too."

"Someone was looking for something."

"My guess is they didn't find it."

"Why do you say that?"

"When you're searching a place, you don't start by punching holes in the walls. That's a last resort."

"But what makes you think they didn't finally find whatever it was they were after?"

"There's a wildness to this, a desperation. It's like whoever did this was getting progressively more and more pissed as they went. There's a line where searching becomes rage, becomes tearing apart. They obviously crossed that line."

Saying nothing, Barton looked around.

"Whatever they were looking for," Miller said, "it must have been important to them. Unless they had a crew, this took time. And it was noisy. But they were willing to risk it. You don't do that because there *might* be something in the walls. You don't do it for a couple hundred bucks."

Barton, once again, felt a chill, felt goose bumps rise on her arms.

"Maybe we should get out of here, Tommy. This might have just happened, and whoever was here might still be around."

Milled nodded, but absently. He said nothing.

"Tommy?"

"Do me a favor, Kay," he said. "Look around for a phone."

"I really think we should maybe get going."

"Please, Kay."

He didn't look at her, was standing by a bookcase that had been emptied of its contents. His eyes were on the heap on the floor before him.

Barton waited, then crossed the room. She figured the best place to look for a phone was the kitchen. She moved down the narrow hallway, saw as she entered that this room was worse than the front room. Cupboards emptied, kitchenware knocked off counters, all of it on the tile floor. Even the contents of the old freezer were there. Barton knelt down beside a carton of ice cream and opened it. The ice cream was soft but not yet melted. Whoever had been here hadn't been gone for long.

There was a jack on the wall by the door but no phone mounted on it. Barton returned to the front room, kicked her way through the debris as she walked to the first bedroom. The holes punched in these walls were every few inches, both high and low. Thorough, but, too, as Miller had suggested, *out of control*. The mattress had been sliced down the middle and pulled off the box spring, which itself had been gutted. The drawers of a single bureau had been removed and turned upside down and emptied, then tossed to the side.

A life in ruins, Barton thought. She could barely imagine how it would feel to come home to this.

In the second bedroom, on the floor beside the bed, among framed photographs, their glass shattered, she found the cradle of a cordless phone. It took her a good minute of looking to find the phone itself. Returning with it to the living room, she saw that Miller was standing with his back to her. By the way he was standing, she could tell that he was looking down at something in his hands.

"I found the phone," Barton said.

Miller didn't answer. She walked across the room to him, stood at his side. In his hands was a small stack a photographs and the envelope that had contained them. He had already gone through the first few pictures, was holding those in his left hand. Barton looked at the photo he was now studying. A young man and a woman, sitting on a couch. Even with the room as it was now, Barton could tell that the photographs had been taken here—close, in fact, to the very spot where they were standing.

Miller said, "The guy's Romano."

"You sure?"

He nodded. "Roffman showed me a Polaroid at the canal."

"Then this must be his girlfriend," Barton concluded. The girl in the photo had dark, curly hair cut bluntly at the shoulders, and a wild smile.

Mid-twenties, slender, in jeans and a red turtleneck sweater. Recent, maybe? Certainly not last summer; the sweater was a heavy, dense knit. She had a beer bottle in one hand, the other clasped around Romano's arm. Adoringly. She was enjoying herself. In love? Maybe, probably.

"Pretty," Barton observed.

Miller nodded, shuffled through the next few pictures. More of the same—Romano and his girlfriend laughing, drinking, kissing. The photos had been taken in a somewhat rapid succession. Not by a timer, then, by *someone.*

Miller shuffled through a few more photographs, then stopped. Romano was no longer in the picture. This photo was of the girlfriend and another girl, sitting together on the couch. Barton recognized her at once.

Abby.

Saying nothing, Miller looked at the picture for a moment. Studied it. Barton tried to read him but couldn't. His face was stone. He shuffled to the next photo. In this one the girlfriend and Abby were laughing and drinking from bottles of beer. Abby was wearing green cargo pants and a white tank top. Ribbed, the tank top clung to her narrow torso, her nipples, hard, all but visible through the thin fabric. Miller moved to the next photo, and then the next. A few photos later he stopped dead again.

In this photo Abby and the girlfriend were kissing, their mouths open, their eyes closed. The next photo showed them kissing still, but trying to do so while laughing. The one after that showed them pulling away from the kiss, Abby reaching up under the brunette's red sweater, the two of them still laughing.

"Well, I guess they know each other," Barton said.

Miller said nothing. He thumbed through the rest of the photos quickly. He'd obviously seen enough, and anyway, this was what they had come here to determine, whether Romano's girlfriend knew Michaels's girlfriend, and if there was something here to lead them to her. Barton stepped away, looking around the room. She hadn't seen a computer anywhere—certainly that might be of help. But she hadn't really been looking for one. She decided to make another pass around and sift through the debris. As she did, she watched Miller pick two photos— each one from different places in the stack—and slip them into the inside pocket of his overcoat. He stuffed the rest of the photos back into the envelope, then dropped it onto the floor. He stood there for a moment, as if lost in deep thought. Barton waited for as long as she could, then said, "I don't see a computer anywhere. In fact, I don't see anything to indicate that she even owned one."

"Does the phone have caller ID?" Miller said. He spoke as if in a trance, one he was certain he wanted to break free of.

"Yeah."

"Scroll through it."

Barton found the buttons, pressed them. "It's empty," she said.

"It was probably cleared out."

"By who?"

"Romano's girlfriend, or whoever was here."

"Why would they clear out her caller ID?"

"Maybe they weren't just looking for something. Maybe they were trying to cover their tracks."

"So what do we do?"

"Hit redial."

Barton did. The phone began to dial.

"Is there a number on the display?" Miller said.

"Yeah."

"When it's done dialing, hang up."

Barton waited, then pressed OFF.

"What's the number?" Miller said.

She read it off to him. It was an East Hampton number. "I should write it down," Barton said.

"No, I've got it."

Miller opened his cell phone, pressed a single button, waited a moment, then said, "It's me. I need you to do a reverse look-up." He repeated the number, then said, "Thanks, Eddie," and hung up.

Neither said anything for a moment. The silence was odd, considering the state of the room they occupied. There should be noise, Barton thought, to go with this mess. Finally, she spoke, breaking the hush.

"You all right?"

"Yeah."

"We're partners in crime now, Tommy. Should you really be lying to me?"

"It's a shock, seeing her after all this time, that's all. Even just seeing a picture of her. I guess it's a shock to see that she's become quite the party girl."

"Is that your fault, too?"

Miller said nothing.

"At least we know now that your business card might have actually *been* in Michaels's wallet legitimately. Abby could have known he was in trouble and gave it to him. It doesn't rule out Roffman being up to something, but—" She shrugged and stopped there. Her thought wasn't exactly the consolation she had thought it would be when she first started to speak. "So what now?" she said.

"Eddie will call back in a minute."

"So why are we still here? Why aren't we leaving?"

Before Miller could respond, his cell phone rang. He answered it, listened for a moment, then said, "What?" Barton watched his face, could see the confusion. It erupted like sudden anger. "Are you sure?" Miller said. He listened a moment more, then thanked Eddie again and hung up. He looked to Barton absolutely bewildered.

"What?" she said.

It seemed almost as if Miller couldn't say anything.

"What?" Barton repeated.

"It's in my name," Miller muttered.

"What?"

"The last number dialed from this phone is a number that's registered to my name."

"I don't understand. Do you have a second number?"

"No."

"So what does that mean?"

"It's Abby. It has to be. She's the only person who ever had access to the information someone would need to get a phone in my name. That's how she stayed hidden all this time."

"Jesus," Barton said. "Did Eddie give you the address?"

"Yeah."

"So do we go?"

"First hit redial again," Miller said. "This time let it ring."

Barton did. The phone rang a half dozen times. Miller waited until it had rung ten times total, then told Barton to hang up.

"No one's there, or someone's there but not answering," Barton said.

"A machine would have picked up before ten rings, right?"

"Yeah, so?"

"So maybe she has call waiting. Maybe someone was on the other line and didn't click over."

Barton could see the look in his eyes. A wild glimmer. A man caught up in bargaining, a man grasping for *something*. To be this close now, suddenly, had to mess with his thinking, she knew that—thinking that probably wasn't all that clear to begin with, thanks to the pain pills. But this was dangerous territory for Miller, there was no escaping that. Everyone has certain behaviors—bad behaviors—that linger always just below the surface, looking, like insurgents, for any reason to emerge or reemerge and take us over like a riot, drive us to do things we should know better than to do. Tommy Miller, as much as he wanted the world to believe otherwise, as much as *he* wanted to believe otherwise, was no exception to this. He was prone to obsession, Barton knew this, everyone who knew him knew this, and when geared toward something constructive, this tendency was a positive force in a town in need of all the positive forces it could get. But when geared toward destruction, as was the case back in Miller's youth, innocent people suffered, Miller himself suffered, and terrible events—events with long-reaching repercussions, maybe even an endless chain of repercussions, like an echo that just won't die— were set in motion.

Miller, then, like everyone, walked the edge of his own dangerous territory, walked it every day and every night of his life. A sentry guarding himself from the worst parts of himself. It was what we all do, Barton thought, there was never any choice in the matter, at least for most of us. The only question, for Miller, was what would it take to unleash the part of himself that waited always for its chance to break free, that followed him as silently and as closely as a shadow? What would it take for the violent child to overrun the man who had finally given up on the notion of redemption?

Barton laid the cordless phone on the bottom of the overturned couch. There was no way she couldn't express the thought that was now foremost in her mind.

"I need to know, Tommy. Is this about getting answers, or is it just an excuse for you to find Abby?"

"It seems to me one will probably lead to the other."

"Maybe. But maybe not."

"Listen, I'm going to make a run out there, see what I can find. First, though, I'm going to take you home."

"Like hell you are."

"You've stuck your neck out enough as it is."

"Look, if you don't take me with you, I'll just follow you. Besides, Roffman's amnesty is no good out in East Hampton. Without me, you're just a guy in a raincoat and baseball cap walking up to someone's door at one in the morning. You need me."

"I don't have time to argue, Kay."

"Then don't. I'm going with you, Tommy, that's all there is to it. In for a penny, in for a pound, you know."

"It's better if I do this alone—"

"Please, Tommy. You need me, okay? You *need* me. That's all there is to it."

It took a moment, but Miller finally nodded. He said nothing, though, what was there to say? They left the cottage together, Barton carrying the mock present in one hand, Miller beside her, her free hand in his. His palm, unlike when they had approached the cottage, was damp now. His grip, though, remained as firm. Walking back to his pickup, he surveyed their surroundings as carefully and as discreetly as he could, the bill of his baseball cap dipped low to obscure his face, the distant ends of the dark street on which they moved barricaded by the slowly rolling fog.

It took close to an hour to reach East Hampton. The village was brightly lit but as still as a ghost town, its shimmering streets and wide brick sidewalks empty. So fashionable, East Hampton was, so *proper.* A New England town at heart. There was less ground fog now, much of it having broken apart as Barton and Miller drove eastward through Noyac and

Sag Harbor. But by the time they had reached the edge of East Hampton, the fog had risen back up to treetop height, where it had been when this night had begun. Low-hanging fog might have proved useful, provided them with some degree of cover, but they would have to make do with the somewhat commonplace appearance of a man and woman—two lovers, to anyone's eye—coming back from late-night drinks, coming back home, hers or his or, if they were lucky, theirs. With the air clear and the village as well lit as it was, this pretense was the only thing they could count on to conceal their intention, if not who they were.

Abby's apartment was on Newtown Lane, a wide side street that led from Main Street to the train station. The exact heart of the village, but nonetheless asleep at this time of night. Barton parked on the far end of the long block, not far from the train station. As she did this, Miller called Abby's number—*his* number, technically—from his cell phone, first entering ★67 to block his information, in case Abby's phone was equipped with caller ID. Again, only a long string of uninterrupted ringing. Barton and he had removed their galoshes before reentering the truck back in North Sea, placed them in the truck's bed. Quickly Miller grabbed them now, rinsed them off with one of several bottles of water he kept behind the driver's seat, then handed Barton her pair. They pulled them on, then walked together down the sidewalk—no gift in hand this time, it was too late for them to play the role of late-showing party-goers. They reached Abby's street door, found that it was equipped with an intercom system. Three buzzers, the first two of which were labeled with names, the third one blank. According to the information Eddie had provided, the third-floor apartment was Abby's. Miller pressed the button for that apartment, the unmarked button, with his gloved hand and waited. Nothing. He pressed it once more. Still nothing. He glanced at Barton, and understanding what the next step would be, she positioned herself to best block him as he removed his pick gun from his raincoat pocket and inserted its long needle into the lock. He pulled the trigger twice and turned the knob. It spun free. They moved inside, closed the door, and started up the stairs, Miller in front, Barton close behind him.

The stairwell was lit by a cluster of small antique lamps mounted on the walls at each landing. Tulip lamps, the amber-colored glass giving off a warm glow. *A nice thing to come home to,* Barton thought. The building was old, the stairs steep, and the planks, no matter how much care they took when they stepped down, noisy beneath their feet. At the foot of the second landing, Miller and Barton stopped and looked up at the door to Abby's apartment. The same warm, inviting glow was there, but Miller waited like somebody suddenly unsure of his footing. Barton couldn't see his face, but there was a stiffness in his shoulders, and that was enough to give her insight into his state of mind. Finally, though, Miller pushed through his hesitation and started up the second flight. Barton followed. At the door he stopped once more, this time to listen. There were no sounds from within, no light visible under the door. Miller knocked. Nothing. He knocked a second time, again got no answer, was leaning down in preparation of picking this lock when something above the door caught his attention. He stood up straight, looked. Barton followed his line of vision, found immediately what it was Miller was looking at.

A photo of a naked woman, securely taped to the molding of the door frame by several pieces of clear tape. It seemed to Barton to be a photo cut from a magazine. At first glance, the woman was flawless. Annoyingly so. Above that was another photo. The same woman, from behind, looking over her shoulder. Above that was yet another photo, this one showing two naked women, a blonde and a brunette, tall, stunning, standing face-to-face and embracing, their breasts pressed together. The brunette was holding the blonde's face with both hands, tenderly, while the blonde was pressing her hands on the brunette's lower back, tugging her close. They were seconds from a kiss, their mouths open, their eyes shut, their heads tilted.

Barton and Miller stared at the photos for a moment. Finally, Barton said, "What the hell's that all about, I wonder."

"I don't know," Miller said.

He looked down at the doorknob, inserted the needle of the pick gun into the lock, opening the door with same ease with which he had opened the street door below. He and Barton then slipped inside, were, just like that, standing in Abby's kitchen. Barton instantly felt a rush upon crossing the threshold, part fear, yes, but something else, too, something more. Her heart was pounding, she could hear it like wind in her ears, a reaction that caught her a little by surprise. She was also caught by the sense of power—no, not power, more like *invincibility*—there was in moving unseen like they were, in entering someone's place without anyone knowing it, passing through obstacles as though they were nothing. Was this part of the draw of being a criminal? she wondered. Was this sense of being a ghost, of *nothing there to hold you back,* at the root of the psychology of the criminal mind? If so, it wasn't a fact she remembered learning back in the academy, nor was it something she had picked up in her ten years as a cop. Of course, there was the chance that this wasn't something criminals thought about at all, was rather something that only mattered to her because of all the doors—doors of every possible kind—that had been closed to her, both when she was a cop and now that she wasn't.

Whatever the case, she felt a rush from her groin to the top of her head, a tingling along her arms and down through her legs. It was good to know, she thought, that there was at least something in this world that could punch through the pleasant cloud that was her Lexapro, bring the edges of her dulled nerves to something that was close to life.

There were no lights on in the apartment, but no real need of any because of the glow of the brightly lit village spilling in through the row of tall windows in the room beyond the kitchen. Miller nonetheless produced a small flashlight from his raincoat pocket, switched it on. He went through the apartment quickly while Barton waited in the kitchen. She had half-expected to find this place ransacked, but it was in perfect order. Abby had apparently become a very neat person. Back when she lived with Miller, at the house his parents had left him and then in the apartment by the train station, she had been as casual about being tidy as Barton was. While Miller explored the other rooms, Barton concentrated on the kitchen. The apartment, though small, was clearly upscale, she could tell that just from the kitchen. Hardwood floors, white walls, stainless-steel appliances. Above a small island in the center of the kitchen was a large skylight, its glass frosted white. Another light source, even at night, even whitened like it was. Miller appeared in the doorway between the kitchen and the front room long enough to tell Barton that the place was empty, to look through the kitchen while he checked out the remaining rooms. Barton began to search through drawers, looking for mail—bills, credit card statements, letters, anything. She opened every drawer there was but found nothing. She even checked the garbage under the sink, but the basket was empty.

When she had exhausted all possibilities, she wandered into the front room. It was a living room, nicely furnished, as clean as the kitchen, with a fully appointed entertainment center. Big TV, stereo, everything. No sign of Miller there, so Barton entered a small hallway, walking past the bathroom, lit by another skylight, and into the only other room, the bedroom. It was small and dark but cozy. A cave for sleeping and making love. Barton couldn't help but wonder if Roffman had ever been here. How long after she had called it off had he come across Abby? That is, in fact, if they were really together at all.

Standing by the bed, Miller was holding a phone in one hand, his unlit flashlight in the other. The phone was corded, Barton could see that, the kind with the caller ID display built into the cradle and not the handset.

"Tommy?"

He looked at her. "Hey."

"You okay?"

"Yeah."

"Did you find anything?"

"Not really." He reached down to the table beside the bed, switched on a small Tiffany lamp. The shade was apples and pears and cherries made of stained glass and thin bars of lead. "The only thing in the caller ID were two calls from the cottage. Mine, and then one a few hours before it."

"No outgoing calls?"

"No. If she made any, they were cleared out."

"What about an answering machine?"

"None. She probably used this phone only for emergencies."

"What makes you say that?"

"It's corded, not cordless. So if the power goes out and cell phone towers go down, she still has a working line."

"That sounds more like the way you think."

"It's where she got it. Plus, a corded phone isn't as easy to eavesdrop on as a cordless."

Barton thought about that for a moment, then said, "Is that the only phone?"

"It looks like it."

"I didn't find any mail or anything in the kitchen."

Miller said nothing, didn't move.

Barton looked around the room. The bed, the nightstand, a bureau. Walls as bare as the walls in Barton's own place. A faint smell of rosewater, and the kind of stillness that is found when the occupant of a dwelling isn't at home.

Finally, she said, "Tommy, it looks to me like she's gone."

He nodded. "Yeah, I checked the closet. An empty knapsack but no suitcase."

"What does that mean?"

"Abby had an old leather suitcase that used to belong to her grandfather. It was one of her prized possessions. She always thought it was, I don't know, romantic." Miller shrugged, thought for a moment, then said, "It was what she packed her things in the night she left. Probably more valuable to her than the things she put into it."

"Maybe she's just gone for a while," Barton said. She felt like she needed to offer him something. This was all she had. "I mean, a lot of stuff is still here. TV, stereo." She glanced toward the open closet door. "Clothes. That's a lot of stuff to leave behind."

"She didn't leave a single trace of herself, though. Not a single trace. No photos, no mail, no computer. Nothing that could immediately identify the person who lived here."

"It could be she's just a freak about her bills. She's obviously a freak about neatness. Maybe she's the kind of person who pays her bills the day they arrive, doesn't like them lying around. As for photos, they can sometimes be . . . unwelcome reminders of things. I don't have any in my place, either."

"I don't know, Kay. It just looks to me like the apartment of someone who very carefully bugged-out. That's not really the act of someone away for a long weekend, is it? That's the act of someone trying to cover her tracks."

"Something else she learned from you?"

Miller's only response was to shake his head. Barton didn't know what to make of that. Was he saying he hadn't taught that to her, or was he just caught up in the confusion, the puzzle he couldn't quite figure out?

Or was it something else, something having to do with his standing so close to her bed.

"C'mon, Tommy," she said. "There's nothing here."

He took another look around the room, then switched off the bedside light. In the gloom he looked down at the bed once more. Finally he turned and left the room. Barton followed him into the living room. He paused, glanced at the large TV, the DVD player, the DVR, the stereo equipment, and stacks of CDs and DVDs. Expensive stuff. Barton wondered how Abby made the money to buy all this. How could she afford this place, these things? She knew that Miller was probably wondering what was she doing with a onetime car thief. How could he not be?

Back out in the stairwell, just before closing the door, Miller stopped, looked again at the series of photos taped above the door. A hunch, come to him suddenly, it seemed to Barton, by the way he moved. He looked at the bottom photo, then the one above it, then the one above that. His head was tilted back so far back that he was all but facing the ceiling. His eyes were now fixed on something other than the photos.

Barton followed his line of vision to a smoke detector directly over their heads.

Before she could say anything, Miller was in motion. He told Barton to wait where she was, then returned into the apartment and came back out seconds later with one of the chairs from the kitchen. He placed it under the smoke detector, then stood on the chair, reached up and carefully removed the detector's plastic cover. He examined it, found two holes in it, one for the indicator light, the other, it seemed, carved out of the plastic by the tip of a knife. With his flashlight held between his teeth he checked the detector's inner workings. Next to the battery, held in place by several pieces of electrician's tape, was a microvideocamera, the width of a dime and less than a half dozen dimes thick. Miller disconnected the camera from the nine-volt battery—the smoke detector's battery—then removed it from the housing. He looked at it closely, then held it for Barton to see.

"Jesus," she whispered.

Miller looked at the device. Built into it was a small transmitter.

"A piece like this has a very limited range," he said. "The receiver has to be nearby."

Back in the apartment, Miller went straight for entertainment center in the living room, pulling out the DVR and turning it around so he could get a look at the access panel in the back. Connected to the RCA inputs, the size of a small penlight, was the receiver.

"I'll be damned," he whispered.

He turned on the TV, then grabbed the remote from the coffee table by the couch and found the button to switch the video input to auxiliary. He then returned to the entertainment center, pressed PLAY on the DVR and held down REWIND.

On the screen, static, and then, in reverse, a bird's-eye view of Miller removing the camera, Barton clearly visible beside him. Playing backward as it was, it appeared that he was installing it.

He turned the TV and DVR off, said quickly, "Give me a hand." Barton helped him disconnect the power cord and connecting cables, then Miller pulled the DVR from its shelf and held it under his raincoat as he started toward the door. Back out on the landing, Miller waited as Barton returned the chair to the kitchen and pulled the door closed. Together they made their way down the two flights of stairs and out into the night. It was raining again, a cold, brittle rain, but Barton doubted Miller even noticed. When they reached his pickup they each peeled off their galoshes and tossed them into the bed again. Miller drove this time, heading for Montauk Highway; Barton sat in the passenger seat with the DVR on her lap and the microcamera in her gloved hand.

Just outside East Hampton, passing one of the hedged-in estates that line Montauk Highway, Miller noticed that a car was suddenly behind them. He informed Barton, and as they headed westward, they each watched carefully, silently. When the road curved, Barton was able to identify the vehicle as a town car with a glossy black paint job. The car followed them for several miles, moving as fast as Miller's pickup, not on his tail but not keeping back, either. It stayed there, made no attempt to overtake or pass. Barton started to consider the possibility that she and Miller had walked into a trap, knew that Miller was certainly thinking the same thing, but as they reached Wainscott, the town car suddenly slowed down, then made an abrupt right turn into the dark parking lot of a restaurant called Helenbach. Barton kept a close eye on the blackness behind them for at least another mile. It was only then that Barton realized she was holding her breath. She let it out and looked at Miller. He glanced at her but said nothing.

For the rest of the ride back to Southampton there was never a sign of any car behind them, let alone the black town car, not even far back in the distance when Montauk Highway became a stretch of straight and well-lit road running through Bridgehampton, and Barton could see at times up to a good half mile behind them.

They rode without speaking, the long drone of the rain interrupted every few seconds by the sweep of the windshield wipers. They sounded, to Barton's ear, like footsteps crunching in frozen snow.

In Miller's apartment they connected the DVR to his small TV and turned both units on, stood together and watched. The camera was obviously motion-sensitive, and there was a time- and date-stamp at the bottom of the screen. The DVR had a program that allowed the viewer to watch the most recent recording first, from start to finish, then move back in time recording by recording. Miller selected this option, started with the recording of him and Barton discovering the camera and removing it from the smoke detector. The next recording, the event prior to that one, was of him and Barton arriving. As they looked up at the photos placed above the door, even with baseball caps on, they exposed their faces to the camera.

"Clever girl," Barton said.

Miller nodded. The recording prior to that one was time-stamped at 8:11 P.M., roughly seven hours ago. It showed a woman leaving the apartment with an old leather suitcase in her hand. She made a point of looking up at the camera, even kind of half-waved at it. She said something, but there was no audio. The woman was, of course, Abby.

"That's a few minutes after the first call from the cottage came," Miller said.

"Someone called her and told her to leave."

"But they called on her landline, her emergency line."

"What does that mean?"

Miller shrugged. "I'm not sure. A call from the cottage on her landline could have been a signal in itself."

"She didn't look all that upset," Barton noted. "She didn't look like someone who was just told her boyfriend was dead."

Miller said nothing. The next recording was time-stamped a little before three in the afternoon, just hours before Michaels and Romano were murdered at the canal. It showed a man leaving Abby's apartment, his face not visible to the camera. The recording prior to that one showed him arriving, a knapsack on his shoulder. He looked up at the nude photos and smiled wryly.

"That's Michaels," Miller said.

"You sure?"

"Yeah."

Barton looked at the screen closely. "He doesn't look like a guy who knows he's going to be dead in a few hours."

Miller pressed the button in the DVR, skipping back to the previous recording of Michaels leaving. He studied it, then skipped to the recording of him arriving.

"Do you see that?" he said to Barton.

"He arrived with a knapsack but didn't leave with one."

"Exactly. It looks like the knapsack in Abby's closet."

"So whatever was inside it is either still somewhere in her apartment or was in Abby's suitcase."

"My bet is the suitcase."

"Mine, too."

The next recording showed Abby leaving roughly an hour before Michaels arrived. The one following that showed her arriving with two bags of groceries in her arms.

"You don't really stock up on groceries when you know you're going out of town, do you?" Miller said.

Barton shook her head. "No."

He pressed PAUSE on the DVR. The screen froze just as Abby was opening her door. Miller stepped away from the TV, thinking. Barton watched him, waiting.

"I should go back to the cottage," he said.

"What for?"

"In case there was a hidden camera there."

"The place was torn apart. If there was, whoever got there before us must have found it."

"Maybe not. They might not have known to look for it. We didn't. If there is one and the cops find it, it'll show the two of us walking in and walking out."

"Are you sure you should go?"

"Better safe than sorry."

"I'll go with you."

"No, I need you to stay here, see what else Abby's camera caught. And I need you to get hold of Spadaro."

"Why?"

Miller grabbed a notepad and a pen from the shelf below his television. "I need the home number of this man." He wrote down a name, handed the pad to Barton. She read it, then looked at Miller.

"Who is he?"

"He owns a supply shop in Riverhead, lives in the apartment above his store. It's on Main Street. I've bought a lot of stuff from him over the years."

"What kind of stuff?"

"Surveillance equipment, tools of the trade."

"Why do you need his home number?"

"Whenever a dealer sells surveillance equipment to someone, he's required to copy down all the info from the customer's driver's license. Name, address, license number. It's supposed to be kept on file along with the serial number of the equipment sold so if it ever turns up where it isn't supposed to be the cops can trace it to its owner. If we're lucky, the camera we found was bought from that shop. He's the only dealer on the East End, so there is a chance it came from there."

"Why do you want to know who bought it? I mean, Abby must have put it there. She looked right up at it when she left with the suitcase. And those photos were there, so she had to have known."

"It's just a hunch," Miller said. "Will you try to reach Spadaro?"

"Yeah, of course." She glanced again at the pad in her hand. "Is this guy a friend of yours?"

"He knows me," Miller said. "It might be best if you call him; he's not all that fond of the police. Tell him you need this information for me, that I'd consider it a favor. And when you call Spadaro, call from a pay phone."

Barton nodded. "Okay."

"I'll be back in an hour, Kay."

"And if you're not?"

"I will be."

Miller looked once more at the paused image of Abby on the screen. He seemed almost reluctant to look away.

"Be careful," Barton said.

He looked at her, nodded, and then crossed his living room and hurried out the door. Barton listened to him on the stairs, then listened to his pickup drive away.

Freshly rinsed galoshes on his shoes again, his pickup parked even farther down the dark road than before, Miller entered the cottage and did a quick search for hidden cameras. All four of the smoke detectors present were actual smoke detectors, and all of the wall- and ceiling-mounted light fixtures were light fixtures. Everything else that could have contained a concealed camera—knickknacks, throw pillows, framed photos and prints—was in disarray on the floor. The way in which this place had been searched seemed even more desperate to Miller now that he was there alone. Such thorough destruction, bordering, really, on vandalism. Maybe it was the contrast between this place and the solemn neatness of Abby's apartment that made Miller feel this way. Or maybe it was the fact that he couldn't help but connect in his mind the chaos around him with the image of Abby leaving with her beloved antique suitcase after being visited by Michaels. Was the item someone was so clearly intent on finding now in Abby's possession? Could that be it, what was in play here, behind all this sudden death and trail of selective destruction? Could all this be a mad grab for some *thing*?

Miller felt suddenly, deeply helpless. He stood still for a long time, letting his mind wander, sifting through free association after free association until a single, crucial thought arose from the clutter. This took close to a minute, but when the thought came to him, Miller was glad he had taken the time necessary for it to be born.

The phone.

The last number dialed from it was a connection to both Abby's apartment and Miller himself, a connection that needed to be, as best as possible, severed. Miller looked for the phone, remembered that Barton had left it on the upended couch, found it there and placed it on the floor. He looked around for something to smash it with, chose a nearby lamp, held it with his gloved hand like a club and brought it down on the phone, breaking it into several pieces. He then broke those pieces into even more pieces. Cops, via phone records, would be able to trace the call from the cottage to Abby's apartment, and then connect Abby's apartment to Miller, but that would take time, and anyway, it wasn't the cops Miller was worried about. It was hard for him to imagine a cop trashing the place like this. Even a rogue cop, even one of the men blindly loyal to Roffman. And a cop would have known to press redial on the phone and collect the last number dialed, found his way to Abby's apartment as easily as Miller and Barton had. No one in the last few hours had been caught on the camera outside Abby's door but Barton and Miller and Abby, and anyone as intent as those responsible for the state of this place would have made a beeline straight for East Hampton if they had discovered the number and in whose name it was listed. That, plus the fact that no one had been tailing Miller and Barton, once the town car had turned off the road back in Wainscott, was reason enough to think that a cop hadn't been here, hadn't been involved in this.

So, then, who was? Too much destruction for this to be anyone who knew what he was doing. Someone with experience at this wouldn't have bothered punching holes in walls covered with paint that was so obviously old, not unless what that someone was looking for had been hidden years ago. And, too, a pro would have pressed redial, gotten Abby's address and shown up at Abby's door, been caught by her surveillance. Unless the pro wasn't thinking, had maybe something major to lose, had been put in a corner and because of this had gone over the edge into recklessness . . .

Stop, Miller thought. *Stop chasing the mice in your head.* The chaos, he knew, was getting to him. So, too, was the pain in his knee. The painkillers were wearing off. Nothing fucked-up your thinking like a dull, unending ache.

He closed his eyes, to get some relief from the mess around him, the sense it inspired him to make of it, took a breath in, let it out. He didn't care who was killing who, not really, not anymore. He didn't care who was looking for what, or why. All he cared about at this moment was Abby, finding her and making certain she was safe, doing that much for her, in the process undoing in some small way what he had done, the choice—the foolish choice—he had made all those years ago. He had no delusions about winning her back, or even earning a night with her in his arms—naked, fully clothed, it wouldn't matter to him. There wasn't a day when he didn't remember her, remember something startlingly specific about her—the smell of her, the feel of her next to him in the night, the way she looked at him, the sudden sweat that would rise from her skin in the seconds before she climaxed, like a fever breaking. He had no delusions, as much as he thought of these things, of ever knowing them again. Still, it would be good to at least see her, to just once say her name aloud while in her actual presence.

He wandered to the other side of the front room then, near to the bedroom doors, and looked down at the envelope of photographs he had left there. He was thinking of picking them up, taking them all with him, when he heard something coming from down the hall.

It was the sound of dripping water.

He paused a moment, then followed the sound, moving down the hallway that led past the bathroom and into the kitchen. He doubted what he heard had come from there; it was the loud, ringing *plop* of a good-sized drop landing in deepish water, certainly that was water landing in a bathtub, not a sink. But he checked the kitchen first, more to make certain that he was in fact alone than anything else. The kitchen was empty, and the back door was closed and bolted, so he backtracked down the small hallway to the bathroom. He had of course checked it when he had first searched the place, when Barton was with him. The shower curtain had been drawn around the tub then, and he had pulled it back on the off chance someone was hiding behind it. No one had been, and the tub was, of course, bone-dry. He couldn't remember closing the curtain, probably wouldn't have done so, but it was closed now, and the dripping sound—slow but steady—was coming from behind it. He didn't want to move any farther at first but knew he had to. The fact that the tub was now full of water could only mean that someone had been here in the time between his and Barton's leaving and now. Why, of all things, would someone fill the tub? Deep down inside he didn't want to know, but somewhere equally as deep he knew he didn't have a choice, he *needed* to know, had asked for this, whatever this was.

He stepped to the curtain, reached out for it. Every part of him now was prepared for something bad. He took hold of the curtain, paused, then drew it back a foot or so, just enough to allow him to see behind it. Having himself ready for something bad wasn't enough; there wasn't anything he could have done to prepare himself for this, something this bad, this terrifyingly horrible.

In the tub, half-submerged in a mix of diluted blood and water, was a woman. Young, naked, both her wrists slashed. Miller in his panic saw those two details first, his eyes going to everything there was, every single thing, that would tell him that this was someone, anyone, other than Abby. He saw curly black hair, full breasts, a rounded face. Once these things had collected in his greedy mind, been sorted out and added together as best as his panic would allow, he recognized the dead woman as Romano's girlfriend, the woman Abby had posed with in the photos, the woman she had kissed and whose sweater she had playfully reached under, to the delight of them both.

Miller stared at her, more from shock than any investigative skill, innate or acquired. He felt the urge to flee but also lacked what it took to move. His feet felt suddenly, ridiculously heavy. He found it impossible to believe what he was seeing, didn't *want* it to be possible, how could it be? Not just the death—he'd been near death, had seen people die before, had *more* than just seen them die—but the mere logistics of it just didn't add up. In the time since his previous visit, this woman had come back, drawn the water, stripped down and climbed in, then opened up both her wrists? Not likely. His brain repeated that, grasping at it. *Not likely, not likely at all.* It was the only sense, and small a piece of it at that, that could be made of this.

He finally found what it took to move, broke free of his paralysis and was heading down the narrow hallway for the living room, desperate to get out of there, to *get away from there,* when he first heard the sirens, far off in the distance but approaching fast. He froze yet again, but for only a second this time. His panic-induced stillness was ended by a surge of adrenaline that hit his legs and, despite his knee, despite everything, he turned and bolted back through the narrow hallway to the kitchen, ran through it, stepping over its debris, to the back door. He fumbled with the dead bolt at first, then spun it open and yanked the door back and burst through it, running across the backyard to the rim of the woods behind the cottage, running almost blindly, running even when his knee started to burn as if from friction. He didn't look back, just locked on what was ahead of him—tree branches, saplings, uneven terrain—and followed the rim of the woods behind several cottages till he found himself at last behind the cottage in front of which he had parked his pickup. It was a dozen cottages down, at the very end of the residential street. He crossed the brief backyard and stuck close to the side of the dark cottage till he reached its front, then peeked around the corner. His chest heaving, he took a look down the street.

Two cop cars, their lights flashing, were parked at odd angles in front of the cottage. A third car was approaching from the far end of the street. It was now or never, Miller thought. He walked across the small front yard to his pickup at the curb—no running now, though it took all he had not to. He stood by the front bumper of the truck, hidden there from sight of the cop cars, and pulled off his galoshes, then stepped around to get in behind the wheel, first tossing the galoshes into the truck bed. Again, he moved slowly, calmly, despite what every nerve in his body was screaming. Once inside, he cranked the ignition—would they hear it over the sound of the rain and across the distance of the long block?—and turned right onto Shore Road, followed it to Cedar Avenue, turned right onto that, working his way back around to Noyac Road. At Noyac he made a left, not a right, which would have been the direct route back to Southampton. Amnesty or no amnesty, he didn't want to risk passing any other cop cars that might be racing toward the scene. He watched his rearview mirror as he drove, keeping an eye out for the first sign of a cop car behind him. But none appeared. He had gotten away unseen. Still, his heart was pounding as he continued forward, putting distance between himself and the cottage, the dead body of a beautiful woman in it and the cops now more than likely moving through the chaos of the hastily searched rooms.

Miller followed Noyac Road to Majors Path, took that south, his heart doing flips in his chest. Just before Majors crossed Sunrise Highway, on the outskirts of the village, he pulled over and got out, grabbing the two pairs of galoshes from the truck bed and tossing them down a storm drain. He was miles from the cottage now, on a desolate road just past the town dump, so there was no one around to see him ditching the incriminating items. He thought he'd feel better once they were no longer in his possession—it had been all he could think about as he drove, struggling not to speed—but he didn't feel any different at all. His heart wouldn't stop pounding, and his mind wouldn't stop thinking, running, chasing a new set of mice. It was, he knew, unlikely that it had been chance that the cops arrived at the cottage while he was there for a second time, and so long after the actual destruction, when a neighbor might actually have been alerted to the possibility of some kind of trouble going on there by the sound of furniture being overturned and Sheetrock being smashed. Of course, since he doubted Abby's friend had committed suicide, maybe the neighbor had heard something, seen someone leave. Maybe that someone had left just minutes before Miller had arrived. There was no way of knowing that now, and when there was no way of knowing something, the safest thing was to assume the worst. Someone must have watched Miller enter the house—a neighbor, or someone else, whose presence on that street was certainly less than innocent. These were the options, the ones that he could think of now, neither good but one maybe a little better than the other, if only a little. At some point in the near future, though, Miller would need to determine which of these had been the actual cause of the cops' arrival, how much the person who had alerted them had seen or knew.

He called his landline as he drove, but Barton didn't pick up. She would have seen his cell number on the caller ID, so that meant she had left, was probably talking to Spadaro right now. He thought of calling Barton on her cell phone—maybe she could find out from Spadaro how the cops had come to be at the cottage—but he didn't dare. So far there was no direct link between him and Barton, and a call to her cell phone from his at this time of night, moments after he had fled the cottage one step ahead of the cops, would require her, should this all go to hell, to do some explaining to the very men who had driven her off the force. He wanted to spare her such grief.

From Majors Path, Miller was only a few moments from the train station. He made his way into the village and parked his pickup at the far end of Powell Avenue, just a few blocks east of his apartment. Powell was as much of an industrial side of town as there was in Southampton—running parallel to the train tracks, it was home to a lumberyard and several small auto shops on one side of the street and a row of working-class houses on the other. Miller ran the length of Powell in less than a minute, paused at the corner of Elm to study his street, what was parked along it now, saw nothing out of the ordinary. He then looked for Barton's Volvo, didn't see it anywhere. He stepped out into the open and walked the dozen steps to his street door, then climbed the steep stairs and entered his cold apartment.

He heard only silence but hadn't been expecting anything else. He moved through his kitchen to the large living room, then checked his bedroom and bathroom, making certain he was alone. He went back into the living room, looked at his TV, saw immediately that the DVR was gone. He took a quick look around; maybe Barton had moved it, or placed it somewhere for safekeeping. But he couldn't find it anywhere. It, like she, was gone.

He stood there in his empty apartment, still laboring to catch his breath, his heart still throbbing. The blue flame in his chest, so long gone now, had been replaced by a burning in his lungs. There was, too, heat in his knee now, but there was nothing comforting about that. Out of habit he thought of his painkillers, the bottle on the table by his bed, but quickly dismissed that idea. He needed a different kind of escape now, an actual route through the trouble ahead and not just a hole in which he could sleep and hide.

He listened to the stillness around him, as still as Abby's place had been, as still as a graveyard. There was only one thought on his mind now. Why had Barton taken the DVR? Had she found something she didn't want Miller to see? Had she witnessed Roffman coming to visit his new lover? Had she, when push came to shove, felt more loyalty—a twisted, neurotic loyalty—toward Roffman than she did toward Miller?

Or, with Roffman's fate in her hands for a change, had she found the idea of revenge too tempting to pass up?

For whatever reasons, had Barton betrayed him?

Another thought came to his mind then, the worst yet. Had Barton been the one to send the cops to the cottage?

There was nothing left for Miller to do but to wait and see. But he had no desire to do so there, sit around like a rat in a trap, so easily found by anyone who might want to do him harm. There was, then, only one place for him to go.

He left his apartment, checking all directions before stepping out onto the sidewalk, out into the open, then made his way around to the back of the restaurant and let himself in through the kitchen door. He sat at a table toward the back of the room, Elm Street and the train station visible through the large front windows but himself invisible to anyone who might pass by. With the lights off and a tumbler of grappa in front of him—for his knee but also for his nerves—he waited there for whatever was to come next.

He'd been there only fifteen minutes when his cell phone rang. The number on the caller ID was one he recognized, one of the pay phones in town. He answered quickly, knew who it had to be.

"Where'd you go?" he said.

"I was getting the information you wanted," Barton said. The sound of her voice was no small relief to Miller.

"Where's the DVR?"

"I have it with me," she said. "I didn't want to let it out of my sight. I swung by my place to get my VCR so we could make copies. And a change of clothes and things. I found something on the surveillance you'll want to see, Tommy."

Miller already knew what it was. He could tell by the sound of her voice. "Hang up and I'll call you right back from a landline."

"Okay."

They hung up. From the phone behind the bar he called Barton back. She answered on the first ring.

"I watched everything there was in the memory," she said. "Abby installed the camera herself about two weeks ago. You can see her doing it. The only people who came and went during that time were Abby and Michaels—with one exception."

"Roffman," Miller said.

"Exactly. But I'm not sure what to make of it."

"What do you mean?"

"He showed up two nights ago, came to the door, knocked, glanced up at the photos, then left. Hardly definitive evidence."

"Was anybody home at the time?"

"Michaels had been there but left about ten minutes before Roffman showed up."

"What the fuck?" Miller said quietly.

"I know. Roffman is up to something, Tommy. There's no doubting it now."

Miller nodded, took a breath, then said, "Did you get hold of Spadaro?"

"Yeah. He got your friend's home number and I called it."

"What did you find out?"

"The good news is he sold a device with that serial number. The bad news is, it was over four years ago."

"Who to?"

"A guy named Bechet. Jonah Bechet."

Miller said nothing.

"Tommy?"

"I'm here."

"I take it your hunch was right."

"Yeah."

"Who is he?"

"He's a guy we need to find as soon as possible. Did you get an address?"

"Yeah. It's just a few blocks from you, actually, on Hampton Road. But the address is four years old, so he might not be there anymore. You know how people move around a lot out here. I can see what Spadaro can find out through the DMV."

"Do that. And find out, too, if you can, why the cops showed up at the cottage minutes after I got there."

"You're kidding me."

"No."

"You obviously got out okay."

"Barely. But there's something else."

"What?"

"Romano's girlfriend was in the tub. Dead."

"Jesus."

"Yeah."

"How?"

"Her wrists were slit."

"That doesn't quite add up, does it?"

"No. Someone put her there and then called the cops when they saw me go inside."

"Where are you now?"

"I'm in the restaurant."

"Downstairs?"

"Yeah."

"What are you doing down there?"

"It's a long story."

"Are you okay?"

"I'm a little shaken. She didn't have any clothes on." He hesitated, then said, "For a second there I didn't know if it was Abby or not. Of the four of them, she's the only one who's left."

"We'll find her, Bobby. How's your knee holding up?"

"It's not."

"Do you have any Tylenol or anything?"

"No."

"I'll bring some. First I'll call Ricky back, then meet you at your place, okay? We need to make some video copies of what's on the DVR, for safekeeping."

"Yeah," Miller said. "See you in a bit."

They hung up. He went back to the table but didn't sit, downed the rest of the grappa standing, feeling its heat move down through him as he looked toward the large front windows. The heat wasn't the same heat he felt when he took his painkillers, but it would have to do. Outside, it was still raining, a mizzling rain, though, as much churning mist lingering in the air as needlelike drops falling. There were blurred halos around the streetlights that lined Elm Street, and the lights that ran the length of the train platform. Miller watched them all for a moment, till his own vision began to blur from exhaustion and everything that cast or reflected even the smallest trace of light took on a halo all its own. He then left the tranquility of the empty restaurant and returned to his apartment above, to the very place he'd been when he last felt Abby next to him in the dark, last heard her voice and the sound of her feet on his floor, was last in her presence when he spoke her name aloud.

Standing at his front window, watching the train station, his overcoat still on, it was difficult for Miller to think of Abby at all and not see in his mind's eye the dead woman in the bathtub. It was difficult, too, not to do the math—first the two men were killed, then, hours later, one of the men's lovers. Assuming the worst—the best and only thing to do in this situation—meant that Abby could be next. *Would* be next. The thought was more than Miller could bear.

Leaving his window, Miller grabbed a lockbox from an upper shelf in his bedroom closet, thumbed in the combination and opened the lid, looked at the Colt .45 semiautomatic and the three loaded clips resting on a cloth inside. Dark, well-oiled metal, a walnut grip, the thing was older than he. Removing the items, he quick-checked the weapon, then slid in one of the clips. Back in his living room, at his front window, the gun hanging heavy in the pocket of his overcoat, Miller looked out at the last hours of night and waited for Barton.

Part Three

Dawn

Seven

A MOTEL ROOM, THE FIRST HINT OF DAYLIGHT A FAINT GLARE around the edges of the drawn curtain. Bechet, his clothes not yet dried, waited in the gloom for the call from Gabrielle. Usually they were asleep by now, had gone to bed together every morning around this time for more than a year. It was a habit that ran deep in him now, but that was what all this had been about, wasn't it, making *new* habits and breaking old ones, the Bechet he used to be replaced forever by the Bechet he wanted to become, *had* become. It was strange, more so than he would ever have thought possible, to witness the pale, rising light beyond the curtain and not sense her—hear her, feel her, smell her—near. Despite the habit of going to bed around first light, Bechet wasn't tired now, there wasn't time for him to be tired, but he knew that closing his eyes for even a few moments wouldn't be a bad thing, considering what was ahead, the miles still left to go, as it were, till this was over and he would be rid of this feeling of *absence*. But he knew that even if he did manage to nod off, take a little bit of rest in preparation for the hours to come, that he would only, upon returning to consciousness, realize all over again that he was a man caught in the last place in the world he wanted to be, a man in secret motion behind enemy lines, separated from his lover, everything that mattered to him now currently beyond his reach.

It would be better, he thought, to spare himself the ordeal of forgetting and then remembering and remain awake as he waited for the time it would take Gabrielle to make it to Manhattan and then into Brooklyn to pass.

As he sat, still naked, a thin motel blanket around his shoulders for warmth, he went through everything he had taken from the two LeCurs. The cell phones were older models, therefore not equipped with GPS tracking devices, so there was no way Castello could use these phones to locate Bechet and come after him. Still, Bechet's general location could be determined via an incoming call, once it was established which cell tower was used for the final relaying of the call, and even that, as complicated and as time ineffective as it was, would be more than he wanted to give away. Bechet, then, powered the phones up only as he scrolled through their respective call histories and address books, to reduce the time that each phone was active and could receive a call. Both phones contained a variety of numbers and names, none of which were immediately useful or recognizable to Bechet, though it was possible that these could prove otherwise at some point down the line, when Bechet learned more about Castello's current businesses. Certainly, at any rate, these names were cogs of some kind in the Castello machine, and going after a cog or two was definitely one way to cause any machine to halt or falter. Bechet hoped, though, that it wouldn't come to that. He didn't want to have to wage a campaign of destruction, simply wanted to do what needed to be done and get away clean. He already had the one number he needed right now, maybe even the only number he would ever need, if he played things right—Castello's cell phone number, an incoming call on the older LeCur's phone, the last call that phone had received. Once Bechet copied that down, along with all the names and numbers from the address books and incoming and outgoing logs, he disconnected the batteries and set them and the phones aside on the motel bed.

The Moleskine notebook he had taken from the older LeCur promised to be much more useful. It was close to three-quarters full of notes, written in a code that Bechet knew well, had learned from LeCur himself. It was a simple sequence based on the telephone keypad. Twenty-one signified *a*, the two representing the key for the numeral two, the one representing the first letter assigned to that key. Twenty-one for *a*, twenty-two for *b*, twenty-three for *c*, thirty-one for *d*, thirty-two for *e*, and so on. It wasn't the most elaborate of codes, could be broken by anyone with any kind of experience with encryption, but it did offer protection from casual readers, should the notebook get lost or end up in the hands of the competition or even a cop. To complicate things, LeCur's code, once deciphered, had to be translated from his native tongue. But Bechet knew enough French to get the gist of what was there. Locations, dates, sizes of shipments and, it seemed to Bechet, an account of how much each shipment had actually contained when it was delivered. Castello had said that the two men found murdered at the canal were couriers who had been stealing from him. The more Bechet decoded, the more he got a picture of the operation. Deliveries from Southampton to various places in New York—Queens, Manhattan, Westchester County, even a few places in New Jersey. Times when the deliveries left Southampton and times when they arrived. Clearly, Castello and LeCur were keeping a close eye on things.

Along with the dates were notations on the weather and traffic patterns—possible explanations, Bechet assumed, why a delivery from Southampton to New York's West Side would take longer than it should. Next to each one of these entries were the code 51–61 or 77–77. JM or RR. James Michaels or Richard Romano, the names of Castello's dead couriers.

There were other entries, too, logging deliveries from points in New York to Southampton, each of these marked with the code for Michaels or Romano, each one of these with dates and times. It would be difficult to see all this and believe that Castello, as he claimed, had nothing to do with these murders. Nearly every entry on every page screamed motive and opportunity.

One of the last entries in the notebook—just prior to the page that contained Gabrielle's license plate number and street address—was a Southampton address, and below it, again, the initials JM and RR.

Bechet recognized it as the place where a girl named Abby had lived, back when she had worked for him, when he had his housepainting business. He remembered taking her there several times, when she was too drunk to drive. Often he and she would slip away from the rest of his crew after a day's work and grab something to eat. He didn't drink, or at least not often, but she did. Maybe the familiar address was a simple coincidence—the gulf between affordable winter rentals and out-of-reach summer rentals meant that the working class usually moved around a lot. Bechet knew of one apartment on Main Street that had over the course of five years been occupied three different times by acquaintances of his, some who knew each other, others who didn't. That was one of the peculiarities of East End life. Certainly Abby had moved out, and at some point after that the two couriers had moved in. Still, there were certain things about her that would make her having been involved with either of those men in no way a surprise to Bechet. She had lived with some private investigator at one point, learned everything she could from him before leaving. Even though they had never become intimately involved, she had certainly learned things from Bechet. It would not have been entirely uncharacteristic for her to want to see, perhaps, what a courier for a man like Castello might have to teach her.

But Bechet couldn't care about any of that. Abby had disappeared when the summer was over and the weather grew too cold to paint outdoors, when his crew was reduced to just himself and Falcetti. What she was up to now wasn't any of his concern; he had problems enough, thanks. Still, he wrote down the address, along with dates and times and locations, and when he was done, he tore from the notebook the page with Gabrielle's information. He tore out, too, the half dozen or so blank pages that followed it, just in case the force of LeCur's handwriting had pressed through and formed indentations on those below. Bechet tore up those pages, flushed their pieces down the toilet, then removed the lid on the back tank, closed the seat and rested the lid upside down on it. He knew better than to carry it with him—it was a possible ace that he didn't want to lose or, worse, have on him if things went wrong. Same with the phones. They would be safer there, easy enough for him to retrieve later on.

The contents of the wallets were the least useful of all the items he had collected, but Bechet had expected that. Fake New York State driver's licenses, some cash, no photos, no business cards, nothing. But of course these men would hardly carry anything that would connect them to Castello, or to anything, for that matter. Cell phones and notebooks were necessary evils, there was no way around that, but wallets filled with items that could add up to some kind of trail would have simply been the careless oversights of the untrained and inexperienced. Bechet removed his clothes from the top of the heating unit, dressed despite the fact that they were still a little damp, and pocketed the cash and the fake driver's licenses, the only photos of the two LeCurs he currently possessed. He then resumed waiting for Gabrielle's call. He should have heard from her by now, but he could also think of several reasons why her trip could take longer than the train schedule claimed it would take. The Long Island Rail Road wasn't the most reliable system around. Still, he was considering calling her from the cell phone he had taken off the charger in the garage he rented, finding out where she was, when his phone finally rang.

He didn't bother to check the caller ID; only she had this number.

"Hey," he said.

"Hey."

"You there?"

"Yeah." She sounded so far away. It wasn't, Bechet knew, just the actual physical distance and the poor signal of a cell phone to cell phone connection that he was hearing.

"You all locked in?"

"Yeah."

"What took so long?"

"The train stopped in the middle of some field. We sat there for a half hour."

"Yeah, it does that once in a while. You okay?"

"Yeah."

"You don't sound it."

"Well, this place isn't the coziest I've seen."

"It's safe, though," Bechet said. No one, not even Eddie, knew of this place. He tried to imagine her there, almost couldn't do it. The building was an old industrial workshop, a nondescript brick structure in a row of nondescript brick structures set along the edge of the East River, unchanged for decades except for what the cycle of season after season after season had done to it. Two stories tall but open inside, its floor cement, one wall comprised of two side-by-side garage-style doors that led from a small indoor loading dock out to the street. These doors were not only locked but bolted. For added security and privacy, there were no windows at street level, and those set high up on the two adjacent walls were smudged by years of pollution and fitted with wrought-iron bars that had long ago begun to rust.

The only enclosed space within the building was an elevated office that overlooked the workshop. It had been built onto the west-facing wall and was accessible by a set of cement stairs. There was a bed and couch in this room and, through a heavy steel door, a bathroom with an old cast-iron tub. The windows in both rooms, each one spanning nearly from the floor to the ceiling, offered a clear view of the river and, beyond it, Manhattan. Bechet had spent a year—longer than a year—in that room, sleeping in that bed, soaking in that tub, watching the skyline light up at night and then dwindle as morning broke. He was drinking a lot back then, did that—and not much else—till he was done with it, done punishing himself. From that point on he spent the rest of his self-exile getting back into fighting shape, readying himself for his return to the *world*. Not the world he had known, but something else. Housepainting, he was thinking, a business of his own, nothing to do with death or vio-lence. In retrospect, yes, maybe he should have gone somewhere other than Southampton to start over. That would have been the smart thing to do. But he knew that a guy could make money painting houses out there. He knew, too, where he stood there, where the dangers—*the traps*—were hidden, and there was, for a man with his past, a real advan-tage in knowledge such as that. But more than all that, he had his deal with the older Castello, his détente, for which he had worked hard, so why not there, why not the place he knew like the back of his hand?

In the end, whatever the reason, Bechet was glad he had returned. If he hadn't—hadn't gone back to the place where he had become, if only briefly, what his father had been, gone back there to become what his fa-ther *hadn't* become—then he would not have met Gabrielle, would not know what he now knew, all the things that there were between them, things the old Bechet could never have imagined.

He thought now of Gabrielle, his Gabrielle, in that place, alone. He wanted to be there with her, locked away in that elevated room, the two of them in the bathtub, watching the skyline together, nothing at all to think about but what and when to eat, no need to listen for a knock on their door or decipher the sounds that made their way in from the street.

He wanted that more than anything, resolved himself to do whatever needed to be done to have that.

"Is it raining there?" he asked.

"Yeah, a little. I'm cold."

"Did you turn the heat on?"

"I don't know how."

He instructed her on how to operate the heater fans mounted high up on the brick walls, then directed her to the elevated office. He could hear her footsteps as she climbed the cement stairs. The door to the office was heavy steel, and the large windows that overlooked both the workshop and the river were thick, a web of wire mesh running through them. Bechet had always felt safe in that room, hoped she would, to some degree at least, feel the same. In times of trouble, people seek high places; even a dozen steps up counted for something. The steel door and safety glass served only to increase the sense of protection that the room offered by design.

A thermostat on the wall inside the door controlled a cast-iron radiator not far from the bed. Bechet told Gabrielle to turn it from its current setting of fifty up to seventy, so the room would warm up quickly. He then told her to go into the bathroom and turn the water heater from its vacation setting to full heat.

"You'll have scalding hot water in about twenty minutes," he said. "It's a good heater, so you can more or less take a nonstop hot bath all night long if you want. Just lie there and watch the skyline."

He wanted to hear that she was at least, if not pleased by the safe room, then impressed by the view. He didn't get either.

"Your father left you this place?" she said.

"Yeah."

"And you can afford to keep it empty like this?"

"He owned the building next door, too."

"The one with the pharmacy?"

"Yeah. The rent from it and the two apartments above is enough to pay the property tax and keep the electricity running."

"No mortgage or anything."

"No. My father bought them both with cash back when I was a kid. I didn't even know about them till after he died."

"What did he use this place for?"

"I don't know," Bechet lied. It had been obvious to him from the moment he first entered what it was his father had done there. What else would a man like him use a place like this for? Thick brick walls, no first-floor windows, a large drain in the floor of the loading dock. Bechet had felt it in the air, a chill that didn't go away, not completely, even with the heaters on. He had felt that chill, too, the year he stayed there, taking bath after bath, looking out the window at the lights on the water, forgetting what he had done.

He would do that again, once he got there. But he wouldn't be alone this time.

"How long will you be?" Gabrielle said.

"It won't be as soon as I had hoped. Probably later on today, or tonight."

"Is anything wrong?"

"No, it's just taking longer, that's all."

"I thought we weren't going to keep secrets from each other anymore."

"I just don't want you to worry, Elle."

"How can I not? What else is there for me to do?"

"I'll be there as soon as I can. I promise."

"Can I call you? I have a feeling I might get lonely."

"Of course. If I don't answer, I'll call you right back. Get some sleep, okay? There are clean sheets and blankets in plastic bags in a trunk at the foot of the bed. I'll be there soon."

"Before that, if you can. Okay?"

"Yes, ma'am."

They hung up. Bechet looked around his motel room for a moment, then took a breath and stood, putting himself and his plan in motion. It was time now. From his shoulder pack he removed a Ziploc bag, stuffed the cell phones and batteries and notebook into it, then zipped the bag closed. With the duct tape he had taken from the dance club storage room he sealed the bag tight, then taped it securely to the bottom of the overturned toilet tank lid. Finally, he replaced the lid, then turned off the ringer of his second cell phone, the phone to which only Gabrielle had the number, and placed it into the pocket of his mechanic's jacket, zippered it closed. His other cell phone, his everyday phone, he shut off entirely as he left the room, then stashed it into the console in his Jeep. He drove the long way around the village, followed Sunrise Highway west for several miles, turning finally onto the north end of Peconic Road and making his way up the hill to its peak. Crossing first the bridge that spanned Sunrise Highway and then the train tracks, he saw that LeCur's car was still where he had left it. The police had yet to find it, but with the sun coming up it wouldn't be long till they did. Even then, with no identification on the man and no registration in the car's glove compartment, it would take a while—several hours, at least—before they identified the body via its fingertips. LeCur, Bechet knew, had a police record, but even so, with his arrest report long out-of-date and no cell phone on his person to guide them, the detectives would have no idea how to contact his next of kin. There were significant disadvantages to living outside the law, and this was one of them.

But it was a disadvantage that Bechet knew he could make use of. Castello and LeCur had no way of knowing if LeCur, Sr., was alive or dead. If not sentiment then commerce would make it in Castello's best interest that the man remain alive; training a man, maintaining a man as seasoned as LeCur, represented a significant investment of time and money. The man's son clearly wasn't there yet, wasn't at the point where he could keep his emotions in check for the good of his employer, might not even ever get to that point, so the safe return of the more mature LeCur would be something Castello should be interested in.

With this in mind, Bechet continued on, following Peconic Road to its southern end, then turning left onto Montauk Highway, heading back toward Southampton. At a motel across from the college, standing on the edge of its driveway, was something that was a rare sight these days—an actual phone booth. Bechet pulled into the motel's lot, grabbed a roll of quarters from his shoulder pack, and walked toward the booth. Inside, he pulled the paper from his back pocket, dropped two quarters into the coin slot, and dialed Castello's number. He waited for the man to answer. It was strange for Bechet, after a year of living as close as he had yet come to an average man's life, to be not only so far away from it now but to have his hopes of returning to it, or to something even remotely like it, hinge on the outcome of a single phone call. He remembered the night he had informed Castello's father that he was leaving, and that it would be in their best interest not to come looking for him, ever. He remembered the way his hands had shaken as he'd held that phone. That was the only time in his life that his hands had ever trembled from fear. Never once before a fight, always a strange kind of calmness then, a deep relaxation that verged on sleepiness, and not even in the moments before he killed for Castello's father, or when he forced an ice pick into the heart of a man who had posed, or so Bechet had been told, some kind of threat to the prosperity of the precious family.

Bechet's hands weren't shaking now, either. This was different, this wasn't like the other call he'd made. Castello, Sr., had been like a father to Bechet, for better and for worse, but Castello, Jr., well, it was clear that he wasn't like his father, just as Bechet wasn't like his. Bechet and Castello, Jr., had been like brothers once, maybe, but that was a long time ago, and anyway, what Castello had tried to do, had threatened to do, that wasn't exactly the act of a loving brother.

Bechet told himself that in a matter of hours he'd be back in Brooklyn, but with Gabrielle this time, and that they would talk as he took a long bath, soaked his naked body till he began to feel clean again, just as he had done before. From there, then what? He didn't know, but he also didn't care. His desire for all this to be done with was like a craving, drove him like a primal instinct. It was all he knew, and all he wanted to know till all this was finally behind him.

The ringing ceased. A pause, then, from the other end of the static-rich line, Castello's voice. Cautious, uncertain.

"Hello."

"We need to talk," Bechet said.

Another pause, a longer one, and then: "Gabrielle Olivo, twenty-six, from Boston originally." Any hint of caution and uncertainty was gone now. "I'll have more later on today, if you'd like to call back then."

That was fast, Bechet thought. Castello had resources, yes, but it had been only hours since he had learned Gabrielle's name—learned it, obviously, from the younger LeCur. Not only had it been hours ago, but it had been during the dark hours of the morning, when most of the people in this part of the world were sound asleep, when institutions that kept such records were closed. But Bechet didn't let his mind get stuck on that, needed his thoughts clear. Nor did he let his surprise at the power and swiftness of the Castello machine show; to do so would have given Castello exactly what he wanted, what he was so used to getting.

"If you thought for a minute that I'd do anything other than what I did," Bechet said, "you were fooling yourself."

"My family is all that matters to me, you know that," Castello said. There wasn't even the slightest hint of apology in his voice.

"And she's all that matters to me."

"So where does this leave us?"

"In the position to make a deal."

"I see." Castello sighed. Bechet wondered then if he had awakened him. "Tell me, is our friend alive or dead?"

"He's alive. We're having a grand old time, actually. Catching up, playing cards. It's almost like the old days."

"What kind of deal, exactly, are you looking for?"

"Gabrielle and I get to disappear."

"And why would I agree to that? There have to be consequences to betrayal, you know this. We cannot afford to be flexible on the matter."

"I'd think self-interest would come before tradition."

"You seem to believe you have something that would be of interest to me."

"LeCur carried a notebook. In it is enough evidence to guarantee the FBI would want to take a good long look at your family for last night's double murder. Frankly, I don't care who killed who or why. But it seems to me a federal investigation would be a detriment to your business."

Bechet waited for a response, got none, then continued.

"Add to that all the numbers in LeCur's cell phone. And the numbers in his son's. You wouldn't want the FBI having access to these numbers, following them to where they lead, would you? I'm sure the last thing any of your business associates would want is to have to explain their connections to you."

"We seem to have taught you well."

"It's the same deal I had with your father, Jorge. If anything happens to me, everything I have goes to the FBI, including the evidence from before. It's a few years old but it's still damaging, still enough to bring your business to a halt. Are we clear on this?"

"Yes, very."

"Our deal of course extends to her. And I'm talking *anything,* Jorge. If suddenly her credit rating gets trashed, or her best friend from high school dies in a car crash—*anything*—then the deal is off. You have way too much to lose, I can't imagine you just throwing it all away for something as petty as revenge. Your father was smarter than that. The question is, I guess, are you?"

"And what about our friend?"

"Once I'm out of town, I'll let you know where to find him. In the meantime, if I see his son anywhere—if I even think I see his son—our friend is dead."

"You seem to have covered everything."

"So we have a deal?"

"No, not exactly. This deal would leave me still needing to know what I need to know."

"That's not my problem."

"Maybe it is, maybe it isn't. It all depends, I suppose, on if you give a shit about that friend of yours or not."

"What friend?"

Bechet heard the sound of shuffling paper in the background. Castello drifted away from the phone for a moment, then returned.

"Robert Andrew Falcetti," he said. "We've got his hack license number, so it won't be so hard to find him when he comes out of hiding. And how long can the guy hide, right? He's got to work, has to make money. From what I understand he has his share of debts around town."

"You can go after him if you want," Bechet said, "but that only means the FBI comes after you."

"You're placing an awful lot on one little notebook, Pay Day. You really expect to get this much from it?"

"You think I'm bluffing?"

"Yes," Castello said flatly. "You expect me to believe that our friend is still alive? You expect me to care either way. He is of a certain value to me, yes, but what's at stake is much more valuable, a hundred times more valuable."

"It's my deal, Jorge. Take it or leave it, it's up to you."

"And what about that business partner of yours? Eddie. I hear he left some enemies when he left Jamaica. It would be terrible for him to wake up and find himself packed in a crate, on his way back to his homeland, don't you think? Don't worry, though, we'd make sure he has company, that his wife packed in there with him."

"Eddie's got friends, Jorge. You don't really want to mess with him."

"Yeah, we know all about his friends. We're not all that worried about them."

Bechet said nothing. The phone booth felt suddenly like a trap. He wanted to flee it but couldn't, had to stay and hear what was next.

"You can't possibly expect me to be held responsible for the fates of a half dozen lives," Castello said. "Shit happens, people get hurt, they die, in accidents, of natural causes even. I mean, that's life, right? The hand you're holding now is, at best, one you can cash in only once. And even then, FBI or not, our business brought to a halt or not, I can still hurt you if I want to, as often as I want to. I can hurt you through everyone you've ever known. Hell, when I'm done with them, I can just find some person at random, some young woman with her whole life ahead of her, and have her killed, let you live the rest of your life knowing that an innocent young woman died a horrible death because of you. You've got heart, Pay Day, but that's the thing about the heart, isn't it? It makes such a vital target."

Bechet muttered, "Yeah, so you've said."

"I'm smarter than my father, Pay Day. And I'm a thousand times smarter than you. I always have been. I've made millions of dollars for my family. I have a country with no extradition treaty to escape to, and more than enough passports to get me there. I have friends all over the world who will do whatever they can to assist me. If I have to flee this country, it only means I get to return to my beloved home, live there like a king for the rest of my life, till I die an old man, just like my father. So the FBI doesn't scare me, never has. Nothing you can do scares me. So what do you say you and I put our heads together and come up with another deal, one that's maybe a little closer to reality."

Bechet waited for what was next, though he didn't need to, knew exactly what was coming.

"You do what I want you to do, when I want you to do it," Castello said, "and no one suffers. More importantly, you do what I want you to do and your girlfriend gets to live a nice long life. With you, without you, that's up to you. Since you won't be working for us officially, it doesn't matter to me what you do with your personal life. What you do for us will be strictly a favor from you to me. Do you understand?"

Bechet stared through the scratched Plexiglas of the telephone booth at nothing. All this time, all this way, only to end up back where he had been once before.

Castello said, "I'll take your silence as a yes. You should know that things have changed somewhat since we last spoke. It's my belief now that we have a traitor in our organization. Or worse, in our family. I want to know who that person is. And I want what was stolen from us, too. I want all of it."

Bechet said nothing, just continued to stare at the world beyond the booth. The two-lane road, the college across it, everything that he could see little more than parts of a ghost town to his tired eyes.

"You there?" Castello said. There was a degree of compassion in his voice, a brotherly softness.

Bechet nodded, then said, "Yeah."

"We'd find her sooner or later, Pay Day, you know that. Slumming it with you might have been fun for a while, but at some point a woman like her will want to reenter the world. Certainly she couldn't live the way she's been living without you. If you did the noble thing and let her go, sent her away for her own good, we'd still find her, do what we had to do. But you know all this, Pay Day. You *know* it."

Bechet thought then of the contents of LeCur's trunk: heavy-duty garbage bags, a hacksaw. The idea of Gabrielle falling into their "machine" filled him with both sickness and rage. But so did the idea of a life spent without her, of his going back to the kind of women he'd known before her, the kind of life he'd known before the life they had made together.

The heart, indeed.

"Don't make this harder on yourself than it has to be," Castello said. "You were a good student, you learned fast, but I've been doing this all my life. There's no shame in losing to the better man. But you don't need me to tell you that, right? What was it they used to write about you back when you fought? You were known more for the punches you took than the punches you threw. Something like that."

Bechet took a breath, let it out. He closed his eyes, didn't like what he saw, reopened them. "Something like that," he said.

"You've wasted crucial time, so you'd better get going. Once you find the traitor we'll know then what needs to be done."

"What has changed to make you think there is a traitor? You didn't say anything about this last night."

"My father always said, the problem with having a lot of people in your pocket is that they all at some point might start talking to each other. In the past few hours we've been receiving some interesting information from one of our men in the department."

"One?"

"It pays to have friends in the right places, and as many as possible. They tend to keep each other honest." Castello paused, then said, "It seems the investigation into last night's murders is a bit . . . single-minded."

"You think a cop is behind this."

"I need evidence, independent confirmation. Being told something is one thing, being shown proof of it is something else. I'd prefer not to take anyone at his word."

Bechet said nothing to that.

"Find the traitor, Pay Day. Provide us with solid evidence and you will have gone a long way toward earning our forgiveness. Do that, get back what was stolen, and you just might begin to earn our gratitude. You remember what that's like, don't you? Our gratitude? A good salary for just sitting around and playing cards, indulging in whatever distractions you desire, whenever you desire them. That girl you used to request all the time, what was her name? Colette? Unfortunately, she's not around anymore, but I'm sure we can find someone to replace her. Someone to help you forget all about your precious Gabrielle."

Neither spoke for a moment, then Bechet said, "As far as what was stolen, it might help me to know what I'm supposed to be looking for."

"Let's just call it merchandise. Merchandise that has a significant street value. Romano's girlfriend is dead, according to our informant. She was killed a few hours ago, so that leaves the other girlfriend, Michaels's girlfriend."

"And if I can't find her?"

"I don't think you really want the answer to that."

"What if she doesn't know anything?"

"She knows."

"What makes you so sure?"

"She's a slippery one. Plus, there's someone in her past. For all I know, he's the one behind all this, pulling all the strings."

"Who is he?"

"His name is Miller. He used to work as a PI. Before that he worked for a man with whom I had an arrangement."

"What kind of arrangement?"

"Let's just call it a treaty of nonaggression. So far it seems this Miller character has been honoring it. For him to suddenly come after me like this means that the sins of our fathers just might be catching up with us."

"I don't understand."

"The chief of police before Roffman was Miller's father. You may remember that he was murdered."

Bechet thought about that. It didn't take long for him to put things together. "My father was hired to kill him."

"Yes."

"By your father?"

"No, he just arranged it, put the person who wanted Miller dead in touch with your father. He put a small team together. But I would imagine that might just seem like splitting hairs to Miller."

"Why now, though? I mean, after all these years of honoring his boss's treaty with you?"

"I don't know. He could have only recently been told who had killed his father. He met with Roffman last night. Or it could have nothing to do with that at all, be about the girl only. Whatever his motivation, I need to know what, if anything, he has to do with this. I need to know if my informant is right or selling me a bill of goods."

Bechet thought about his father, the building in Brooklyn. That, of course, made him think about Gabrielle, waiting for him in that desolate, rundown place, hiding, alone, scared. No way to live, even for one night.

"It's interesting, though, don't you think?" Castello said after a moment's silence. "Your having left us like you did is what makes you the only man I can come close to trusting right now. You're not part of my family, so you can't be the traitor in my family. You went your own way, got out of reach and stayed there, are therefore clean because of that." He paused, then said, "I remember when you came to us. As far as the rest of the world was concerned, you were a man with nothing to offer. You knew how to hurt, you were a savage, but what use is that in the civilized world, right? We offered you a chance to be useful, paid you more than minimum wage, *a lot* more than minimum wage, which is all you would have gotten working any of the jobs available to you. Dishwasher, day laborer, some dingy loading dock somewhere. You needed us and we needed you. It seems to me now that we—you and I—need each other again."

"So who is she?" Bechet said after a moment. "Michaels's girlfriend. A name would help."

"Shepard," Castello said. "Abby Shepard."

Again, Bechet said nothing.

Castello must have sensed something different about this silence. "Do you know her?"

"No," Bechet lied.

"Well, as I said before, she's a slippery one. No address, no phone number, no trail at all. She doesn't even have a car registered to her."

"So how exactly am I supposed to find her?"

"That PI is still around. He owns a building by the train station, lives in the apartment above."

"Which building?"

"The last one on Elm. The one with the restaurant."

"L'Orange Bleu?"

"Yeah."

Bechet thought about that. He had stood in sight of that building mere hours ago, while he and Gabrielle had waited for the train to Hampton Bays. He had studied it, searched its doorway and windows for any sign of someone taking note of them. How many other times, he wondered, had their paths almost crossed?

"I want to hear from you in twelve hours," Castello said, "whether you find anything or not. Sooner, of course, if you've found what we want. If I don't hear from you then, we go after one of your friends. It's as simple as that. You can't warn all of them, get them out of town. Even if you could, we'd just pick a stranger." Nothing for a moment, more than enough time for his point to sink in. Finally, Castello said, "You're calling from a pay phone now, right? In Southampton?"

Bechet hesitated, then answered, "Yeah." There was no point in denying it.

"I want your next call to come from a local phone as well. I don't care if it's a pay phone or not. I don't want any calls from a cell phone, do you understand? I need to know that you haven't said the hell with everyone but you and your girlfriend and skipped town. Also, remember, you don't work for me, so there can be nothing connecting me to you. Otherwise, this whole endeavor is pointless. Is that clear?"

"Yeah."

"You should have listened to me before, Pay Day. I told you, I'm not my father."

And I'm not mine, Bechet thought.

"You'd better get going. The clock's ticking."

The line went dead.

Bechet stood there for a while before hanging up. He felt numb, the way he used to feel after a twelve-round fight, his body and mind past beaten, past tired, off in worlds all their own, nothing at all to do with him, nothing at all to do with each other. But he couldn't give into that feeling now, wouldn't. He headed back toward the village, the drizzle that had started just a few hours ago now a steady rain again. At least it broke up the ground fog, made it easier for him to make his way around. In his motel room, he retrieved the notebook and cell phones and batteries from the toilet tank, removed them from the Ziploc bag and put them in his shoulder pack, then powered up his cell phone—his everyday phone, not his emergency phone—and keyed in a number.

His precaution, despite everything Castello had said, still needed to be put into place. There was always the chance now that Castello wasn't sending him to find the girl and the traitor and what had been taken but instead setting him up to take some fall, or to be in the position where he had no choice but to make a hit, take out someone Castello wanted taken out without having to worry about it being connected back to him. There was the chance, too, that Bechet was being sent to be the target of a hit, that this was retribution for his having done what he had to do to get away, both years *and* hours ago. Everything and anything was possible now, and should something happen to him, Bechet wanted the evidence, all that he had collected, to find its way to the proper authorities. Maybe, as Castello had insisted, it would accomplish little, but the fighter in Bechet—the fighter he had been, the fighter he was still—was all too aware of the fact that if one must go down, if there was no way to avoid that, then it was always better to go down swinging. Maybe he couldn't bring Castello down with him, but he could at least hurt the man, maybe even like no one else had ever hurt him, in a way his onetime brother would not ever forget.

But I'm not there, Bechet told himself. Not yet, not by a long shot. There was still plenty of fight in him, and still ways this could turn to his favor. There had to be. It was just a matter now of waiting for the moment to present itself, of being in the right place at the right time, and doing then whatever it was that needed to be done. In the meantime, he would do enough to appear as though he was obeying Castello, keep this up till the time came for him to make his move, whatever that move might be.

After the third ring the phone was answered by a voice Bechet hadn't heard in a long while.

It paid, indeed, to have friends in the right places.

"Hello." It was a male voice, groggy. Bechet had clearly awakened him but didn't care.

In fact, he cared about very little at all now.

"It's me," Bechet said. "Listen, I'm going to need a favor."

Miller watched from his window as Barton crossed through the straining morning light toward the Southampton train station. The rain was steady but weak, and the Tylenol Barton had brought for him of course did little to ease the pain in his knee. But while a dull ache had a way of distracting Miller, all-out pain had a way of clearing his mind, doing so like nothing else. He needed that right now, needed it in a way he hadn't in a while, since he had retired two years ago, let his beard grow, and made the choice of wanting nothing more than to live his life within the tight perimeter of Elm Street and Railroad Plaza, in the privacy of his unchanging apartment above, enjoying when he felt like it the sometimes chaos of the French-Moroccan restaurant below.

Once Barton reached the station she climbed the short steps leading to the empty platform and placed a call from the pay phone. Soon after she dialed, the station lights went out, and then the streetlights lining Elm blinked out as well, one by one down the length of the road. Morning, then, was officially here. Miller watched Barton as she spoke, then watched the two streets leading to the station, checking for cars—cop cars, any cars, at this point, anybody, anything. The early westbound train had left a half hour ago, so none was due from either direction for another hour. This meant any car approaching the station now carried the potential of trouble. No, *probably* was trouble. But none did approach, and when he was certain that Barton was okay, Miller grabbed his corded phone and, still watching his friend, dialed a number from his landline.

He didn't want to make this call, was hoping for another way to get what he needed, but with the clock ticking there was no point in taking any chances. If it turned out that he didn't need the person he was calling, if Barton got the information they needed from Spadaro, then he'd call back, say thanks but never mind. No harm done. In the meantime, though, he wanted this in motion, wanted help on the way, just in case.

The phone rang twice, then was answered.

"I need to talk to you," Miller said.

"What's up?"

"Can we meet?"

"I'm driving tonight. One of my drivers was a no-show."

"I only need a few minutes. Can you maybe swing by?"

"Are you in trouble?"

"I'm not sure."

"I'm in Water Mill. I can be there in ten minutes."

"I'll be looking for you. Park at the train station, I'll come down."

Miller hung up. Behind him, Barton's VCR, which she had brought along with a three-pack of blank videocassettes she had purchased at the 7-Eleven on her way over, was coupled with Abby's DVR. Miller and Barton had made one copy already, and a second one was in the machine, in the process of being made. They were duplicating the contents of the entire DVR, not just the segment showing Roffman but all of it, everything recorded from installation to discovery. The two weeks' worth of comings and goings totaled just more than fifteen minutes.

Miller glanced at his watch. There was about another ten minutes left to go on that copy. Then he looked through the window for Barton again. She talked for a few minutes more, then hung up and made her way back to his building's street door, a solitary woman in a dark leather jacket and jeans and work boots moving through the raw light of a rainy morning.

Miller was still at the front window when she entered. He turned sideways so he could face her as she stood in the kitchen and keep the train station within his peripheral vision. His front room was so large, there were a good fifteen paces between him and Barton. Neither made an attempt to bridge that gap.

"What did Spadaro have to say?" Miller asked.

She shook the rain from her sleeves and hands. "Someone called in a disturbance. That's how the cops showed up at the cottage when they did."

"Who called it in?"

"They don't know."

"How do they not know that?"

"It was an anonymous call."

"But where'd the call come from?"

"A pay phone in town. Either someone had left the cottage, didn't know you were there and made the call from town, or someone watching the cottage had seen you go inside and called a second person in town, and that person called it in. But either way, why call the cops?"

"So I'd be found in a house with a dead woman."

"But that's if someone was watching and called someone else. What if the person who had killed her had driven to town and called the cops from there. Why would he do that?"

"He wouldn't."

"So that means someone was there, watched you go in and called someone else. There wasn't enough time for the person watching to drive to town and make the call himself."

Miller thought about that, then said, "What else?"

"Whoever called it in didn't identify you by name. So they either didn't know who you were or did but didn't want the cops to know."

"But then why call them in the first place?"

"Yeah, I know, it's all fucked-up. At least we know no one's looking for you. You don't have to leave your truck parked at the end of Powell anymore."

"What did Spadaro tell you about Bechet?"

"He's pretty sure Jake Bechet and Jonah Bechet are the same guy."

"How does he know that?"

"The address on Bechet's registration is a garage behind a private residence on Hampton Road. Three floors of apartments above, a four-car garage below. The garage has been divided up and rented out as individual storage units. Ricky says there's nothing but stuff in Bechet's. Surveillance equipment and old boxing gear and clothes. Between the surveillance equipment and boxing gear, he figures Bechet goes by Jake instead of Jonah."

"Spadaro went inside?"

"I guess, yeah."

"When?"

"I don't know."

"Did he get a warrant?"

"He didn't say."

Miller thought about that. "Anything else?"

"Bechet seems to change vehicles about every six months. All different kinds of cars—a sedan, then a truck, then a station wagon. Right now he's driving a Jeep Wrangler. Green, with a black hardtop, according to the registration. That should be easy enough to spot."

"Were his cars old or new?"

"They were all older models. The Jeep's a '94. Some were even older than that. Why?"

"The first thing I think of when I hear that someone keeps trading in one old junk for another is that he's probably trying to keep somebody from picking up his trail."

Barton thought about that, didn't understand what Miller meant, then realized his point and said, "You think he's the one who taught Abby how to live the way she was living."

"Yeah."

"So who the hell is this guy?"

"I'm not sure."

"But you had a hunch the camera was his almost from the moment we found it, so you know something about him."

"I know that Abby worked for him one summer."

"Doing what?"

"Painting houses."

"How long ago?"

"A few years."

"I don't understand. What's a housepainter doing with surveillance equipment?"

"Yeah, well, that's the thing. He wasn't always a housepainter."

"What do you mean?"

"It looks like at one point he may have worked for Castello."

"Doing what?"

"I don't know for sure. But he used to be a boxer, one of those fighters who after ten years of almost making it realizes he isn't going to. There aren't exactly a lot of options for someone like that, are there?"

"You think he was an . . . enforcer."

"You look at the guy and it's hard to imagine him doing anything else."

"You've seen him?"

"Once, yeah."

"When?"

"Back when I found out Abby was working for him. I went out to where they were painting to get a look. That's when I decided to find out what I could about him."

"And you found out he used to work for Castello."

"Nothing conclusive, but, yeah, everything pointed to that."

"And yet you let Abby keep on working for him?"

"I didn't want to, but I didn't really have a choice."

"Because of your promise."

Miller nodded. "Partially, yeah. I know you think it's stupid, Kay, but it's best for everyone if I leave Castello alone like I was asked to. But anyway it was more than that. Bechet was running a kind of halfway program, hiring troubled kids, working them hard and paying them well. He was obviously trying to do some good. So maybe what I'd heard about him was wrong, or maybe it wasn't and he was trying to make up for his past. Either way, I knew it would piss Abby off if I interfered. I didn't want to run the risk of giving her a reason to not come back to me. I guess back then I was still thinking she might."

"Does Bechet still paint houses?"

"No, he got out of that business. The last thing I heard he and Eddie went into partnership together."

"The cab company? That Eddie?"

"Yeah."

"So why don't you call him, ask him what he knows about Bechet?"

"I did. Call him, I mean."

"When?"

"While you were on the phone with Spadaro. He's on his way over, should be here any minute."

Barton waited a moment, watching Miller. She took a few steps into the living room.

"What exactly are you hoping to find out? By locating this Bechet guy, I mean."

"Abby installed a surveillance camera he had purchased. She did it two weeks ago. They might still be in contact."

"You think he's just going to tell you where she is?"

"If he gave her the camera, taught her what she knows, then he was trying to help her. I'm trying to help her, too."

"Yeah, but that's my point. Who the hell are you? Unless he knows you and Abby used to live together and that you're still in love with her, why should he tell you anything?"

"I'm not still in love with her," Miller said.

"Whatever." Barton shrugged. "That's not the point."

"What is the point?"

"The last time we saw Abby she was leaving her apartment with a suitcase full of something."

"Yeah. So?"

"A lot of people have been killed tonight, Tommy. By someone who knows what he's doing. Maybe what they're being killed for is inside that case. Maybe this Bechet guy is the one doing the killing."

"He's partners with Eddie," Miller said. "Eddie wouldn't get mixed up with someone like that. Not in a million years."

"Maybe Bechet tried going straight, but it didn't take. That happens, you know. People turn over a new leaf, then find themselves falling back into old behavior for some reason."

Miller chose to ignore the comparison Barton was obviously trying to make.

"I mean, think about it, Tommy. Bechet could be working for Castello again. Or worse, he and Abby could be up to something. He could have killed all those people so the two of them could end up with whatever is in that suitcase. Even worse than that, he could want it all for himself, which would mean he's probably looking for Abby right now, if he hasn't already found her."

"So there's only one way to know for sure if he has."

"Tommy, don't be foolish. Please. Let's just take off, go somewhere, and let this run its course. Let's just go somewhere and never come back."

"I can't."

"Why?"

"Because I can't."

"That's a little boy's answer."

Miller shrugged. "Then I'm a little boy."

"She's gone, Tommy. She left you a long time ago."

"Do we have to do this, Kay?"

"I just don't want you to get hurt. Or killed."

"I'm sorry, but whatever the hell is going on, Abby's the common denominator. She was dating Michaels, gave him my business card; she once worked for Bechet, learned a thing or two from him; and Roffman knocked on her door two nights ago. She's the key to all this, Kay, whatever this is. I know it."

Neither said anything more for a long moment, just stared at each other and thought and listened to the rain. Finally Miller turned his head and glanced out the window at the train station. No cab there yet.

"I think there might be more than one common denominator here, Tommy," Barton said.

Miller looked at her.

"Abby was dating Michaels, yeah," she said, "but Michaels was also working for Castello. She knew Bechet, is maybe even still in touch with him, but Bechet apparently has his own history with Castello, too. And like I said yesterday, Roffman made his own deal with the devil a long time ago. He's been in Castello's pocket pretty much since the day he took over as chief. You had to have noticed that you weren't the only one looking the other way when it came to that family."

Miller said nothing.

"Anyway, Tommy, every link to Abby that you see, I see as a link to Castello and Roffman. So if you really want to help her, I think you're going to have to get yourself to a place where you're able to forget about that promise of yours. I just don't think there's going to be any way around that. Everything seems to be leading you there. I know you think it's to the benefit of us all that you keep it, and I love you for that, but I have a feeling we're past that now. I have a feeling the war you've been trying to prevent has already begun. And it looks to me like maybe it's time for you to pick a side and fight. Before the wrong side has a chance to pick you."

Barton's words were still in Miller's ears when he looked out the window and saw the cab parked at the train station. He told her he'd be right back, to take the second tape out of the VCR and get the third one started, grabbed his overcoat and put it on as he went down the stairs. He'd almost forgotten about the Colt in the pocket, was caught a little off-guard at first by its presence there. Though his PI license had lapsed, he still had a carry permit, so he was legal, but that knowledge didn't seem to ease the sensation in his gut, the feeling, eerie and quietly startling, that he was stepping out into the middle of something—some greater conflict—that, despite all his efforts so far, he wasn't even close to understanding. Was he a pawn? Was he a target? One of several targets?

Was his apartment being watched now, was he being watched? Once he stepped outside, would he be walking into someone's sights, his life's end just seconds away? The gun hanging heavy in his pocket somehow stripped him of the neutrality that had been for years now his best line of defense against who he used to be and what he used to do, the thing inside him that had once *driven* him. By carrying the weapon it was as if he had accepted an invitation to become once again part of what the man who had taught him the trade called the "mischief and misery of others," a world that was nothing less than violence and destruction. People at their most vulnerable, and people at their worst—that had always seemed to be how these things were cast. There was now, it felt to Miller suddenly, nothing he could do but push forward, make his way somehow through the maze that surrounded him, and hope for some kind of victory that didn't cost too much, didn't leave the world as he knew it a smoking wasteland.

Stepping through his street door, Miller walked toward the station with his head down, eyeing his surroundings. Nothing, but it was only a quick look, and anyway, if it came, when it came, he wouldn't see it coming, knew that much at least. His father, a man with more experience than Miller could ever hope to have, had been murdered by a team of hired killers, a team he hadn't seen coming. Half-expecting to hear at any moment a shot—*something*—and not hearing it, hearing only his footsteps and the rain, Miller reached the station, passing the parked cab without looking inside it and stepped up onto the platform. He walked to its edge, standing as if waiting for the train even though none was due. *A man confused about the time, or early but with nowhere else to go in the rain.* After a moment of standing there, his hands deep in the pockets of his overcoat, looking up and down the tracks, Miller heard from behind him the sound of the cab door opening and then swinging shut. The sound echoed, muffled a little by the rain. Miller glanced over his shoulder, saw Eddie walking toward the steps, his unlit but half-smoked cigar clamped in the corner of his mouth.

Eddie was close to sixty, a small scrap of a man with a clubfoot and hobbled legs, who walked these days with a cane. Miller had known Eddie for years before ever seeing him outside of his cab, hadn't known till that moment that the man had a deformity at all. Eddie's skin was dark and cut with deep creases, mostly around his eyes, the whites of which were the color of milk. He wore baggy cargo pants and a work shirt, over it a tank driver's jacket, Second World War surplus. Nylon with a wool lining, lightweight but water-repellent and warm. Despite his decidedly scruffy appearance, Eddie was now something of a well-to-do man; after decades of eking out a living as a cabbie, he had partnered up with Miller's former boss, a man who went by the name of Gregor. Gregor had helped build up Eddie's cab business while at the same time buying his way into several local businesses—key, profitable businesses since 9/11. When Gregor took off with his wife Liv to a small gentleman's farm in Vermont, he had handed many of his businesses over to Eddie. The PI firm went to Miller, under the condition that Miller never pursue the Castello family. More than that, though, that he cut them a wide berth. As with all businesses, a new owner took possession of the assets as well as the debts. Miller understood this, that Castello had once done Gregor a favor. The Castellos weren't all that easy to ignore, but Miller kept the promise he had made to the man who had made him who he was. Running the business for as long as he could bear it, Miller finally sold out to a private security firm from New York eager to cash in on the newfound fears of the wealthy. The promise to his former boss had somewhat remained, though. Things such as these were important to him—too important, yes, but he was who he was.

Miller, still looking over his shoulder, watched Eddie make his way up the steps. He felt bad making his friend leave his cab and walk, but now wasn't the time for recklessness. If Barton was right, if Roffman and Castello were at war, or on the verge of it, then danger was no longer an abstract thing. Protecting himself and others from it was no longer a ritual, like meditation or prayer, a daily practice followed to give him peace of mind. It was, now, a matter of nothing less than life or death.

Once on the platform, Eddie paused to light his cigar, then wandered toward the edge, a cabbie stretching his troubled legs and taking a moment to have a smoke. He came to a stop eight feet from Miller, close enough for them to speak without looking like they were anything more than two strangers chatting. Eddie was as familiar with all this as Miller was, had always helped Miller out when he could, and helped Gregor before him, seeking out the two of them, respectively, whenever he knew of something he thought either of them might do well to know. After a second attempt at lighting his cigar, Eddie spoke finally, his voice, as usual, deep for a man his size, his Jamaican accent carrying with it the ring of music.

"What's up, my friend?" he said.

Miller looked up and down the tracks, wanted to look like a man waiting for the train, nothing more than that. "I need to talk to you about your partner."

Eddie drew on his cigar, or tried to, removed it from between his teeth and checked its end, then returned it to his mouth, lit it a third time. "What do you need to know?"

"I need to know for certain if his real name is Jonah. If Jake Bechet and Jonah Bechet are the same man."

"Can you tell me why?"

"If they are, then he's linked to the murder victims they found at the canal last night."

"Linked how?"

"Through a woman. She was dating one of the victims. The other victim's girlfriend was found dead a little while ago."

"You back at work?"

Miller shook his head. "No."

"Then this trouble you mentioned on the phone is personal."

"Yeah."

"Bad?"

"It's looking that way, yeah."

Eddie waited a moment, then said, "Jake Bechet and Jonah Bechet are the same man. But no one I know of calls him by either name. To everyone he's Pay Day."

"Why Pay Day?"

"It was the name he fought under when he was a boxer. How is he linked to this woman?"

"She used to work for him, back when he was painting houses. And last night I found a surveillance camera outside her apartment that had been purchased by him. She had installed it two weeks ago."

Eddie nodded. "What else do you know about him?"

"That he probably worked for Castello a while back. Can you tell me what he did exactly?"

"Everyone makes mistakes, Tommy. In our youth, out of desperation, we've all done things we shouldn't have done. I've always thought anyone asking for a second chance deserves it."

"I need to know exactly what he did, Eddie."

"I don't know exactly. I do know, though, that he'd never go back to working for Castello."

"How can you be so certain?"

"Would you go back to the person you were before you started working for Gregor, back when your father was still alive? When you and your friends had your little club and you used to hurt women?"

Miller shook his head.

"Some things just can't ever happen," Eddie said. "Pay Day going back to work for Castello is one of those things."

"Still, he's connected to Abby. I'd like to talk to him, ask him a few questions. Could you arrange it?"

"I could if I knew where he was."

"He's missing?"

"When my driver didn't show, I tried to call Pay Day to cover the shift, but his phone was shut off. I swung by the place he was living at but no one was there."

"Has he ever disappeared like that before?"

"Not in the time I've known him. He doesn't stray all that far from home these days. He's like you that way. And he's always been reachable by phone, has to be in case a driver calls out, that's part of our deal."

"I'd really like to speak to him, Eddie."

"The last I heard from him was yesterday evening. He was looking for Bobby."

"Who's Bobby?"

"My missing driver. Bobby Falcetti. He was watching the cops process the scene at the canal. A friend of his owned that restaurant right across from where the bodies were found."

"Tide Runner's," Miller said.

"Yeah."

"Falcetti knew the owner?"

"Yeah, why?"

"The owner's dead, Eddie. He was killed a few hours after the two bodies were found. He'd been strangled."

Eddie looked directly at Miller then. "You think maybe Bobby and Pay Day are in trouble?"

"If they saw something they shouldn't have, yeah, they could be. They've both disappeared on you."

"Pay Day I'm not worried about, he can take care of himself. But Bobby, that guy's just walking bad luck. And he's got a serious gambling problem."

"If Bechet were in trouble, is there anyone he'd call?"

"Not likely."

"Are you sure? Somebody, anybody."

Eddie thought for a moment, then shrugged. "He might call Scarcella."

"Who?"

"Paul Scarcella."

"The salvage yard? That Scarcella?"

"Yeah. He's how Pay Day and I met. If you ask me, they're two of a kind."

"What do you mean?"

"Let's just say you wouldn't want to mess with either of them."

Miller thought about that. "How do you know Scarcella?"

"We have a contract with his wrecker company. And his auto shop services and repairs our cabs."

"He's the one Bechet gets all his vehicles from," Miller said.

"Yeah." Eddie paused again, then asked, "How'd you know about that?"

Miller shrugged the question off. "Do you think you could give him a call, Eddie? Scarcella, see if he's heard from Bechet at all?"

"Who's this woman anyway? The one you're looking for."

"Abby."

"Your Abby?"

"Yeah."

"Shit."

"Exactly."

Eddie glanced back at his cab, then looked forward again, down at the tracks. "What time is it?"

"It's just a little after six."

"Scarcella opens up the yard around now. I can try him there, see what he knows. My phone's in my cab."

"I can get it for you," Miller offered. He was in a hurry now, tried not to let it show.

"No, I'm okay. Doctor says I need to walk more."

Eddie turned, crossed to the stairs. Back at the driver's door of his cab he reached into his pocket and removed something. A piece of aluminum foil, folded flat. He unfolded it, held it in his palm and used it like an ashtray to put his cigar out. He returned the dead cigar to his mouth, refolded the foil and slid it into his pocket. Back inside his cab he made the call. Miller watched him through the windshield as he started to speak, then looked toward his apartment. He could see Barton standing in one of his front windows, the last one in the row, watching over him as he had watched over her. He stared at her for a moment, at the shape of her, then took a look around again, studying his surroundings.

Nothing that shouldn't be there, no car that didn't belong to a neighbor, hadn't been there at this time every other morning. The only variant visible was Barton's Volvo, parked directly across from his place. Not that any of this really meant anything. Still, for now Miller felt safe, moved, he believed, unseen. But he didn't expect that feeling to last for very much longer, not if Eddie got him what he wanted, and not if he was to going to do what needed to be done, whatever needed to be done to save the woman he had once so foolishly abandoned.

Barton watched as Miller waited for Eddie to finish his call. From the window she could see Eddie behind the wheel of his cab, talking on his cell phone, could see, too, Miller's impatience in the way he stood. Could anyone have seen that or was it just her? A good two minutes went by, Miller on the edge of the platform, his hands in the deep pockets of his overcoat, glancing up the tracks expectantly but also glancing now and then at the cab. When he saw that Eddie was off the phone, Miller crossed the platform, stepped down to the street, went to the cab's passenger door. Eddie lowered the window, and Miller leaned in, held up what looked to Barton to be money. It didn't take long for her to realize that Miller was pretending to ask Eddie for change. They chatted as Eddie broke the bill and handed Miller change. Eddie then picked up his phone in a way that made Barton think it must have been ringing. He spoke briefly, then hung up, nodded to Miller. Miller leaned back, watched as the cab drove away, then started back toward his building. Barton could see the slight limp that plagued him whenever it rained or was humid. Even from the second-floor window she could see, too, his effort at trying to conceal it. A habit of his, one that she knew well.

Once he reached the street door and started up the stairs, Barton walked into the kitchen, ran some water into a glass, then stepped over to the table on which lay the VCR and DVR. She opened her overnight bag, dug out her prescription bottle, and downed a single pill. The sight of Miller's wound had reminded her of her own. Seven o'clock was earlier than she usually took her pill, and she was supposed to take it at the same time every day, but a few hours' difference couldn't matter that much, and anyway, with everything going on, she didn't want to forget. *Blessed Lexapro did to the brain what love did, caused the same cascade of chemicals and kept them flowing steadily throughout the day and night.* The nights were what were important. Barton was placing the empty glass in the sink when Miller walked through the door.

She could see by his eyes—inflamed along their edges, red flesh surrounding whites that were a little glassy—that he was tired, more though from physical pain than from lack of sleep. Unlike her, he couldn't take his pill, not now, not yet. His dark hair and beard were wet from the rain, and in the somber morning light the drops repelled by the wool of his dark overcoat, clinging to the fine hairs of the fabric, glistened like winter dew.

"What did Eddie say?" she asked.

"Bechet's going to meet me."

"Jesus, Tommy. Where?"

"At a salvage yard in Noyac."

"That was fast."

"Eddie called a friend of Bechet's. Turns out Bechet was on his way over. They set up a meeting."

"That was . . . lucky."

"There are certain conditions I have to follow, though."

"Like what?"

"I have to go alone."

"Why?"

"Bechet won't meet me otherwise."

"Tommy, c'mon."

"It's the only way, Kay. There's no time to argue, okay? I'll be back as soon as I can."

"I could ride with you, get out before the salvage yard. That way I'd at least be nearby."

"He's sending someone to pick me up."

"When?"

"Right now."

"I don't like this, Tommy."

"Neither do I. But we don't have much choice. Bechet is all we have."

Miller quickly emptied the pockets of his jeans. Wallet, a handful of change, keys to his pickup, cell phone. Then he removed his overcoat, laid it on the table. By the way it landed on the wood Barton knew there was something heavy in one of the pockets. Miller ignored the sound, did so in a way that made Barton think he wished he had been more careful laying the coat down and was therefore hiding whatever it was that pocket contained. She looked at the coat but said nothing. Miller, too, was silent. He stepped into his bedroom, was returning with his field jacket, pulling it on fast as he walked, when Barton finally spoke.

"Where are you being picked up?"

"At the station."

"I could tail you in my car. For all you know, Tommy, this could be a trap."

"He knows I'm a friend of Eddie's."

"You think that's going to matter?"

Miller ignored the question. "I don't want to see your car anywhere behind us, Kay, do you understand?"

Barton nodded. "Yeah."

"Stay here, keep an eye on the tapes. I'll be back as soon as I can."

"And if you're not?"

Miller apparently couldn't think of an answer to that.

"Be careful, Tommy."

"I will."

Miller walked to the door, went through it and started down the stairs. He was moving slowly because of his knee. Barton returned to the window, watched him walk to the platform again. Once he was there and waiting, she dialed Spadaro's number on her cell phone as she hurried to Miller's bedroom, opened his closet and knelt down in front of the foot-locker. She searched fast through its contents with one hand as she waited for Spadaro to answer.

He picked up after the third ring. "Hey."

"I need the name of the salvage yard in Noyac," Barton said. She knew she sounded a little frantic but didn't care.

"What's going on?"

"I don't have time to explain. An auto yard, a junkyard, out in Noyac, do you know of one?"

"Yeah, sure. Scarcella's."

"Where is it?"

"What the hell's going on, Kay?"

"Just tell me where it is, Ricky."

"It's the same yard where we have our holding pen for accidents pending an investigation. We went there once, remember?"

"Oh, Jesus, yeah." She saw it now, saw the way to it. More important, she saw the layout of the place, or the way it had been laid out years ago, when she was taken there. Acres of piled-up wrecks, rows and rows of them, a ridge on one side of the property, a dirt road running along it. She doubted that much about the place at all had changed since then.

"Thanks, Ricky," she said. "I'll call you in a little while and explain."

"Are you okay?"

"Yeah. I just need to check something out. I'll check back in with you in a little bit."

She flipped the phone shut, pocketed it, had two hands now with which to search. She didn't find what she was looking for in the foot-locker, stood and searched the shelves above. It wasn't there, either. She stepped out of the closet, surveyed the room. Miller's bed by the window, a night table, a bureau. On the bed was an open lockbox. Barton went to it, checked it out of curiosity. It was empty. She got down onto her hands and knees, looked under the bed. Nothing. Stepping to the bureau, she pulled open the top drawer. Clothes. The second drawer was only more clothes. As she grabbed the handles of the bottom drawer, she felt that her plan—less of a plan, more of a wild urge—was on the verge of falling apart. But when she opened the drawer, saw that it contained not clothes but more equipment, she felt a rush of hope. Almost right away she could see among the clutter what she was looking for.

A long-distance listening device, laser-sighted, and beside it a pair of binoculars. The eavesdropping device was the kind that allowed one to listen to either a conversation between people standing out in the open or one between people inside a building. A dish, shaped like a satellite antenna and fitted with a microphone, picked up conversations outdoors while the invisible laser, when aimed at a window, detected the vibrations made on the glass by those speaking and bounced the signal back to the receiver, where it was converted into audio. Barton turned the unit on, quick-checked the battery, then grabbed the binoculars and hurried into the living room, emptying her overnight bag of her things and placing the equipment inside. Taking one of the two finished videotapes, she tossed it into the bag as well. Better to have a copy with her, in case someone broke into Miller's apartment while they were gone. The second finished tape she placed into the empty lockbox in the bedroom, closed the lid, checked that the lock had caught, then tossed the box into the locker at the bottom of the closet, closed and locked that. It was the best she could do, better certainly than doing nothing. Back in the living room she checked on the progress of the third tape. It was still recording, so she left it in the machine. On the table, next to the machine, was Miller's overcoat. She looked at it for a second, a long second, then picked it up, located in the pocket what Miller had tried to hide from her.

A Colt .45 and two clips.

She removed them from the pocket, checked to see that the Colt was loaded and that the safety was on, then placed the gun and the two clips into the overnight bag. As she laid the coat back down she remembered Miller putting the photos he had found at the cottage into the inside pocket. She wondered if he had taken them out at some point, wasn't sure exactly why she wondered that, reached into the pocket and found them both there still. She pulled them out, looked at each one. The first one was of Romano and his dark-haired girlfriend. He'd probably taken that in case he needed it to show to someone and ask if either person was someone they knew. The second photo was of Abby and the dark-haired girl, not one of the photos of them kissing, just of them sitting beside each other on the couch. Barton gave her friend credit for not taking one of the more racy photos, but then thought maybe that wasn't such a good thing, that such discretion was maybe an act of love. She laid the photos on the table beside the coat, looked at Abby once more. Finally, grabbing the keys to Miller's pickup from the table, Barton returned to the front window.

He was still at the station. She waited for what felt like a long time but was probably only a few minutes. Finally a car approached from North Main, an old sedan that looked like it had probably been a cop car once. Too old, though, to be part of the chief's fleet still. The sedan parked at the station, and Miller walked down to it. A man got out from the passenger door. He and Miller nodded to each other, then Miller, as casually as he could, raised his arms. The man—larger even than Miller, in jeans and a nylon pilot's jacket, his head shaved clean—frisked Miller thoroughly. When he was done, the man nodded toward the back passenger side door. Miller opened it, climbed into the backseat. The man climbed in beside him, pulled the door closed.

Barton bolted then, her overnight bag in her hand. At the bottom of the stairs she opened the street door just enough to watch the sedan coasting down Railroad Plaza. It stopped at the Stop sign, turned right onto North Main, and disappeared from sight. She hurried out into the rainy morning, running to the corner, rounding it and heading down Powell. She ran as fast as she could, her heart throbbing like a fresh wound by the time she reached the street's end, and got in behind the wheel of Miller's pickup.

There were two ways to the salvage yard in Noyac, one longer than the other. Barton opted for the longer route; it was more complicated than the first one and she figured whoever was driving Miller wouldn't take it for that very reason. Her only hope was that the driver would drive as cautiously as Miller had when she and he had made their way to East Hampton. This would maybe allow her to make up the time she had lost by leaving after them, and the time she would further lose by following the roundabout way.

She needed to arrive first, find her spot and get set up. From there, what? She didn't know, didn't care. There was an overwhelming sense of purpose running through her now, and she hadn't felt that, or anything even remotely like it, for a long time.

She trusted it, even if a little blindly.

SALVAGE.

The sign was visible through the bare trees that lined the back road, posted high on a twelve-foot cyclone fence topped with rusted razor wire. The auto yard was an eighty-plus-acre compound in the middle of the north woods, no houses for at least a mile in any direction. A world of its own, all on its own. Barton drove past the main gate, wasn't sure yet if she had arrived ahead of Miller, strained to get a glimpse beyond the fence as she negotiated the long curve in the road. She didn't dare slow down, didn't want the pickup to look like anything other than a vehicle passing, heading somewhere, anywhere. She didn't see the sedan through the fence, only a three-bay garage with an office attached and, behind that, a large storage shed. The buildings were cinder-block constructions with metal roofs, looked like military barracks. For all Barton knew, the sedan was already inside, parked behind one of the bay doors. And Miller, too, alone and unarmed, at the mercy of these men.

Beyond these buildings were stacks and stacks of vehicles of all kinds, cars and pickups and SUVs, bashed and rusted wrecks in rows for as far as the eye could see. Barton had sped the entire way there, pushing Miller's pickup into sharp back road turns, pressing the accelerator to the floor whenever there was even the slightest hint of a straightaway ahead, risking, she realized now, adding the very vehicle she was driving to this collection. But she didn't care about that. Just past the salvage yard, exactly as she had remembered it, was a long ridge, and running along it was a narrow dirt road that made its way up into the vast woods that bordered the yard. A hunter's road, gutted by the winter's rain. As Barton turned onto it she was glad she had taken Miller's pickup and not her Volvo, wouldn't have gotten far otherwise. Shifting into four-wheel drive, she followed the inclining road, driving as quickly as the uneven terrain allowed till the road veered away from the edge of the ridge suddenly and the truck, heading into the deep woods, was out of sight of the cluster of buildings. Barton parked and grabbed her overnight bag, made her way back on foot through the cold morning rain till she was back at the ridge's edge. Elevated by a good thirty feet, she had a clear view of the buildings and the gate, all half a football field or so away.

She found a grassy spot under a tree, to keep her out of sight but also to protect her from the rain. She crouched down, removing the listening device from her bag. As she turned it on and slipped the headphones over her ears, the sedan arrived at the gate. Her heart jumped at the sight of it. She'd just made it. The earphones blocked out nearly all the sounds around her; all she could hear was her own breathing. In this surreal void she aimed the binoculars at the gate and watched the driver of the sedan get out—a young guy with a shaved head, dressed and built like the man who had gotten into the backseat with Miller. He unlocked and opened the gate, then got back behind the wheel and drove the sedan into the compound and parked in front of the garage. Climbing out again, he walked back to the gate, was about to close it when a Jeep appeared on the back road. Green, with a black hardtop. The headlights—rectangular, not round—told Barton that it was a '94 or older. The Jeep pulled into the compound and parked alongside the sedan as the younger of the two men closed and locked the gate.

Miller was now theirs, at their mercy, if these kinds of men even had any.

Miller and the older man, the one who had sat beside him on the ride over from the train station, emerged from the back of the sedan. They took a few steps, then stopped and waited as the driver of the Jeep got out and approached them. This man, wearing a dark jacket over a hooded sweatshirt and jeans that strained against thick legs, was holding over one shoulder a small, military-style backpack. His hair—brown with gray at the temples—was buzzed close to the scalp. He was a big man, not the biggest man there, but bigger still than Miller. Not taller, just *bigger*. A onetime boxer, that much was obvious by the width of his shoulders and the way he carried himself. So, then, Bechet.

Barton studied him as he approached Miller. The binoculars were equipped with a built-in digital camera, so Barton snapped several photos of him, as well as the others, just to be thorough. Bechet looked older than she had thought he would be, in his late thirties, maybe even early forties. In her mind boxers were young men because young boxers were all she had ever seen. For years she had watched the fights with her father, on TV mostly, though a few times he had taken her to the local arena to experience them firsthand. Bechet, despite the fact that he was older than she had thought he would be, seemed no different at all from the men Barton had seen as a youth. He had the same hard face, wore the same stare as he faced Miller that boxers wore when they stood toe-to-toe with their opponents.

A stare-down, between her friend and this man. Not overtly hostile but not friendly either. Barton's stomach tightened at the sight of this. Miller was tough, yes, had played football when he was younger, possessed now the innate strength of a natural athlete, the kind of strength that never really goes away, but he had that bad knee, and anyway, he was outnumbered, and by the kind of men who seemingly knew how to hurt, were maybe even themselves impervious to being hurt, as was so often the case with those who caused suffering for gain. To be numb to the pain of another, Barton had learned a long time ago, required one to become, to some degree at least, numb to his or her own pain. A trade-off that was unavoidable.

With all her running around, blindly trusting the sense of purpose driving her like an uncontrollable urge, Barton hadn't really come up with a specific plan beyond getting to where she needed to be. Seeing now that these men were barely in range of the Colt in her bag, and too close to Miller for her to fire upon them with anything other than a hope to hit *someone,* she had no choice but to ask herself what exactly would she do should things suddenly turn bad? Not only was the distance between her and Miller an issue, there was a fence between them, one topped with coils of razor wire. She felt now the need to have something in mind beyond lying still and listening, a witness only. Something *to do* should something more need to be done. Her thoughts edged toward the frantic, and it took all she had to keep them from giving in to all-out chaos. For all her racing thoughts, though, she could think of nothing more that she could do except watch.

She told herself to focus, cleared her head. Miller didn't seem intimidated by Bechet, returned the onetime boxer's stare with one of his own.

Eventually Bechet said something to Miller, but Barton couldn't hear what, nor could she hear Miller's response to it. The volume was turned down. She turned it up, watched as Bechet waited a moment, taking his time studying Miller, sizing him up. Finally Bechet nodded and looked over his shoulder toward the older man behind him. *Let's get moving.* She heard this. Surrounding Miller with roughly the same formation guards employ to escort a prisoner, these three men guided him toward the garage. Entering through a metal door between the adjoining office and one of the large bay doors, they one by one disappeared from Barton's sight, leaving once they were gone only the eerie stillness of a junkyard in the moments after dawn. As she looked upon it, Barton felt suddenly, deeply alone, but maybe that was something due to the fact that all there was for her to see now were the countless remains of so many violent crashes stacked in tall rows that spanned the acres below her.

Monuments to uselessness, as it were.

The door swung closed with a dull clack. The sound echoed briefly—Barton could hear it, muffled, through the headphones—then was gone. She removed the Colt from her overnight bag, chambered a round, and laid the weapon upon the exposed root of her sheltering tree, well within reach. It may come to that yet, and she still didn't know what she would do if it did. But she didn't think about it now, did instead the only thing she could do, the only task there was at this moment before her.

She shouldered the listening device, aimed its invisible laser at the window nearest to the door through which Miller had been taken. She adjusted the volume until she began to hear sounds. Footsteps, shuffling, indications so far of nothing more than casual movement, everyone getting settled, taking their places.

But no words, not yet.

Motionless, holding her breath, she waited for someone to speak.

Eight

CINDER-BLOCK WALLS PAINTED GRAY AND LINED WITH TALL
metal shelves upon which sat hundreds of cardboard boxes filled with
starter motors, alternators, carburetors, solenoids, all of them used parts
that had been stripped from the vast collection of wrecks outside. A
workbench with a variety of mechanic's tools scattered upon it, tall
Craftsman toolboxes at both ends, the overwhelming smell of old motor
oil with just a hint of gasoline in air as dormant and cool as the air inside
a cave. The dim morning light bleeding in was made even more so by
windowpanes layered with a thick dust of grime and engine exhaust,
years and years of it, Miller thought.

He was standing in the center of the work bay nearest to the small adjoining office. This bay was empty, but the two beyond it, to his left,
housed an old pickup and a sedan, respectively. The sedan was nearly
identical to the one that had brought him to this place. The hoods of
both vehicles were raised, but the truck, in the bay farthest from Miller,
was up on a hydraulic lift, suspended high enough for a man to stand
beneath. Its front wheels were removed, and an unlit work light was
hooked to its undercarriage.

Just as he had done outside, the younger of the two men stood behind
Miller. He was Miller's age, maybe a little younger. There was no doubt,

though, that he was Scarcella's son, just couldn't be anything else, was easily a carbon copy of the man. He had the same powerful build—not the body of an athlete, like Bechet or Miller, but of a laborer, more a solid bone structure and bulk than symmetrical muscularity. He wore the same type of clothing, had, too, the same stony face—round, framed by a cannonball head. The only difference between Scarcella and his son was the fact that the son did not shave his head but wore it buzzed close like Bechet. Unlike Bechet, though, the younger Scarcella was obviously balding.

Still, rough-and-tumble men, the two of them, the very kind you'd expect to rule over a place such as this.

Miller knew little about the older Scarcella, had heard once or twice that he was "connected," but had never crossed paths with him till now. Not only had Miller not crossed paths with Scarcella, he hadn't even crossed paths with anyone who, to his knowledge, had crossed paths with Scarcella, that was how far off his radar the man was. Miller had always assumed that the rumor about Scarcella being "connected" had to do with the fact that Scarcella's company had a contract with the town to service and repair all its vehicles, which included cop cars. A connection such as this might have allowed Scarcella certain access to police, but to what extent, Miller didn't know or care.

Scarcella and Bechet had moved to the far end of the work bay, put a dozen feet between themselves and Miller. They faced each other, spoke together in whispers, then adjusted themselves so their backs were turned completely to Miller, spoke some more. After a moment Bechet slipped off his shoulder pack, removed something from inside and handed it to Scarcella. Miller couldn't see what the item was, but it was important, whatever it was, that much was clear, because Scarcella nodded quickly and called to his son, who walked past Miller and joined his father and Bechet in their huddle at the other end of the bay. Scarcella said, "Lock this up," not as softly as he should have, and handed to his son what Bechet had handed to him. Miller looked as the younger Scarcella carried the item into the adjoining office, saw that it was a half-gallon Zip-loc bag. He couldn't, though, make out its contents. Once in the other room, the younger Scarcella started to close the door, but before it shut Miller glimpsed beyond the threshold, saw a desk and filing cabinet, both of them old, made of cheap metal. Beside the filing cabinet, though, was something that by contrast stood out. A large antique safe, black with gold scrollwork and the name of some certainly now long-out-of-business company stenciled in ornate and bold letters across its door.

The office door closed, and Miller looked at Bechet and Scarcella. Neither, as far as he could tell, had noticed his glance toward the office. Looking at them again, Miller thought that Eddie had been right, that these men *were* two of a kind. Russian dolls maybe, all three of these men, each enough alike and just slightly larger than the other—Scarcella larger than Bechet, Bechet larger than Scarcella's son.

Bechet said to his friend, "Give us a few minutes," then waited till Scarcella had stepped into the office and closed the door before taking a few steps toward Miller. The stare-down that had occurred outside continued. For a moment all there was to hear was the rain on the metal roof above. Miller waited; this was Bechet's world, the first words should be his.

"You're Miller," Bechet said.

"Yeah."

"Tommy?"

Miller nodded.

"Eddie seems to think you and I have some things to talk about." Bechet laid his shoulder pack at his feet, let both his arms hang loose at his sides. Miller noted that his hands were large, his knuckles like jagged stones pressing against thick, calloused skin.

"Thanks for meeting me," Miller said. "I'm not sure how much Eddie told you over the phone."

"Only that I should listen to what you have to say. And that I can trust you." Bechet looked at Miller for a moment more, sizing him up—not as a boxer now, a man facing his opponent, but as something else, something more along the lines of one man attempting to understand another, getting the sense as quickly but as thoroughly as possible of who he was and where he stood, doing so only by what he sees.

Still, overt aggression gone, for now at least, Bechet's caution—what little Miller knew about the man said *cautious*—remained. "I don't really have a lot of time," Bechet said.

There was no reason then for Miller to do anything other than what he wanted to do, which was to just *jump in*. He didn't care about where it might take him, what dangers doing it would create for him. He'd come too far to play coy, to dance around, particularly with a man like this.

"I'm looking for someone," Miller said. "She used to work for you."

Bechet paused before responding. "Who?"

"Abby Shepard."

Though Miller couldn't tell exactly what it meant, Bechet nodded slightly, as if thinking about that. Finally, he said, "What do you need to find her for?"

"There was a double murder at the canal last night. She's connected to it."

"How?"

"One of the victims was her boyfriend."

"How do you know this?"

Miller shrugged. "It's what I've heard."

"You haven't been in touch with her?"

"No."

"When was the last time you saw her?"

"A few years ago."

Bechet nodded again, thought about that. "Not sure how I can help you," he said.

"When was the last time you saw her?"

"Why do you ask?"

"She installed a surveillance camera outside her apartment door two weeks ago. The camera belonged to you."

"What makes you think that?"

"It was sold to you four years ago. We traced it from its point of sale."

Bechet took in a breath, let it out. He looked away for a moment, toward the bays to his right, then looked back at Miller. "You found the camera?"

"Yeah."

"Who has it now?"

"I do."

"Do the cops know about it?"

"No."

"You sure?"

Miller thought about Spadaro. He knew, but there was no reason to mention that, no reason at this point to involve him.

"Yeah," Miller said. "This has nothing to do with them. I'm just trying to help out an old friend."

"You and Abby used to live together, didn't you?" Bechet said.

"For a while, yeah."

"She used to talk about you. Back when she worked for me. Not much to do when you're up on ladders except talk."

Miller resisted asking what it was she had said. It took, for a second, everything he had. Instead, he said, "I'm curious, how did she end up with a camera that belonged to you as recently as two weeks ago?"

"I keep most of my things in storage. She must have let herself in."

"You told her where your things were stored?"

"No. But I don't have a hard time imagining her following me. Most likely back when she worked for me."

"Why don't you have a hard time imagining that?"

"She was . . . obsessed."

"With you?"

"No. With what I could teach her. All she wanted from any man, as far as I could see, was what he could teach her."

Miller considered that. "Have you been to your storage unit in the past two weeks?"

"Yeah."

"Any sign of a break-in?"

"No. But there wouldn't be, would there?"

"Why not?"

"Abby knew how to pick locks. According to her, she learned how from you."

Miller remembered having done that, the afternoons they had spent together, him teaching her things, her asking to be taught. They used to make love afterward, as the sun went down. At times he used to think it was her way of delaying his leaving for work.

"You said she was obsessed with learning things from men," Miller said. "So what did you teach her?"

"If you've been looking for me, then you know I'm not so easy to find."

"You taught her how to do that."

"Among other things, yeah."

"Did you know her boyfriend at all? Michaels. Or his buddy Romano?"

"No. Abby and I had fallen out of touch."

"From what I understand Michaels had a police record."

"What does that mean, 'from what I understand'?"

"I've been told, haven't actually seen it."

"What was he arrested for?"

"Grand theft auto."

"I guess Abby wanted to learn how to steal a car."

"Maybe she was just in love with him."

Bechet shrugged. "Maybe both."

"Did you know that Michaels and Romano were working for Castello?"

Bechet didn't answer. He and Miller stared at each other for a moment.

Miller didn't back down, said, "From what I hear, you used to work for him, too."

Bechet remained silent.

"Any idea what they might have done for Castello?"

"How would I know that?" Bechet said flatly. "Like I said, I've never met either of them."

Miller decided to let that go for now. "One of the recordings Abby made with your camera shows Michaels coming to her door with a knapsack. When he left again, he was empty-handed. Later on, Abby received a call on her landline, after which she bolted from her apartment with a suitcase."

"You've been to her place?"

"Yeah."

"How'd you find it?"

"Does it matter?"

"Maybe not, but I'd still like to know."

"Romano had a girlfriend. We went to her cottage—"

"We?"

"A friend of mine is helping me."

"Who?"

"Just a friend."

"You trust him?"

"Yeah." Miller didn't see the point in properly identifying his friend's gender.

Bechet nodded. "So you went to this cottage . . ."

"We found evidence there that Romano's girlfriend and Abby knew each other. The last call from the landline was to an apartment in East Hampton. We got the address and went there, found the camera."

"Any sign of Abby?"

"No. Not a piece of mail or a bill, nothing at all to indicate who was living there. Not even photos."

"What was the evidence you found at the cottage?"

"Photographs of Abby and the girlfriend. And Romano, too."

"What else did you find?"

"Not much. The place had been trashed."

"Searched?"

"Yeah."

"Any sign of violence? Blood, anything like that?"

"Not the first time."

"What do you mean?"

"I went back a few hours later."

"What for?"

"To see if there was a camera there that we had missed. I found Romano's girlfriend in the bathtub. Her wrists had been slashed."

"I take it you don't believe it was suicide?"

"She wasn't there the first time, but *was* there the second. Somehow I doubt between the time I was there and came back she had walked in, drew a bath, undressed, and opened her wrists."

"Was Abby's place trashed, too?"

"No. In fact, it was in perfect order."

"You said Abby had a landline."

"Yeah."

"Did you check the incoming and outgoing calls?"

"There were only the two calls from the cottage—when I had hit redial, and the call before it. With what the camera recorded it looks like Abby got the call from the cottage not long after Michaels and Romano were swung off the bridge."

"And the camera shows her bolting with a suitcase."

Miller nodded. "We found the knapsack Michaels had entered with. It was empty."

"And that was the last recording made?"

"Except for me and my friend entering and finding the camera, yeah." Miller waited a moment, then said, "It looks like Michaels and Romano were caught with their hands in the jar. Which means they were probably couriers. And the way they were murdered has a South American ring to it, don't you think?"

Bechet said nothing.

"Frankly, I don't care who killed who and why," Miller said. "But it's pretty obvious to me that Abby is in some kind of trouble. I would like to help her."

Still thinking, still nodding, Bechet continued to study Miller. He had been listening like a man who hadn't expected to hear what he was hearing. Listening, too, like a man who wanted to believe what he was being told. *If only he could.*

"You really think someone like Castello would string up two of his employees so close to a building everyone in town knows he owns?" Bechet said finally.

"If he wanted to send a message, yeah, maybe."

"There's sending a message and there's broadcasting your involvement in a double murder."

"Triple."

"What do you mean?"

"The owner of the restaurant across the canal was found strangled a few hours later. Everyone seems to think that the two men who had killed Michaels and Romano killed the restaurant owner as well."

"You seem to know a lot about what's going on."

Miller shrugged. "I hear things."

"What have you heard about me?"

"That you used to be a boxer, fought under the name of Pay Day Bechet. After you quit, you worked for Castello for a while. After that you painted houses. Now you're partners with Eddie."

"And that's it."

"Yeah. That and you're friends with Bobby Falcetti, who was friends with Dennis Adamson."

"The guy who owned the restaurant by the canal."

"Yeah." Miller paused, then said, "So you think the fact that the bodies were found where they were means Castello had nothing to do with the murders."

"If I wanted people to believe he was behind a murder, I'd probably do something like that."

"It's a long way to go to set someone up."

"So maybe it's about more than just setting him up. Maybe it's also about what was taken. What Michaels gave to Abby, and what Abby stashed in her suitcase before leaving her apartment."

"Any ideas what that could be?" Miller said.

"Castello has his hands in a lot of different things. It could be anything."

"Something worth murdering four people for?"

"For some people it wouldn't necessarily take a whole lot for them to kill four people. What else did the camera show?"

"Abby coming and going, bringing home groceries—not long before she took off, actually. So I don't think she was expecting to have to bolt."

"Anything else?"

"At one point someone came to her door and knocked, then left."

"Who?"

Miller waited, then said, "Roffman."

"The chief of police."

"Yeah."

"When was this?"

"Two nights before the murder."

"Is it possible he and Abby were . . . involved?"

Miller shrugged. "I don't know. Hard to imagine."

"He's someone she could learn things from," Bechet said.

"He's married, though."

"That doesn't seem to stop him, from what I hear."

"I'd like to think it would stop her."

"People sometimes do things they wouldn't normally do. Particularly if they think it will make themselves safe."

Neither spoke for a moment. Miller wondered then exactly what Bechet knew about him, his past, *the things he had done.*

"What do you know about Roffman?" Bechet said finally.

"Enough."

"What do you know about him and Castello?"

"There's supposed to be some kind of deal between them."

Bechet nodded. "It's more than a deal. Castello has Roffman in his pocket."

"How do you know this?"

"When Roffman took over as chief, Castello didn't waste much time making certain Roffman needed his help."

"They set him up?"

"Everyone has a weakness. I assume you know what Roffman's is. He got involved with a woman who turned out to want to make trouble for him. Castello waited till Roffman was up to his neck in shit, then offered to help make the problem go away. Roffman went for it in a heartbeat, didn't even know the woman had been working for Castello the whole time."

"You know this for certain?"

"Yeah."

For some reason Miller took that to mean that Bechet had actually been there, was working for Castello at the time.

"You think maybe Roffman is trying to get out of Castello's pocket," Miller said.

"It could be. It certainly looks that way."

"That's the problem, though."

"What?"

"Everything looks exactly the way it should. It looks like Castello is behind four murders, but according to you he's not. It looks like Roffman is up to something, a lot of people are eager to think he is up to something, but in my experience things are seldom how they look. Anyway, I'd need more than him knocking on a door and then walking away to think that he's behind four murders."

"If not Roffman or Castello," Bechet said, "then who?"

"I don't know. But I'd like to hear what Roffman has to say for himself."

"He'll talk to you?"

"I think so. Anyway, we have footage of him coming to the apartment of a woman who was involved with someone who had worked for Castello and is now dead. A woman who has taken off with something stolen from Castello. He'll either talk to me now or to the feds tomorrow."

"You can play hardball like that?"

Miller nodded. "Yeah."

"I'd like to hear what he has to say," Bechet said. "But he shouldn't see us together."

"I can record the conversation."

"I'd rather hear it live. No offense."

"None taken."

"I have gear for that."

"So do I," Miller said.

"I'd rather use mine, if it's okay."

"Yeah, no problem."

"Can you set up a meeting for this morning?"

"Probably."

"I'd like to see the video of him coming to Abby's door. Like you said, hearing is one thing, seeing for yourself is something else."

"I can get you a copy."

"Appreciate it," Bechet said. "I'll give you a ride to your place, park down the street. You can run up and get it for me, okay?"

"Yeah."

"Wait here." Bechet picked up his pack, started toward the office door.

"Hold on," Miller said. "I have a few questions."

Bechet stopped, turned, looked at him. "What?"

"My friend thinks you might be working for Castello again. Are you?"

"No."

"How do I know that?"

"You don't. But you can ask Eddie. Anyway, I don't do that kind of work anymore."

"You used to, though?"

Bechet nodded once.

"And you have nothing to do with him now?"

"No."

"So then why are you doing this? Why are you getting involved?"

"Let's just say we both have someone we want to protect."

"What do you mean?"

"Castello went to a lot of trouble recently to make it so I had no choice but to do what he wanted."

"What is it he wanted you to do?"

"Find the traitor in his family. And get back what was stolen from him. He seemed to be under the impression that finding Abby might help me do both."

Miller thought about that. "How'd he give you no choice?"

"He threatened to hurt everyone I know, everyone in my life, including Eddie and his wife."

Again, Miller said nothing, thinking.

"Castello has more than just Roffman in his pocket," Bechet said. "He has other cops, too, each one there to keep the others on their toes. To keep the others honest. It looks to me like one of those cops is making a move. It might even be all of them, working together."

"Do you know who these other cops are?"

"No. But it's someone who knows enough about Roffman's connection with Castello to play them against each other. Probably someone with something to gain by either of them falling on his face. Or both of them."

"That could also be anyone in Castello's organization. Why do you think it's a cop?"

"There's something in the way the investigation is being handled."

Miller thought about what Mancini had told him, about the quickness with which Adamson had been killed, how only a cop could have known Adamson had witnessed Michaels and Romano being hanged off the bridge. Miller thought, too, of something else.

"The problem with that is it just brings us back to Roffman," he said.

"So maybe it is him after all. Or him and someone else, another cop or someone in Castello's family. Either way, I'd like to hear what the man has to say. You're positive you can ask tough questions?"

"There's no love lost between Roffman and me."

"If that's the case, then it's possible that's why you got dragged into this in the first place."

Miller nodded. "Maybe."

"We should get moving," Bechet said.

Miller didn't move. "I need to know something first."

Bechet waited.

"If you aren't helping Castello, then why are you looking for the traitor in his family?"

"If someone is looking to start a war between Roffman and Castello, I want to make sure I'm on the right side."

"And which side is that?"

"Whichever side is trying to smash Castello and his family to pieces. Hearing what Roffman has to say just might give me an idea which side that is."

"And then what?"

"Then I do whatever I can to help them. I don't care about what was stolen, or who the traitor is. All I care about is that no one gets hurt. No one who doesn't deserve it, anyway. Not Eddie, not Abby, not anyone. You can understand that, right?"

Miller nodded. "Yeah."

"My storage unit isn't far from where you live. I'll drop you off, you bring down the tape, then I'll get my gear and meet you somewhere safe."

"I'll call Roffman, set something up."

"Just tell me where, I'll be there before you."

"How will I get in touch with you?"

"When you come down with the tape, I'll give you a number." Bechet waited a moment, sized Miller up one more time, said finally, "I hope Eddie's right about you, that I can trust you."

"I'm hoping he was right about you, too," Miller said.

Bechet stepped into the office. Miller stayed where he was, could hear Bechet talking to Scarcella and his son. It was obvious that they had heard everything that had been said, despite the closed door. Bechet asked when the sedan was going to be ready, Scarcella told him it would be done by the afternoon. Miller assumed they were discussing the sedan in the next bay. Bechet was in the process, then, of changing vehicles again. A smart move, but Bechet was a smart man, not at all what Miller had expected.

Bechet told Scarcella that he was going leave his shoulder pack with them, and that he'd be back in a couple of hours. Scarcella instructed his son to unlock the gate for them. When Bechet returned to the bay, he was sliding a single cell phone into the pocket of his jeans and the younger Scarcella was behind him. The guy could have been, Miller thought, Bechet's shadow.

Together they stepped through the heavy steel door and out into the morning rain. Bechet and Miller headed for the green Jeep, Scarcella toward the gate. He reached the gate and unlocked it, sliding it back on its rollers. He waited there as Bechet steered his Jeep through. In the passenger seat, Miller glanced at Scarcella as they passed him. They made eye contact, Scarcella nodding once. It was, strangely, an almost gallant gesture, easily as friendly a gesture as Miller had seen the guy make so far. Miller looked behind as the Jeep pulled onto the back road and drove away. He saw Scarcella tugging the gate closed, wondered then what it would be like to live and work in a place such as that—isolated, fenced-in to the point of being as secure as a fortress, various ways of escape right there for his choosing.

Bechet said, "You live at the end of Elm Street, right? By the train station?"

Miller nodded. There was no point in asking how Bechet knew this. What they knew of each other, and how exactly they had come to know it, that was all irrelevant now, had to be, maybe would *always* be, maybe *should* always be. The past was, after all, the past. Wasn't it? Miller, these two years spent alone in his apartment, living his cold neutrality, had counted on that being the case, had built his limited existence around the very belief that a man could stop, strip his life bare, start over again from scratch. His years as a PI, and the years before that—terrible years when he was a young man running wild, morally bankrupt and causing harm, poisoned by a notion of privilege and indestructibility—those years amounted to *different* lives, each one a separate life unto itself, the first life having nothing at all to do with the second life except for the fact that it had made that second life necessary. *This,* then, *now,* was the life that had to count; a third chance was more than one could ask for because most didn't even get a second. So the past had to be past, that was all there was to it, for himself, for anyone who even looked like he was trying to begin again, or make good, anyone trying to resist what he was for that which he could be, if only fate would let him. And anyway, of the things that Bechet knew or might know, all that mattered to Miller was what would help him locate Abby. Nothing more, nothing less. He'd make whatever deal he needed to make with any variety of devils to get that, to get to *her.*

As if reading Miller's mind, Bechet said, "You know, she could be long gone already."

He glanced in the rearview mirror as he followed the curving back road through the woods, heading toward Noyac Road. There was kindness in Bechet's voice, Miller thought. A real thoughtfulness, concern. This all caught Miller just a little off guard. A man with Bechet's appearance—*savage,* somehow, and cunning, like some animal—wasn't supposed to sound like this.

"She could have taken off with whatever's in that suitcase of hers," Bechet continued. "Or if she's working with someone, she could have run to him. I could see her doing either of those things. I'm just saying, we might not find her. Ever."

Again, Miller nodded. "If she's long gone, then she's safe. If she's with the man she wants to be with and he protects her, then good for her, this is none of my business. But if not, if she's alone and scared somewhere, I don't want to leave her like that."

That was the previous Miller, the younger Miller, not the Miller—the *man,* bearded, almost thirty, retired, finally smarter—that he was now.

Bechet checked the rearview mirror again, then looked ahead. The off-road tires of his Jeep hissed on the wet pavement, water spattering against the undercarriage like shrapnel from an explosion whenever the vehicle crossed a part of the road that had been washed over by more than an inch of rainwater. The ride was bumpy, ridiculously so, but that was a Jeep, Miller thought—its stiff leaf-spring suspension was meant more for trails and dunes than curving back roads or, for that matter even, highways. Bechet held the wheels with both hands, steered with small, nearly constant gestures. A Jeep was, at best, a top-heavy and overly responsive vehicle, made that way by its high center of gravity and narrow wheelbase. A single bold stroke by the driver at the wrong moment could easily send the thing wildly out of control. Bechet seemed to Miller, though, to be a cautious driver. But then again, why wouldn't he be? Everything about the man, everything he did and said, seemed to be informed by that particular need, and that need alone.

They were maybe a mile from Noyac Road, fifteen minutes, give or take, from Southampton, when Bechet spoke again. It seemed to Miller that Bechet had needed a moment to decide whether or not to say what he was now about to say.

"You know, back when she was working for me, there probably wasn't a day when she didn't talk about you."

Miller heard that, didn't know what to make of it. Finally he looked over at Bechet.

Bechet thought for a moment more before deciding to continue.

"There wasn't a day when she didn't talk about whether she should call you or not," he said. "There wasn't a day when she didn't wonder whether or not she should show up at your place and wait for you to get home from work. She'd go back and forth a dozen times in one day— hate you, love you, glad it was over, miss you. Every morning when she arrived for work I'd ask her, 'Well?' Meaning, 'Did you cave, go to his place?' I expected her to at least once say, 'Yeah.' But she'd just shake her head." Looking at the road ahead, Bechet shrugged. It was more a gesture of decisiveness than indifference. "As far as I could tell, leaving you wasn't an easy thing for her to do. She just couldn't stand her nights alone. It was as simple as that. And staying away from you was . . . a struggle, clearly. Just thought you might want to know that."

Miller looked out the passenger door window, said nothing. He thought about what he had just heard. The summer Abby had worked for Bechet was the summer Miller was finally coming to the realization that being a PI wasn't for him, that maybe Abby had been right when she'd told him that redemption was to be found elsewhere, if it was to be found at all. Her last words to him, more or less, before packing her grandfather's suitcase and walking to the station to wait for the evening train. There were nights that summer—a season with a half dozen weeklong heat waves, some seemingly right after another, and a string of jobs that only confirmed the worst that people could do to each other—that Miller would find himself hoping against hope that he'd come home to find Abby waiting for him in his bed. *Their bed,* once. How he had craved that, like nothing else. *The shape of her beside him in a room so dark that the only shapes one could know were those that could be felt.* It was odd now for him to know that there had actually been a chance of his getting what he had wanted, what he had hoped for knowing there was no hope of it, that he might have come home one night to discover her presence in their empty bed, hear her words in the silent darkness, feel her breath upon his face. . . .

Miller closed his eyes now; doing so allowed him to put himself there, with Abby and what *could have been, if only.* There wasn't, after all, much else for him to do, nothing for him to see except the bleak, mizzling morning rain and the bare trees moving past his window. He was done talking for now, done listening to this man beside him, and to the questions in his head, done considering the pieces that added up, or at least looked like they did, and the pieces that didn't.

Miller kept his eyes closed for a long moment, lingering in thoughts that weren't really thoughts, memories that weren't really memories. *Such a vivid night, for one that had never been.* When he finally reopened his eyes, Miller saw that Bechet was looking in his rearview mirror. He appeared to Miller to be puzzled by what he was seeing now behind them. Deeply puzzled.

"Where the hell did he come from?" Bechet muttered.

Miller glanced at Bechet, then turned and looked through the rain-smeared back window. What he saw made as little sense to him as it had to Bechet.

A vehicle was right on their tail.

But not just any vehicle, Miller realized. A Volvo sedan. *Barton's* Volvo. On their tail and closing fast.

"Hang on," Bechet said, but it was already too late, the front bumper of the Volvo had slammed into the Jeep, not dead center but to one side, the passenger side, as if the driver of the Volvo were trying to nudge the Jeep into a spin. Not that it would take a nudge even, a single panicked pull on the wheel by the driver would, at this speed, on a road this slick, be more than enough to set disaster into motion. Bechet didn't panic, though, held the wheel firm, straining to keep the Jeep from veering off the back road. Miller looked at the driver of the Volvo, didn't see a face, only segments of one showing through the eye and nose and mouth slits of a dark ski mask. Miller's mind, as if it had just been stirred from a complex and pleasant dream, struggled to make sense of this strange reality. *What the hell was going on? What did Barton think she was doing?*

But a second nudge by the Volvo, harder than the previous one, jolting Miller like a shove, made her intentions clear. The Jeep skidded forward, then shuddered wildly as Bechet downshifted and hit the accelerator, the engine screaming beneath the hood. The Jeep lurched forward again, this time under its own volition, putting distance between it and the Volvo. The distance, though, didn't last; the Volvo's engine screamed as well and it came after the back quarter of the Jeep a third time, ramming it with its steel-reinforced nose. The Jeep was shoved forward once more, but this time, since it was in a low gear and in the process of accelerating, the extra force was just too much. Miller felt another shudder, a different one this time, the shudder that comes with the loss, regaining, and loss yet again of traction. He saw Bechet laboring to keep control, doing all the right things, but there was at this point nothing that could be done. The Jeep began to spin, and even in the best of conditions—dry roads, no Swedish-engineered car ramming him from behind, a skilled driver behind the wheel determined to take him out—there would have been little that Bechet could have done. Jeeps were simply not built for maneuvers such as these.

Miller reached for the handle mounted above the glove compartment, clung to it as the Jeep slid passenger's side first down the road. Bechet tried to steer his way out of that, and then, suddenly, the Jeep was sliding driver's side first. It went back and forth like that for what felt like forever, fishtailing, sideways and facing one direction one second, then sideways and facing the other direction the next, the Jeep's light rear end always prying its nose away from wherever it was aimed. At last, when the front tire, angled sharply, caught something resembling traction by straying from the paved road and sinking into the muddy shoulder,

Bechet made a last-ditch attempt at regaining control by turning the wheel with everything he had, trying to guide the Jeep into the soft mud. His large shoulders flexed, and his knuckles, white from grabbing the wheel, looked to Miller's eye like a tiny range of snow-capped mountains. The instant Bechet spun the wheel Miller heard a dull *clunk* from the front end, knew right then that a tire rod had snapped under the strain. Despite which direction Bechet turned the wheel now, the Jeep would remain in its current sideways slide. Miller braced himself as they rode that slide, waited for the Jeep's top-heavy design to succumb to physics and unleash the roll that was inevitable.

He felt it begin, the shift in the center of gravity, like the pull at the start of some carnival ride. Then he felt the Jeep pitch to a degree that told him the driver's side tires had given up the road. Within seconds the vehicle—he and Bechet trapped inside it—was well past the point of no return. Miller was flung against the passenger door, his hands torn from the safety handle. In an instant he was upside down, had no sense at all of the movement that had to have occurred between those two positions. As the roll continued, Miller was flung in the other direction, his shoulder colliding with Bechet's, and then, an instant later, their heads smacked together, hard skull against hard skull. Miller had never felt anything like it. Pulled back into his seat as the Jeep came over and onto its wheels again, Miller still had enough sense at this point to know that the ride had only just begun, that this one roll hadn't come close to expending all the energy that had been built up. The Jeep turned over once more, with the same speed as before, and then again, three rolls in as many seconds, maybe less. Miller's seat belt held him in place, but his limbs and head flailed as if he were in the midst of some violent fit. He couldn't hope to control them, felt as if the centrifugal force generated as the Jeep spun and spun and spun might at any minute tear his arms from their sockets.

When finally the Jeep had slowed enough that the rolling came to a stop, it was resting on its top, in a cluster of young trees a distance from the road. Miller, Bechet beside him, was hanging upside down, folded almost in half by the seat belt that held him suspended. His mind, still back in the terrible spin, was on the verge of tumbling off into darkness. He fought the unconsciousness, though, reached up and followed the seat belt to its buckle and pressed the release button. He was instantly let go, fell like a child dropped to the ceiling below. He landed hard, in a slump, little more than a pile of body parts, and it was then that he first felt the pain.

His knee, his bad knee, had already begun to swell. He could barely move it. Even when he kept it still, cradling it with two hands, pain radiated from it like heat. The pain was so severe that he gasped, then winced, drawing a breath deep into his lungs through clenched teeth. When he finally let it out, the breath quivered as if he were in extreme cold.

He looked through the windshield, cracks running through it like branches of lightning across a stark sky, tried to orient himself. His head was throbbing, from deep inside, his vision blurred, but still he managed to see through the young trees back to the road. Barton's Volvo was now at the muddy shoulder, not far beyond the curve where the Jeep had begun its roll into the woods, but it wasn't parked. Its driver, too, must have lost control on the wet pavement, or in the mud running alongside it, and had slid sideways into a tree. Miller could see enough to see this, could see, too, someone climbing out from behind the wheel of the Volvo. *Barton?* If not, then who? That person didn't waste any time, started running toward the Jeep. By the way the masked person ran, and by the shape of him as he got closer, Miller could tell that this was in fact a man, not a woman, not Barton. Running to help them? No, that wasn't likely; he had just run them off the road with a degree of expertise. As the masked man got nearer still, Miller could see that he was holding something in his right hand. A blur at first, but then Miller focused hard and was able to make out what that something was, knew once he saw it clearly what it was the man was rushing toward them to do.

Handgun in hand, the man was coming to finish the job.

He reached the overturned Jeep in a matter of seconds, stopped and looked at Miller through the cracked windshield. They made eye contact. The masked man was breathing hard. He took a few steps closer, raised the handgun, aimed at Miller. The gun was fitted with a silencer. The masked man glanced over at Bechet—still hanging upside down in his seat, unconscious, as far as Miller could tell—then back at Miller.

Slumped on the roof of the Jeep, unable to move in the confined space, Miller just stared at the masked man. He saw the man's eyes narrow, but it looked to Miller more like he was wincing than taking aim. The man lowered his gun, then raised it again. His hand was shaking. He lowered the gun once more, only a few inches this time. It was obvious to Miller that the masked man was trying to summon the guts to kill in cold blood but was unable to. The man raised the gun once more, took aim, then all but closed his eyes. He remained that way for several long seconds before suddenly turning his head, looking back toward the road.

Instantly, the masked man took off, not in the direction of the road but away from it, deeper into the woods. Miller watched him go, could barely see more than a blur by now, a dark blur—dark pants, dark jacket, dark ski mask—moving away, disappearing finally from his line of sight. When Miller looked toward the road, what he saw made even less sense than what he had just seen, what had just occurred. He saw his own pickup parked behind the Volvo, its driver's door open and someone running down the path of overrun saplings the Jeep had formed during its roll. That person yelled something—stop, Miller thought, but he couldn't be sure, there was ringing in his ears now—then stopped by the Jeep, where the masked man had stood, and assumed a shooter's stance, aimed a .45 Colt in the direction of the fleeing driver.

But that second person, whoever he was, didn't fire. Instead, he lowered his weapon, then dropped to his knees and looked at Miller through the windshield.

This wasn't a man at all, Miller saw. *This* was Barton.

"I'm here," she said. Miller could barely hear it over the sound of the ringing. "Everything's going to be okay. Just hang on, okay?"

Miller looked at Bechet then. The man was conscious now but only just. One hand was pressing against the roof below him, the other searching for his seat belt, fumbling for the buckle. There was blood running down the side of his face, and the steering wheel was little more now than a crescent moon. Bechet must have slammed into it at one point, done so with enough force to break it into pieces.

"Hang on," Miller said. But he didn't think Bechet even heard him. The man continued to fumble about, his thick arms all but useless, his eyes glazed over as though he were drunk.

Miller's eyes fluttered as he was hit with a powerful wave of nausea. It came from deep within him, ran ice-cold, overwhelmed him fast. Suddenly there was nothing to hear but silence, nothing to see but blackness, nothing at all to feel but a sickening lightness as he at last lost his hold on precious consciousness.

Part Four

Day

Nine

BECHET AWOKE IN A ROOM HE DIDN'T IMMEDIATELY RECOG-
nize, looked toward a shaded window beyond which glared a light that
was to his straining eyes both somber and harsh.

His head hurt, a dull, throbbing ache that made every inch of his skull
all but vibrate. After a moment he realized that his left hand hurt as well,
this pain the sharp, pinching pain that meant damaged bone, though to
what degree the damage was he didn't know. He closed his left hand into
a fist, or tried to anyway, had to stop just past halfway when he felt the
pain increase suddenly from pinching to blinding. Broken, then, or
maybe fractured or just splintered, but the exact nature of the injury
didn't matter, the fact that he couldn't make a fist was all Bechet needed
to know.

His first thought was that he should wrap the hand up—he was in a
strange place, couldn't remember how he had gotten there, didn't know
yet what he might need to do to get out, so an injured hand was a disadvantage he didn't really need right now. He looked around the room for
his Alice pack—there was duct tape in it, he was able to remember that.
Duct tape would do, hold his fragile bones in place and prevent him
from inadvertently closing his hand into a fist and triggering yet more
blinding pain. But Bechet didn't see the shoulder bag anywhere, nor did

he see anything at all that was familiar. He looked at his watch—if not where he was, then he could at least know when he was—and saw in the gloomy light that it, like his left hand, was busted. The crystal was shattered, the cracks like frosted veins, the luminous hands beneath frozen at 7:32. What the hell had happened at 7:32, he wondered, to stop his watch and mess up his hand and cause such a steady pain to radiate against his aching skull like an echo that would not dissipate?

When he finally tried to sit up and felt a flash of yet more pain from deep inside his chest—a real pain that stopped him dead—Bechet suddenly remembered the cause of his injuries. He was shirtless, and as he lay back down he saw a sickly bruise across his broad chest, a shocking stain of purple and black and green—inhuman colors—where his sternum had struck the steering wheel as his Jeep had begun its roll into the woods. It took him several moments—he moved in stages, carefully—but Bechet finally managed to sit up and swing his legs off the bed and place his feet on the floor. Once there, once seated, on the verge of standing, he took another look around Tommy Miller's bedroom.

The rest came to him, or much of it, he couldn't be certain; it was all as elusive and fragmented as bits of a dream close to fading from memory. He remembered a woman helping him out of the overturned Jeep, and that at first he'd been barely been able to stand. Then he remembered the woman—in her thirties, pretty in a plain way, moving fast but not frantically, not panicked—telling him to help her drag Miller free of the wreckage. Bechet, his blood still surging with adrenaline, was more or less oblivious at that point to his injuries and did what he could. Though Miller was unconscious, the rain on his face, once they had gotten him clear of the vehicle, brought him around long enough for Bechet and the woman to get him to his feet and help him back to a pickup waiting on the side of road, behind the Volvo that had rammed them and then itself crashed. Miller was limping, significantly favoring one leg, the woman and Bechet propped beside him like crutches, his arms wrapped around their necks. Bechet remembered asking where the driver of the Volvo was and the woman telling him that he had taken off on foot. The next thing he knew after that the three of them were in the front seat of the truck—its only seat—Miller slumped over between them. The woman drove them straight to Miller's apartment. Miller was unconscious again by then, and the woman had been unable to awaken him. He was too big and too heavy for even Bechet to carry—the injuries Bechet had sustained had finally begun then to register—so the woman got help from the restaurant below, a dishwasher and someone else. The owner, Bechet had gathered. These two men carried Miller up to the second floor and laid him out on a couch. Bechet remembered then being in a bed—Miller's bed—and the woman leaning over him, tending to a cut on his head. She said something, but Bechet now couldn't remember what. He looked down at the pillow upon which he had rested his head, saw a bloodied towel covering it. His blood, of course. His first thought upon seeing it was that he shouldn't forget to take the towel with him when he left. His blood was proof, should anyone need it, that he had been there.

Despite what he had been through, he was at least thinking with some degree of clarity now. That, Bechet told himself, was something.

He stood then, in stages again. Boxers work to develop an instinct that is contrary to human nature, an instinct to remain standing *no matter what,* and Bechet was running on that contradiction now. In the bathroom he splashed his face with cold water, moving only as much as his injuries would allow. He leaned against the sink, bracing himself with his good hand, and looked in the mirror, first at his face and then at the cut on the side his head. His left side, so he had probably struck the window or the door frame above it during the crash, had more than likely brought his hand up to his head at some point, as if to cover himself against a right hook. Another boxer's instinct, that particular motion. He'd been cut enough times to know that scalp wounds bleed like crazy, which was probably why he was without his sweatshirt now. Covered with his blood, someone—that woman?—had removed it so he could rest comfortably. He would need to find that, too, and take it with him. He would need to find his mechanic's jacket as well; bloodied or not, there was part of his five grand in one of its pockets.

Bechet dried his face and hands, then returned to the bedroom. The clock on the table beside Miller's bed said 9:16. It must have taken them twenty minutes or so to reach to the apartment and get Miller inside, and the accident had occurred at 7:32, so Bechet must have been unconscious on Miller's bed for about an hour, maybe a little more. Not a lot of time, but still the clock was ticking, he had less than seven hours left till he was supposed to check in with Castello, tell him something, give him something, anything that would serve as a reason for Castello to believe that Bechet was in fact doing what he'd been ordered to do, what Castello needed him to do.

That something, Bechet realized now, was right here in this very apartment.

He found a T-shirt in Miller's bureau, pulled it on. There wasn't anything about the motions involved that didn't cause pain. He found his socks and work boots, pulled them on as well, each task taking time, certainly longer than usual, though he got better at it toward the end, as he grew familiar with his various pains, recognized their specific patterns, which movement would hurt where. There were, he knew, ways around pain. When he was finally done, he stepped into Miller's kitchen, beyond which was a large front room, rows of tall windows at its far end, a few support beams down its center. Bechet saw Miller stretched out on the couch, a garbage bag filled with ice draped over his knee. Motionless, Miller was either asleep or unconscious.

Bechet looked for the woman but didn't see her anywhere. He listened, too, but heard only the rain. The exit—the only door that he could see in the entire place other than the bedroom door—was off the kitchen, opened to a set of steep stairs that led down to the street door. He remembered coming up them, someone helping him. Since there were no doors except these, there were no other rooms for that woman to be in, which meant she had left. Where she had gone and why, Bechet didn't know, but he assumed she probably wouldn't be gone for long. He needed to look around while he could.

Stepping into the kitchen, he first saw an amber-colored prescription bottle on the counter near the telephone. It was empty, the prescription, for painkillers, in Tommy Miller's name. Bechet then caught sight of his sweatshirt, caked with dried blood, in the sink in the center of the counter. He saw his mechanic's jacket, too, hanging on the back of a nearby chair, bloodstains on its collar and left shoulder. He could tell by the shape of its pocket that his money was still there.

Moving into the front room, Bechet spotted right away what he was looking for, on a table just inside the wide doorway. A DVR and VCR, coupled by RCA cables. He went to them, found his microcamera beside the DVR, fought the urge to grab it right then. He noticed that the power lights of both units were lit. He glanced at Miller, saw that he was still out, then pressed the eject button on the VCR with the knuckle of his index finger. First the whirring of gears, then out came a cassette tape. Bechet glanced again at Miller. When he was satisfied that Miller was still asleep, Bechet removed the tape, using the end of Miller's T-shirt like a glove. Could this actually be the tape Miller had agreed to give to him? It had to be. Bechet laid it on the table beside the microcamera—easy grabbing for when it came time to leave—then noticed two photographs near the edge of the table, by a pile of change and a stack of clothing. Women's clothing. Using the T-shirt again to prevent leaving fingerprints, Bechet picked up the photos by their corners. It took effort for his eyes to focus, but finally he was able to see the images clearly enough.

One photo showed an unknown man and woman, the next that same woman—dark, curly hair, an inviting smile—with another woman, the two of them sitting together on a couch. The other woman was, Bechet saw right away, Abby. He looked at her for a moment. White tank top, green cargo pants. He recalled the summer she had worked for him, remembered teaching her what he knew about guarding one's identity in this age of information, and the way to escape this island without leaving so much as a trace. She listened casually yet closely, and he had quickly gotten the sense that this was more than just conversation to her, a means of passing the long hours of work. She was looking for nothing less than ways—any way, all ways—to feel safe. She had, he had gathered over the weeks—talking while painting was something akin to therapy, or confession—always sought men out for the sense of security being with one gave her. These were her words. She had always needed someone—a man, once she reached a certain age—near, particularly at night. *So afraid of the dark, of being left alone in it.* There were worse reasons to keep someone near, Bechet thought, but he understood her conflict. He understood, too, that she simply didn't want to do that anymore, to *be* that, didn't want to have to rely on a man for anything since, in her experience, they couldn't be relied on for anything. A cynical joke, especially from one so young, but Bechet had learned a long time ago not to argue with someone about their own experience. Leaving Miller had obviously caused her anguish, so the drive to feel safe, to have someone nearby at night, was for her greater than the need for love. That was, at that point in his life, something Bechet could easily understand.

Still looking at her photo, he remembered the few Friday nights after work that he and Abby had gone to happy hour at Buckley's, the Irish pub on Job's Lane. Employer and employee at first, then finally close friends, but never anything more. They were that summer two people in flux, what would have been the point? She was beginning then to be drawn to men for what she believed they could teach her, that and nothing more than that, and he had always only seen women as temporary companions at best, so the temptation was there. But it was, that summer, for Bechet, time for *more than just that,* for something other than the less he had only known so far.

He recalled, finally, one specific night in late August when they had found themselves in what is known as a pub crawl: starting at Buckley's, then moving across the street to LeChef, then up Job's and around the corner to 75 Main, ending the night at Red Bar a few blocks east of the village. Bechet had known better than to drive home that night, instead made his way to his storage unit next door, sacked out alone on a foldout cot he kept there. Was that the night, he wondered now, that Abby had learned where he kept the gear he had told her about over the summer, the devices necessary to ensure one's safety? Was it shortly after that night that she had let herself in and helped herself to what she needed? Or had she done that recently, as recently as two weeks ago, when the camera, according to Miller, had been installed? Bechet hadn't touched his gear since putting it away at the start of that summer, when he went "legit," confident in his arrangement with Castello, Sr., and his habit of always taking the long way home, his eyes on his rearview mirror. There was, then, no way of knowing how long the camera had been missing, no way of knowing now if more than just that had been taken.

Bechet looked at his microcamera and the videocassette, considered grabbing them both, grabbing, too, his sweatshirt and jacket and the bloodied towel back on Miller's bed, then bolting from this place and calling Castello, arranging a hand-off. This tape might be enough to draw Castello out, drive him to some reckless action the result of which would be his own destruction. If that was too much to hope for, then maybe the tape would drive Castello to an action that would at least expose him, do so in a way that Bechet could take advantage of and put an end once and for all to this nightmare. A lot of *mights* and *maybes,* yes, but it was all Bechet had. With his Jeep wrecked, though, and more than likely at this moment in the custody of the police, secure in their holding pen in Scarcella's salvage yard, then how was Bechet to get anywhere? The sedan he had arranged for was not yet ready—serial numbers needed to be filed down, he wasn't messing around now, and newer tires had to be installed—and anyway the sedan, too, was back at Scarcella's garage. Bechet knew he could call Eddie, have a cab sent, but his partner was involved enough as it was. He thought about calling another company, having them send one of their cabs, but then there'd be a record connecting Bechet to Scarcella—or at least a record of a fare from Elm Street to Scarcella's Salvage. Someone, at some point, might piece that together, and Bechet couldn't take that risk. *Leave no trail.* Now wasn't the time to just forget everything he knew.

It was then, standing at that table, feeling just a little trapped, that Bechet realized something he should have realized when he had spoken to Castello hours ago, when he'd been told by Castello that there was, in fact, no record of a vehicle registered in Abby's name. Bechet knew he might not have realized this, with all that was going on, if he weren't himself facing the dilemma he was now facing—the need to leave but no means by which to do so, at least none within immediate and easy reach. If he was right, though, if what had just occurred to him was the case, then maybe there was a chance of finding Abby after all. Again, a maybe, but there it was. And not that he wanted to find her, not that he wanted it to come to that. But if *Miller* found her, put her somewhere safe, far beyond anyone's reach, even Bechet's . . .

He returned the photographs to the table, looked over at Miller, saw that he was still out. Moving past him to the kitchen, opening cupboards till he found a stash of empty supermarket bags, some paper, some plastic,

Bechet grabbed two of the plastic ones, walked into the bedroom, stuffed the bloodied towel into one of the bags, then, back in the kitchen, stuffed his sweatshirt in as well. He went through the kitchen drawers till he found a roll of silver duct tape, grabbed it, then returned to the table and put the microcamera and videotape into the second bag, tying that bag closed and putting it in the bag that contained the bloodied sweatshirt and towel. From the pile of change he picked up all the quarters there were and stuffed them into the pocket of his jeans. Finally, with the duct tape, he wrapped up his left hand as quickly as he could. He was finishing that task when he heard a sound come up from the street, the muffled *thump* of a car door closing.

He went to one of the front windows, looked down and saw a pickup parked at the curb below. The sound of the street door opening and closing was followed by the sound of someone coming up the stairs. The woman, he thought, it had to be. Alone, by the sound of her footsteps. Bechet remained by the window; there wasn't much else he could do. And anyway, there were things he wanted to know, needed to know, things that would determine exactly what his next move would be. Glancing toward the train station as he waited, he remembered standing there hours ago with Gabrielle, waiting for the last night-train west, holding her close and looking up at this very apartment for any sign that someone was watching.

Bechet turned toward the door as it opened, saw the woman who had saved Miller and him enter and go straight for the couch to check on her friend. She was carrying a small paper bag in one hand, the kind of bag prescriptions are put in, and an overnight duffel in the other. She had reached the couch when she realized Bechet was in the room. Startled, she stopped short, quickly looked down at Miller, then back at Bechet. Her eyes shifted briefly to the bag in his hand.

"Didn't mean to scare you," Bechet said.

She didn't say anything, just looked at him. Finally she walked around the couch, laid the pharmacy bag and small duffel on the coffee table in front of it. She sat on the edge of the couch. One of Miller's hands was resting upon his chest. She laid her hand on his, looked at his face for any sign of consciousness.

"He's out like a light," Bechet said.

"I gave him two painkillers. He woke up just long enough to take them. He was out of it, otherwise I don't think he would have let me give them to him."

"How's his knee?"

"I don't know. I might have to take him to a doctor."

The woman was wearing a black leather jacket. Bechet noted that one of its pockets hung heavy. By that, and the distinct shape the leather was taking, he knew the item was a gun.

"How long have you been up?" the woman asked.

"Not long."

Still seated on the edge of the couch, she glanced at the plastic bag in his hand again.

"It's just my sweatshirt," Bechet said. "And the tape that was in that VCR over there. Your friend was going to give me a copy of what the surveillance camera caught. That's why we were coming back here."

"I know," she said.

Bechet nodded, then found himself thinking about that. Something didn't quite add up. It took him a moment—he was tired, his brain crowded with all the pain signals rushing to it from various parts in his body—but finally he said, "How do you know that?"

"What do you mean?"

"You said he only came to long enough for you to give him a pill, and even then he was out of it. How did you know what he and I had talked about?"

"I heard everything you two said."

"How?"

"Tommy used to be a PI."

Bechet remembered then what Miller had said about owning his own gear.

"You work for him?"

The woman shook her head. "No."

"But you just happened to know how to operate surveillance equipment. And the way you handled yourself back there in the woods. A lot of people would have panicked, but you didn't, you took charge."

"I used to be a cop."

Bechet nodded. "That explains it, then." He waited a moment, then said, "Southampton cop?"

"Yeah."

"You're the friend he was talking about, the one helping him."

The woman nodded.

"What's your name?"

"Kay."

"Kay what?"

"Barton."

She seemed to Bechet to be waiting for his reaction, watching for it, as though her name was supposed to mean something to him. It didn't mean anything at all, but then again it shouldn't, really; he stayed away from all things having to do with the cops, kept to himself and the small life he and Gabrielle were, day by day, making for themselves.

"How long were you a cop?" he said.

"Almost ten years."

"Why aren't you one anymore?"

It became obvious very quickly to Bechet that Barton had no intention of answering that question. She looked at Miller instead, her hand still covering his. It was clear that she was looking to—needed to—comfort her friend in any way that she could, and that this caring gesture, as simple as it was, seemed for now all that she could do.

"Did he tell you to follow him?"

"His name is Tommy." She said this without recrimination or hostility, was simply stating a fact, in case Bechet had forgotten.

"Did Tommy tell you to follow him?"

"No. He was told to come alone, so he said he was going alone."

"But you followed him anyway."

"I wasn't going to just let him walk into what could have been a trap. Anyway, I couldn't just sit around and do nothing. I've done enough of that lately to last me for a while."

"If you heard everything we said, then you know what's going on. With your former boss."

Barton nodded.

"The thing is," Bechet said, "the guy who ran us off the road, he drove like a cop. That quarter tap thing he did, that's what cops are taught to do to end a chase. But you'd know that, wouldn't you?"

"Cops aren't the only ones who know how to run people off the road," Barton said. "You aren't a cop, but apparently you know about quarter tapping."

She was right, of course, Bechet thought. He had been taught that technique by LeCur, Sr., back when Bechet was in Castello's employ, when he was being made into what they needed him to be. Someone had taught LeCur. And certainly LeCur had taught his son. But that didn't really add up, did it? If Bechet was doing what Castello wanted him to do—or at least appearing like he was—then why would LeCur have run him off the road? And how would LeCur have known to wait outside Miller's apartment, unless he had been sent there knowing that Miller's place was more than likely Bechet's next stop. But, again, why? There was no reason for that, at least none that Bechet could think of. No, this had to be something else, *someone* else, someone who had both the skill necessary and something to gain, something important enough to risk an ambush in the light of day.

But *who?*

"You were behind us, right?" Bechet said.

"Yeah."

"Would you mind telling me what you saw?"

Barton shrugged, looked at Bechet, her hand still on Miller's chest. "He pulled in behind you guys when you left the salvage yard. I got into Tommy's truck and followed. By the time I caught sight of you again, he was running you off the road."

"Then what?"

"He crashed. Lost control, slid off the road and into a tree. When I pulled up, he was standing by the Jeep. It looked like he was aiming a gun inside."

"Did you see a gun?"

"No."

"Was he aiming it at me or Tommy?"

"I don't know. Like I said, that's what it looked like, but I can't be sure. He turned and looked at me when I pulled up, then started running."

"What direction did he go?"

"Into the woods. West, I guess."

"Did you get a look at him?"

"He had a mask on."

"What about his build, though?"

"He was too far away for me to see how tall he was. It all happened too fast."

"Was he fat, thin, what?"

"Thin. Average. Athletic, maybe." She thought for a moment. "He was young. I mean, he wasn't old. He ran like a man in shape."

"Could it have been Roffman?"

"No."

"Why not?"

"I would have recognized him."

"Even with a mask on, from a distance?"

"Yeah."

"Why's that?"

Again she didn't answer, looked back at Miller, clutched his hand a little tighter. Was there more to her gesture than care? Bechet wondered then.

"Anyway, I imagine you'll trace the car to its owner," he said.

"No need to."

"Why not?"

"Because it was my car," Barton said flatly. She let out a breath, then looked at Bechet.

"*Your* car?"

She nodded. "I followed Tommy in his pickup. My car was parked out front here. Someone must have been watching Tommy's place, stole my car after I left and followed me."

Again, things didn't quite add up to Bechet. It took a moment, though, before he could articulate exactly what it was that bothered him.

"But how is that possible?" he said.

"What do you mean?"

"Your car was parked out front?"

"Yeah."

"Was Tommy's truck parked out front, too?"

"No, it was around the corner."

"Where?"

"At the end of Powell."

"Could someone see his truck from where your car was?"

"No."

"How long did it take you to get to his truck?"

"Less than a minute. I ran to it."

"So unless whoever stole your car was already sitting in it when you left here, waiting with the engine running, it's doubtful he would have been able to follow you. He would have had to wait till you ran around the corner, then get to your car and break into it, get it started and somehow catch up to you. I don't really see how anyone could have done that."

"He had to have already known where I was going," Barton said.

"That's what I'm thinking. But how could he have known that?"

Barton looked at Miller then. It seemed to Bechet as if she thought doing so might help her find the answer.

"Did Tommy tell you where he was going?" Bechet said.

"Just that it was a junkyard in Noyac."

"But you knew which one."

"Not right away."

"How'd you figure it out?"

Barton's face went white.

"What?" Bechet said.

She closed her eyes, as if to prevent herself from seeing something she didn't want to see.

"What?"

"I called a friend of mine in the department," she said. "He told me about the salvage yard."

"So this friend of yours knew where you were going."

"Yeah."

"And he's a cop."

"Yeah."

"He knows your car, I assume."

She nodded. Thunderstruck, she said nothing.

"What's your friend's name?"

"Ricky," she said absently.

"Ricky what?"

"Spadaro." She started shaking her head then, a gesture of desperate denial. Her body was suddenly very stiff, her shoulders tight. "It's not possible," she muttered.

"Why not?"

"I've known Ricky for a long time. He wouldn't . . . use me like that."

"Someone might not have given him any choice."

She stood, took a few steps, stopped. She seemed now almost panicked.

"But he's just a patrol cop," she said. "There's no way he could manipulate an investigation. You said yourself that there was something in the way the investigation was being handled that was suspicious. Ricky couldn't do that, he couldn't affect an investigation one way or the other, there's just no way. Plus, Roffman hates him, and he hates Roffman. They'd never work together, not in a million years."

Alliances, Bechet knew, were often not what they seemed.

"Could he have been the man you saw running away?"

Barton struggled with that, couldn't easily find an answer—or, at least, speak the only answer there was.

"Is he fat?" Bechet said. "Is he not average or athletically built?"

Barton quickly grew flustered, pushed close to a breaking point. This was too much, too fast. She seemed almost angry now—at Bechet, for proposing such a terrible thing, yes, but also at the fact that his suspicions were, clearly, dead-right. There was no way around that, as much as she wanted one, scrambled in her mind to find one. Finally she took a breath, then let it out and, reluctantly, nodded.

"Have you called him for information before this morning?" Bechet said.

"Yeah, he's been helping Tommy and me all along."

"How, exactly?"

"With information, mainly. Things we needed to know, sometimes even which direction we should go. Also, Roffman sent him to pick up Tommy last night."

Bechet remembered then that Castello had told him that Miller and Roffman had met the night before. He remembered, too, that Castello had an informant in the department.

"What for?"

"To bring him to the crime scene."

"The canal?"

Barton nodded. "Yeah."

"Why?"

"One of the murder victims—Michaels, I think—had one of Tommy's old business cards in his wallet. Roffman wanted to know how it got there."

"How did it?"

"At first it looked like maybe Roffman had planted it. But then we started to think that Abby might have given it to Michaels."

"And that was all Roffman wanted. To know how Tommy's business card got into a dead guy's wallet."

"Not exactly. He offered Tommy amnesty if Tommy agreed to help."

"Help how?"

"I don't know."

"Spadaro and Roffman may hate each other, but Spadaro is still a cop, right? He works for the chief, would have to do what the chief says if he wants to keep his job."

"But I can't imagine Ricky doing something like this. I just can't."

"Someone built like him ran Tommy and me off the road, did so by using a technique taught to cops. And that someone had to have already known that Tommy was going to Scarcella's salvage yard. If not Spadaro, then who?"

"But why would he run you and Tommy off the road?"

"Maybe Roffman didn't like the idea of Tommy and me talking."

"So he had Ricky do that as, what, a warning?"

Bechet shrugged. "He might have done more than that if you hadn't showed up like you did."

"I'm sorry, I just don't believe Ricky could do that. He's a friend of mine, he helped me out when I was in trouble, when no one else would. And Roffman's an asshole, no argument from me, but I can't see him doing that, either. Say what you want about them, they aren't cold-blooded killers."

She stopped herself there. Neither of them said anything for a moment. Then, finally, Bechet said, "Yeah, well, like I said, sometimes people do things they wouldn't normally do."

Barton said nothing. Bechet could sense her frustration. He could sense, too, her anguish at the thought that her friend was maybe not who she thought he was. She returned to her place on the edge of the couch, looked at Miller, then reached out and laid her hand over his again. This gesture was, Bechet thought, more of an attempt to get assurance than to offer it. Or maybe it was a half-plea for Miller to wake up.

"I don't really see the point in Tommy meeting with Roffman any- more," Bechet said.

"Roffman showed up at Abby's door," Barton said. "You don't want to know why?"

"I just don't think he'd tell us. I wasn't sure what his involvement in all this was before, if he wasn't maybe being set up or something. But everything just keeps bringing us back to him. Everything points to him being the one behind all this."

"Behind what, exactly?"

Bechet took a breath, let it out. "Someone coerced or convinced two of Castello's couriers to steal from him. That someone had to have had some kind of influence. Michaels had a record, Roffman is the chief of police. Roffman could have threatened him somehow—or better yet, promised him protection. People who work for Castello know what will happen if they betray him."

"If that's the case, then stealing from Castello, even with Roffman's promise of protection, is a pretty big risk for someone to take. What they were stealing had to have been valuable to make it worth the risk."

"It was."

"How do you know?"

Bechet shrugged. "I just do."

"So what were they stealing?"

"Drugs."

"What kind of drugs?"

"I don't know for sure. My guess would be Ecstasy."

"Why?"

"Castello's couriers run the drugs from here into the city, then bring raw materials back. That means the drugs are being made out here, by someone in Castello's organization."

"He has a lab somewhere."

"Yeah. Which might explain why he keeps a property like the Water's Edge vacant."

"So Roffman somehow convinces these two couriers to steal a shipment?"

"Probably small portions of several shipments, spread out over a period of time."

"But that would be suicide. I mean, whoever the couriers hand these pills to in the city must count them, right?"

"Yeah."

"So Castello would know that shipments were arriving short, which means he'd have a motive to kill his couriers."

"Exactly."

"So then maybe Castello did."

"Right next to a building he owns, with a profitable Ecstasy lab running in the basement?"

"How profitable? What are we talking about here?"

"The materials are easy enough to get, if you know where to look. And unlike crystal meth, Ecstasy can be mass-produced. I'm talking millions of pills. Tens of millions. It takes about a dollar to make one hit of Ecstasy. Five years ago a single hit was going for twenty-five bucks. Nowadays, in places like the city, it's closer to fifty. So an investment of a million dollars can return fifty million."

"Jesus."

"Yeah."

"How much was stolen from Castello?"

"About twenty thousand pills, over a period of about a month."

Barton's eyes looked away as she quickly did the math. "That's a street value of a million dollars," she said.

"Right."

"And Castello let the stealing continue?"

"He knew someone in his organization was behind it, someone other than his two couriers. He wanted to know who, was getting close to finding out when the couriers were killed."

"In a way that would make people think Castello ordered it."

"Right. But someone witnessed the murders—a fact, at the time, only a cop could know. Not long after he made his report to Roffman, the witness was killed."

"And you think Romano's girlfriend was murdered because of that South American ethic, that 'screw with me and I'll kill you and your whole family' thing. To maintain the illusion that Castello is doing what Castello does."

"I think that's what it's supposed to look like, yeah. But I also think there's more to it than that."

"More to it, how? What do you mean?"

"I think the stolen pills went astray. I think Roffman wanted them, that his getting them was part of their deal, and instead of handing them over, Michaels kept them for himself, put them in Abby's apartment for safekeeping. Abby gets a panicked call from Romano's girlfriend telling her that their boyfriends are in trouble, so she loads up her suitcase with the goods and takes off. And ever since Roffman has been scrambling to get his hands on that suitcase. That's probably why he tried to get Tommy involved, so he'd have someone who could go places he couldn't, someone who wasn't in any way connected to him. That way no one would ever suspect he was working on Roffman's behalf. Think about it. Setting up your enemy to take a fall for murder is one thing, but making a nice little profit from it, fuck, that's just icing on the cake."

"I can't imagine Roffman selling Ecstasy on the street. Or Ricky, for that matter."

"They wouldn't have to. All they'd need to do was find someone who'd take the whole lot off their hands. Say, twenty-five bucks a pill. That's a cool half million for their troubles. Being cops, I'd imagine they'd know how to find someone who might be interested in a deal like that."

Barton was nodding, thinking about everything she'd just heard. It didn't take her long to come back again to the one problem she had with all this.

"The killers were two men," she said. "On the bridge, that's what the witness reported. That means Roffman and Spadaro—" She couldn't even finish the sentence.

Bechet watched her struggle with that, saying nothing. For a moment it looked as though she were about to speak, that she wanted to speak, to say something. In the end, though, she remained silent, her face dulled by, to Bechet's surprise, sadness.

"This tape gives me an idea of how to make what I need to happen actually happen," Bechet said. "But once everything is in motion, things are probably going to turn bad pretty fast."

"What are you going to do?"

"If Roffman wants Castello so bad, he can have him. Enemy of my enemy is my friend, and all that. Listen, you might want to convince Tommy to lay low for a while. You guys should probably even get out of town. I'm going to tell Eddie the same thing."

"I don't think I could get him to leave even if I tried. I assume he's built up a pretty high tolerance to his medication, so I don't imagine he'll be out for long. When he comes to, he'll want to go looking for Abby again, even if he has to crawl."

"What if I told you there's a chance you might be able to find Abby? Find her right now. Or at least confirm that she's gone, which would mean there's no point in Tommy looking for her, no point in either of you getting any more involved in this. Would you be interested in that?"

"Yeah, I probably would," Barton said. "What do you know?"

"When Castello tried to convince me to find Abby, he told me that she didn't have a car registered in her name. It didn't click at the time, but a little while ago it finally did."

"What do you mean?"

"When she bolted with the suitcase, after she got the call from the cottage, how did she get away without a car? If she was leaving the is-land, she would probably have walked down the street to the train sta-tion, caught the next one to the city. If she did that, then she's long gone, out of reach—for now, at least."

"But if she wasn't leaving the island?"

"Then she either had to call a friend for a ride or a cab. If she called a friend, that leaves us with nothing. But if she called a cab, there should be a record of the pick-up and drop-off."

"But if she knows that, if she was so clever about not leaving a trail, why would she do that?"

"If she had no one to call, how else would she have gotten wherever it was she was going? She probably would have taken precautions, though."

"What kind of precautions?"

"She would have had the cab pick her up somewhere in town, somewhere just far enough away from her place to be safe. You know by the surveillance camera what time she left her place, and you know the pickup would have been somewhere in East Hampton. If we're lucky, you can use that information to find out where she went. If we're really lucky, the person she spoke to was Eddie."

"Call him right now," Barton said, "and find out."

"It's better if you do it."

"Why?"

"It just is," Bechet said. He left it at that. "If there was no pick-up in East Hampton, she might have taken the train to Bridgehampton or even Montauk. Check the schedules and figure out the right times, then see if there are any records of a woman matching her description being picked up at either of those stations."

"And if there are none?"

"Then she called a friend, someone we don't know about. If that's the case, all we can do is hope she's safe. Tommy said he wanted to know that wherever she was, she wasn't alone. If she called a friend, then she isn't and he can rest easy. Or at least easier."

"Tell me something, though. Do you want Abby found so you know where she is, in case you need her?"

"No. I don't even want to know where you take her, if you find her. I just want to know she's somewhere safe."

Barton squinted. "Why?"

"Let's just say it would be better for me if she was out of reach."

"You mean out of Castello's reach."

"If things go the way I want them to, he won't be able to make good on any of his threats. But just in case, I want her safe."

"I should give you my cell number."

"It's better if you don't."

"Why?"

Bechet didn't answer.

Barton looked at him, then said, "How will I let you know if I found her or not?"

"Hang a blanket over this window if you found her," he said. "No blanket, and I'll know you haven't."

"And if I don't find her, then what?"

"Like I said, by then maybe it won't matter either way." Bechet took a breath, let it out, then said, "You eavesdropped on our conversation back at the salvage yard. Did you by any chance record it, too?"

"No."

"Take any photos?"

She paused. "No."

Bechet watched her for a moment, couldn't tell if she was lying, knew it didn't matter. He looked out the window, made a quick survey of the area. No train was due for more than an hour, so the station was empty. Living in Gabrielle's cottage by the tracks for the past year, he'd come to know the schedule by heart.

"Listen," Bechet said, "thanks for before. For the help."

"Yeah. Just so you know, I called your friends at the salvage yard the minute we got back here. They were able to tow your Jeep and my car to their lot, so as far as the police are concerned, the accident never happened."

"Jesus," Bechet said. He was more than impressed. He looked at her, then nodded. "Good thinking."

"I assumed they wouldn't have a problem with it, despite the fact that it's as illegal as hell."

"They're good friends."

"Good men to know, at least." Barton said. "You know, you should maybe get looked at. Your chest, I mean. It looked pretty bad to me. It must hurt like hell."

"It does."

"Do you have a doctor?"

"Not exactly," Bechet said.

Barton half-smiled. "What does that mean?"

"Don't worry about me. I'll be fine." Bechet crossed the long room to the kitchen. He removed his jacket from the back of the chair and walked to the door. His head was still throbbing; motion didn't help matters, was easily, in fact, making them worse, but what could he do about that? There were places to go, things that needed to be done.

He stopped at the door, looked over his shoulder. "I hope you find her," he said.

"Everyone calls you Pay Day, right?" Barton asked.

Bechet nodded. "Pretty much, yeah."

"Good luck, Pay Day," she said.

"You, too, Kay."

At the empty train station Bechet deposited two of Miller's quarters in the pay phone, punched in Scarcella's number. The short walk from Miller's apartment to the platform may as well have been a long one as far as Bechet was concerned. He had to move slowly, like an old man; a single too-quick step jarred his insides, sent a whole new burst of pain crashing through him. No fight in his professional career had left him quite like this—close, maybe, but not like this, not this broken, not this spent. But that didn't matter. It couldn't matter. Bechet told himself this, thought it with each careful step. *Too far to turn back now, too much to lose.* If anybody knew how to ignore pain, how to push through it, it was Jake "Pay Day" Bechet. He wasn't that far past his prime, that far from the man he used to be, for better and for worse.

Scarcella, Sr., answered on the second ring.

"It's me," Bechet said.

"You all right?"

"Yeah."

"What the hell is going on? I've got your Jeep here, and the Volvo."

"Yeah, I know." Bechet looked down at the plastic bag in his hand. "Listen, I'm going to need my things from your safe. As soon as possible."

"No problem."

"You think Junior could come get me?"

"He went out on a call. Actually, he should have been back by now. I just tried him on the radio, but he didn't answer."

"Did you try his cell?"

"Yeah. It's shut off."

"Where'd he go?"

"Pennies Landing, out at the end of Ox Pasture Road. Someone stuck in the mud."

Bechet knew the spot. It was a boat launch, fed into an inlet called Heady Creek, at the dead end of a road lined with tall hedges beyond which, on wide lawns, stood giant estates. Directly across the inlet from Pennies Landing was the Indian reservation, acres of unused, still wild land. If not a desolate spot, then at least a private one.

"I was about to go looking for him," Scarcella said. "He's got some married woman in town I'm not supposed to know about, probably swung by to see her. He's done this before, will probably come back and try to tell me it took this long to pull some idiot out of the mud."

"I'll go," Bechet offered.

"You sure?" Scarcella said.

"Yeah. Keep working on the sedan."

"I appreciate it, Pay Day. His lady friend lives out there somewhere, rents the gatehouse on one of those estates. He took the big wrecker, so he shouldn't be too hard to spot."

"I'll call you when I find him."

"I'll try to have the sedan ready by the time you get back."

Bechet hung up, stared down at his feet for a moment. If he didn't have the pay phone to lean against, he just might have slumped down to a heap on the cement platform. The pain was only getting worse—not just his chest but in his head and hand as well, both of them throbbing as if they, too, contained their own small but hardworking hearts. Not one of these throbs was in sync, though, had the effect then of an endless series of ex-plosions being followed by endless after-echoes. *A war within, all his own.* Bechet wondered if the prescription bag Barton was holding when she re-turned to Miller's apartment contained a fresh batch of painkillers. The idea of going back and asking for one or two was tempting. But Bechet knew he needed to think clearly, needed every bit of his smarts now, more than ever. He was down, after all, to just one good hand. And anyway, he doubted he would have been able to make it back across the hundred or so feet to Miller's street door, let alone up the narrow stairs to his apartment.

He dug into his jeans pocket for two more quarters, the last two he had, deposited them into the phone and dialed another number. This call was answered at the very end of the fourth ring.

"It's me," Bechet said. It was more of a single grunt than two words articulated. Making an effort to speak more clearly, he said, "I need you to come get me. I need you to take me somewhere."

"Yeah, man, sure. Where are you?"

"The train station."

"I'm not that far away. I'll be right there."

Bechet hung up and waited. He thought of calling Gabrielle from his emergency cell phone, wanted now to hear her voice, wanted that very much, but that meant she would have heard his, and there was no way he would have be able to hide his condition from her, not that they were supposed to hide things from each other anymore. But she was worried enough as it was, that much was certain, and anyway Bechet was maybe only an hour from leaving. Maybe even less. He decided to wait till then to call, let her know that he was on his way to her when he was actually on his way to her.

Less than five minutes later a familiar car turned onto Railroad Plaza from North Main. It was a ten-year-old Camaro, beat to shit. Bechet was glad to see it, if only because he would have a place to sit down for a few minutes. The Camaro pulled up to the platform, and as he stepped down and got in, Bechet did his best to conceal his injuries; no one, not even his friend, needed to know of his sudden frailty, the extent of the limits that his own damaged tissue and battered bones now imposed upon him.

"Shit, man," Falcetti said, "you look like how I feel."

Bechet looked over at his friend. Falcetti's face still bore the marks of the beating LeCur had given him the night before.

"Nice face," Bechet said.

"What the hell happened?"

"It doesn't matter. Just take me out to the end of Ox Pasture Road."

Falcetti shook his head from side to side, as if to say *what the hell for?*

Bechet remembered then the gambling debt Falcetti owed to Scarcella, Sr., that this whole nightmare, really, had begun when Falcetti swerved to avoid some dog and crashed his cab but didn't want to call Scarcella for a tow, didn't want to have to face him. A long way to go, then, Bechet thought, to end up exactly where one didn't want to be. Once they found Scarcella's son, Bechet would need Falcetti to drive him to the salvage yard, but there was no way around that, no one else Bechet could call. And anyway, one could only, it seemed, expect to run from one's debts for just so long, particularly out here.

"I just need to check something out," Bechet said.

"What?" Falcetti asked. He didn't get an answer, though. He waited a moment, watching his friend, his eyes on the cut on the left side of Bechet's head. Finally, though, Falcetti shifted into gear and pulled away from the station.

Bechet felt gravity tugging at him as the Camaro made a U-turn, felt it pulling him deeper into the bucket seat as Falcetti drove just a little faster than the posted speed limit toward North Main Street. Once there, Falcetti turned left and headed toward the village, on the other side of which was Ox Pasture Road.

Inside the warmth of the Camaro, its dull wipers dragging noisily across the windshield, the two old friends began their last ride together.

A long, wide boulevard one block south of Hill Street and three blocks north of the ocean, running for a little more than a mile from Agawam Lake in the village to the edge of Heady Creek. A different world, this part of town, always has been, always would be. In the summertime Ox Pasture was usually lined from early morning to dusk with trucks and trailers—landscapers, roofers, painters, tradesmen of every kind. Driving down it meant having to weave from one side to the other. Now, though, the street was empty—only those who lived on it had any reason to use it—and the Camaro rode between the towering hedges and ancient trees. A shady road in the summertime, it was almost gloomy now within the valley of the tall hedges, the battleship clouds crowded above. This being Tuesday morning—a rainy one at that, and in the last days of winter—it was unlikely that there would be anyone around, either here at the end of Ox Pasture or across the inlet, in that unused stretch of Indian land. No one, then, to hear anything, no one to see anything.

Bechet suddenly wasn't so sure if he liked this.

As they approached Lee Avenue, the last road off of Ox Pasture before it curved sharply and came to its abrupt end at Pennies Landing, they drove into a bank of ground fog, visibility instantly down to just several feet in any direction. Bechet told Falcetti to pull over, but even without the fog the landing wouldn't have been visible from where they were, only the sharp turn itself and the water beyond it and the reservation beyond that. With the fog, though, they could barely see past the nose of the Camaro.

"So what the hell are we doing out here?" Falcetti said.

Bechet didn't answer, just sat there, looking into the slowly churning mist ahead.

"Jake?"

"I don't like this," Bechet muttered. He thought for a moment, said finally, "Do you have a flashlight, Bobby?"

"What for?"

"Do you have one?"

"Yeah." Falcetti reached under the driver's seat, removed a heavy eighteen-inch Maglite, handed it over.

Bechet knew it was probably his condition—the paranoia that always came with not being at one's best, to say the least—that was causing his mind to see the potential for an ambush here. He could see the potential—even without the ground fog this would have been a private enough place for one—but he could not see who would do such a thing, nor could he see a reason, what someone could possibly gain by it. He'd been drawn out the night before by a similar ruse, lured to a secluded place on the pretext of a friend in need. But that was Falcetti, hardly a match for Castello and his thug. This was Scarcella, Sr., and Scarcella, Sr., had nothing to do with this, had no allegiance or affiliation with Castello. More than that, he wasn't at all the kind of man who could be persuaded to do something he didn't want to do, never mind bait some-one for Castello, never mind that someone being Bechet. And why would Castello even want to bait Bechet if Bechet was doing what Castello wanted him to do, what Castello had gone to such trouble to make sure Bechet had no choice *but* to do? How could Castello possibly know what was in Bechet's mind?

It was possible now, Bechet realized, that he wasn't thinking as clearly as he had believed he was back in Miller's apartment. Or maybe this last half hour of activity and thought were just too much for him, were wearing him down. Maybe he had finally reached his limit, physically and intellectually and every other way possible, had passed it and was now in a realm that was far beyond his abilities, beyond anything he'd ever known before.

The only thing that was for certain was the fact that there was no way of determining what, if anything, was going on at the landing from inside this Camaro. Bechet reached for the door handle, pulled up, wincing as he did so. The door swung open a few inches by its own weight, and Bechet nudged it with his shoulder to open it the rest of the way. He wanted to wince then, too, but didn't.

"Where are you going?" Falcetti said.

"I'm just taking a little walk. Wait here."

"What the hell's going on, man?"

"Just wait here, Bobby, okay," Bechet said calmly. "I'll be right back."

Outside, the rain fell on Bechet's bare head. He thought of his bloodied sweatshirt in the bag with the videotape back in the Camaro, that if he was wearing that sweatshirt now he could have pulled the hood up and saved himself from getting rained on. But as he stepped away from the Camaro, the drops landing on his head actually had the effect of soothing his pains. Cool, soft, like brushing fingertips in summer, *Gabrielle's fingertips.* Bechet wondered then if he had a fever, if that was why his thoughts were so muddled and the rain so comforting. Or was the cut in his scalp simply radiating heat, the way cuts sometimes did? Either way, he almost felt good, felt his agonies washing away. There was something, too, about the sound of the rain pattering on the thick fabric of his mechanic's jacket. It gave him something other than those endless echoes to listen to.

On him and around, then, a steady, soft hissing, just enough to drown out his own chaotic inner world.

He was maybe ten steps from the Camaro when he stopped. The sense that this was somehow wrong returned suddenly, overriding whatever sense of well-being the rain had created in him. The feeling ran deeper now, deeper even than the one he'd had moments ago. How could he ignore that? He wasn't used to doubting himself, but he wasn't himself now, was he? So maybe this wasn't a feeling that was to be trusted, was instead one that had to be doubted, born as it was from that inner chaos.

Bechet moved again, walking slowly. He passed Lee Avenue, looked down it, saw no houses, no cars, nothing but just a few feet of glistening pavement disappearing abruptly into fog. He had walked for close to a minute, was approaching finally the sharp turn at the end of the road, when something began to emerge out of the mist ahead. A glimpse of dulled chrome. After a few more steps Bechet saw a shape that could only be the bumper of a vehicle. It wasn't more then twenty feet ahead of him now. He knew by the sight of it, by its height and size, that this was Scarcella's wrecker. It had to be. As he closed the remaining distance, he was able to determine that the large truck was parked with its nose, not its back end, toward the water. Its back end toward the water was the position the truck would have been in had its operator been preparing to tow someone from the muddy bank of the narrow boat launch. Maybe Scarcella, Jr., had parked there with his lady friend, Bechet thought, had taken her there for the privacy this spot offered. No traffic, certainly no one launching a boat on a day like today. Scarcella, Sr., had said that the woman his son was seeing was married, so maybe her place wasn't safe and there just wasn't anywhere else for them to go. Maybe this was, in fact, *their* spot, the place where they often met.

Bechet reached the back bumper, stopped. The wrecker was large enough, the fog by the water thick enough, that Bechet was barely able to see the entirety of the vehicle. The back window of its cab was visible, though, and Bechet saw no one in it. He looked around quickly, saw nothing within the limits of the fog but the wrecker, the tall, thick hedge that bordered the property to the left of the launch, and the short reach of shoreline to the right of it. From what he could see and hear, he was completely alone here at the water's edge.

So far he hadn't encountered anything to justify his belief that this was some kind of trap. If anything, he was close to being convinced now that this was nothing more than what it seemed: a young man compulsively stealing an hour with his lover. Bechet wanted to turn around and head back to the Camaro, call Scarcella and tell him that he had found the wrecker, that Scarcella could come out here if he wanted and chide his son. But that would mean a delay in the sedan being made ready for Bechet's escape. He decided, considering what he'd been through in the past few hours, that the embarrassment of interrupting a tryst was nothing. He walked along the left side of the wrecker, came to the driver's door. High up as the truck was on its industrial-sized tires, Bechet couldn't see into the truck's cab through the window. In a way, he was grateful for that. He knocked on the door with the heavy knuckle of his middle finger. The younger Scarcella was certainly inside, he and his lover more than likely lying together across the seat. When Scarcella responded, Bechet would tell him to call his father and that would be it, Bechet's part would be done. But Scarcella didn't respond, didn't appear in the window above, to see who was there. Bechet knocked a second time. Again, nothing. He stepped back a little, to see if he could see into the cab, and it was then that there was a brief break in the churning fog, a break that allowed something to his left to catch his eye, something beyond the nose of the wrecker, in the mud alongside the boat launch.

Boots, angled in a way that told Bechet that whoever was wearing them was facedown.

He took a few steps toward the front of the wrecker, stopped when he saw someone sprawled out on the edge of the shore, one side of his body on land, the other in the shallow water.

Bechet hesitated, but only for a few seconds, tucked the end of the Maglite into the back pocket of his jeans as he hurried toward the body. He was leaving his boot prints in the mud as he approached the water, but there was no time to waste, no time to be careful. He grabbed the arm drifting in the water with his good hand and pulled as he stepped back onto land, rolling the body out of the water and turning it onto its back.

Scarcella's lifeless face—eyes and mouth opened, mud-smeared—lay before Bechet. Bechet took a few steps back, leaving even more tracks in the mud, but there was no avoiding that, either. He knew enough about death to know that Scarcella had been dead for a while, so there was no point in trying to resuscitate him, no reason for Bechet to have rushed to him and moved him like he did. But how could he have known that at the time? The last detail Bechet saw before stepping away from the only son of his friend—a face so passive yet staring at him—were the two puncture wounds in Scarcella's chest, one right beside the other. Bechet knew the weapon that had made them. An ice pick. Scarcella's shirt and jacket, where they had been punctured, were only slightly bloodied, and the water where he had lain facedown was clear. Bechet knew that Scarcella's heart had been stopped instantly by the long shaft of the ice pick, and because of that very little blood at all had run from the tiny wounds. What had come out of him had only done so by the force of gravity as he lay facedown.

But that didn't really matter to Bechet. All that mattered was that he get out of there, now. He left the body on the shore, hurried toward the wrecker. There was a radio inside, and he thought of using it to contact Scarcella, Sr., felt compelled to tell the man as soon as possible what had happened. But that would only have delayed Bechet's departure from the scene, and no good would come of that. He ran, as best he could, past the wrecker, turned the corner onto Ox Pasture Road, couldn't see the Camaro but knew it had to be there in the fog, headed toward where his rattled memory said it should be waiting for him. As he did, he saw a figure coming toward him, just the vague shape of a man in the mist. Bechet had, of course, told Falcetti to stay in the car, but what reason, really, did he have to expect Falcetti to listen? The figure was still only a featureless shape directly ahead, moving swiftly, when Bechet said, "We have to get out of here." But before there was a chance to say another word, the figure emerged from the fog and Bechet saw suddenly who it was approaching him with such directness, saw that this face was no less than the face of the man, he realized, too late, that he should have expected to now see.

The younger LeCur. The man who had bruised and cut Falcetti's face, bearing the very bruises and cuts Bechet had made on his. More than that, though, the man whose father Bechet had killed to keep Gabrielle safe. Certainly LeCur knew that, or had, like Castello, assumed it by now, because here he was, coming at Bechet with everything he had, moving with the swiftness of a sudden storm, intent—and there was no mistaking this—on killing Bechet right there where he stood.

One could only expect to outrun one's debts for so long.

Bechet reached back for the Maglite with his good hand, had just enough time to pull it free and take a wild swing at the opponent before him. It was just by luck that Bechet struck with the heavy end of the metal flashlight the hand that was lunging for his chest, fast, striking the knuckles of LeCur's left hand, connecting with it as though it were a baseball and Bechet a major-league hitter. The blow landed with a solid *crack,* and the force alone, never mind the damage to LeCur's many small bones, was enough to send the foot-long ice pick flying. But LeCur hardly registered the pain at all, made no sound and changed in no way the expression on his face, which was that of pure, focused rage. He continued toward Bechet, closing the little distance there was left between them, grabbing the back of Bechet's right forearm with his own right hand before Bechet could counterattack with a backswing. He threw himself into Bechet, or tried to; Bechet, despite his battered upper body—bruised sternum, gashed scalp, useless left hand—still had his strong legs, his boxer's footwork. He retreated, but not in a straight line, moving instead in a circular motion, giving no place for LeCur's tackle to land, while at the same time keeping LeCur within range of Bechet's favorite weapon, a looping overhand right.

He swung, all his weight and body mechanics behind the motion, slamming his large fist into LeCur's face, catching his nose squarely. Bechet heard the fine bone break, saw the blood coming instantly from LeCur's nostrils. Without wasting any time, Bechet followed up with a left hook to LeCur's head, a punch he intended on missing because his left hand was of course lame and by missing with it but still following through his left elbow would strike LeCur, an old and dirty trick. An elbow, if it hit right, was like a razor, would open skin up, and it did so as it grazed just above LeCur's right eye, in that narrow space below the eyebrow. Blood seeped from the cut, rolled fast into LeCur's eye, but by then Bechet was well into his third blow, a shovel punch—a half hook, half uppercut—with his right that landed as LeCur began to cower in an attempt to avoid more blows. It hit him flush in the solar plexus, and Bechet would have done more, wanted to do more, was feeling no pain now, feeling nothing at all but the desire to remain standing at all costs while causing as much damage as he could, as often as he could, to his opponent. The old, brutal Bechet, the savage peekaboo boxer he had once been, was after all these years back, had been unleashed for one more time.

But LeCur was already on his way down to the pavement, so Bechet did what he could to keep the brutal savage in check; this wasn't the time to become reckless. He stuck close to LeCur but held back his punches, scooting around his opponent as the man began to fall, moving with him as though they were partners in some strange dance, which, of course, they were. This restraint took all Bechet had, and because of this he knew it wouldn't last for long, couldn't last for long; a decade as a fighter, cultivating the killer instinct, the ability to hurt while ignoring being hurt was just too much to keep down. LeCur hit the pavement, was out when he had begun to fall, lay now unconscious at Bechet's feet. Bechet looked down at him for just a moment, then ran to where the ice pick had landed, grabbed it and picked it up. He felt the too familiar shape of its handle against his palm but ignored what that made him remember. He turned to start back toward LeCur, to finish this once and for all, couldn't have stopped himself if he wanted to, he was all savage now, the old Bechet again, conditioned for violence, but it was too late; LeCur, his face bloodied, flat on his back on the wet pavement, had come to, or close enough to it, and was drawing a handgun from the holster under his jacket. Not the Desert Eagle Bechet had taken from him, not even close to that, but it was still enough to make Bechet stop in his tracks when LeCur, through tearing, barely focused eyes, held it up and pointed it toward him.

"Drop it," LeCur said. Between his thick French accent and his slurring speech, the words were barely audible. But Bechet understood them well enough. He lowered his hand, then let go of the ice pick. It hit the pavement with a clanking noise.

LeCur sat up, slowly, then got to his feet, moved faster as he did that—faster but with less control. He staggered as he stood, but somehow that only served to make him more dangerous in Bechet's mind. The broken nose was causing LeCur's eyes to water, already had caused, too, dark bruises, like the black smears athletes wore, to appear above his cheekbones. Most men, Bechet knew, wouldn't have stood up after a beating like that. As tough as his old man, then, this Algerian was. LeCur's right arm was fully extended, his grip on the gun tight, his knuckles bloodless-white. Bechet's good work had only seemed to increase LeCur's rage, but that just might be a good thing since, when pissed off, LeCur obviously tossed all his training out the window. The extended arm, the gun held in Bechet's face, the fact that LeCur's weight was shifted back on his heels and not on the balls of his feet where it belonged—these were the mistakes of an amateur, mistakes Bechet was looking now to exploit.

But it never actually came to that.

Through his sneer—blood from his mouth and nose staining his clenched teeth—LeCur said, "Kill him."

Bechet looked at the young man. What he had said had made no sense at all, not till Bechet realized that LeCur wasn't talking to him, was talking instead to someone else, someone behind Bechet. Looking over his shoulder, Bechet saw a figure standing ten feet away, on the threshold of the fog. A faceless figure, his right hand hanging by his thigh, in it the unmistakable silhouette of a handgun. The figure stepped forward, its features suddenly becoming clear.

Falcetti.

Bechet looked down at the firearm, the gloved hand holding it, then back up at Falcetti's face. There was nothing Bechet could think to say.

"Shoot him," LeCur ordered. "Now."

Falcetti didn't move, just stood there, staring at Bechet. Taking a few steps back, LeCur kept his arm raised, still holding the gun level with Bechet's head.

"Shoot him," he repeated.

Again, Falcetti didn't move. A long moment passed.

"I can't," he said finally.

"Just fucking do it."

"Bobby," Bechet said. It was as much a question as a statement.

"I'm sorry," Falcetti said, but Bechet wasn't clear on who Falcetti was saying it to.

"Prove yourself, right here, once and for all," LeCur said. "Kill him."

Falcetti was shaking his head.

LeCur was losing the little patience he had. "You want your share or not?"

"Keep it."

"Kill him!"

Falcetti raised his gun, aimed it at Bechet. The gun was fitted with a long silencer. Bechet stared at his friend. The only thing he could say was, again, *"Bobby."*

His gloved hand shaking, Falcetti winced, his mouth clamped tight, his lips all but seamless. He looked as if he were trying to keep himself from crying.

"Just pull the trigger," LeCur said. "That's all you have to do. He'd kill you if he knew the truth, wouldn't hesitate for a second, trust me. You don't have a choice now. Kill him or he'll kill you."

Falcetti tried to steady his hand, failed. LeCur took another few steps back, just in case, looked from Falcetti to Bechet, and the instant he did, Falcetti swung his arm to the right a few inches, aimed his gun at LeCur and fired fast. The silenced shot was barely audible over the rain. Falcetti had fired too quickly, though, missed his target completely. LeCur spun and aimed at Falcetti as Falcetti aimed once more at LeCur, this time taking the second needed to do so with greater care. Bechet saw the look on Falcetti's face—fear, an almost baffled surprise—as he and LeCur both fired, LeCur's gunshot a flat, sharp *crack* that echoed out over the still water.

Bechet had dropped into a crouch between the first shot and the second two, watched as both men, their legs instantly buckling beneath them, went down. Nothing more happened then; neither man tried to get up or even moved. LeCur was the closest, so Bechet went to check him first. Falcetti's second aim was much better than his first; LeCur had been shot in the throat, was struggling to breathe as fine, narrow arcs of blood spurted from the gash. Bechet stood and kicked the handgun from LeCur's reach, then hurried to where Falcetti had fallen. He had been hit, Bechet determined quickly, in the left thigh. By the amount he was bleeding, though, Bechet knew that Falcetti's femoral artery had more than likely been severed, and that if Bechet didn't do something, Falcetti would bleed out, at best, in a matter of minutes.

"Shit," Bechet whispered.

Falcetti looked up at him. His face was already white. "He got me, right? I didn't just fall down."

"Yeah, he got you."

"I thought maybe I just fell. Did I get him?"

"What the hell is going on, Bobby?"

"I'm fucking bleeding." Falcetti was looking down at his own thigh now. He seemed as much repulsed as he was scared.

"That's usually what happens."

"I'm sorry, man," Falcetti said. He laid his head down on the wet pavement. There were tears in his eyes, his breathing was shallowing. "I'm sorry."

"Tell me what's going on, Bobby."

Falcetti's eyes began to flutter.

"Bobby, tell me what's going on. How long have you been working for Castello?"

No answer.

"Bobby, c'mon. How long have you been working for Castello? Why did he have Scarcella killed? Bobby, c'mon, stay with me, tell me what's going on."

Again, Falcetti didn't answer, couldn't. He was on the verge of passing out, Bechet saw this. Pulling off his belt, he made a quick tourniquet, secured it as fast as he could around Falcetti's thigh, as high above the wound as he could get to slow the bleeding. There wasn't time to be delicate, and Falcetti screamed as Bechet pulled the tourniquet tight. At least he was conscious now. With his good hand, Bechet grabbed Falcetti by the collar of his jacket and dragged him down the street to the Camaro. There was no way in hell that he could carry him. He pulled Falcetti up into a seated position and leaned him against the back tire, then saw there was another car parked twenty or so feet back. It was an unmarked sedan, similar to the one LeCur's father had been driving, no one visible through the windshield.

Without hesitation, Bechet dragged Falcetti to the sedan, propped him up against it, and looked inside. The car was empty, no keys in the ignition. Bechet opened the back door, then, squatting beside Falcetti and wrapping Falcetti's right arm around his neck, he stood, got Falcetti to his feet and shoved him through the door and into the back of the sedan. Falcetti screamed out again as he fell upon the seat, his torso inside but his legs still hanging out, his feet still on the pavement. Bechet ran around to the rear passenger door, opened it and leaned inside, grabbing Falcetti's collar again and pulling him the rest of the way in. Taking off his mechanic's jacket, knowing that shock was inevitable and that he needed Falcetti alive, at least long enough to tell Bechet what he needed to know, Bechet laid the jacket over Falcetti's torso. Closing the passenger door, Bechet took a quick look around. No one to be seen, nothing but the same rainy morning quiet, same shifting curtain of fog limiting the world. Nonetheless, it was time to get out of there, Bechet knew that.

Back near where LeCur lay, Bechet grabbed the ice pick, wiped its handle clean of prints with Miller's T-shirt, then dropped the weapon again. He picked up the Maglite, thought of his muddy boot prints by the wrecker, decided to leave them, take care of that vulnerability by tossing his boots into the East River upon his return. Between now and then, wearing them was a risk he would have to take. He stepped then to where LeCur was lying, looked down at him once more.

They made eye contact again, LeCur's stare a vague one, not like Scarcella's stare yet, but that was only a matter of time. Bechet held LeCur's stare for several seconds, watched as the last bit of cognition faded from the Algerian's eyes. Finally they went cold, his stare the blank stare of a dead man, his gasping for air done. Bechet watched LeCur's chest, waited for it to move. When it didn't, Bechet crouched down, searched through LeCur's pockets, emptying them. A wallet, another cell phone, a ring of keys. The last thing he found was the key to a motel room. The plastic tag identified the motel and the room. THE VILLAGE MOTEL, ROOM 9. Bechet collected these things together, pocketed all of them except for the ring of keys. He found the key marked GM, the key to the sedan, just to be certain he had it, then looked at LeCur once more before standing and walking finally away.

Back in the sedan, Bechet turned right onto Lee Avenue, heading toward Hill Street. Maybe two minutes had passed since LeCur's gun had been fired, maybe more, and Bechet knew that it was possible no one had been around to hear the gunshot, but that if someone had heard it, it may have been assumed that the sound had come from the Indian reservation. There were nights—often, actually—when random shots were heard coming from there. Another reason why LeCur had lured Scarcella to that very spot? Bechet wondered. As he drove down Lee Avenue, careful not to speed, Bechet listened but didn't hear any sirens in the distance, was certain he would have, even over the sound of the rain and the hissing of the tires on the wet pavement, if there were any right now to hear. He had pretty much pressed his luck enough for now, though, didn't count on that solemn peace lasting for very long. One way or another, from one part of town or another, a dead Algerian was waiting to be discovered, and once one or both were, all hell was certain to break loose.

Turning left onto Hill Street, Bechet headed west. A mile later, at the college, he turned onto Tuckahoe Road, followed that to Sunrise Highway. At the train crossing, waiting for the light to change, Bechet looked over the seat and back at Falcetti. Trembling, white, the mechanic's jacket staining with the blood seeping from the wound, Falcetti met Bechet's eyes.

Neither said anything at first. The edges of Falcetti's eyes were red, the skin raw, the eyes themselves already beginning to sink deep into their sockets. The wiper dragged across the wet windshield. The light, a long one, remained red.

"Where are we going?" Falcetti said finally. His voice was little more than a whisper.

"We're going to get you patched up," Bechet answered. He spoke flatly, then looked forward again, his eyes on the red traffic light.

"A hospital will call the cops," Falcetti said.

"I know."

"So who's going to patch me up?"

Bechet ignored that. When the light finally turned green, he made the left turn onto Sunrise Highway, continuing west.

"You've been working for Castello from the start," Bechet said.

"There's so much blood."

Bechet glanced back at him. "You've been working for Castello from the start, Bobby, haven't you?"

Falcetti shook his head, the gesture a small one. "Not Castello," he whispered.

"What do you mean?"

"I'm really fucking bleeding, man."

"Stay with me, Bobby."

Though he nodded, Falcetti was about to pass out again. There was no way to keep him conscious now; at this point, not even pain—all the pain in the world, all the pain he did or didn't deserve—would do that. There was no knowing, either, if Falcetti would survive a two-hour drive west, if the one answer Bechet had gotten—*not Castello*—would be all that he would ever get.

"Why was Scarcella murdered?" Bechet said. "C'mon, stay with me. Why was Scarcella murdered?"

Falcetti didn't answer.

"Bobby, c'mon, stay with me, man. Stay with me."

As always, though, Falcetti wasn't listening. Even when it was obvious that his friend had lost consciousness, Bechet kept calling back to him, trying to wake him. Eventually, though, Bechet gave up, focused his attention instead on keeping the sedan between the lane lines and maintaining an even speed. The last thing he needed was to get pulled over for erratic driving in a vehicle that was certainly unregistered, with a man bearing a fresh gunshot wound stretched across the backseat. *No faster than the posted limit, then, but no slower, either, and between the two lines.* This was all that was required of Bechet now, and yet, after what he'd been through, it was more than enough. He was a little grateful for his injuries, knew they would keep him from caving in on himself like a gutted building, which was what a part of him wanted to do, craved to do. But another part of him, the deepest part of him, knew that this was still so far from over. Bechet would not rest till it was, and only if it meant that Gabrielle was safe once and for all.

Whatever that took.

He followed Sunrise Highway through the desolate Pine Barrens, connecting with the Long Island Expressway at Manorville. From there it was a straight line, more or less, to Brooklyn, where the only hope for keeping Falcetti alive was waiting.

Ten

BARTON PULLED HER THERMAL SHIRT OVER HER HEAD, dropped it to the floor of Miller's bedroom, then stepped out of her socks and damp jeans, dropped them as well. Standing in that unfamiliar room, the cool air against her bare skin, she pulled her hair into a pony-tail, then got into the change of clothes she had brought with her this morning. Back in the front room, Miller still unconscious on the couch, she pulled on her work boots, laced them tight and grabbed her green parka. Slipping the Colt into the right pocket and the fresh pair of ga-loshes she had taken from the locker at the bottom of Miller's closet into the left, she walked to the couch, sat on its edge again, and reached out and touched Miller's hand as it rested on his chest. His eyes fluttered open this time, wandered for a moment, then found her above him. He focused on her as best he could, his eyelids never managing to part more than halfway. Two painkillers meant he'd be like this for a few hours still. She smiled at him but didn't say anything, and neither did he. There wasn't really enough time; Miller's eyes fluttered closed after a few sec-onds and he was out again, adrift in that murky world he knew too well. Eventually Barton stood and went to the nearby table, took one of the photos of Abby, pocketed it, and pulled on her oversized parka as she headed out the door.

Across the street, at the train station, just as she had done at her apartment last night, she waited for the cab to arrive, did so long enough to start wondering again if it was going to arrive at all. But it finally came into sight, moving toward the train station, and she stepped down from the platform, pulling up the fur-lined hood against the rain—a drizzle now—as she went to meet it. She approached the driver's door, Eddie lowering the window. Without saying a word, he handed Barton a piece of notebook paper. On it was handwriting that, to her surprise, was elegant and refined.

> No record of our drivers picking up a fare in East Hampton. Called a friend's company in Hampton Bays, had to wait for him to come in to get dispatch information. Told that one of their drivers took a fare from East Hampton to Montauk at the time in question, description of passenger matching one you gave me. Ocean View Motel, Old Montauk Highway.

Barton folded the note, slipped it into her pocket. They had agreed to communicate only via notes; after everything that had occurred, Barton figured that was the only safe thing to do. No conversation, she realized now, was ever totally invulnerable to eavesdropping

She took a look around, surveying the area, saw Miller's building, saw, too, the building to its right, and the one across Powell from Miller's place, the old brick feed barn that had been converted into an office building. Nothing, at a glance, unusual there. Looking at the station parking lot, she studied the few cars there; not one of them, from what she could tell, had anyone seated inside. It was the same with the cars parked along Elm Street. No one was watching her and Eddie, at least no one that she could detect.

Looking at Eddie again, Barton nodded her thanks. He indicated that he needed her to wait, wrote something else on the notepad, tore out the page, and handed it to her.

> You aren't the only one asking about a fare in East Hampton.

Barton looked at him. Eddie wrote down a single word on the pad, held it up for her to see.

Cop.

Barton shrugged, as if to say, *Who?*

Eddie wrote on the same page. This time it was more than just one word. He tore the page out when he was done, handed it to her.

Called my company and company in Hampton Bays. Cop said name was Roffman. Told that both caller IDs read "Town of Southampton." Number police department number.

Barton folded and pocketed that paper, too. *So there it was.* How much more did she need? Roffman, or maybe Spadaro, either way the two men, for better and for worse, to whom she had been to one degree or another close. Maybe she was lucky to have gotten out when she did. If she hadn't, would she, too, have been corrupted? If Spadaro, the Boy Scout that he was, could be, then so could anyone.

Barton said softly, "Thanks, Eddie." What would it matter who heard that?

Eddie matched her tone. "Call if you need anything," he said. "And be careful."

He raised the window and shifted into reverse, backing away from the platform. Barton watched as the cab pulled away, turning from Railroad Plaza on Elm Street and heading south. When it was gone from sight she looked once more at Miller's building, at his row of front windows and his pickup parked at the curb below. She crossed to the pickup, got in, surveyed her surroundings once more, then followed Elm to its end, turning left onto Newtown. Less than a mile later it became Montauk Highway. Watching the rearview mirror as the two-lane road carried her eastward, she made sure, just as Miller had on their way from North Sea to East Hampton, that no one was tailing her.

Montauk, at the very end of the island, was about an hour away, but despite the cautious manner in which she drove, and the intermittent banks of fog that crossed her path now and then and caused her to slow, Barton managed to reach the motel by a little past noon. Its parking lot—cracked pavement, strands of dead sea grass poking through—was empty, and the place itself looked closed. More than that, it looked abandoned.

As the name had promised, it was an oceanside motel, a single-story, ten-unit tract set on the Atlantic's edge, between the low dunes and the narrow beach-line. Though it appeared to be shut down for the season, Barton pulled over to the shoulder and parked. She put on the galoshes, watched the place as she did, then got out and stepped to the edge of the lot. The rain had stopped, but the air, grainy with fog, was still full of moisture, left a cold, thin film on her face.

She walked the length of the motel, past all the rooms, heading toward the door marked OFFICE at the far end of the unit. To the left of the door was a large picture window, reflecting the bleak Long Island sky behind her, but the reflection didn't prevent Barton from seeing inside when she got near enough. There were no lights on, no sign of anyone anywhere. Barton wondered if Abby had expected to find the place open for business, only to arrive and discover, after she sent the cab away, that she had been mistaken. Could she have called another cab from the pay phone past the office, then gone elsewhere? Or maybe she had already known that this place was closed, came here to throw off anyone who might know how to trace her trail, cause them to waste their time coming all the way out to Montauk. For that matter, instead of calling for another cab, she could have been met here by someone, some unknown friend, and taken elsewhere. She was supposed to be clever, to have learned the art of staying one step ahead from Miller and Bechet, not to mention God knows who else she had crossed paths with in the years since she had disappeared on them.

At the office door, nowhere to go from there, Barton turned and scanned the empty parking lot behind her, looking for something, *anything*—tire tracks, footprints, some piece of luck. This was all that was left for her to do. It was then that she spotted someone on the other side of Montauk Highway, a man dressed in a dark overcoat and dark pants. Behind him, parked on the shoulder of the road, pointed west, was an unmarked police car. It hadn't been there when Barton arrived a moment ago, she was certain of that. The man waved to her, then crossed the road and started walking across the parking lot toward her. She recognized him then, more by his shape—a bull of a man, solid except for his round gut—than his face.

Detective Mancini.

She headed toward the middle of the lot to meet him. It seemed, for some reason, despite her ill-feelings for the man, the thing she should do. They stopped just feet from each other, Barton's back to the motel, Mancini's to the empty road.

"Long time, no see, Kay," he said.

"Detective," Barton said flatly.

He stood with his hands in the pockets of his overcoat, smiled at her but did so guardedly. *Happy to see you, I think.* He would have, had she remained on the force—and had she, somehow, miraculously, been promoted to detective—become her boss; he had, in fact, been the one to encourage her to take the detective's exam, was pleased but not at all surprised when she aced it on the first try. But in the months leading up to Barton's resignation—when all the other cops, save Spadaro, had turned on her—Mancini had made a point of remaining abruptly neutral, doing nothing to hurt Barton but also nothing to help her. A ghost, present but seemingly, suddenly helpless. She had always considered that restraint nothing more than the act of Mancini's true self—a politician protecting his backside, playing both ends of a tricky situation, just to be safe. The whole postaffair thing could have gone badly for the department— Barton could have sued—or it could have, somehow, worked itself out, no one hurt, not permanently, anyway, in which case Mancini's behavior would have passed for, at least, appropriate.

But as proper and true to his self as Mancini's neutrality may have been, it still had hit Barton hard, like the betrayal that it was, the betrayal of a mentor. Nothing quite like that—she, of course, should know. By that cautious smile of his, she knew that there was the potential for this meeting to go a way that was less than pleasant. Which meant Mancini knew—fully knew—exactly what it was he had done to her. Somehow, that only seemed to make it all the worse. At least Roffman had acted from scorn and fear—honestly, in its way. Mancini had acted out of cold necessity, turned a blind eye to the wrong that was being done to someone who so much wanted to be his student.

Tense, then, to say the least, this crossing of paths in the empty parking lot of a shut-down motel at the edge of the world.

"What are you doing out here, Kay?" Mancini said. He was dressed, as usual, in expensive clothing—quality materials finely cut. Barton noticed that galoshes, not unlike the ones she was wearing, covered his shoes. *Always pristine, Mancini's shoes, as shiny as jackboots.*

"I'm just checking something out."

"Looks to me like maybe you and I are on the same dead-end trail."

Barton looked at him, said after a moment, "Roffman sent you out here?"

Mancini nodded, looking toward the motel behind her. "Not the best use of head detective, wouldn't you say? This might as well be Siberia. But we go where we're told, right?"

Barton looked toward the road, just to avoid his eyes. "Not fun, being left out in the cold, is it?" she said. She looked around the lot once more, then concluded, "Nothing here, I guess. I'll see you, Detective." She started toward the road.

"Tommy sent you out here, didn't he?" Mancini said.

Barton stopped, was standing shoulder to shoulder with Mancini now. He hadn't moved, kept his back to the road. She looked at him, said nothing.

"I mean, he sent you out here to find his ex-girlfriend, right?"

"I'm here on my own," Barton said.

"If you are, that means you found out where the girl lived. How else would you have known to come here, right? You traced her here, just like Roffman did, didn't you?"

"What do you want, Mancini?" Barton said.

"I want to help."

"You want to help yourself, is what you mean."

Mancini nodded. "You're still pissed off about that, fine, I understand that. I'm sorry about what happened to you. It was a stupid thing for you to do to begin with, but you didn't deserve what Roffman did to you. I mean, it takes two to tango. If there was anything I could have done, I would have, you have to know that. It's fucked-up, yeah, but women are still punished for ambition while men are rewarded for it, that's just the way it is."

Barton felt a cold chill of anger. She did what she could, though, to hide it. "What happened between Roffman and me wasn't me being ambitious."

"I get it, I do. A woman like you would be drawn to a man like Roff-man."

"A woman like me?"

"We all have our issues, Kay. I don't think there's a person walking around who doesn't have some kind of father issue, man or woman. Roffman had all the power in our little world; he could help you, teach you what he knows, make sure you get the attention you deserve."

"What does that mean, the attention I deserve?"

"You're a smart woman, talented, even. You would have made a fine detective, clearly. But our department is a boys' club, always has been. You had to have known, on some level, anyway, that you were going to have to do something to make yourself stand out."

"So I woke up one morning and decided to have an affair with the chief of police."

"Of course not. He picked you to be his driver, you two spent a lot of time together. Your issues made him attractive to you, and his issues made you attractive to him, it was only a matter of time and all that. But it's seldom what something really is on the inside, Kay, it's how it looks on the outside, you know that, or should by now. That's what matters, that's what your friend is about to find out the hard way."

"What do you mean?"

"Roffman claims he got an anonymous tip early this morning that led him to where the Shepard girl was living. That's why I'm out here in no-man's-land, wasting my time. But if you ask me, Roffman already knew where she lived."

Barton thought of what the camera outside of Abby's apartment had caught. She looked at Mancini, said, "So what does this have to do with Tommy?"

"Roffman searched her apartment this morning, found out that her phone was registered in Tommy's name."

"That was fast."

"No need to involve the phone company. One of the cops with him called his own cell phone from her phone. Tommy's name as clear as day came up on the caller ID."

"Roffman has cops with him? He's not doing this alone?"

"There are a handpicked few he apparently trusts. Patrol cops, no one higher than that. If he doesn't trust them, then he at least controls them or holds something over them."

Before Barton could ask the inevitable questions, Mancini continued.

"So first there's the business card connecting Tommy to one of the murder victims, and then one of the murder victim's girlfriend's phones turns out to be in Tommy's name. If Roffman didn't think Miller was involved before, he has to now."

"Involved how, though? In what?"

"Roffman doesn't actually confide in me these days, you know, but he must think Tommy is trying to set him up or expose him or something. He never believed that Tommy was retired, figured he was just lying low, waiting for his chance. Roffman's been keeping a close eye on Tommy ever since. The guy's paranoid, I'm telling you, Kay. He's like Hitler in his last days. A real bunker mentality."

"Tommy has nothing to do with this, Mancini. Not a single thing. He just wants to find his ex, make sure she's okay."

"Like I said, it's how it looks, Kay. That's what matters."

"But why would Roffman think he's being set up?"

"He's owned by Castello, everything he does is on Castello's behalf. Whatever he's up to now—it looks like he's manipulating an investigation—he's got himself out on a limb, is probably looking for somewhere to land in case the limb breaks. Someone setting him up—if not proof of that, then at least the suspicion of that, circumstantial evidence indicating that—just might be the best place for him to fall. A onetime PI who has a well-documented history with Roffman and a chip on his shoulder, who better for the job, right?"

"Roffman came to Tommy, asked for his help."

"Yeah, and promised him a twenty-four-hour amnesty. What kind of bullshit was that?"

"Why would he do that if he thought Tommy was out to get him?"

"Maybe he was hoping Tommy would lead him somewhere. Maybe he wanted Tommy to get caught somewhere he shouldn't be, to add to the illusion that Tommy was conspiring against him."

Barton thought of the cottage in North Sea, the fact that the police had arrived just as Miller was looking through the place for a second time. It all added up, what Mancini was saying, but so had what Bechet had proposed. There could only be one true sum to that equation, though. But whose sum was it? The onetime enforcer for Castello, or the detective with the heart of a politician?

After a moment, Barton looked at Mancini and said, "You think Castello is behind these killings after all, that Roffman is trying to cover up for him."

"Roffman took over the case, Kay. Locked me and certain others out, is keeping yet others very close to him. Low-level cops, desperate to prove themselves loyal, for a promise of promotion."

"Which others, exactly?"

"Your buddy, for one."

"Ricky."

Mancini shrugged. "It looks that way, yeah."

"I don't believe that."

"Spadaro pretty much shot himself in the foot by sticking up for you, Kay. It'd take a grand gesture for him to make up for that with Roffman. I mean, Spadaro has to have realized by now that his career is heading nowhere, that for him to keep his job, let alone move up, he has to play nice with Roffman."

It made sense, it all did, but when push came to shove, Barton still refused to accept it.

"What else could it be?" Mancini asked.

"Something else."

"Yeah, but what?"

"Do you think it's possible that Roffman could be trying to bring Castello down?"

"What do you mean?"

"You think Roffman has taken over the case so he can sweep things under the rug and protect Castello. Someone else thinks Roffman is behind these killings, that he coerced the couriers into stealing and then killed them or had them killed so people would think Castello was behind it."

"Who thinks that?"

"It doesn't matter. But there's a third possibility here."

"What?"

"That Roffman sees what's going on as a chance to get out of Castello's pocket."

"What makes you think that, Kay?"

Barton shrugged. "It's just a . . . hunch."

Mancini looked at her closely. "What do you know, Kay?"

"Nothing. I just can't see Ricky doing either of the things you guys suspect him of doing. I don't see him being part of a coverup or going along with murder. I just don't see that."

"Roffman could have given him no choice."

"That wouldn't matter."

"So what do you think is going on?"

"I think Roffman is trying to keep the investigation on track by taking charge of it, and Ricky is helping him."

"That's a stretch, Kay."

"To me it's less of a stretch than what I've heard so far."

"Tommy came running to you after his meeting with Roffman. Did you tell him something? About Roffman? Do you know something?"

"No."

"Then why the hell do you think all this is some elaborate plan of Roffman's to get rid of the man who has been buttering his bread for the last ten years?"

Barton didn't answer at first. Then, finally: "Tommy and I found a surveillance camera outside Abby's apartment. It was wirelessly linked to a DVR inside."

"Yeah, so?"

"On it were two weeks' worth of recordings. One of the recordings shows Roffman coming to Abby's door once."

"When?"

"Two nights before the murders, before last night. He knocked on the door and then just left."

"So Roffman did know where the Shepard girl lived. He lied about getting the anonymous tip this morning."

"That's the thing, though. I don't know if that necessarily means he knew her."

"Why not?"

Barton shrugged. "Something about the way he knocked on her door.

Like he was there for the first time. Like maybe he wasn't even sure why he was there."

"What do you mean?"

"I know Roffman. You're with a person for a time, you know them, right? It's just a hunch, I know, but what if someone tricked Roffman into going there, lured him there so there'd be a record of him coming to Abby's door?"

"Why would someone do that?"

"I don't know. I just know Roffman, and I know Ricky, and none of what anyone is telling me adds up."

"No offense, Kay, but female intuition doesn't really impress me. It sounds like your grasping at something to clear your friend and your ex. And *that* doesn't really make sense to me. I mean, I'd think of all people, you in particular would be glad to see Roffman fall flat on his face."

"Not if it means two killers go free."

"If not Roffman and Spadaro, then who was on the bridge last night? Who killed the restaurant owner?"

"Castello was under the impression that he had a traitor in his organization."

Mancini said quickly, "How do you know that?"

"I just do. Maybe this traitor and someone else killed the two couriers. Maybe they killed the restaurant owner and Romano's girlfriend."

"Hayes," Mancini said. "Her name was Hayes. She had a police record."

Barton thought about that, the photos of the girl, her and Abby together, laughing, kissing. She was glad now, at least, that the poor girl had a name.

"Maybe whoever is doing all these killings is playing Roffman and Castello against each other."

"Again, why would someone do that?"

"I don't know. To start a war. Or maybe to expose their relationship."

"That's a great theory, Kay, but how could we prove that?"

Barton looked away, toward the empty road, Miller's truck pointed in one direction, Mancini's car on the opposing shoulder, pointed in the other.

"I wish I knew," she said.

"Did you and Tommy take the DVR with you? The one you found in Abby's apartment."

"Yeah."

"And the camera?"

Barton nodded.

"That's a real piece of luck," Mancini said. "If you hadn't gone there and found it, Roffman would have it now. Whatever it turns out to mean, we might never have known it even existed. Do you still have it?"

"It's safe," Barton said.

"However this turns out to be, Kay, that's evidence—of something, at least. Whether Roffman is covering up for Castello or he's trying to nail Castello, the tape means *something*."

"Like I said, it's safe."

"So tell me, how does it feel?"

"How does what feel?"

"To hold in your hand the life of the man who ruined yours?"

Barton said nothing.

"Where will you be?" Mancini said. "In case I need to find you."

"Back at Tommy's."

"I'm surprised he didn't come here himself. Is he okay?"

"He's fine. I was hoping to find Abby so there would be no reason for him to get any more involved than he already is. At least we would have done everything that could have been done."

"Roffman will probably keep me here all night. I'm out of his hair out here but, for the record, on the case. I doubt I will, but if I hear anything, I'll let you guys know, okay? If you hear something, you know how to reach me."

There was a part of Barton that hoped there would be no reason to hear from Mancini again, ever. There was, too, a part of herself that wanted her and Miller's part in this to end here and now. *Nothing more than that, nothing left to do but heal.*

She said, "I'll see you, Detective," and left Mancini in the middle of that empty parking lot. She took several strides before he spoke. When he did, she stopped, listened without looking back.

"You know, if Roffman falls on his face, I'll probably be appointed acting chief while they look for his replacement. If that happens, I'll be

able to hire whomever I want. Do you think there's a chance you might
be interested in coming back? I'll probably need all the allies I can get.
Smart ones, even more so."

Barton said nothing.

"Like I said, I've always believed you'd make a hell of a detective. So
at least think about it, okay? I hate to think of all your talent and hard
work going to waste. I mean, you can't want to work at a liquor store for
the rest of your life."

Barton said again, "I'll see you," then crossed the parking lot to the
street, got into Miller's pickup. She didn't look back as she went, wanted
only to get the hell out of there, get away not just from Mancini but also
from the last known whereabouts of Abby Shepard and her antique suitcase.

It was one thirty and raining still in Southampton when Barton
reached Miller's apartment. He was exactly as she had left him. She sat
beside him again, touched his hand, but he didn't wake up this time. She
needed to wash away the cold film still clinging to her face, felt it now on
her entire body, so in Miller's bathroom she undressed and ran the
shower, stepped under the heavy stream. The sound of the water relaxed
her, allowing her tired mind to wander, and it wasn't long at all before it
came to her, before everything suddenly clicked and the true sum of the
equation and what it meant—what it had to mean, could only mean—
was right there before her.

Despite the warm water washing down her, she felt a chill spill
through her, tumbling down from her head to her groin. Her slender
legs were suddenly very weak, and her heart ached as if she had just run
for miles and miles in frigid cold.

It took a while for her to shake off the inevitable physical reactions
that came with knowing what she now knew. Still, even as she recovered
from them—strength returning to her slender legs, her heart calming—
she was faced with the question of what to do with this knowledge. She
wasn't certain if there was anything that could be done, anything *she*
could do. After all, who was she? Just a nobody. That much had been
made painfully clear. She felt, though, a sense of purpose as she dressed,
felt it growing inside her, into an urgency. To think this through, she
went to Miller's front windows, stood at one and looked across to the

train station. There, staring out but not focusing on anything, letting everything in the visible world smear into a soft, rainy blur, she realized eventually what it was she would have to do, the only thing, now that she knew the truth, that she could do.

If Mancini wanted help, then maybe that was just what she would give him.

By the table upon which the equipment lay, she opened her cell phone and dialed a number, waited for her call to be answered. A risk, but at the same time, not really, not if she was right, which she knew she was.

When the call was finally answered, Barton said softly, "It's me." She looked at Miller, making sure he was still unconscious, then continued. "You and I need to talk. I'll meet you anywhere you want, but it has to be right now. This can't wait." She listened for a moment, then said, "All right, I'm leaving now. I'll meet you there in a few minutes."

Ending the call, she looked at her watch. It was just after two o'clock.

Though the afternoon sun was obscured by colliding clouds with steely black hulls, Bechet could still find its place above the crooked city skyline. Visible like a wound bleeding through bandages, its position, sinking bit by bit, told him that he had still a few hours till nightfall, when he would need to call Castello from a Southampton pay phone. There was time yet, but not much—less, of course, with each moment Bechet spent standing around and waiting for what he needed before he could make the return drive east.

In the elevated office he had converted into a bedroom and storage area—a fortress within a fortress, the safest place in his world—he waited for Gabrielle to finish checking Falcetti. The sedan was parked in the small loading dock, the garage-style door leading out to the street locked and bolted again, Falcetti, at last check, unconscious in the backseat. Bechet had called Gabrielle from his cell phone once he was a few streets away—he didn't want to tell her that he was on his way till he had actually entered his neighborhood—and told her that Falcetti was badly hurt, to get the first-aid kit from the bedroom and ready everything she would need to treat a gunshot wound. She wasn't surprised, then, when she saw

Falcetti curled up in the backseat, but she hadn't expected there to be so much blood. Just looking at it was enough for her to know that there probably wasn't much she could do. Falcetti's paper-white face and sunken, glassy eyes, once she looked up at them, only confirmed this.

Still, she and Bechet tended to the guy, moving quickly as they cut up the leg of Falcetti's jeans to expose the wound, then cleaned and dressed it. Bechet's kit, of course, was more than complete, contained even what Gabrielle would need to remove the bullet. But there was, she had said, no point in that; Falcetti had lost too much blood, and cutting into him now would only make matters worse.

As he waited now in his bedroom for Gabrielle to return from below, Bechet felt hungry and stepped away from the window, found a box of Clif Bars among his supplies, opened it and removed one, eating it as he stood back at the window, not far from the bed in which Gabrielle had spent her lonely night. A few minutes after he finished she was standing in the bedroom doorway, her arms folded low across her stomach.

Still looking out the window, Bechet said, "How is he?"

"Not good. I don't think it will be long now."

"Any chance he might come to first?"

"I don't know. Why?"

"I need to talk to him. I need to know what he knows."

"I thought you guys were friends."

"We were."

Gabrielle took a step into the room. "We should have taken him to a hospital, Jake. He might have had a chance if we took him when you first got here."

Bechet shook his head. "It would have been too much of a risk, Elle."

"Because it's a gunshot wound."

"Because it would have meant leaving a trail. Even if we had just dropped him off outside the emergency room and driven away, their security cameras would have caught us and the cops would be looking for us. We don't need that right now."

Gabrielle waited a moment, then took a few more steps into the room, stood at the opposing window, the one overlooking the interior of the building. She looked at the wire mesh running through the plate glass, then past it, first at the sedan in the loading bay, its back doors open,

Falcetti visible through the back window, and then toward the far end of the open room, the corner where a speed bag platform was mounted on the brick wall and a heavy bag hung on a long chain from a crossbeam high above. Leaning up against a wall not far from that corner, under a tarp of clear plastic, was an old motorcycle.

Gabrielle studied all this, remnants of a life she knew so little about. Finally she looked back at Bechet.

"Are we going to talk about what's on, Jake?"

Bechet thought for a moment, nodding. "You should have been a doctor, Elle," he said. "The way you handled yourself down there." He looked over his shoulder at her. "Your hands never shook once."

She shrugged. "I wasn't ever bothered by the sight of blood, even when I was kid." She paused, then said, "How about you?"

"How about me what?"

"Does the sight of blood bother you or are you used to it?"

There was no way Bechet couldn't know what she really meant by that. He looked out at the skyline again.

"It wasn't like that, Elle."

"It wasn't like what?"

"What I used to do."

"What exactly did you used to do?"

Bechet took a breath, let it out. "I've killed two men in my life, Elle. The first one was years ago. I did it for Castello." He held out his left arm, showed her the dark star tattooed on his inner forearm. "That's what this means. One kill. Like fighter pilots. Five of these means you're an ace. The second man I killed was the man who taught me how to kill and get away with it. When I last knew him, he had nine of these on his arm, one kill shy of a double-ace. That was years ago, so he probably had more when I killed him."

"And when was that?"

"Last night." He turned to face her. "I did it for you."

Gabrielle winced slightly, saying nothing.

"The guy who shot Bobby in the leg, he had three of these tattoos. He was the son of the man who taught me. The man I killed."

"Why would he shoot Bobby?"

"Because Bobby was working with him."

"Doing what?"

"That's what I need Bobby to tell me."

"So if Bobby was working for him, why'd he shoot Bobby?"

"Because Bobby wouldn't kill me."

Gabrielle thought about that. "This guy, where is he now?"

"He's dead."

"How?"

"Bobby killed him."

"Jesus, Jake."

"I put that life behind me, Elle. I've tried every day to make up for that first man I killed. Everything I do is to . . . separate me from that. But I make no apologies for the second man. He was a dog, would have killed you and cut you into pieces and scattered them God knows where."

"Stop, please."

"You need to know this, Elle. I need you to understand what it is I'm trying to protect you from."

"If you left that life behind, then why was this man going to kill me?"

"Because my old boss wanted me to come back to work for him. I've been living the way I live so he wouldn't be able to find me. That's how much I was determined to never go back."

"But what were you doing there to begin with, Jake? How could you . . . ?" She didn't finish her sentence, couldn't.

Bechet walked into the bathroom. The old tub by the large window, the industrial-sized water heater in a corner, even more dry goods stacked in boxes. In another corner, a dark one, stood a metal filing cabinet. With his good hand, Bechet opened the top drawer, removed a heavy file, carried it into the bedroom, then dropped it on the unmade bed.

Gabrielle looked down at it, reached down finally and opened it. Inside were newspaper clippings. She read the top one. It was about a man called the Iceman.

"What are these?" she said.

"Articles about my father."

Gabrielle flipped through a few of the clippings on the top of the pile.

"He used to kill people," Bechet said. "It was his job. I didn't know it, barely knew him, in fact, but after he died it all came out. It turns out the feds were closing in on him, suspected him in close to fifty murder-for-hire cases, most of them in the city."

Gabrielle glanced at a few more articles—headlines, for the most part, a few paragraphs here and there—then looked out the window at the open space below. The loading dock, the drain in its floor, the lack of street-level windows. She understood then what it was Bechet's father had used this place for. A sudden chill made her shiver.

Closing the file, Gabrielle looked at Bechet. "How'd your father die?"

"Heart failure." He shrugged. "Natural causes."

She nodded, waited for more.

"When my boxing career was over," Bechet said, "I didn't know what to do. I'd made okay money as a fighter, but after paying managers and taxes—and just the general cost of living in the city—it was pretty much all gone. I'd inherited these buildings by then, but they were my security, you know. I figured when I was an old man, I could always come here to live. Or maybe one day turn this into a neighborhood gym, find fighters of my own, train them and manage them. So even though I needed the money, I didn't want to sell out, not unless I had to. I mean, they'd only get more valuable, right? So I hung onto them while I tried to keep the life I had made for myself going. I was used to a certain way of living, you know?" Bechet shrugged. "Pride, I guess. People tell you that you're the next big thing long enough and you start to believe them, start to count on it, think you deserve to live like the next big thing. The question was, how? Then one night a friend of mine introduced me to a man named Jorge Castello. A South American businessman, he reeked of money, living the life. He tells me he's got some businesses out on the island, would I like to come work for him? Security, he called it, but I knew what he meant. What else would someone hire a man like me for?"

"So you knew from the start what you were getting into."

Bechet nodded. "Yeah. I don't expect you to understand this, Elle, but it wasn't just a job, it was a chance to be part of a family. Castello was this fatherly kind of guy, he and his son and the man who trained me, they took me in to where they lived, treated me like one of their own. I knew what kind of men they were, I wasn't being fooled or tricked, but still there was something . . . seductive about the whole thing. Money, travel, living higher than I'd ever known. Living the way I would have lived had I become what everyone said I was going to become, the next big thing. Any . . . distraction I wanted I could get. Castello and his son, they knew what they were doing, in every possible way."

"What do you mean?"

"Picking me in the first place. To be a boxer, you need a certain mentality. They recruited me because I was already preconditioned to violence, already so used to it. It would be easier for them to make me into what they needed me to be."

"And you let them."

He nodded. "The step from boxer to what they wanted me to be, it wasn't really that much of a stride. And since there was nothing else I could do to earn money—the kind of money I was used to—the step seemed even shorter."

"And then one day you just quit."

"One day I found a way out, yeah."

"How long ago was this?"

"A long time. Over six years."

"And all of a sudden, after all these years, they want you back?"

"More or less, yeah."

"How'd they even find you?"

"Through Bobby. Somehow he got mixed up with them."

Gabrielle thought about all that, watching Bechet closely, nodding. "So now what?" she said finally.

"I need to talk to Bobby to know that."

"And what if you don't get to?"

Bechet looked out the window at the city. "I don't know."

Gabrielle walked to him then, stood beside him.

After a moment, Bechet said, "I'm curious about something, Elle. Why didn't you go back to school after your parents were killed?"

"I told you. I didn't have the money."

"Your folks were wealthy, though. They didn't leave you anything? There wasn't any life insurance?"

"They were living the American dream."

"What do you mean?"

"They were living far beyond their means. Even people of means can do that, it seems. They had nothing but debt. Their debts had debts. Whatever didn't go to paying what they owed went to the lawyers."

"Why didn't you take out a student loan?"

Gabrielle shrugged. "I was debt-shocked, the idea of owing anyone anything freaked me out."

"Couldn't you have gotten a fellowship or grant or something?"

"Probably."

"So why didn't you?"

"Maybe I just didn't want to go back. Maybe I was in med school because my father wanted me to be."

"Do you think that that's true?"

"I don't know. Maybe the reason I keep myself so busy now is so I don't have to think about it too much."

"I can't imagine you want to wait tables the rest of your life."

"It's not that bad."

"For now, maybe."

"Our life was good, Jake. Simple, honest."

"Was?"

"I'm not so sure we could go back to the way things were."

"So what do we do?"

"I love you. Not much that can change that."

"I love you, too, Elle."

"So we've got that going for us." She smiled, waited for his. He offered her the best that he could manage. She watched him for a moment, then said, "This is going to sound weird, but I've never been with anyone before who hadn't known me as a daughter. I mean, that's what I was for so long, my parents' daughter. It wasn't such a bad thing—my parents really were my best friends, part of my everyday life, there for pretty much every major decision I ever made. When they were killed I was . . . lost. I was just . . . lost. I didn't have a clue who I was without them, I really didn't, but the one thing I did know was that my life as I knew it was over. *I* was over. It was more than just being broke, more than having to leave school to make money and pay my bills. It was simply that what had been there all my life was suddenly gone—I mean, like it had never even been there. When you and I met, we agreed not to talk about our pasts. For you it was because you had a past you didn't want to remember. But for me it was because I didn't have a past at all. Every-thing and everyone was gone. The idea of living . . . adrift with you, be-ing a mystery to someone who was as much a mystery to me, was more than a conscious choice, it was all I could do. Every day I'd wake up and realize that what you knew of me—*all* you knew of me—was what you had seen the day before, and the day before that, going back to the day we'd met. It was surreal, literally, and that was probably what appealed to me the most about it. We were living in our own little world, never straying too far from where we felt safe, saying so precious little about ourselves, who we were before. Eventually what you knew of me be-came what I knew of myself. Eventually Gabrielle Marie Olivo the daughter was replaced by the woman you call Elle, the woman who works six days a week and sleeps a lot and loves this guy named Jake who likes to live in a way that will allow him to take off at any moment and leave no trail."

"What are you trying to say, Elle?"

"All the time we were hiding, it never really dawned on me that it was death we were both hiding from. Deaths in our respective pasts—different sides of it, though, you know?" She waited a moment, then said, "If we're going to continue, we're going to need to be a little more . . . realistic, we're going to need to know things about each other. Everything."

Bechet nodded. "Fair enough."

"Don't get me wrong, Jake. It was fun, there was something . . . grat-ifying in not being burdened by our pasts, not being identified by them. In its own way, oddly enough, it was healing. But like I said, it's just time now to be realistic again."

"You should really think about going back to school, Elle. I mean, if a doctor is what you want to be, don't let fear stop you."

"Debt makes me nervous still."

"I could pay for it."

"How?"

"I could sell these buildings. Or just this one, keep the one next door for security's sake. Don't need both, and the rent I collect from next door would more than pay for a decent enough place in Cambridge."

Gabrielle smiled again. "Thanks, Jake, but if I decide to go back to school, I'll find a way to do it. I'm a big girl."

"A doctor in the family might be a good thing, is all," Bechet said. "Anyway, we'll talk about it. I think maybe there's a difference between accepting help and relying on it." He had stepped to the opposing window as he spoke, was looking now down at the sedan.

"So what's next?" Gabrielle said.

"I'm going to need to go back to Southampton in a little while."

"What for?"

"There's one loose end I need to tie up."

"I want to come with you."

"You better not."

"Why?"

"Because alive or dead, I'll be bringing Bobby with me. If I get pulled over, I'd rather you weren't sitting next to me."

"How long will you be gone?"

"Not long."

"I don't want to wait for you here. Not now."

"Take a cab into the city, check into a hotel, don't tell me which one. Stay there till I call you, okay? If when I do call I call you Elle, it means everything is okay, tell me where you are and I'll be there in two hours. If I call you Gabrielle, though, hang up and get out of town."

Bechet, always cautious, always thinking steps ahead.

"And what if you don't call at all?" Gabrielle said.

He knew by her eyes what she was thinking. One evening her parents had gone out for dinner and never come back. That was a drive on a foggy night that turned bad. This would be a drive on a foggy night in a stolen sedan with a dying gun-shot man in the backseat, not to mention a driver with an injured hand, cracked head, and bruised sternum working on no sleep.

"You'll hear from me, Elle," Bechet said. "I promise."

He phoned for a cab, took all the money from his pockets and put it into Gabrielle's ditty bag, the one she had carried with her when she fled their old life. When the cab arrived a few minutes later, he led her outside. It had stopped raining, and at the open back door, while the driver watched them, Gabrielle kissed Bechet, hard, as if, somehow, they had never been lovers and this kiss, initiated by her, was their first. Then she got into the cab, sat with the bag on her lap. Bechet closed the door, and she looked at him through the window in the seconds before the cab pulled away.

When it was gone from sight, Bechet surveyed his street. A row of two-story brick buildings like his own, most of them unoccupied, their windows boarded over. Three blocks to the east was the heart of Williamsburg, an enclave for artists and young hipsters. To the west, just feet from his heavy steel door, was the edge of the East River.

Back inside, in his bedroom, Bechet searched till he found a handheld digital recording device, loaded in a fresh battery, then grabbed a tube of smelling salts from his first-aid kit. Back down on the loading dock, he crushed the tube and held it directly under his friend's nose till he regained consciousness. It took a moment, but once Falcetti was alert enough, Bechet tossed the broken tube away and then sat behind the wheel of the sedan, facing forward. Looking over his shoulder into the backseat, he watched Falcetti struggle to make and maintain eye contact. There was, finally, cognition, but Bechet knew by the look of his friend this was not only his chance, it was the only chance he was going to get.

He switched on the recording device, laid it on the seat beside him.

"I need you to tell me what's going on, Bobby," he said. "I need to know what you know, and I need to know it right now."

Falcetti was wrapped in an old blanket, his head propped up on a pillow. His breathing was labored, there was a rattle in his chest, and his lips were dried and cracked. The marks of the beating he had taken the night before, though still visible on his face, were the least grave-looking thing about him now.

"I don't really feel so great," he muttered. "Can I have some water?"

"We don't have a lot of time, Bobby. We'll talk first, then I'll get you some water."

"What do you want to know?"

"Is LeCur the traitor in Castello's family?"

Falcetti nodded. "Yeah."

"I need to know what was he up to."

"He had a scheme to rob Castello. Him and someone else."

"Who?"

"I don't know his name. I never met him."

"What was the scheme?"

"Force Castello's couriers to skim off the top. If they didn't, LeCur's partner would make sure they went to jail for a long time."

"Was LeCur's partner a cop?"

"I don't know. I never saw his face. Maybe. That would make sense."

"If these couriers got caught stealing from Castello, they'd be killed. Their girlfriends would be killed. Why would they risk that, even with the threat of going to prison hanging over them? Why didn't they just take off?"

"LeCur promised them a cut once they were done. Plus, he convinced them they wouldn't get caught, that his father was in on it, too, and they'd be protected."

"Was his father in on it?"

"Not really."

"What do you mean?"

"He kept tabs of everything that went out and came in, so he knew stuff was missing. He had to have suspected that his son was involved. Who else would know enough about the organization to pull an inside job like that? LeCur counted on his father saying nothing. What was the old man going to do, turn in his only child to Castello?"

"So what went wrong? Why were the couriers killed?"

Falcetti took a breath, began immediately to cough. Bechet listened to the rattle of the fluid collecting in his friend's lungs, building. After the coughing finally stopped, Falcetti closed his eyes, seemed to need a moment. Bechet gave it to him, or as much of it as he could, then said again, "Why were the couriers killed, Bobby?"

Falcetti opened his eyes again, took a careful, shallow breath, and continued.

"It turned out they were skimming more than what they were supposed to," he said. "Double, in fact, and keeping the extra for themselves. LeCur's father could only cover for part of what was being skimmed, the amount LeCur told the couriers to take. LeCur knew that, knew how much the old man could fudge. But there was no way he could cover for the extra. Castello eventually found out, and naturally he wanted to know who was behind it."

"And since the couriers knew, LeCur and his partner killed them."

"It was their contingency plan all along. The couriers being killed in the way they were would look like Castello's work. It was their way out if it all turned to shit."

"LeCur and his partner were the two men on the bridge."

"Yeah."

"You're sure about this?"

"I saw them."

"How?"

"I was in on the plan, was supposed to be their alibi. They called for a cab, and instead of picking them up I was supposed to park somewhere out of sight and wait. If something went wrong, I was supposed to say I was driving them out to East Hampton at the time of the murder."

"But you didn't park somewhere and wait?"

"No. I hid in the woods behind the train tracks and watched."

"You did more than that, though, right?" Bechet said. "You video-taped it, didn't you?"

"Yeah. My share for providing them with an alibi would have paid off my debts, but nothing would have been left over. I figured one way or another, a tape of the murder might be worth something."

"How close were you?"

"Close enough. Plus, the thing has a zoom."

"It would be helpful if we knew who LeCur's partner was. Do you still have the tape?"

"No."

"What happened to it?"

"You took it, remember?"

Bechet nodded, thought about that, then said, "So what did you see?"

"The whole thing. LeCur and his buddy chopped those guys' hands off and then hanged them. I'd never seen anyone killed before, let alone like that."

"That's why you were so jumpy. When I was towing you out of the ditch, I mean. That's why you were acting the way you were. That's why you were dressed the way you were."

"My hands were still shaking, I kept trying to hide them from you. That fucking dog ran out in front of me, just came out of nowhere. I was so spooked by what I'd seen that I totally overreacted, spun myself out of control. The crash was nothing, I'd been in worse back in my smashup derby days. Still, I thought my heart was going to explode, I was so freaked-out."

"The bar in Wainscott, then, if you and LeCur were buddies, what was that all about?"

"He was still working for Castello, had to do what Castello wanted him to do. When they snagged me, I thought it was because of what we were up to, that that was it, I was a dead man. Turned out, though, Castello needed me to bring you out in the open so he could talk to you."

"And LeCur beat you up even though you guys were partners."

Falcetti shrugged. "He had to. Castello didn't know he and I knew each other, it had to stay that way. There was so much money at stake."

"You told Castello about Gabrielle. That's how he got her information so fast."

Falcetti nodded.

"Who else knows about her?"

"Just Castello."

"Are you sure about this?"

"LeCur and his father knew, but that doesn't matter now, does it? You killed the old man, right? LeCur assumed you did, said he didn't care that Castello wanted you alive, that he was going to kill you the next time he saw you. It doesn't matter to me, man, but you killed the old man, right?"

Bechet ignored the question. "What do you know about Romano's girlfriend?"

"What about her?"

"Was she murdered?"

"Yeah."

"By LeCur and his partner?"

"Yeah. The partner took the girl away, and LeCur and I stayed and searched the place. I didn't know what I was doing. Neither did LeCur, really. We couldn't find what we were looking for, and then the partner came back with the girl. He and LeCur put her in the tub and killed her, made it look like a suicide."

"You were there?"

"Yeah. It was terrible."

"Did you see the partner's face?"

"No, he had a ski mask on the whole time."

Falcetti started coughing again, these coughs worse than ones before, like seizures. Bechet waited till these passed, watching his friend, then said, "How was his partner built? Was he tall, short, what?"

"Stocky, big shoulders. He had this round gut, like a pregnant woman."

"What was he wearing?"

"An old raincoat. It was covered with the girl's blood when he left. You should have heard her while they were cutting her. And I thought what I'd seen on the bridge was bad. I knew then I was in over my head. The partner had taken some Polaroids of the girl back at the Water's Edge, when he was making her tell him Abby's number. Staged them to look like bondage photos. He planted them in the cottage, I guess to explain the bruises that were made when they held her down in the tub. 'S and M freak kills self,' is what the headline was supposed to read, I guess."

Bechet thought about that. LeCur had certainly learned his old man's tricks. But then Bechet pushed that thought—every element of it—out of his head.

"Then what happened?"

"I was left to watch the place, and when that Miller guy went in, I called LeCur. He told me to get out of there. I guess LeCur or his partner called the police for some reason. I heard the sirens as I was driving away."

"You were the one who ran Miller and me off the road, weren't you?"

"Yeah."

"Why?"

"LeCur's partner had seen Miller talking to some cop or something, and then suddenly Miller showed up at that cottage. They didn't know what he was up to, figured it wasn't good whatever it was, so they wanted him dead."

"But you didn't shoot him."

"I couldn't."

"Did they want me dead, too?"

"They knew Castello had asked you to find the traitor."

"So that's a yes."

Falcetti nodded. "They didn't want to take any chances. There was no way I could have done that, though, man. I couldn't even kill that Miller guy." He paused, closed his eyes, then reopened them again. His face was covered with sweat. "How could someone do that? Just kill someone 'cause they're told to."

Bechet looked through the windshield for a moment, then back at Falcetti again.

"Abby has what the couriers took for themselves, doesn't she?" Bechet said.

"Yeah."

"Ecstasy pills, right?"

"Yeah."

"Do you know what it's worth? What the couriers took for themselves?"

"A million, give or take."

"And that would fit in a suitcase."

"Easy, yeah."

Bechet thought about that. "Where is she now, Bobby?"

"I don't know. LeCur's partner has been trying to find her."

"Because she knows too much."

"That, and he wants the extra the couriers took for themselves, thinks it belongs to him."

"Do you know if he's found her?"

"Last I knew, no. She's probably long gone, though. That was the plan—she and the girl and Michaels and Romano, they were going to take off with their share, sell it for the quick cash, go somewhere and never be heard from again. Not a bad plan, actually."

"LeCur and his partner didn't know where Abby lived?"

"No, they did."

"How?"

"They followed Michaels there one night, or something like that. They don't miss a trick. But by the time they realized Michaels had given her the stuff it was too late. She was long gone, and someone had already been to her place."

"How'd they know that?"

"Something that should have been there wasn't."

"Do you know what?"

"No. Before they killed Romano's girlfriend, LeCur's partner tried to get her to tell him where Abby went, but apparently she didn't know."

Bechet thought about the other tricks LeCur certainly had learned from his father—or from Castello, for that matter—the many ways of getting someone to talk. A soaked rag stuffed deep into the mouth, a few gallons of water poured over it. Or, if not water, then gasoline. Fear of drowning as well as the fear of, at any minute, being set on fire. Bruises left by the restraints holding the victim's hands down would certainly look like the marks of rough sex play.

Again, Bechet had to will his mind clear.

"We're almost done, Bobby," he said. "I need you to tell me exactly what you saw on the bridge last night."

"They came out of the basement of that bar."

"The Water's Edge?"

Falcetti nodded. "Yeah. That's where they took the couriers to try to get them to talk, tell them who had the goods. That's where Castello's lab is, too. Way underground, in some subbasement or something. The train tracks run right behind that place, so they walked the couriers onto the tracks and then out onto the bridge. Just far enough out so they'd be over the canal. They hacked their hands off, tossed the hands into the water, then hung them by their necks. First one, and then the other."

"What did they do when it was done?"

"They walked up the tracks, stepped across a board they had put there so they wouldn't leave footprints in the mud, then crossed the pavement and went back inside the bar. They got blood on their coats and burned them in the furnace."

Bechet remembered the black smoke he had seen rising from one of the three crumbling chimneys as he stood behind Tide Runner's, looking across the canal.

"You're sure it was them? LeCur and his partner?"

"I heard LeCur, that accent of his, when they were walking by. And the other had that round gut. Solid guy, big shoulders, but this round gut. I remember that he had galoshes on over his shoes. At the canal, and at the cottage, too. Those were the only two times I saw him. LeCur said the guy always wore expensive shoes, kept them shiny, didn't like getting them dirty."

Bechet thought about that, but not for long; it meant nothing to him.

"Listen, I don't really feel all that well, man," Falcetti said. "I could use some water."

"Just one more question, Bobby."

Falcetti waited.

"Why did LeCur kill Scarcella?"

"He wasn't supposed to. He was just supposed to grab him, for Castello."

"Why did Castello want Scarcella grabbed?"

"There was something Scarcella's father had that Castello wanted. He was going to trade Scarcella's son for it."

"Do you know what it was Scarcella had that Castello wanted?"

"It was evidence or something."

Bechet nodded, looked through the windshield again. After a moment, he said, "If LeCur was supposed to grab Scarcella, why was he killed?"

"I guess he put up a fight and LeCur ended up taking him out. If you ask me, I think LeCur was just looking for an excuse to do it. Once his partner found Abby and they split up what she had, LeCur was going to blow town. He already had his share of the cash-out from what he and his partner got from the couriers. The last thing he probably wanted was to be stuck watching Scarcella."

"Where did LeCur live?"

"I don't know. But the last few days he was hiding out in a motel somewhere."

"Do you know where?"

"No."

"Did his partner?"

"No. One never knew where the other was. That way they couldn't turn on each other."

Bechet thought about that, then switched off the recorder. He looked back at Falcetti.

"How much do you owe Scarcella?"

"Ten grand."

Bechet nodded, looked forward again. "Thanks, Bobby, you did good. I'll get you some water now."

He got out from behind the wheel, was passing by the open back door when Falcetti said, "Hey."

Bechet stopped, looked at his friend.

"I'm sorry, man," Falcetti said. "I didn't know you'd get caught up in this. I needed the money, you know. It was only about the money."

"You knew people would get killed, though, right? The couriers. That other girl. And not just strangers, but Abby, someone we both knew. You knew that, right?"

Falcetti nodded. "Scarcella isn't the kind of guy you want to owe money to."

"I don't know, Bobby. Scarcella, it turns out, was the least of your problems. He's a scary man, but he wouldn't have killed you over ten grand. LeCur, though, he wouldn't have thought twice about cutting you open if it served his purpose. His partner, too, by the sound of it. Hell, killing you meant they wouldn't have to pay you your share. Plus, you knew too much. They were probably going to kill you next anyway, once they knew they didn't need you for an alibi."

Bechet waited but Falcetti had nothing to say to that. What more, at this point, needed to be said? Bechet walked to the far end of the loading dock, where there was a stainless-steel sink mounted to the wall and some paper cups in a clear plastic sleeve on a small shelf beside it. How many times, Bechet wondered, had his father washed his own hands here, after cutting up the bodies of the men he had killed for money? How much blood had the man hosed toward the drain in the floor? How many men had died here, the face of a man with not one speck of kindness in his heart the last thing of this world they saw?

Bechet ran the tap till the water was cold, then filled the cup up. As he did this he heard Falcetti enduring another fit of coughs, these, though, different from any that had come before, weaker, shorter, more like gasps. Bechet listened to them—even after the cup was filled and the faucet was turned off he remained there at the sink, his back to his friend, and listened. Falcetti was dying now, there was little doubt about that, and even if Bechet was somehow able to prevent it, he couldn't. In the end, he did the only thing he could do. He poured the water down the sink, tossed the cup aside, and walked back to the sedan, stood there and looked at his friend as he drowned in his own fluids. It took a long moment for Falcetti's gasping to stop—his eyes were closed and thankfully, never opened—but when the gasping finally did, when Falcetti's life was at last gone, Bechet turned away and got to work.

Opening the trunk of the sedan, he found a box of garbage bags and a bone saw, just as he knew he would. He removed them both and tossed them aside. Moving quickly, he pulled the clear plastic tarp from his old Triumph motorcycle and spread it out on the cement floor alongside the sedan. Keeping Falcetti's body wrapped in the blanket, he laid it on the tarp, then rolled it over several times, wrapping it up. Things would be easier, Bechet knew, if he did what he had been taught to do—sever the limbs and the head with the saw from the trunk, stack these pieces onto the torso, and *then* wrap the whole thing up. Easier to move that way, easier to load into the trunk—and, too, the remains could be scattered in a number of far-off locations. But it just wasn't in him to do that, not to anyone, never mind a friend, even one who had betrayed him. Bechet lifted the body—there was just no weight like deadweight, and he only had one good hand—and placed it in the trunk, the rear shocks compressing slightly. With the hose Bechet sprayed the backseat, washing the blood off its nylon covering. What had spilled down to the carpet had already dried, and no amount of scrubbing would get that out, so Bechet grabbed an old blanket from a locker and laid it over the stain. After that he washed the blood he had hosed out of the sedan toward the drain, then aimed the hose down the drain itself, making sure to flush all trace of the blood away. Finally he found the industrial cleaner that his father had left behind and poured it down the drain. Emptying the container, he tossed it in the trash.

Back in his bedroom, Bechet removed a laptop computer from the bottom drawer of the filing cabinet and turned it on. While he waited he removed his boots, grabbed a new pair from storage, and put them on. Opening the window in the bathroom, he dropped the boots into the East River. By the time he came back to the computer, it was running. Connecting the digital recorder to the USB, he uploaded the file containing his conversation with Falcetti and then transferred it to a flash drive. Shutting the computer down, he returned it to the cabinet drawer, then, pocketing the flash drive, climbed down the concrete stairs to the open workshop.

He looked at his watch, had forgotten that it was broken, so he removed it and tossed it into the trash. He looked toward the clock mounted on the brick wall in the corner where his boxing equipment was, had used that clock to time his rounds back when he had first come here to nurse his wounds and get back on his feet—rounds on the speed bag and heavy bag, rounds jumping rope, rounds of shadowboxing till the sweat poured from him, of sit-ups and squats. Now this clock told him that there were less than two hours till sundown. Just enough time, then, to drive back to the East End—Noyac first, to get rid of LeCur's sedan and what it contained, then leave Scarcella's salvage yard with his own untraceable one—and, after that, Southampton, Miller's apartment first, and then, if he dared, if all looked right, a certain motel before finally calling Castello, setting what needed to be done into motion. The next two hours would require, considering what was now in the trunk, great care, but Bechet was nothing if not careful.

Just these things left, Bechet thought, and then all this would be done.

He opened the garage door, backed the sedan out, then pulled the door closed from the inside, locking and reinserting the bolts. Back outside, after one more look around, Bechet got behind the wheel and made his way through the narrow streets of Williamsburg to the Brooklyn-Queens Expressway, the flash drive in one pocket, the key to LeCur's motel room in the other. *One thing left to do, maybe two.* Fifteen minutes later Bechet was eastbound on the Long Island Expressway, the late afternoon sun, or what could be seen of it through the shrouding clouds, looming in his rearview mirror. It descended just a little bit with each dozen or so miles the sedan crossed. Moving in this way, the dulled sun seemed to Bechet like some kind of natural odometer, as ominous as it was patiently relentless.

During the last moments of daylight—the somber end to a somber day—Barton steered Miller's pickup into the parking lot outside Tide Runner's. Mancini's car wasn't there yet, and though the rain had stopped, for now, at least, Barton chose to wait behind the wheel. Even with the windows closed she could hear the low rumble of the canal, the sound of the water rushing from Peconic Bay to Shinnecock Bay, moving with the force of a deep and unobstructed river. The locks, then, were open. Barton waited for a few minutes, her stomach tight, her heart racing just a little bit, then finally got out and walked across the lot to the wide but short set of stairs leading down to the restaurant. She heard not only the rumble of the water, the unrelenting force of it, but also the high-pitched hiss of its movement through the concrete channel as well. It echoed off the flat walls, was the kind of noise that, when first heard, scrubbed the mind of all thought, if only for a quick moment. Barton's thoughts, however, remained with her.

She waited at the bottom of the stairs, a little lost in all that sound, watching the canal lights reflecting on the choppy surface. She thought of news footage she had seen of the tsunami in Southeast Asia a few years ago, the way the wave had come in and swept away lives. That footage had replayed over and over again on her television, and each time she saw it all she could think about was how easily, and so often without warning, lives could be, by act of man or act of nature, erased.

She heard the sound of someone on the steps behind her and glanced at her watch. It was 6:38. Turning, she saw Mancini at the top of the stairs. He walked down to her, and they stood face-to-face, a man with shoulders like a bull and a round gut and a woman who for too long now had been frail, been what she didn't want to be, less than she could be. Both in dark coats—Mancini in his wool overcoat, Barton in the leather jacket Miller had given her—and both wearing galoshes—over work boots for Barton, something of a silly sight, but she didn't care about that, and over Italian loafers for Mancini. The parts of his shoes not encased in the dull black rubber were immaculate, as shiny as a clear summer night.

"What's going on?" Mancini said. He had to speak up to be heard over the din filling the space around them. Barton hadn't heard his car approach, hadn't heard his door close, so maybe he had parked not in the lower lot, where she had parked, but in the upper, secondary lot, an overflow lot, the farthest border of which was just feet from the train tracks, where the bridge met solid land again. His vehicle would not be seen from the road there, a precaution she realized she should have thought of and taken herself.

Mancini surveyed the area around them, did so quickly, then turned his line of sight across the canal. She followed it to the western end of the bridge, where the bridge met the opposing bank and last night around this time two young men had been mutilated and then hanged.

"Thanks for meeting me, Detective," Barton said.

"We shouldn't really be here, Kay, you know that."

"I thought it would be good for us to have a look around."

"What for?"

"It might help make things clearer."

"What things?"

"The things I've been thinking about this afternoon."

"I don't have a lot of time," Mancini said. "Roffman's in his office right now, and I thought I might follow him when he leaves, see where he goes."

"I'll come right to the point, then." Barton watched his face as he surveyed their surroundings again. "I know what's going on," she said. "I know what you've been up to, and what you're up to now. I just wanted to let you know that if there's anything I can do to help, you can count on me to do it."

Mancini looked at her, not right away but after a moment, when he was done with his second visual search of the area. He looked at her almost casually, but she knew that was just a mask. He looked first at her face, lingering there for a bit, then up and down the length of her body before returning again to her face. It seemed at any moment that he might smile, but he didn't. Barton felt suddenly, oddly, in this stare of his, naked.

"You look tired, Kay," he said finally. His voice was flat, almost dismissive. He sounded like a father telling his child it was getting late, time to go to bed now. "You should probably go home."

"You might want to hear what I have to say."

"Maybe another time."

"No," Barton said, "I think we should do this now. Out in Montauk you offered me something. I've had time to think about it, and it's something I very much want. I'd like to know tonight whether or not I can actually have it."

"I'm sorry, I don't remember offering you anything, Kay."

"Just hear me out, Detective. If I'm wrong, I'm wrong, and that's that.

But if I'm not, if what I think is going on really is going on, then maybe you and I can help each other."

Mancini studied her for a moment longer, then said, "Let's get out of this damp." He nodded toward the restaurant. Barton looked at it, its darkened windows and its entryway blocked by a waist-high line of yellow police tape. Before she could state the obvious, that it was a crime scene and the tape was a line they shouldn't cross, Mancini said, "Don't worry, I'm still head detective."

Lifting up the yellow police tape, Mancini let Barton step under it first, then followed her, lowering the tape behind him. He walked to the restaurant's front door, which was fitted with a latch and padlock and sealed with a single strip of yellow adhesive tape. The latch and padlock were new, department-issue. Barton stayed where she was and watched as Mancini opened the lock with a key, then, with a pocketknife, cut the tape where the door met the frame. He was wearing, she noticed now, leather gloves. Expensive, of course, thick stitches at its seams. They were stretched tight over his large hands. He held the door open for her but she hesitated one more.

Again, before she could express her obvious concerns about contaminating a crime scene, Mancini said, "It's okay, we both seem to be wearing our galoshes tonight. Anyway, they're done." He took another look around, then nodded toward the open door. He was a stern parent now. "C'mon, Kay, get inside."

The interior of the restaurant was an open space—no tables or chairs, nothing here except for signs of an ongoing restoration—ladders, canvases, cans of paint. Unlit, yet not dark, either, not totally.

Barton moved through the door and into the empty, echoing space, stopped after a few steps. Mancini pulled the door closed behind them, cutting off the rumble and hiss of the canal.

With the lights off, the row of oversized windows at the far end of the room was the only source of illumination, letting in the bluish white canal light, no brighter than the light from a fish tank. Enough, though, for Barton to see by. She quickly got the layout of the room, determined that the only other way out that she could see—a double door made of panes of glass, located just past the bar to her right and leading to the deck—was chained shut. Her eyes went to the cans of paint in the corner farthest from where she stood. Was one of them full enough, she wondered, to shatter a window, if it came to that?

"Step to the middle of the room," Mancini ordered.

Barton walked, reached what seemed to her the center, and stopped. She turned and faced Mancini. He held back ten feet or so, lingering in what was the darkest half of that room.

He unbuttoned his overcoat, let it fall open. Barton saw his round gut, saw, too, the handgun holstered to his belt.

"Take off your jacket," Mancini said.

"What for?"

"Just do it."

She could feel the tension in her brow and around her eyes, clear indications that her face had shifted now into a puzzled expression. She looked at Mancini, got the exact sense that he wanted her to get, that he was near the edge of his patience, geared up, from this moment on, for quick decisions and quick decisions only. *No bullshit, moment of truth, one thing he didn't like and he was out the door.*

Barton unzipped the leather jacket, then removed it.

"Toss it over," Mancini said.

She did. He caught it, turned it around as he ran his thick fingers around the inside of the collar and cuffs, then over the pockets. He was, she knew, looking for some kind of recording or listening device. He felt something in one pocket, unzipped it and reached inside, removing Barton's cell phone. He checked, she assumed, to make sure no active line was open, then returned it to the pocket and dropped the jacket to the floor.

"Turn around, Kay," he said flatly.

She told herself that she had come too far to give up now, had walked too far out on this limb as it was just by making the call she had made before calling Mancini, never mind actually meeting Mancini, and here of all places.

Mancini walked up behind her, and as he did she felt the shift in the still air caused by his motion. Cold stirred by cold. He was just inches from her, must have taken off his gloves because his bare hands were suddenly on her, touching her shoulders, the back of her neck, her ponytail. She made herself hold steady. His hands then moved down her back and around her waist to her lower stomach, moving finally up to her breasts.

She had nothing on beneath her thermal shirt, and she felt her nipples harden under his palms. She closed her eyes. *Two years without a man's touch, and now this.* There was nothing overtly sexual in the way Mancini groped her, it was strictly a professional pat-down, rough and thorough. Still, it was an unpleasant invasion nonetheless. Once Mancini was certain no device was hidden on her torso, he moved down her legs, one at a time, from top to bottom, lingered in a crouch as he searched through her socks and the rubberized tops of her work boots with his thick fingers.

When he was done, he stood behind her again, and she knew what was next, braced herself for it.

His hands moved down her lower back to her ass, then between her legs from behind. He was skimming fast now. Moving up her narrow hips, he dug his fingers into the waistband of her jeans, made a half circle with each hand till his fingers met in the back, then retraced the motion till they met again in front. Finally he moved one hand down and placed it between her legs, searching her from the front. His hand lingered there, his fingers pressing against her pubic bone, and then suddenly it was gone, Mancini was no longer standing behind her. He walked back to where he had been standing. Barton turned and faced him as he picked up her jacket and tossed it back to her. It landed short. She stepped to it, picked it up and put it on.

"So what is it you think you know," Mancini said finally.

"Someone I know thinks that everything that's happened since last night points to all this being the simple matter of Roffman going after Castello. Roffman took over the investigation of last night's murders, the only witness to the murders was himself killed, and at the time he was killed only a cop would have known that there was a witness and who the witness was."

"Who exactly is this someone?"

"It's not important."

"Maybe not, but I'd still like to know."

"It's not Tommy. That's all I'm going to say."

Mancini said nothing, so Barton continued.

"This whole thing started when two of Castello's couriers began stealing from him, and this friend of mine thinks that someone with some kind of authority had to have coerced them to do it. Everyone who steals from

Castello knows what's going to happen to them if they get caught. My friend even thinks Ricky Spadaro is involved, passing along information— things only Miller and I could have told him—to Roffman. This all adds up, looks great on paper. But there's one thing my friend doesn't know."

"And what's that, Kay?"

"It is impossible for Ricky to be working with Roffman like this."

"Nothing's impossible."

"No, this is. Ricky's a Boy Scout, everyone knows that. Even if Roffman somehow threatened him, he wouldn't go along with it, certainly not with something like this. He wouldn't follow Roffman out on that bridge there and kill two men in cold blood."

"People do surprising things sometimes, Kay. You should know that better than anyone."

"You said it yourself, Detective. My affair with Roffman was only a matter of time, him being who he was and me being who I was back then."

"Back then?"

Barton said nothing.

"You're putting an awful lot of faith in Spadaro's character, Kay. And Roffman's, for that matter."

"Even when push comes to shove, we can only ever do what we're capable of doing, what we already have deep down inside us."

"That's what you think, huh?"

"Yeah."

"So if Spadaro and Roffman aren't capable of what your mysterious friend thinks they are, then who is?"

"When the shit hit the fan, when I broke it off with Roffman, he reacted the way a jilted man who was used to having the power would react. And Ricky, being a Boy Scout and my friend, reacted the only way he could. For better or for worse, they remained true to themselves. You, though, there was no . . . passion in the way you reacted. You went cold, detached yourself from the whole thing. You left me out there to dangle in the wind."

"And you think that means something."

"I think it means everything, yeah."

"So because I didn't come running to your rescue like Spadaro or turn against you like everyone else, I'm capable of cold-blooded murder. Because I let you, as you put it, dangle in the wind, I must have hanged two men last night."

"Again, you said it yourself. Roffman loses his job, you become chief. Roffman gets killed—by Castello or anyone else, for that matter—and you become chief."

"Maybe you aren't as smart as I thought you were, Kay. You honestly expect me to just come out and tell you that you're right, you got it all figured out. I'm supposed to be inspired by this wild theory of yours to confess to multiple murders."

"I'm not looking for a confession, Detective. I want in."

Mancini shook his head in disbelief. "Don't embarrass yourself, Kay. You call me, tell me we have to meet, suggest that we meet here. You're not wired, so maybe this place is. Or maybe your buddy Miller is some-where outside with one of his gizmos, listening to everything you and I are saying, recording it for all posterity."

"Why would I want to trap you, Detective? You're my only way back to where I want to be. You get what you want, I get what I want. Enemy of my enemy."

"You left Montauk, Kay, at, what, one? Which means you would have gotten back to Southampton by two. You didn't call me till a half hour ago. Plenty of time in between two and six for you to make some plan with Miller or your mysterious friend. Hell, for that matter, you could have even called Roffman, made a deal with him."

"Tommy's on his couch, out cold, Detective. He was run off the road this morning, banged up his knee pretty bad. And as far as calling Roff-man goes, I'd rather work at a liquor store for the rest of my life than go crawling to him."

"You actually believe he took over the investigation because he's de-termined to find out what's going on. He didn't know who to trust so he's doing it all himself. That's what you said in Montauk, right?"

"Yeah."

"But you said Roffman had information only Spadaro knew, things Spadoro could have only learned from you and Miller."

"I said that's what my friend thought."

"What information, exactly?"

"Someone knew Tommy was on his way to Noyac this morning. Someone who wanted him dead. The only person who could have figured out where Tommy was heading was Ricky. On his way back from Noyac someone ran Tommy off the road. I think that person would have killed him if I hadn't shown up."

"So let me guess. Spadaro hasn't been tipping Roffman off, he's been tipping me off."

"He wouldn't have to tip you off."

"Why not?"

"Maybe you've been listening in on Ricky's calls. If there's a bug on his line, it should be easy enough to find, right?"

Mancini said nothing for a moment. Barton waited.

"Humoring you," he said finally, "why exactly would I want Miller dead?"

"Because he found the surveillance camera and DVR at Abby's apartment. If Miller was murdered, you, as head detective, would search his apartment and, lo and behold, there would be a DVR showing Roffman knocking on the door of one of the dead couriers' girlfriends two nights before the murders. The fact that one of these girlfriends was murdered, too, only makes it worse for Roffman. You'd enter the DVR into evidence, like the good cop you are, and that's it, your part would be done. Suddenly Roffman has a lot of explaining to do. Suddenly everything he's been doing looks like he's either covering up for Castello or trying very hard to frame him so he could slip out of Castello's pocket. Whichever way it falls—whichever way Roffman falls—you win."

Mancini nodded. "There's a problem with your theory, Kay. I didn't even know there was a camera till you told me this afternoon."

"So you say. So you made a point of pretending. You were convincing, I'll give you that. But if you were the one coercing the two couriers, you would have known where Abby lived. She was in hiding, but her boyfriend, Michaels, knew, so he could have told you or you could have followed him there one night. He could have been the one to tell you that she had installed a camera outside her door. After that all you needed to do was figure out a way to get Roffman to show up so the evidence you needed would just be waiting there to be found by you after Abby was killed. Of course, Roffman locked you out, and if he found the evidence, he would have been certain to lose it, so it *was* lucky that Tommy and I found it, that much of what you said this afternoon was true."

"I think you should quit this right now, Kay."

"And how easy would that have been, to get Roffman there? A phone call from her apartment, an East Hampton number on his caller ID that turns out to be listed under Tommy Miller's name, that would have been bait he couldn't ignore. 'Come alone, there's something here you need to see' is all someone would have had to say, and that would have been something he couldn't resist. Roffman's a man with a guilty conscience, trust me, I know. Caution is his religion. Not all cautious men are guilty, but all guilty men are cautious. It would have been so easy for you to play upon that. If there had been a call from Abby's apartment to Roffman's home phone or cell phone, there'll be a record of it."

"And how exactly did I let myself in and make that call without being caught by that camera?"

"You didn't have to. The DVR shows Michaels entering the apartment about an hour before Roffman showed up—leaving, in fact, right before Roffman got there. If you were controlling Michaels, coercing him, then it wouldn't have been difficult to get him to do that. Again, if I'm right, the phone records will confirm this."

"You're way out of your league, Kay."

"Only a few of us are as smart as we think we are."

"What is that supposed to mean?"

"Someone calling cab companies from inside the department and claiming to be Roffman could have just as easily been someone other than Roffman. Those calls were made early this morning. Maybe Roffman was in then, maybe he wasn't. Again, it shouldn't be too difficult to find out for sure."

Mancini said nothing. Barton took a step toward him. "Look, I don't care that two drug runners were killed," she said. "I can even get to the point where I don't care that some poor idiot was killed because he was in the wrong place at the wrong time. Shit happens, right? Roffman's corrupt, Castello has a team of hired killers working for him, these are bad men, it's war, I understand that, I understand that sometimes innocent people get hurt or killed. I understand, too, that there are millions at stake, and that . . . changes things somehow. Our own government allows innocents to die so their cronies can get rich. This is the world we live in, the way things are, so, really, right now I don't care who killed whom or why. All I care about is the fact that Roffman ruined my life, took away everything I worked for, everything I was. I'd be more than happy to see him fall on his face, and I'd be more than happy to do something to help make that happen. But even more than all that, Detective, I'll do what needs to be done to put a stop to any more attempts on Tommy's life. You sent someone to Noyac to kill him so you could get your hands on that DVR. I'm here to tell you that if you want it that bad, you can have it."

His face blank, Mancini said calmly, "We're done here, Kay."

She took another step toward him, a fast one, a desperate one. His calm demanded that she be otherwise.

"All right, then I got it all wrong," she said, "you had nothing to do with any of this, it's all Roffman and Ricky, it's exactly how it looks on paper. I'm coming to you then because you're the head detective and I have in my possession evidence I would like to turn in."

"You'll hand over the DVR, just like that?" Mancini said.

Barton nodded.

"You'd have to testify in court how you found it."

"I don't care. Like I said, whatever it takes to make Roffman fall on his face."

"And this wild theory of yours, you'll drop it?"

Again, she nodded.

Mancini watched her face for a moment, then gestured toward the door. "Let's step outside."

"What for?"

"Just do what I say, Kay."

"Do we have a deal?"

Mancini said nothing, simply stood there and waited, watching her. *A portrait of neutrality.* Finally, Barton started toward the door, Mancini following her.

She stepped under the tape and stood at the foot of the stairs leading up to the parking lot. It was full night now, all hint of natural light gone. Mancini locked the door, then stepped under the tape and stood face-to-face with Barton. His overcoat was still open, his holstered gun, like before, clearly visible.

"Just one last thing I need you to do, Kay."

"What?"

"Tell him to come out now."

"What are you talking about?"

"Whoever is out there listening in on us, I want you to tell him to come out and bring his equipment with him."

"There's no one out there, Detective. Really. I came alone."

"I'm head detective, Barton, which means I'm smart and I'm experienced, I'm used to seeing through the bullshit people try shoveling at me. I'm also a card player. I put myself through college playing poker in Atlantic City, spent every weekend I could at the casinos. So even people who are very good at bluffing can't really fool me. And you, my sweet, ain't all that good at bluffing."

Barton took in a breath and let it out. If she gave Mancini what he wanted, then that would be it, Miller would be, as far as Mancini was concerned, out of this, and there would be no need for anyone to come after him again. Miller and Mancini were, after all, men of neutrality, they had that in common, it might serve to allow Mancini to trust that Miller would not pursue him. With the knowledge that Abby was long gone, Miller would have no reason at all to remain involved, not to any degree, would simply slip back into his early retirement then, into the quiet life of landlord and friend. Mancini would have nothing—once he possessed the item he wanted and it had been entered into evidence—to fear from anyone.

Roffman would fall and Miller would be safe, Barton thought. These two things were what mattered to her. She wasn't, after all, a cop anymore, Mancini had, in his way, seen to that. What did she need to care about justice, particularly when those still sworn to uphold it clearly didn't? She wondered, though, if she could find what it took to live with knowing what her personal gain had cost so many others? Did she already have that in her somewhere?

For now, though, what choice did she have but to play the hand she'd been dealt?

Speaking to the noisy air, Barton said, "Come on out." Her voice was only as a loud as it needed to be for her to be heard over the sound of the canal. There was no point in speaking in any way other than how she had been speaking to Mancini all this time. "It's okay, come on out."

She looked toward the border at the top of upper parking lot, past it to the line of scrub pines on the other side of the train tracks. Mancini followed her line of sight. After a moment a figure appeared, walking out of the darkness and into the influence of the canal lights, which fell just above where the upper lot connected with the lower lot. When the figure was close enough to be recognized, Mancini said to himself, "Spadaro. Of course."

Dressed in dark street clothes and carrying the recording device Barton had used to eavesdrop on Miller and Bechet, Spadaro reached the top of the steps, stood there looking down at Mancini and Barton.

"Come on down," Mancini said.

As he walked down the stairs, Spadaro looked at Barton. Neither of them said anything. When Spadaro reached the bottom step, he and Barton looked at Mancini.

It was then that they saw the handgun in the detective's hand.

"What's going on?" Barton said.

"Hand her the gizmo," Mancini ordered. The gun was aimed at Spadaro. Despite the fact that everything had suddenly, obviously changed—the presence of the gun alone was enough to do that— Mancini remained cool.

"What are you doing?" Barton said.

Mancini ignored her, talked directly to Spadaro. *Like she didn't exist, suddenly.* "Hand it over to her, Ricky."

Spadaro looked at Mancini, then finally held out the listening device. Barton hesitated a moment before taking it.

"Is there a recording device attached?" Mancini asked.

Barton eventually checked, found the output jacks, but there was nothing connected to them.

Mancini smiled. "Where is it, Ricky?" *Tell me, it's all right, I can still be your friend.*

Spadaro shrugged. There was, Barton thought, something punklike in his attitude now. "Where's what?" he said defiantly. Like a kid, almost. Was Spadaro's change in demeanor—boldly defiant—a reaction to the lack of change in Mancini's?

"Hand it over, Ricky. Okay? Hand it over now and things don't have to get ugly."

Spadaro reached into the pocket of his black denim jacket, did so with a deliberate slowness, both cautious and contemptuous, then removed a small digital recording device, the RCA cables still attached to its input jacks.

"Let me have it," Mancini said.

Spadaro tossed it to Mancini. When Mancini caught it, Barton noticed that the detective had his gloves on again.

Glancing at the device, switching it off, Mancini said to Barton, "Get his gun, please, Kay."

She looked at Spadaro. His eyes were locked on Mancini. Barton had never seen her friend quite like this. It was more than a reaction to the gun aimed at him, much more than that.

She reached inside Spadaro's jacket and removed his handgun from its holster. He never once looked at her. She then offered it to Mancini, who took the weapon and slid it into the left pocket of his overcoat. Careful to keep his eyes on Spadaro, he threw the digital recorder over the top of the single-story building, chucking it with everything he had, like a soldier lobbing a live grenade. Even with the rumble and hiss of the canal—it echoed off the banks, was all around them—Barton could just make out the gulp as the rushing water took the device.

So that was it, all this for nothing, she thought.

"I need you to take out your cell phone, Kay," Mancini said.

"What for?"

"Just do it."

Barton glanced at Spadaro again, saw the same defiance in the way he stood, in his eyes. Looking back at Mancini, she didn't make a move for her jacket pocket.

"You're going to call Miller," Mancini said calmly. Again, he spoke to Barton but wasn't looking at her, kept his eyes on Spadaro. "You're going to tell him to bring the DVR here."

"I told you, he's out of commission."

"Then let's hope the sound of his phone ringing is enough to wake the little addict up."

"I'll get it," Barton offered. "I'll go get it, bring it back."

"No."

"Then send Ricky."

"Just make the call, Kay," Mancini said.

"I don't understand," Barton protested. "What good will that do you?"

"Just make the call," Mancini repeated. *No change in his tone.*

"Don't do it, Kay," Spadaro said, warning in his voice.

Barton looked at him. He was shaking his head.

"Don't call him, Kay. If you do, you and me and Tommy are as good as dead."

Mancini aimed his gun at Spadaro's face. "Stop talking, Ricky."

"If Tommy brings it here," Spadaro said, "all Mancini needs to do is kill all three of us and there it is, everything he wants just handed to him. The DVR is his and the three people who are on to him are shut up for good. Doesn't get much neater than that."

"But the DVR has to be entered into evidence independent of him," Barton said. "Otherwise it's no good to him."

"Exactly. He waits nearby till the bodies are discovered. Or maybe he has one of his lackeys call in that they heard shots, and he arrives shortly after the first cop, says he heard the call on his radio, gets there before Roffman can and directs the cop's attention to the DVR lying there next to one of us. By the time anyone knows what's on it, it's too late for Roffman to lose it."

"He's going to kill all three of us, just like that?"

"He can suggest any story he wants. He could say it was a love triangle gone bad, Tommy killed you and me and then shot himself. There'd be the record of you calling Tommy from your cell phone, maybe Tommy figured out you were here with me, came to confront us. You were involved with Roffman, so it wouldn't be that much of a stretch for someone to think you had been involved with Tommy and were now involved with me. Everyone loves to think the worst of the woman, don't they? The fact that I stuck up for you all this time would only convince people that you and I had something going on."

"But he'd have to kill three people. I mean, three people he knew."

"You give people too much credit, Kay," Spadaro said. "He's a psychopath. Think about it. Ever see him anything other than cool and detached? I swear to God, I've never seen him sweat, not once. I guarantee you he has no anticipatory anxiety. I guarantee you he's fearless. Look at him."

Barton did. Nothing about Mancini's demeanor, despite everything that was going on and being said, had changed. Finally, Mancini looked at her. *Like she was nothing.* For the first time, she understood how he had been able to remain neutral as she had suffered, while everything she had worked for was stripped from her.

"I'd offer to kick you a share, Kay, in exchange for your silence," Mancini said, "but there'd really be no point in that, would there?"

Barton said nothing.

"I'd rather not kill you if I don't have to. It's not too late to be reasonable. We'd all benefit from Roffman falling on his face, as you put it. You'd be a cop again, Spadaro would have for once bet on the right horse."

Barton, puzzled again, looked at Spadaro. *Bet on the right horse?* Before she could say anything, though, Mancini spoke.

"I didn't need to tap his phone, Kay. I didn't need to bug his desk. He was more than happy to tell me everything I needed to know, whenever I needed to know it. He's been doing that for a while now."

Barton stared at Spadaro, dumbstruck.

"In his defense," Mancini said, "he did think he was helping things, that Roffman was up to something and that he and I were going to catch him in the act. It seems that manipulating a Boy Scout isn't all that different from manipulating a man with a guilty conscience. You tell the Boy Scout what he wants to hear and the guilty man what he doesn't want to hear, then let them do the rest."

"Ricky," Barton said finally.

"I didn't know he was in Castello's pocket, Kay. How could I have?" Spadaro looked at Barton for a moment, then at Mancini. "More than likely Castello was paying him to keep an eye on Roffman. At least that's the most popular theory. Insurance against Roffman making a move against Castello. That's how he would know to play them against each other. That's how he'd be able to handpick the right people to help him set this whole thing up. He's a smart man, all right, but he's not the smartest man."

All eyes were on Spadaro now.

"You think I'd just come here, Mancini, without checking into some things," he said. "And not just your relationship with Castello, other things, like those calls to the cab companies this morning. They were made from Roffman's office all right, but when Roffman wasn't in. And I think once we check his cell phone records we'll find that he, in fact, got a call from Abby Shepard's apartment two nights before the murders. All that's left is a warrant to search your house, which shouldn't be difficult to get now. My bet is we find a whole pile of cash stashed somewhere inside, your split of what the couriers stole. Maybe even more. God knows what you've had your hand in before this scheme."

"You're a smart man, too," Mancini said, "good for you. But you're also a dead man, so little good your smarts will end up doing you. As far as what I'm going to do now, the one thing you got wrong, really, is that I'm not going to kill all three of you here. That would be too much bloodshed in the same place, would look suspicious. Maybe a suicide—if Miller is stoned out of his mind, that would be easy enough to set up and more than enough to accomplish what I need. That would leave you, Spadaro, and your friend here. After I march you both back across the bridge, walk you into that big basement, it'll be like you two never even existed. I close the door behind us and no one will ever see you again, not even the pieces of you."

Spadaro said nothing.

"The advantage of being a psychopath, as you put it, is it's easier to do what needs to be done."

"No fear to slow you down."

"If you ask me, Ricky, the world was made by men who were willing to do what it took."

"That makes you, what, Brutus to his Caesar?"

"Something like that."

"Why not just kill Roffman then? Why all this?"

"Bringing your enemy down is one thing. Profiting handsomely from it is something else altogether." Mancini glanced back at the dark building behind them. "I've always wanted a restaurant," he said. "Apparently this one might be going into foreclosure soon. I look at it as an unexpected bonus."

"You killed him, too. Adamson."

"Maybe he saw something, maybe he didn't. Roffman kept his statement under lock and key, so there was no way of knowing. Better safe than sorry, right?"

Spadaro nodded for a moment, almost absently, then reached for his other jacket pocket. Mancini raised the gun, extending his arm and aiming it at Spadaro's face. *Take it easy.* Pausing for a second to establish that he wasn't up to anything, Spadaro resumed reaching for his pocket, moving with that same deliberate slowness as before. With two fingers he reached in and removed his cell phone, held it up for Mancini to see.

Barton looked at it, recognized what was on the display.

An animation of a phone off the hook and a series of moving arrows indicating that a line was open and active. Below the animation was the word *VOICE MAIL.*

"I made this call the moment I started recording," Spadaro said. "The digital recorder you tossed into the canal, that played everything you guys said from a little built-in speaker. All I had to do was hold my phone up to it. I thought it might be smart for us to have a backup—you know, just in case."

"Smart man, indeed," Mancini said. "Hand it over, please."

Spadaro ended the call, then tossed the phone to Mancini. Catching it without taking his eyes off Spadaro, Mancini glanced quickly down at the display. It was clear to Spadaro what Mancini had in mind.

"I didn't call my cell phone voice mail, Detective, so don't expect to just hit redial and erase the message. I called the voice mail system at the station. No way you can erase that, not without my password. If anything should happen to me, Roffman gets the system administrator to access my voice mail. Standard procedure, right? He does that and he hears everything that's been said here."

Mancini didn't miss a beat, swung his arm a few feet to his right and pointed the handgun at Barton.

"I guess I'm going to need that password, then, huh?" he said. "You can give it to me now or she can start taking bullets in places that hurt."

"You being a hotshot card player and all, Detective, I would have expected your bluffs to be better than that. You're not about to start shooting out here in the open like this."

"It's a good thing, then, that I know of a place nearby that's nice and private. Why don't the two of you be good kids and start walking up toward the tracks."

Neither Barton nor Spadaro moved. Even now Mancini wore that blank look of neutrality. Not a trace of sweat, not a tremor in his hand, eyes as steady and dark as a bird's. How could Barton not have seen that before? Now she could see nothing but that. The man was ice, everything he was doing, everything she had ever seen him do, said that, screamed it.

"You're out of time," Spadaro said.

"Just the opposite, actually. We've got all night to work this out among us."

"You kill us, you lose."

"You'd be surprised how much hurt a person can take without actually coming anywhere near dying. I've realized recently that it's not just the pain that fucks with you, there's a big humiliation factor as well— that is, when you're being made to suffer in front of someone else, someone close to you. They see you scared, see you cry, hear you scream and beg. Ugly, ugly stuff for everyone involved."

Barton's heart gunned suddenly. She thought of what she had told Miller when they met at Cooper's Neck. *It's easier to suffer alone.* She had kept to herself, stayed away from Miller, from everyone, so the scars of her disgrace would, if not heal, then at least go unnoticed. But the terror of her depression being known was nothing compared to the thoughts of violation that Mancini promised and that flashed now in her mind like scenes caught in lightning.

"Of course, you're both forgetting something," Mancini said. "I know where Miller is. I agree with you, Ricky, it is smart to have a backup."

"You think we didn't make sure he was safe before coming here?" Spadaro said. "You think we didn't stash the DVR somewhere you'd never find it?"

Mancini smiled. "Now who's bluffing?"

"And if I'm not?"

The detective's smile grew just a little. "What can I say, I like to gamble."

"It's an awful lot to lose," Barton said.

Mancini looked at her as if he had forgotten she was there. "Then it wouldn't be much of a gamble, would it?" he said. He nodded toward the stairs. "C'mon, let's all of us start walking to the tracks."

Spadaro opened his mouth to speak, got a few words out, something about all this being over, but Mancini had had enough, lunged without warning toward Spadaro with his extended gun hand, shifting the angle of his wrist just as he reached Spadaro's face so that he smacked him in the nose with the butt of the gun. Mancini had moved with more speed than Barton would have thought possible for a man built as he was. *The savage lashing out of an animal, no hint of thought before it.* As Spadaro staggered back from the force of the blow, he stumbled on the bottom step and fell onto the stairs leading up to the parking lot. Quickly recovering his shooter's stance, Mancini aimed the gun at Barton's face just as she took a step toward him.

"Get him up," Mancini hissed, "and start walking."

Spadaro was already halfway to his feet, though, when Barton reached him. He had gotten up quickly, the way a son might, Barton thought, after having been struck down by his own father for what, the son was determined, would be the last time.

Spadaro faced Mancini, glaring at him. "Admit it," he spat. "You've been outplayed. The hand you're holding is shit, we all know it."

"I've held worse," Mancini said.

"You're going to have to kill me right here."

"It doesn't have to be this way, Ricky. It doesn't have to be this way at all. You helped me out, I'll remember that. I make good on my promises. Just give me the password and Roffman goes down like he should, we all get what we want."

Spadaro was seething. "Fuck you."

"Jesus, Ricky, forget about being a Boy Scout for once, forget about your little friend here. This isn't just your job this time, this is your life. Don't make the same stupid mistake again, not for a slut like her. I don't care how good with her mouth she's supposed to be."

"You're insane, Mancini. You know that, right?"

"She's not worth it. You don't have to make the same mistake twice. Tell her to call Miller and give me the password. That's all you have to do. Make the right choice for once in your life."

In the end, Spadaro did the only thing he could.

It happened fast, Spadaro lunging at Mancini with even more speed than Mancini had lunged at him. Barton wasn't even sure if Mancini had meant to fire, or if Spadaro's sudden movement had caused Mancini's trigger finger to twitch, but whatever the cause, the gun went off just as Spadaro, ducking under Mancini's outstretched arm, was moving in for a tackle. The sound of the gunshot, so close to his ear, caused Spadaro to shout *"Motherfucker"* in pain. Then the two men collided, Spadaro tall and athletic and in his mid-thirties, Mancini a bull of a man in his fifties. Though Mancini was older and, compared to Spadaro, out of shape, he was also more experienced, more—and maybe this was all that really mattered—vicious. Low and squat, he kept his balance as Spadaro charged him, then stepped slightly to the side, pulling Spadaro with him, pulling Spadaro off balance. As they faced each other, Mancini brought his knee up, a sharp, sudden motion, landing his thigh with tremendous force squarely into Spadaro's groin. There was nothing Spadaro could have done, and he grunted when the blow landed, sinking in deep, and heaved forward, his legs buckling beneath him immediately. Barton was in motion by then, launching herself into the fray, grabbing Mancini's gun hand and going for a wrist lock. She was, though, just too weak. Stunned and gasping for air, still clinging to Mancini, Spadaro started to go down, bringing Mancini with him. Barton, holding on to Mancini's wrist, went down as well, all three of them a tangle of bodies on the wet deck planks—grasping arms and kicking legs, a frantic and brutal struggle for nothing less than who lived and who died.

Mancini quickly went to work on Spadaro, striking him several times with his free hand—open palm strikes, all but bouncing Spadaro's head off the hard wood. As he did this, Barton made another attempt at a wrist lock, was close to getting one when Mancini abandoned his attack on Spadaro and mounted Barton like a schoolyard bully. *So fast, so goddamned fast.* She did then the only thing she could do, gave up on the joint lock and pulled on Mancini's wrist, not to bring it toward her but to use it to lift herself to it. When she was close enough, she turned her face sideways and locked down on Mancini's knuckles with her back teeth, where her jaw was the strongest and she could grind his skin without breaking it and risking getting his blood in her mouth. Mancini, caught off guard by this, shouted but still held on to the gun. He did nothing for a few seconds, his thoughts scrambled by the pain, and then he recovered and wound up to strike Barton with his free hand. A fist this time, not a palm strike. But before he could throw the punch, Spadaro, on his back, stomp-kicked Mancini with both feet, sending him sailing off Barton and onto the deck. His knuckles remained in Barton's grip as his body landed and started to slide, pulling Barton with him a good foot or two. When they came to a stop—Mancini on his back, Barton on her stomach, holding on to Mancini's hand not only with both her hands but with her teeth—Barton saw, lying on the shimmering planks between them, Mancini's handgun.

She let go of him and lurched for it, grabbing it by the barrel, but Mancini was already on his feet and bolting up the short stairs. By the time Barton gripped the handle and was able to aim, Mancini was out of her line of sight, running, by the sound of his footsteps, toward the upper lot.

The train bridge.

Barton scrambled to her feet, looked down at Spadaro. He was curled up in pain, his head bleeding from several cuts.

"Ricky, you okay?"

"He parked across the canal," Spadaro gasped. "Behind the Water's Edge. I watched him walk across the bridge." He found her eyes, held them. "He's going after Tommy, Kay. You have to stop him."

Barton hesitated, was unable, for a second, to move or even, for that matter, breathe.

"Go, Kay," Spadaro urged. *"Go."*

She looked at him once more, then stood and, Mancini's gun in her hand, took the stairs two at time. Running across the packed mud and broken shells of the lower lot toward the upper one, she could see Mancini ahead, watched him cross the threshold where the light from the canal no longer had any influence and the blackness of a clouded night erased all details. After that she had only the vaguest sense of Mancini, saw only a lone figure moving as silently as a shadow through a dark place.

Barton reached the top of the incline and stepped onto the tracks as Mancini was closing in on the halfway point of the bridge. She wasted no time, continued after him even though she was already winded from the uphill run. *So slight, so weak.* Covering the distance of several feet, she was suddenly out over the choppy black water, felt a real sense of disorientation because of this drastic shift in perspective. *Up in the air, suddenly, wind rushing past her, water rushing below her.* She looked down at her feet as she ran, to help her adjust to the change from softened dirt and crushed shells to the wooden ties that were spaced too close together with brief patches of loose gravel placed evenly between them. She was afraid now of stumbling, almost preoccupied by that possibility, felt her pace falter as doubt caused her to slow. The train tracks were themselves wide enough for two people to walk shoulder to shoulder, and the gridwork of the trestle's frame complex enough to serve as a railing, so it wasn't a matter of fearing that she might fall from the bridge itself and into the dangerous water below, more a fear of tripping and taking a bad spill onto the hard ties and gravel. If she did that, Mancini would no doubt get away— even if she didn't fall, even if she kept her footing and continued to run with everything she had, he could still get away. As out of shape as he may have been, it was nothing compared to her condition, so what hope, really, did she have of catching the man, and what exactly would she do if she caught him?

For several crucial seconds, she looked not at the man she was pursuing but down at the threatening terrain beneath her feet. When she finally did look up again, expecting to see Mancini pulling away even farther, or maybe already off the bridge by now, she saw instead that he had in fact stopped, was standing not all that far from where he had been when she last looked at him. His right side facing her and his left hand out of sight, there was less than twenty feet between them now and nothing around them but the cold and deafening air. Barton, too, stopped, or began to, realizing quickly that Mancini was in mid-turn, that his left hand, unseen till this very second, was holding Spadaro's gun. As Mancini was completing his quick turn, facing Barton almost full-out now, he raised his left hand, was just a second, maybe less than that, from taking aim and firing.

Barton, slowing but not yet stopped, decided to do the only thing she could do.

She took a bad fall.

Pitching forward, she dove onto the tracks, landing belly first on the hard ties. The leather jacket did little to protect her from the gravel—she felt the sharp stones bite her elbows and knees as she hit, felt, too, her ribs and thighs slam against the unforgiving ties, her body ringing suddenly like a tuning fork. Still, she kept her arms outstretched in front of her, Mancini's gun firmly in both hands, and took quick aim and fired once, doing so before Mancini could even adjust to her tactic. He was hit, somewhere, Barton wasn't sure where. He reeled from its impact, staggering back a few steps before stumbling and taking his own awkward fall. Landing in a heap on the edge of the tracks, he rolled over to his side, almost like a man in his sleep, and suddenly, quietly, he was gone from Barton's sight.

She got to her feet, ignoring the pain vibrating through her, and hurried to the spot where Mancini had landed and then disappeared. Looking down, she saw that he had slipped between the edge of the tracks and the wrought-iron trestlework, was caught on a steel girder several feet below the tracks, folded over it sideways and teetering. His left hand was empty, and blood spurted from his right. It didn't take long for Barton to see that two of Mancini's fingers were missing. His middle and ring fingers. This was, she realized, where he had been hit by her shot.

Barton got down to her knees, really felt the pain then, and laid Mancini's gun on the tie. Dropping down to her stomach again, she reached over the edge, straining for Mancini's empty hand. He reached up with it, and they locked grips. She tried to hang on to him, but his balancing act on the girder was precarious at best, only a stall in his descent. Mancini began to slip, scrambled to grab onto something with his other hand, his wounded hand, but it was useless. Still, he clutched for something, cried out from the pain as what was left of his fingers came in contact with a small support girder. As he was dangling there, held only by the girder wedged under his armpit and Barton's grip on his wrist, it was very clear to the both of them that neither of those things would be enough. Mancini looked up at Barton, their eyes met. He wasn't smiling now, wasn't smirking, wasn't the cool iceman he had been moments ago, and for every minute of the years she had known him and worked with him. He was frightened now, but more than that, he looked almost bewildered, unable, it seemed, to accept the fact that after a lifetime of winning, he was, simply, about to lose—to lose big, lose everything.

Barton tried to hang on, but she simply didn't have the strength, Mancini was too heavy. His hand began to slip through hers, and as it did, he tightened his grip, did so almost viciously, crushing her with his power. She felt herself begin to slide forward, first to the edge and then over it. With her free hand she grabbed for something, but there was nothing for her to grasp, no anchor to hold her steady. As she continued to slide, the pain of Mancini's desperate grip was nothing compared to the pain in her shoulder, the deep tearing as muscle and tendons strained to keep the bone from being wrenched from its socket. Mancini slid down the girder a few inches, pulling Barton's shoulder out even farther and dragging her that much farther over the edge. He maintained his eye contact, and it was clear now to Barton that his intent wasn't so much to save himself as it was to bring her with him. *A last-ditch effort to win—or, at least, not be the only one to lose.*

Barton's torso was hanging over the edge, only her legs remaining on the bridge, was slipping now, about to go over when she felt suddenly someone grab the back of her jeans, a strong hand closing around her belt and holding her fast. Then she sensed that someone was over her, saw a foot on her right and a knee on her left. It was Spadaro. He had Mancini's gun in his hand, held Barton fast as he aimed point-blank at Mancini's head. Without hesitation he fired once, the shot like a slap against Barton's ears. The bullet hit Mancini dead center in the forehead, and he dropped like a hanged man, falling toward the rushing water below and landing with a splash that sounded and then was immediately absorbed by the rumble and hiss of the water and the howling of the rushing air. He went under, was once again gone from Barton's sight. *There, and then not.* A life, for better and for worse, ended, *just like that.* With Spadaro's hold on her belt anchoring her, Barton pulled herself back from the edge and onto the solid ground of the train tracks. Spadaro let go, and she lay there for a moment, then rolled onto her back and looked up at him and the gun in his hand, a thinning wisp of smoke, like a last strand of fog, rising from its barrel.

Part Five

Night

Eleven

MILLER SAT ON THE EDGE OF HIS BED, LEANING OVER BARTON and watching her eyes, only barely visible in the darkness of his bedroom, soften as the effects of the painkiller he had given her for her injuries took hold.

She and Spadaro had arrived around seven, but she hadn't said much at all, had let Spadaro do all the talking. He was the one who told Miller what had happened at the canal, and how it was Mancini all along, that Roffman was only being set up. Spadaro, too, was the one to first wonder what their next move should be, whether they should come forward with what they knew and what they had done or cover up their presence at the canal and let it all end there. There were, both Miller and Spadaro knew, certain advantages in keeping what they had learned to themselves. And there was the fact that Spadaro and Barton had left the scene of a homicide—a justifiable one, certainly, but a homicide nonetheless. Spadaro was afraid how it would appear if they came forward after having fled like that. But Miller had pointed out that, considering how corrupt the department was, Spadaro's need to secure crucial evidence first should clear him and Barton of any suspicion of wrongdoing. And anyway, if they came forward, it wouldn't be to anyone in Roffman's department, it would be to the FBI.

It was then that Barton spoke, stating flatly, decisively, that there was simply no way they would cover this up, that doing so would make them just like all the others, and that she'd rather face whatever would need to be faced by coming forward than live the rest of her life like some criminal, like someone with something to hide. She was, as she had said to Miller the night before, *done with all that.*

At that point she didn't say anything more, and it wasn't, Miller understood, because she was shaken or in shock. She was in fact lucid, present, composed. *The strongest person in the room, easily.* She simply didn't want to dwell on what she had done, what *had* to be done. She was injured, in pain, wanted now only to rest. Whatever happened from here would happen, there was no avoiding that, no point, then, in worrying about it or talking about it over and over.

While he waited for Spadaro to return with copies of what was on the voice mail system at the station, Miller helped Barton undress and clean up her scrapes. It was as if she had been beaten, her shoulder, despite the painkiller she had taken moments before, aching, growing stiff. Once she was patched up, he helped her into his bed, covered her with blankets and watched over her just as she had no doubt watched over him during the day, before running off to search for his obsession. Barton had done so, Miller knew, for no other reason than to maybe cut him free, once and for all, if she could, from all his various, lingering pasts, give him his new life back. His search for Abby had pulled him back into the world he had worked very hard to put behind him. He was beginning, just as he had done before, to lose himself in it again, in that dark and troubled world. He would never forget, then, what Barton had done for him, and what, in the end, it had cost her. How could he?

Her breathing was growing more shallow when Barton looked up at Miller with soft eyes. They watched each other for a moment, and then Miller whispered, "Thanks, Kay."

She smiled, a drowsy smile, oddly intimate in its own way. Miller smiled back. He hadn't sat with a woman as she fell asleep in a long time, since that night Abby, with her grandfather's suitcase, had left him and waited for the late train, took it when it finally came, heading for God knows where, God knows who.

"I wasn't about to let anything happen to you," Barton said.

Miller nodded toward his open bedroom door, and his living room beyond it, where Barton had put to an end to Miller and Spadaro's confusion over what would be done next. "Thanks, too, for what you said out there."

"We save ourselves from ourselves," she said. "It's what we do, Tommy. Promise me that we'll keep on doing that."

Miller promised.

"Try to keep this one, though, okay?" Barton joked.

Miller laughed. "I'll do my best." He looked at her for a moment more, brushed a stray strand of hair from her eyes with the tip of his index finger. "You should rest now, Kay."

She took in a breath, let it out, was moments from unconsciousness. *Did she feel the blue flame in her chest?* Miller wondered. She would sleep deeply, he knew that much. And when she awoke, he would be there, to talk to or not to talk to, whatever she wanted, whatever she needed.

"I'm sorry I didn't find her," she said. "I know how much she means to you."

Miller shook his head. "No, you did good, Kay. You did great, actually. And anyway, what matters now is you."

She smiled again. The drowsiness was in her eyes now, which glistened in the weak light like polished stones in a river.

"I do like the sound of that," she cooed.

"Rest up."

"You know what, I think I like your pills better than mine."

"Go to sleep, Kay."

He watched her drift into unconsciousness, stayed there on the edge of his bed till he was certain that she was out, then took hold of his cane and got up, making his way through the kitchen and into his unlit front room. He limped badly, and his head, for the most part, was still a little awash from the double dose Barton had given him in the morning. But he managed to remain upright and make his way to the front windows.

It took Spadaro close to an hour to return. Miller began to worry that maybe something had gone wrong. As he waited, he looked out his window, watched as a black town car with a broken taillight pulled up to the station and waited, Miller assumed, for the 9:10 train. He watched, too, a young couple walk onto the platform and stand face-to-face, embracing, kissing, laughing. As the westbound train pulled up—they were running on time tonight—the driver of the black town car got out and walked his passenger—a tall Latin-looking man in expensive clothes—to the station. They waited, along with the couple, for the train to stop, and then the tall man boarded it as the driver returned to the town car and got back behind the wheel and waited. This didn't make much sense to Miller, but there was no reason that it should, no reason at all for him to even try to make sense of it.

He was relieved when the old Bronco turned onto Railroad Plaza from North Main and headed his way. The restaurant below was busy for a Tuesday night—the familiar and comforting murmur of voices rising up through the old floorboards, friends and loved ones gathered for something to eat and something to drink, *time spent together.* Blessedly oblivious, all of them, Miller thought, to the things he and Barton and Spadaro knew, the things they had done for the sake of this small part of the world they all shared. Oblivious, at least, for now, but soon enough everyone would know.

With both sides of Elm Street lined with cars, Spadaro drove down Powell Avenue and parked somewhere out of sight, then made his way back on foot. Miller heard him enter through the street door, then climb the steep stairs. Still at his front window and leaning on his cane when Spadaro entered the apartment, Miller took one last look at the train station, gave one last thought to what had been for so long his only consistent thought: Abby. There was no hope of finding her now, he knew this. Maybe another lead would present itself, but he didn't count on that. *Too many maybes last night, so few now.* If she didn't want to be found, by him or by anyone else, then there would be no finding her, of that much Miller was certain. He didn't realize till now that he had been harboring a kind of wild hope that she had in fact planted his business card in Michaels's wallet so that it would be found, that this was some grand plan of hers to orchestrate the opportunity for him to rush in and save her, as though she would know that was what he would want, even after all this time, and knowing this, she would want to give this to him. Strange how a hope is sometimes recognized only when it is at last put aside. Strange, too, that he thought of Abby as someone who would be concerned with his salvation enough to go out of her way to gift him with a second chance. What did that, then, in his mind, make her exactly? Just like him? His two years of sitting still and playing landlord, caring nothing about the affairs of others—none of this apparently had changed his obsessive nature that much, had only, it seemed, quelled it for the time being. He had once been driven to prove to those around him that he had become at last a *worthy man,* had seen helping as many as possible as his way of doing so. A scattershot approach at redemption, at best. Now, yes, his target was more precise, his aim more focused—instead of others, it was one he wanted to help, instead of *strangers,* it was the last woman he had loved, touched, slept beside—but it was still obsession nonetheless. Maybe this was the last of it, he thought, the final hurrah of *who he used to be.* He could see this as being that—the final spiking of a fever at last about to break. What would it be like, he wondered, to wake one morning and find it *gone,* his mind free of it, free of her.

Still, wild hope or not, Miller would have liked to have at least laid his eyes upon Abby once more, if only to see her off to some place no one would ever find her and know once and for all that she had gotten away clean and was going to be okay. He would have liked that, would have liked, too, to have been able to tell her that he was, more than anything, sorry for having given her reason to leave him in the first place, to have played his part in sending her on such a dark journey as the one she had been on.

Spadaro closed the door behind him, and Miller reached down and switched on the lamp standing on a table by the window. His view of the train station was replaced suddenly by his own reflection in the dark and distorting glass.

Nothing left to chance.

Bechet left Scarcella's salvage yard at seven and headed in his own sedan toward Southampton. No registration, no insurance, all the serial numbers filed down, the out-of-state plates, taken from some abandoned car, provided by Scarcella. *A car for leaving town in, a drive and drop, but nothing more than that.* Because it was in every way possible an illegal vehicle, Bechet drove as cautiously as he had on his way to the yard in LeCur's sedan, the dead body of his old friend wrapped up in a blanket and clear plastic in the trunk. It wasn't an easy meeting with Scarcella, considering the news the man had received earlier in the day, and considering, too, what Bechet needed Scarcella to do—right now, with LeCur's sedan and the body in it, and later on as well, if all went right and Castello took the bait. But Scarcella was the kind of man who did what needed to be done, had always been that way, was the man who made Bechet want to be like that as well. Bechet knew that he could count on him. It had helped that Scarcella's own brother was there; Bechet didn't have to leave his friend alone with his mourning, and the plan Bechet had proposed would go better with two than it would with just one.

As he drove away from the yard—his Alice pack, along with the evidence he had collected against Castello's family, both years ago and recently, on the seat beside him—Bechet told himself that now wasn't the time for recklessness. He'd told himself that before, not all that long ago, actually, but it was even more so now. To accomplish what he needed to accomplish—for himself and Gabrielle, for Eddie and his wife, for Miller and Barton, and, maybe most of all, Scarcella—he would need all the skills that he possessed.

He reached his storage unit on Hampton Road, opened the garage door and pulled the sedan inside. Closing and bolting the garage door, he made his way on foot across the village, staying off the main streets as much as possible. It was seven fifteen, he should have called Castello by now, but first things first. In less than ten minutes he reached the motel in which LeCur had been staying, and after hanging back in a shadow and studying the window of room number nine, getting the sense of the place, Bechet used the key he had taken from LeCur and quickly slipped inside. The room was dark and still, no one there. Bechet looked around, found a leather duffel bag and searched through it. Some clothes and toiletries, nothing that would be useful to him. He opened the drawer of the nightstand by the bed. In it were two ice picks and several packs of French cigarettes. Bechet left them there. The bureau drawers were empty, and there was nothing under the bed. All that was left was the bathroom.

He found a toothbrush and toothpaste, nothing more. He looked at the toilet tank then, went to it and lifted up its lid.

There was nothing in the tank, but something was taped to the bottom of the lid. Bechet turned the lid over, rested it on the seat. He had found exactly what he had expected to find—a dark garbage bag, folded over several times and sealed with silver duct tape, the same kind of tape that secured it to the lid. Bechet pulled the bag free, knew by the feel of its contents—bulky but not heavy—exactly what was inside. He didn't bother to confirm that, just stuffed the bag into his Alice pack and left the key on the desk and got the hell out of there. He headed back toward Hampton Road via the same back streets and empty parking lots, his heart beating a little as he walked. On the edge of the village, from a pay phone outside Sip 'n' Soda, Bechet dialed Castello's number.

"You're pushing it," Castello said when he answered. "I was beginning to think you took off, left all your friends high and dry."

"I've been a little busy," Bechet said.

"I hope so."

"I have the information you want."

"Good work. How shall I get it?"

"Have your driver drop you off at the Southampton station. Get on the nine ten westbound. A car will pick you up in Hampton Bays. The driver will give you what I have and take you back to the station."

"Why the runaround?"

"Because you taught me well. And because I don't trust you. It's this way or it's nothing."

"All right, Pay Day, whatever you need. I'd like to talk to you, though."

"I'll be on the train. We'll talk on the way to Hampton Bays."

"I'll see you then."

Bechet hung up, walked the two blocks down Hampton Road to his storage unit. Inside, the lights low, he removed the garbage bag from his Alice pack and tore it open. It contained another bag, this one a clear, heavy plastic, the same kind of material Bechet had used to wrap up Falcetti's body. It was sealed tight with duct tape, and though he could already see what was inside, Bechet opened it anyway, doing so carefully and spilling its contents onto the workbench.

Twenties and fifties and hundreds, not neat bills wrapped with paper bands, not bank money but used money, dirty bills folded together into wads and secured by thick rubber bands. Laundered money, then, untraceable. LeCur's share, no doubt, of the cash-out from the Ecstasy the couriers had stolen. Bechet made a quick count of the wads, keeping his mind focused even as the amount grew and grew. When he was done he had to take a step back; he simply couldn't believe what was there.

Just over three hundred thousand dollars.

He stood there, shaking his head. What else could he do? Then he counted the money a second time, getting the same figure. *Just over three hundred thousand dollars.* He set aside two wads, one worth ten thousand, the other worth twenty, then packed the rest back into the plastic pouch, sealing it tight again. From a storage container in the back of his unit he removed three large manila envelopes, put one wad in one and the second in another. In the third envelope he stashed the flash drive containing Falcetti's confession and the cassette tapes and photographs from his days with Castello, along with the notebook he had taken from LeCur and the cell phones he had collected. From a drawer beneath his workbench Bechet removed a watch, checked the time as he put it on, then stuffed the plastic pouch containing the wads of bills into his Alice pack. He put the three manila envelopes in after that, then closed it tight and turned off the light. Locking up, he left.

He walked down Hampton Road, past Red Bar on his right and then the motel in which he had stayed briefly last night on the left. At the diner where Hampton Road became Montauk Highway, Bechet spotted Eddie waiting in the parking lot, just as planned.

Nothing left to chance.

On the way to the Bridgehampton train station, Bechet dropped the envelops one at a time over the seat. Eddie watched him in the rearview mirror, saying nothing.

The first one contained the ten grand. "This is for Scarcella," Bechet said. The next envelope contained the evidence against Castello. "This is for Miller." And the third contained the twenty grand. "And this one's for you."

Eddie glanced down at it. "What is it?"

"Just open it later, okay." Bechet leaned back, took a long breath. There was just one thing left to do now.

"Is everything okay?" Eddie said.

"It's about to be. We probably aren't going to see each other for a while."

Bechet removed a notebook and pen from one of the outer pockets of his Alice pack, tore out a piece of paper and wrote down the number to his emergency cell phone, handed the paper to Eddie.

"If you need me, call me from a Southampton pay phone. Otherwise I won't pick up. If anyone asks, I didn't tell you where I was going."

Eddie read the number, then folded the paper and put it into the pocket of his shirt. He looked back at Bechet, chewing on his unlit cigar, his yellow teeth, in the dashboard light, as dull as old bones.

"Bobby's dead," Bechet said finally.

"How?"

Bechet looked out the window. They were passing through Water Mill. "He got mixed up with the wrong guys."

"Was he murdered?"

"Yeah."

"He wasn't long for this world, was he?" Eddie said. "I'll have Angel pray for him."

Bechet nodded. "That'd be nice."

They didn't speak again till the cab was pulling up to the Bridge-hampton train station. Bechet was so close he was beginning to feel tired, beginning almost to relax. *Not yet, not yet.* When the cab stopped in front of the station, Bechet grabbed his Alice pack and got out, stood by the driver's door. Eddie lowered the window, and he and Bechet shook hands.

"You've got my number," Eddie said.

"Take care of yourself. Angel, too."

"Be good, my friend."

The cab drove away, and when it was out of sight, Bechet walked to the edge of the tracks, waited there for the train. It didn't take long, though; everything was planned pretty much down to the minute now.

When the train came, Bechet boarded it, easily found an empty car, just as he knew he would, took a seat. Sitting back, closing his eyes for now, he felt the tug in his gut as the train began to move and this final journey of his was, at last, in motion.

The black town car with the broken taillight was visible in the station parking lot as the train pulled into Southampton. Bechet saw four people waiting on the platform—Castello and his driver, and a young couple standing face-to-face. Castello and the couple boarded the same car, two ahead from where Bechet was seated. As the train pulled away, Bechet glanced out the window at Miller's building. His windows were dark, but Bechet thought he saw the shape of someone standing in one.

When he looked forward again, Castello was entering the empty car. He made his way toward the middle of it, where Bechet was seated on the aisle. Bechet stood, and, without speaking, he and Castello embraced, not out of fondness, though, simply so they could search each other for weapons and wires. When they were done, Castello sat across the aisle from Bechet. He crossed his legs and settled back in his seat, leaning his right elbow just a little on the armrest.

Two old friends—family, once—about to have a friendly chat.

"You don't look too worse for the wear," Castello said.

"No thanks to you."

"Not that I owe you an explanation or anything, but I didn't want the Scarcella kid hurt."

"No, but you sent a killer to kidnap him. You didn't order his death, but you still caused it."

Castello shrugged. "A technicality."

"He was a friend of mine."

"It looks to me like you've made new friends, though. Miller, that friend of his."

"Why?" Bechet said. "Why drag Scarcella into this?"

"You did that."

"How?"

"I suspected that he was the one holding your precious evidence. Of your friends, he'd be the one I'd go to for something like that. I couldn't be sure, though. But you went straight to him after our conversation this morning, and that confirmed it."

"I thought you weren't afraid of the FBI."

"I'm not, but business is just too good to be interrupted by such nonsense. It is as if we struck a gold mine."

"How did you know I went to Scarcella's after we talked?"

"LeCur told me."

Bechet nodded. "He was the traitor, by the way. LeCur, Jr. He and some partner."

"Who?"

"That I don't know."

Castello thought for a moment, then said, "What about Roffman?"

"It looks like he had nothing to do with this."

"He was being set up?"

"It looks that way."

"You will provide me with the proof of that, right?"

"It's all in an envelope," Bechet said. He looked out the window, at the wilderness rushing by.

"The police found LeCur's father early this morning," Castello said. "Dead, in the trunk of his car. It seems they found his son a few hours later. Dead, too, but in the middle of a road."

"Bad day for your workforce, I guess."

"Did you kill them both?"

Bechet didn't answer.

Castello shrugged again. "It does not matter, I suppose. Anyway, I still have you."

"I did what you wanted, Jorge."

"There's still the matter of LeCur's unknown partner."

"Find him yourself."

"I seem to be a little shorthanded at the moment. And there's also the matter of what was stolen from me. I must get that back, you know that."

"I don't know what to tell you," Bechet said. "It's long gone."

"That is bad news."

"Maybe you should imagine it going to some good cause. School for some orphans or something."

"Your Gabrielle, she is an orphan, is she not?"

Bechet looked at him.

"I thought I made myself understood, Pay Day. You work for me, do what I want you to do when I want you to do it, no questions asked. *That* was the deal."

"Things have changed."

"Not as far as I'm concerned."

"Well, it's not about you and me anymore, now, is it?"

"What does that mean?"

The train sped past the Peconic Road crossing then, where Bechet had left LeCur, Sr.'s vehicle, his body in the trunk. Seconds later, on the other side of the train, in the dark woods just feet from the tracks, they passed Gabrielle's cottage, too fast to even try to find it in the dark. Ahead of them, seconds down the line, was the Shinnecock Canal.

"What does that mean, it's not about you and me anymore?" Castello said.

"You brought Scarcella into this."

"That was unavoidable."

The blur of woods outside the windows gave way then to open sky. They had crossed onto the canal bridge. Visible through intricate trestles, a dark hulk in the bright, watery lights, stood the Water's Edge. Bechet's glimpse of the place lasted less than five seconds, and then it was gone, the view once again a blur of scrub pines and broken patches of night sky.

"Scarcella isn't a man to take lightly," Bechet said.

"Maybe, but I'm not all that worried."

"Why not?"

"A man like that is easy to see coming," Castello said. "He's a brute. He's not smart, not like us."

Bechet looked ahead. "You shouldn't have threatened Gabrielle," he said after a moment. "This might have gone better for a lot of people if you had done things differently."

"I only know the one way of doing things, Pay Day. But as long as you work for me, she's safe. Everyone you know is safe. I promise you that. And, for that matter, as long as you work for me, your new friend never finds out that . . . uncomfortable connection you two share. How long would the peace you two have made last if he knew the truth?"

"We're not our fathers," Bechet said.

"Maybe not. Still, if I were you, I'd rather a guy like Miller didn't know something like that."

"Well, you're not me," Bechet said.

The Hampton Bays station was only a minute or so away now. *Close, so very close.* Bechet took a breath, let it out.

"It was a good life you had, Pay Day, wasn't it? Your life with us, I mean. Good money, whatever distraction you needed, women when you wanted them. You could do a lot worse."

The train began to slow for the station. Bechet sat still, saying nothing. He would rather die than go back to that life, that utterly meaningless existence of pleasure and violence, of things he would give anything to forget.

"We'll set you up good," Castello said. "We're a lot bigger than we were six years ago. International. We'll bring in some men for you to train. If you do well, I probably won't ever need you to do a 'job.' I know how difficult that was for you. I am not without feeling."

"Feeling is not compassion," Bechet said. "Animals feel."

The train came to a stop, the doors opened. Castello and Bechet stood, paused to see who'd go first. Castello, as if it were an act of grace, led the way. Bechet followed him up the aisle. Castello stepped down to the door and onto the platform. Bechet, however, remained aboard.

Turning, Castello looked up at him. "Well?" he said.

Bechet didn't move. Castello realized that something was up but too late. A man was standing beside him.

It was Scarcella. He put one hand on Castello's shoulder, the gesture, seemingly, of an old friend. With his other hand he pressed the muzzle of a .45 into Castello's right kidney. Scarcella standing so close to Castello made the gun all but invisible.

Castello glanced back at Scarcella, stared at him for a moment, at the face of man whose only son had been murdered hours ago. Then Castello looked up at Bechet.

"So much for seeing him coming," Bechet said.

Castello smiled, an awkward smile meant to conceal his fear but not accomplishing that. Before he could say anything, the doors closed and the train began to move. Bechet stepped to the first seat, sat by the window, watched, as the train pulled away, Scarcella leading Castello toward a black van and the man, not unlike Scarcella—not unlike Scarcella's son, not unlike Bechet, even—waiting by the open door. Scarcella's brother, there in his brother's time of need.

In the empty car, the Alice pack on his lap, Bechet opened his emergency cell phone and hit redial.

Gabrielle answered at the end of the second ring.

"Hey, Elle," Bechet said, "it's me."

She told him what hotel she was at, then asked if whatever was going on was finally over. Bechet said it was, and that he'd be there in two hours, then hung up.

The train brought him to Penn Station, and then he ran the five blocks to the hotel. Her room was on the top floor. He knocked, just a little out of breath, and waited for her to open the door.

At midnight Miller awoke to the sound of a dog barking in the distance. A neighbor's dog, he heard it once in a while. He had been pulled from a dream but could not remember what the dream was about, only that in it he was happier than he had ever been. He would, he knew almost right away, be unable to get back to sleep, so he got up, careful not to disturb Barton, and grabbed his cane hanging on the headboard, then walked to his bedroom window. Old habit, and nothing else, really, for him to do at this time of night. His view was of the well-lit train station, and looking down at it, he didn't at first understand what he was seeing. Finally, though, it became obvious to him that what he was looking at was, in fact, what was there and not just some memory or fragment of a vague dream.

Just as she had the night she left him, Abby was standing on the platform, waiting alone for the last train, her grandfather's suitcase standing beside her.

Miller hurried on his cane to his front room, found his boots and pulled them on, made his way to his door and then down the stairs. It was slow-going because of his knee, because of the cane, terribly slow, just one step and then another, and when he reached the landing and pulled open the street door, he saw that the last train to New York had pulled to a stop at the station. From where he stood, Miller could see Abby climbing on board. He crossed Elm Street at a diagonal—didn't even looked for traffic when he stepped off the curb—then started across Railroad Plaza, half-walking, half-hopping, moving as fast as he possibly could. He reached the platform stairs and climbed to the top of them—one at a time, the knuckles of the hand grasping the cane bone-white—as Abby took her seat and the doors closed. She was looking down at her lap as the train began to pull away, looking intently, as if reading something, and Miller raised his hand to get her attention, but in the end he didn't wave, didn't bother, just let his hand linger in the air a moment before falling again to his side. There was no way she was going to see him, he sensed that, but as her window passed him, as he got a clear view of her profile, she lifted her head, doing so casually, it seemed, just by chance, then glanced out her window and caught sight of him. Surprised, she stared for an instant, then smiled once, the smile of an old friend, fond and intimate. Raising her right hand, still a little stunned, she offered Miller the peace sign, then opened her hand all the way and touched the glass with her palm. She said good-bye, or maybe she had simply mouthed the word, Miller didn't know. Raising his hand again, Miller waved and mouthed, "Good-bye, Abby," back to her.

A few seconds later the train was gone, Miller left behind in the lingering silence. L'Orange Bleu was closed now, everyone long since headed home, so he was the only being in this part of town, would be till morning. Well, not the only being, he remembered. Barton was there with him now.

Back in his apartment he took off his boots and wandered around his living room for a time. The table on which all the evidence he had collected had been laid out was empty again. Nothing now for him to do but reclaim his old life, the quiet existence of a landlord. Without the rain beating down on the roof and windows, the silence around him was nothing less than consuming. Not a bad thing, really, by which to be consumed.

Later, he climbed into bed next to Barton. She had uncovered herself during her sleep, her breasts exposed to the cool air of his dark bedroom. He drew the blankets up to her shoulders, covering her, then lay beneath them himself, in the warmth she generated, got as close to her as he could and made himself as comfortable as his aching knee would allow.